W9-AHF-949

BENJAMIN FRANKLIN'S BASTARD

BENJAMIN FRANKLIN'S BASTARD

Sally Cabot

WILLIAM MORROW
An Imprint of HarperCollins*Publishers*

BENJAMIN FRANKLIN'S BASTARD. Copyright © 2013 by Sally Cabot. All rights reserved. Printed in the United States of America. No part of this book may be used or reproduced in any manner whatsoever without written permission except in the case of brief quotations embodied in critical articles and reviews. For information address HarperCollins Publishers, 10 East 53rd Street, New York, NY 10022.

HarperCollins books may be purchased for educational, business, or sales promotional use. For information please write: Special Markets Department, HarperCollins Publishers, 10 East 53rd Street, New York, NY 10022.

FIRST EDITION

Designed by Lisa Stokes

Library of Congress Cataloging-in-Publication Data has been applied for.

ISBN 978-0-06-224192-4

13 14 15 16 17   OV/RRD   10 9 8 7 6 5 4 3 2 1

To Timbo. None of it happens without you.

BENJAMIN FRANKLIN'S BASTARD

I

Philadelphia, 1723

IT WAS ONE OF those days that struck the fifteen-year-old Deborah Read from time to time—she could work away most mornings without complaint, through heat or cold or even spinning flax, the worst kind of domestic tedium—but then an itch would come up in her and she couldn't bear to be inside at her work a single minute longer. She'd been scrubbing a hearth spill and had gone to the door with the bucket of dirty water, intent on dashing it into the gutter and returning to her task, but the sights and sounds and smells of the street grabbed hold of her. Most of what she saw was the usual drab Quaker gray, but of late Philadelphia had added other colors and tongues: Irish, German, Scots, free Africans, all come to see if it was true—this Quaker promise of peaceable commingling of all peoples and beliefs.

Perhaps it was. Deborah looked along Market Street and saw Brock Mueller teasing his oxen along in his usual off-note singsong; farther on, past the bakery, John McKay was just sweeping his stoop. Opposite the courthouse, two small Quaker boys chased a loose pig grubbing in the mud for whatever it was loose pigs always grubbed in the mud for, and in the other direction, toward the river, an old Negro woman sat on a crate under the covered market, empty on the off day, rolling a stone between her palms and muttering to herself. Deborah's gaze was about to travel past the old woman to the waterfront and the ever-present masts poking against the sky when she saw someone coming down the street in her direction, a stranger not much older than herself but already tall and broad backed, with a strong, lively face. His clothes showed the dust of travel, and leaking out of his pockets she spied what looked to be all his worldly goods—a dirty shirt and a pair of stockings. He strode along chewing on a roll while carrying two others beneath his arm, as if determined to keep a full day's ration on tap. Later she would tell this story of her first glimpse of the great Benjamin Franklin—how she, Deborah Read, stood in the doorway of her father's house on Market Street, looked at this comely young man walking by with his laundry and his rolls, and dismissed him as beneath her notice. But when telling the tale Deborah always took care to tell the whole of it—that the man had bent down and offered one of his rolls to the old Negro, as if to prove he wasn't in as great a need of it as he looked.

WHEN DEBORAH NEXT SAW Franklin, he was standing on her father's stoop asking after a room to let. The rolls and dirty clothes were gone, and he was claiming a fair wage as assistant in a printer's shop; the day was hot and Deborah had been walking around limp as a dishrag, but when the stranger appeared on the stoop she felt herself taking in a little starch.

Franklin peered around the father to examine the daughter. "I remember you," he said. "Standing in the doorway with your dirty wash water."

Deborah opened her mouth to snap back something about Franklin's dirty linen, but she took note of a look in Franklin's eye that told her he expected her to do it, that he'd laid out the dirty wash water just so she'd have a chance to lay out the dirty linen, that he was proud of how far and how fast he'd come and wanted her father to know it. Deborah stayed silent.

DEBORAH'S FATHER LET FRANKLIN the room, but at first Deborah hardly noticed—it seemed Franklin had already made a lot of friends, and he met nearly nightly with them at one or another tavern—but after a time he began to appear at the kitchen table or the family fire as if he'd always been part of it. From that point onward, life in the Read home changed. One morning Deborah came in from hanging the wash to find Franklin at the table, filling glasses with different amounts of water from a jug. He caught Deborah's hand as she walked by, spread her fingers apart, dipped her forefinger in the water, and guided it to the rim of the glass, moving it around and around. Then the glass began to vibrate, the finger to tingle, the glass to let out a sound like a cat fallen into a molasses barrel. Franklin added water to the glass; Deborah tried to pull her hand away, but Franklin held tight to it. He rimmed the glass with her finger again, and she noticed the sound had mellowed. He let go of her finger and took up a glass of his own, adding and subtracting water until he'd made a new note. When Deborah's mother came in from the shops, they'd created eight separate sounds, dried out the roast, and scorched the newly washed napkins hanging by the fire for drying. Benjamin took the blame—and the credit—for the whole of it.

THEY ALL LIKED IT when Franklin was around—Deborah's father and mother and Deborah—but Deborah suspected she was the only one who listened for his step on the stairs. She took care not to show

Franklin any special attention and felt she did a fair job of it, but after a time it seemed clear that Franklin was showing *her* some special attention. He met her out at the well and carried in the bucket, he noticed when she tied back her hair with a new ribbon, he sat up with her while she did her sewing after the rest of the family had gone to bed. On those nights alone together he told her about Boston, the town where he was born, how it was laid out over old, winding cow paths, so unlike the neat grids of Philadelphia. He talked too of a wind-racked island called Nantucket, where his mother was born, and how his grandfather had bought his grandmother out of indentured servitude to marry her. And one night he told her his astounding secret—that he was a runaway indentured servant himself. If Deborah's father had known, he would certainly have warned Deborah away from the man, perhaps even evicted him from the house, but the problem was simply enough solved; Deborah told her father nothing of it. Already, she didn't like to think of a day without this man's attentions in it.

Another night Franklin came in with news that Deborah was glad enough to share with her parents—Franklin had met the governor! The governor had by chance seen a letter Franklin had written and had been so impressed with it that he'd requested a meeting. At the meeting the governor suggested that Franklin set up his own print shop in Philadelphia—when Deborah told her father this news, she looked to him in the hope of an offer to assist the young printer, but no such offer came. Afterward Deborah wished she'd looked harder at her father, or talked longer, or made him his favorite custard for dinner; in the morning she found him dead in the yard, halfway between the house and the necessary.

DEBORAH'S MOTHER TOOK CHARGE of the lease of the carpentry shop and paying off the creditors, but it was Franklin who kept them afloat above the waves of grief that pounded them from all sides. He made sure to spend time in gentle chat with her mother, but it was Deborah who was clearly his main concern; he began each morning with just enough words to warm her and ended each night by walking her up the stairs to her chamber, always saying a proper good evening at the threshold. At first Deborah only thought of how nice it was not to have to walk past her parents' chamber door alone, not to have to think of her mother lying in there beside an empty bolster. But after a time Deborah's thoughts began to veer away from the dead to the living, to the tall, solid form that accompanied her. She began to feel queer things when he happened to brush against her thigh or when his hand rested low on her back, just above the curve of her buttocks, to guide her up the steep stairs.

One night Deborah opened her chamber door and discovered she'd left her window open in the rain. Franklin stepped into the room to wrestle with the sash, but he wouldn't close it all the way down.

"Fresh air is healthful," he said. "No one catches cold from cold; in fact, a close, overheated room is the more likely culprit." He went on about the healthfulness of certain airs, and Deborah pretended to listen, but she only really caught up again when he crossed to the bed and began to admire the embroidery on her coverlet.

"I wonder if you know how often I think of that coverlet and the treasure that lies beneath it," he said.

Some number of nights later—it was *not* that same night, Deborah was almost sure of it—she found herself lying under that coverlet with Franklin, discovering all the things that could happen to a woman unaware, as long as a man went about it politely enough.

BENJAMIN WAS ON THE RISE—Deborah could feel it—even before he clattered his way up the stairs and into her room one night way too loudly, almost shouting: The governor had offered to send him to

London with letters of credit to purchase the press and types needed to set up his own print shop in Philadelphia!

It was exciting news, no doubt of it, but Deborah couldn't help it. Her father was dead and her mother only just afloat on the shop rent; Deborah had gone too far, and all that could save her if trouble came was this man who was about to leave her behind on a distant continent. A thick, dark, panicked grief dropped over her, stopping her tongue.

"Well?" Benjamin asked. "Don't you have something to say of your fine fellow?"

"Are you?" she asked. "Are you my fellow?"

He heard. He knew. He took her hand and pulled it tight to him. "We'll marry before I go," he said.

The cloud over Deborah lifted. She would have married Benjamin Franklin no matter what he was, but marriage to Benjamin Franklin, print shop owner, could be all her father would have wanted of her.

When they spoke to Deborah's mother, however, she didn't see any print shop owner—she saw only an eighteen-year-old printer's assistant and a sixteen-year-old, restless daughter; whatever her affection for the man, it would not allow of any financial risk for her daughter. Or so she explained it to the pair of them.

"Go to London, Benjamin," she said. "Come home. Set up your shop. Then talk to me of marrying my daughter."

Deborah considered telling her mother what she'd already risked with Benjamin, but she wavered, thinking of the disgraced Sue Kent's exile to relatives in Virginia, her mother's firm endorsement of the parents' actions in the matter. In the end, Deborah decided she didn't trust her mother as much as she trusted Benjamin.

2

DEBORAH WOKE IN THE old anticipation that lasted only as long as it took her to come fully awake and realize that the day would have no Benjamin in it; she'd guarded herself against total despondence over Benjamin's leaving—she would *not* erase herself from life in his absence—but she hadn't been prepared for the blandness that was left. To pull herself up she fixed her sights on Benjamin's first letter, practicing in her mind her possible answers to it. She was not skilled with words and anticipated much to live up to from a man who made his living at them; if he wrote in long sentences of all the fine carriages in the London streets, she must counter with something of equal interest, if not with equal skill. But what? Deborah's days were full of the things they'd always been full of: spinning, washing, sewing, cleaning, the Wednesday trip to the covered market that ran two full blocks down the middle of Market Street, the Sunday trip to the butcher's shambles for a fresh leg of mutton or a haunch of beef. It had been enough; she'd always put her best effort into her chores, proud of a full skein and a clean house and a good meal, but she couldn't imagine writing of such things in a way that would make them interesting to Benjamin.

So Deborah went, marking the days in her head—the four to six weeks that he would be aboard ship wouldn't hold promise of a letter unless they crossed with a homebound ship and hauled up to exchange mail sacks. Four weeks came and at the end of it Deborah reminded herself of how foolish she'd been to hope of such an exchange at sea; at the six-week mark she reminded herself that a six-week voyage was a good voyage—there were many bad voyages that went on into months. At the two-month mark Deborah reminded herself that even once in London, Benjamin would still have to wait for a return ship to deliver the letter he would of course sit down at once to write.

At the four-month mark Deborah's mother began to say things that Deborah took as ominous. "Young and vigorous men do not always possess vigorous memories," she said, or, "That potter, John Rogers, seems to be making a good living out of his shop."

After six months a letter came. It made no mention of a prolonged voyage, or an illness, or any other inconvenience that would have explained the delay. He wrote of the governor's letters of credit proving worthless, of finding employment at a quality printer's, of the vastly greater opportunities London offered over Philadelphia; between those lines lay the only explanation Deborah was to receive of the last one: "I am unlikely to return to Philadelphia anytime soon."

Deborah answered the letter, taking great pains over it, but in reading it back she saw clearly enough that it didn't even measure up to Benjamin's disappointing offering—she sensed that the words didn't look right, but they gave no hint as to how they could be bettered. She almost didn't put the letter out for the post, but she knew how she'd felt in all those months of waiting. In the end she decided that a poor letter was better than none and mailed it anyway. After six long months with no answer she mailed another. She didn't write again, but she couldn't say that she didn't continue to wait. It wasn't that she believed Benjamin would come back or that he would even write again, it was more that she wasn't able to erase him as easily as he'd erased himself. She'd long envisioned what her future life would be like, and it varied little from her mother's: a modest but well-kept tradesman's house, a full pantry, a warm hearth, and every other year an infant in a cradle beside it. Since he'd first slipped himself under Deborah's coverlet, the man she'd pictured on the other side of that hearth had been Benjamin Franklin, and she couldn't seem to move him out of that seat.

DEBORAH'S MOTHER HAD NO such trouble moving Benjamin; she kept up her talk of John Rogers's agreeable nature, his mastery of his trade, his interest in Deborah. "What more are you after?" she asked.

Musical glasses, Deborah thought. Astounding secrets. Lectures about healthful and nonhealthful airs—although in truth Deborah didn't miss the lectures so much. But as Deborah's mother said, John Rogers was there, and Benjamin Franklin was not.

John Rogers was invited to dine; Deborah's mother set out to make him feel welcome and did so; John Rogers set out to make himself welcome, and he did that. He used the visit to good purpose, making a fair account of himself to Deborah's mother—not long arrived from London, he was already making forty pounds a year out of his shop. He made no pressing demands for speech from Deborah but included her in his talk with the mother with the kind of look that expressed well enough his intent. In fact, he seemed unwilling to take his eyes away from her face and form, and Deborah could not help but feel the compliment in it.

As the night wore down, Deborah's mother made an excuse to retreat to the kitchen, and Rogers proved himself the gentleman by asking Deborah's leave to call upon her again; once it was granted he stood up and bid her good night.

John Rogers called five times before declaring his desire to make Deborah his wife. She'd by then learned he was proper and pleasant and attractive enough in his person, although he had a habit of licking his hair behind his ears that she didn't like, but it seemed a small enough fault. Still, Deborah answered Rogers, "I'm not of a mind to marry yet."

When Deborah's mother heard of her answer, she said, "Very well, there's an advertisement in the newspaper for someone to scrape skins at the hatter's shop."

When Deborah's eye widened she said, "I can't afford to keep you. 'Tis one thing or the other—you go to wife or you go to work."

That night Deborah lay in bed with her eyes tightly closed and tried to reimagine her old hearth, the cradle at one side, the chair at the other, but with Rogers sitting in it instead of Franklin. The room seemed dim and cold, the fire weak, with Rogers little more than a dull gray shape; but when she tried a second trick, putting her mother into that chair, the room grew too close and overhot. And what of an empty chair? The minute she tried to picture it the scene went black.

John Rogers returned. Deborah never did know if her mother had summoned him or if he'd come of his own accord, confident enough that he'd not be turned away twice. Deborah's mother left them alone in the parlor, and John Rogers stood before her and spoke in his most earnest voice. "My disappointment at our last meeting was great. But here I am again, in hopes that perhaps you've had a second thought."

"Perhaps if we talked of it again in a year—," Deborah began, but John Rogers shook his head.

"I'm not so young as to have a year to waste."

"But my daughter is." Deborah's mother had come through the door. "She's young and unused to the idea as yet. Surely another month or two could be allowed her."

"I could not object to a month."

The talk went back and forth, Deborah saying little, until belatedly she realized just what it was they talked of—not a renewed suit in a month but a marriage in a month. Deborah leaped up from her chair to correct the plan while she could, but her mother turned on her such a bright smile of satisfaction that Deborah could see in it the clearest reflection of the reverse—the face she would be staring at across her mother's hearth if she chose to remain at it single yet. She also saw the hatter's shop. She turned from her mother's smile to Rogers and saw that he waited on her word, understanding that nothing could be settled until she said it herself; Deborah's mother talked on, and still John Rogers watched her and waited. Perhaps after all it was not such a poor prospect, life with a man who would grant her her own mind? Indeed, if she kept Benjamin Franklin out of it, this man would measure up well against the rest, and, as her mother repeated again and again, Benjamin Franklin was indeed out of it.

"A month," she said.

DEBORAH'S MOTHER AGREED TO a dowry she could ill afford, culled out of the sale of the remaining inventory at her husband's carpentry shop. Deborah's mother offered no money for wedding attire, but Deborah didn't object—she'd already discovered the sum of her assets lay in a full figure and a fresh face that would show up just as well in her unadorned lavender bombazine and navy cloak. The justice of the peace said the necessary words over them in the parlor, and Deborah's mother made a roast of the last of the freshly slaughtered pork. After he'd cleaned two plates, John Rogers stood up, swiped his hair behind his ears, said his thank you to Deborah's mother, and pointed Deborah to his cart. He hoisted her trunk in after her and geed his horse into the street; Deborah turned to say a last word to her mother, but the night was cold and her mother had already gone back inside the house. Looking at the door of the place where Deborah had lived the whole of her life, she began to think that perhaps she'd given up a known thing for an unknown thing without sufficient thought, but it was, as her mother would certainly have told her if she'd voiced the idea out loud, too late.

Rogers's house was on Warren Street, at the far end of Market, the houses growing smaller and darker as they progressed. Rogers spoke little on the short ride and made no grand announcement of any kind as they entered. Deborah didn't particularly mind, as she'd occupied herself with her own thoughts, or perhaps better said, with one particular thought: Would Rogers be able to tell that another had already explored parts of her he might well expect to explore first? A memory of her last time between the sheets with Benjamin caused her to flush with double shame—at the act itself, and at thinking of Benjamin Franklin hours after she'd wed someone else.

Rogers handed her down at the door, raked the trunk across the threshold, grinned at Deborah, and pulled her up the stairs. Two closed doors greeted her at the landing and Rogers opened one of them, unleashing a cold, damp draft. Deborah would have liked a few more words with her new husband, or better yet, a cup of tea, but neither was offered, and Deborah, feeling herself already in the wrong, made no fuss.

It turned out not to matter. There was, Deborah discovered, a not-polite way to bed a woman, and if Rogers noticed any lack in her it didn't slow him. He fell asleep, woke and kneed her legs apart again, drained himself, slept again. Deborah now saw the great advantage of remaining chaste till marriage—the night would have been a good deal less disappointing if she'd had no comparison to make.

The second disappointment was her new husband's empty pantry. Deborah managed their breakfast out of toast from an old crust of bread and the dregs of beer from the beer barrel; she offered them up to Rogers with what from her mother would have sounded like apology but from her came out as accusation: "Your pantry needs stocking."

"Gray's has my account," Rogers said, the only words he'd spoken to her since she'd arrived at his house. He swiped his hair behind his ears again and left for his shop.

LIVING WITH ROGERS PROVED to be little different from living alone, and alone, Deborah turned to her thoughts. That her thoughts were too often of Benjamin Franklin she knew to be wrong, but she didn't care. Her thoughts, at least, were hers, and she'd do with them as she liked. The first sign of deeper trouble came a month into her marriage when Deborah put a sack of Indian meal on the counter at Gray's and was told that John Rogers no longer had an account. Deborah told Rogers that night.

"I'll square it," he said, and went out.

That night Deborah learned another new thing—that there was something besides Benjamin Franklin's good nature that could be brought home from a tavern—but when she went to Gray's the next day there was no trouble over the account; it was another month before she discovered from Gray's store that all her purchases were now being charged against her mother's account. Deborah returned home, went straight to her husband's desk, and prized it open without compunction, hunting out his ledger book. Deborah was not good with words, but she was good with numbers, having helped her father from time to time in his shop, and she could soon track the spending of the entire dowry she'd brought with her to her marriage, as well as the long list of remaining debts. She closed up the desk and sat long in thought. As affairs now stood, the only advantage to her marriage to John Rogers went all to John Rogers, with her mother forced to keep the pair of them at her own expense. Deborah thought longer, and could see only one way to improve her state as well as her mother's: She climbed the stairs, packed her trunk, and wrestled it back down the stairs with greater ease than she'd wrestled it up. She found a cart boy at the corner and gave him a coin to take it and her to her mother's house.

Her mother heard the racket and came out into the hall. "What in heaven is this?"

"We're done with Rogers," Deborah said, "and you'd do well to inform Gray before he takes all you own to pay off the man's debts."

"What!"

Deborah explained. And explained again. Her mother was the sort who had her own idea of a thing and didn't like to give it up; in the end she went out to Gray's and came back the color of sour milk, apparently drained of ideas altogether.

"What are we to do? You still bear his name."

"He may keep his name," Deborah said. She climbed the stairs to her old room, opened the window, and breathed in the cold, healthful air.

SOON AFTER DEBORAH'S FLIGHT John Rogers disappeared, and in time the rumors began to fly around Market Street from every point on the compass. John Rogers had a wife in London. John Rogers had fled to the West Indian Islands to escape his creditors and had taken a third wife. John Rogers was dead, beaten to a pile of bones by one of his creditors. Or the third wife. At first Deborah didn't care where he was or whom he was with or, indeed, whether he was alive or dead—her earlier rage had washed away under a crashing wave of relief—but after a time Deborah realized that what had happened to her husband had to matter to her. If she had no proof of his death, if she had no proof of that London marriage, Deborah was herself as near dead as any living woman could get. She had no husband, but neither was she free to marry another unless she could afford to legally investigate either the first wife in London or the possible death in the West Indies. The dowry for Rogers had taken all that the Reads owned in the way of assets. Any legal fees were as beyond Deborah's grasp as the tops of the masts that lined the Delaware River.

DEBORAH'S MOTHER BEGAN TO have difficulty on the stairs, and with the washing, and with balancing over the fire to lift the skillet; she began to tremble as she worked her needle. Deborah took on the main of the chores, settling her mother in her chair with some wool to wind or some dough to knead; at night she helped her to bed and returned below stairs to sit alone with her sewing. The relief that had washed away her anger over John Rogers was in turn washed away by a hopelessness that had heretofore been entirely alien to her nature. She got out of her bed and did her chores and her nursing but didn't go out beyond what was needed; she could see the looks on the faces she passed, as if she were lame or disfigured. Nothing moved her until one day on her way back from her errands her eye happened to fix on the masts dissecting the sky.

Deborah walked toward the water. From a distance the river looked still, but as she drew closer she saw how fiercely it ripped into its bank, that she was the thing that was still. She wondered what happened when a still thing hit a moving thing, where the still thing might end up. Benjamin would have known; Benjamin was a strong swimmer, had even experimented with paddles on his hands and feet to make him an even stronger one. He'd once hitched himself to a kite and let it drag him across the pond, testing the power of the wind against a few sticks and pieces of paper.

"But how did you get back?" Deborah had asked.

"Paid a friend sixpence to carry my clothes around the pond and walked." Benjamin chatted on about this and that amazing thing he'd discovered about wind and water as he blew across the pond, but Deborah only wondered that as he'd walked home wet and cold and short an entire sixpence it hadn't occurred to him how foolish it was.

THERE MUST HAVE BEEN a dozen ships lined up along the river, but every one sat with sails furled, as stagnant as Deborah, having long since discharged its passengers and cargo—if Benjamin Franklin had been aboard any one of them he certainly hadn't come looking for her. Deborah stared down at the angry current again, so dark and rough she couldn't see bottom, and shuddered. She should go home— her mother grew nervous when Deborah left her alone too long—but she felt too old and achy and worn out to even make the turn against the wind. She was seventeen and finished.

3

Philadelphia, 1726

WHEN BENJAMIN FRANKLIN RETURNED to Philadelphia, Deborah Read discovered it only along with the rest. Philadelphia had grown in his two years gone—it was not uncommon to see forty masts at one time against the river skyline. An upholsterer, a clock maker, and three new taverns had all sprung up along Market Street; the Scots-Irish had almost caught up to the Quakers in numbers, although not in money or influence. Deborah, watching all the new bustle from her window, one day spied the familiar mane of hair, the wide shoulders, the rollicking gait. She stepped back, hands flying to loosen her apron, but he walked on past her house without stopping. The hot flush of mortification was followed by a realization so cold that she shivered from it: She was no longer of account. But how could she be? Franklin would have heard of her marriage and seen it for the tar pit it was.

A number of weeks passed before Deborah saw Benjamin Franklin again. Her mother required her constant attention, and she found it easier to send a boy to do her marketing; this was what she told herself, but the truth was, she hid. After a time, however, the old itch drove her back into the street, and it wasn't many days before they passed each other face-to-face. He appeared to have gained in size, as if all he'd experienced in London had added an extra inch to his height, an extra few inches to his already broad back. As he walked he was engaged in intense debate with another man, so it was understandable that he would smile, nod, dip his head, and pass without slowing. This was Deborah's first thought; her second was a rage so hot it burned her teeth. She whirled around. "Mr. Franklin!"

He turned, smiling yet. The gentleman with Franklin touched his arm and moved off. Franklin stopped smiling. He took a reluctant step toward Deborah. "Mrs. Rogers."

"Miss Read," Deborah said.

Franklin looked over his shoulder as if in hunt of a friend. Finding none, he turned back. "Indeed, I heard of your abandonment, and I am truly—"

"Then you heard wrong," Deborah said. "I left my husband, if he ever was, and I left his name with him, long before he fled. I only stopped you now to ask if you received my letters. Two, it was. Fearing the first one lost, I wrote another. I'd like to know if two got lost. If they did, I'll not waste more paper on letters."

Franklin's face danced through a series of changes that Deborah discovered she could read better than she could read any book: surprise, guilt, something like admiration if not quite the thing itself, and, last, calculation. But he was, after all, an honest man. "Two letters did not get lost," he said.

"Thank you," Deborah said. "In that case, perhaps one day I'll chance another." She moved off.

THE NEXT TIME DEBORAH came upon Franklin he was walking briskly ahead of her in a northerly direction, as if he'd just come from dinner at a tavern and was on his way home, or as if he'd seen her first and turned away. His being in front of her for several blocks, she could watch who he'd become, how he had a word of greeting for nearly everyone he passed, how nearly everyone moved on with a new smile, or an old smile made bigger; if he happened to pass two people walking together, their talk grew more animated after he'd gone by—talking of Franklin, no doubt.

The fourth time Deborah saw Franklin's unmistakable form ahead she felt all the fire that had seen her through their previous meeting wash out of her; she'd done well then, letting him see she was not yet beaten down by him or Rogers or anyone else, but now she couldn't summon a single word of address that could match his. Deborah crossed to the other side of the street, and they passed as if they'd never met.

IN TIME, DEBORAH DEVELOPED a public face of indifference whenever she saw Franklin or whenever his name came up in her hearing, but in private she found she was far from indifferent. She even took some poor comfort in the fact that her mother had been wrong about Benjamin Franklin and she had been right, but she took less comfort in the fact that the man's rise took place right there on Market Street, where she was forced to watch. He opened a print shop that at once began to thrive, which no doubt gave him some new ideas about his worth. Rumor traveled Deborah's way that he'd made a marriage offer to a relative of his landlord but had overreached himself with a demand of a hundred-pound dowry and was rejected. The next rumor Deborah heard was that Benjamin Franklin, the runaway printer's apprentice, was now the owner and editor of the *Pennsylvania Gazette*.

The paper was, of course, a great success. As word of its growing influence swept up and down the street, Deborah found herself taking a queer pride in it and, queerer yet, a sense of some small claim to it. She'd done nothing but believe in Benjamin Franklin, but surely that must have counted for something in his life; indeed, if she were to look back over her own life, there were times when that seemed her only accomplishment. She watched Franklin's name leap from mouth to mouth until all Philadelphia seemed to ring with it; she expected daily to hear of his marriage, Franklin now being one of Philadelphia's brighter prospects, but she heard no such news. She believed she knew enough of the man to know that he must be seeking—and no doubt finding—physical comfort from someplace, but if he did, she heard no name attached to it.

4

Philadelphia, 1730

SHE WAS NAMED ANNE, for the queen. From what she came to know of Franklin in later years, she knew he no longer approved, but back then he delighted in a king or a queen as much as anyone else. He delighted in many things—the heat of the fire on his back; the rich, greasy slice of goose on his tongue; the kick of the cider as it slid down his throat. She supposed that was part of what drew people to him— his childlike delight in things. In *them*. Simple enough, when you thought of it.

She saw him first at the hanging. She'd been to the butcher's for soup bones when she saw the cart with the two boys seated on their coffins in the back of it. One of the boys was crying uncontrollably, the other was murmuring to him in a voice too low for Anne to hear the words, but the tone sounded brave and she decided to follow the cart to see how he managed. The bells had already begun to toll, and by the time Anne and the cart arrived at the prison the crowd had gathered into thick knots. The cart reached the hanging tree and pulled up close under it; the ropes were thrown over the beam and the sheriff addressed the boys. Anne didn't hear the sheriff's words but she saw the brave boy shake his head, the sheriff speak again, and then she heard the brave boy shout back: "What would you have me say? I am innocent of the fact and it will appear so before God!"

That was when Anne noticed Franklin, standing at the front of the crowd but also standing out from it—taller and handsomer than most, with thick hair the color of dark gold and curious gray eyes, a strong face and stronger shoulders, taking down the boy's words in a small notebook. The sheriff raised his voice and began to read, the death warrant Anne assumed, until she fixed her attention on the actual words of it. Reprieve! At the good news the brave boy's courage failed him and he fainted. Franklin—although she didn't know it was Franklin then—was one of the first to reach the cart, and with one strong arm swept the boy off his coffin and into the street, laying him in the dirt; it would seem a poorer location to some, but Anne approved of it.

ANNE HAD BEEN SERVING at the Penny Pot two months when she next saw Franklin. She'd been driven to the tavern the same way every girl her age ever was—by hunger—and by the fact that she'd seen the sign in the window of the Penny Pot and in none of the other taverns: GIRL WANTED. Not the Penny Pot, her father said, but her mother paid him no heed; by then Anne's father was good for nothing but coughing blood into a pewter cup, and Anne's mother had gotten used to leaving the few words he managed to offer unanswered. Anne minded her father's words better—studied them, in fact—even copied them as best she could, hearing in them something finer than those she heard elsewhere in the house; her father had once been a tutor at Philadelphia's finest school for boys until the consumption struck. But in the case of the tavern, Anne took her mother's tack. What did her father know of hunger? Anne saw to it that he got first pick at whatever food her mother managed to push together—a watered broth, a meatless pie, a thin custard. Anne never begrudged her father his lion's share, nor did she begrudge whatever small child wasn't still at breast being fed next and on up through the seven—but it did prove to Anne that if she wanted something better for herself she'd have to go out and get it for herself.

Once they were alone in the kitchen, Anne's mother made her own argument in favor of the tavern. "Past time you earned," she said. "But if he thinks I'll be waiting on him like you've been, he can get himself another thought. Not with the rest of this lot to wash and feed and dress."

In truth, that was the argument that almost swayed Anne against the Penny Pot, but the greater argument was getting the food and clothes in the first place, and besides, she'd made up her mind already, on her own, as she usually did. She dressed herself in her best linen, or what she could find of it that came closest to fitting; in her sixteenth year she'd grown another surprise inch up and two more out, and there were gaps below the hem and between the lacings that couldn't be bridged. She took a piece of not-clean toweling and scrubbed her face and neck, tipped herself upside down and ripped the comb through her hair until it lay smooth down her back, then tied it with a piece of shoe binding because it was less frayed than any of the ribbons her work box offered up. Her next oldest sister, Mary, lent Anne her shoes in exchange for the brightest of the ribbons; the shoes were too small but less scarred than Anne's, and she knew she could walk in them at least as far as the Penny Pot. Her mother stopped her at the door and covered her in her own shawl. "'Tis cold," she said, as if Anne didn't know what a Philadelphia January was, but Anne also knew the greater meaning of the gift and softened her look.

Anne set off along the alley, taking care to keep her sister's shoes wide of the gutter that ran down the middle, wishing it would rain and wash away the dead thing that still floated in it. She would *not* take up the creature and lug it to the river—not this time—there were two dozen others in the alley who could take a turn at it, just as they could take more care in disposing of their own refuse. She turned onto Second Street and braced herself against the turn onto Vine, straight into the river wind; she considered a longer walk to one of the inland taverns but decided she'd make better use of her time in less walking and more earning. As soon as she made her turn onto Vine she could look down the street and see the Penny Pot, a two-and-a-half-story brick building with an odd-shaped multifaceted roof, too near the river landing for winter comfort but good for trade no doubt. She walked through the door without pause, the way she used to drink down her mother's tincture for the canker throat.

A roomful of men seated at a mix of long and short tables faced Anne, those nearest the fire packed tightest, but the heat of the fire didn't reach Anne at the door. She went up to the first server she crossed, a woman her mother's age but with enough flesh on her for the two of them, although this woman's face showed the same fatigue. Despite the outer chill the woman's forehead and upper lip were beaded with sweat.

"I should like to speak to the proprietor," Anne said.

"He's over there." The woman pointed to a man passing out sloshing-full pewter tankards at the tap. "But if you're looking to speak to the one who runs the place, you're doing it."

Anne looked to the man at the tap. He was perhaps the age of her father, but a far more robust version of it, with strength in his arms and color in his face, and the kind of free and easy laugh that Anne had never heard out of her father in all her life. When he looked up from pumping the tap, he caught her look and grinned; Anne was still so disconcerted that she only managed to twitch her cheeks into the beginnings of an answering smile when the woman in front of her spoke.

"Well? What are you after? Work?"

Anne returned her attention to the woman. "Yes, work."

The woman looked her up and down and handed her a tray holding assorted pewter tankards and mugs. "Table at the corner," she said. "They owe sixpence. Don't hang about for chat. I'll be watching; I'll know soon enough if you'll work or you won't." She moved off, wiping the sweat from her lip with the back of her hand, as if too tired to even lift the hem of her apron to her mouth.

Anne moved to the table in the corner, left off the contents of her tray, collected the sixpence, turned around, and saw herself being hailed by a table near the fire. She hurried to it, collected the empty tankards, and worked her way to the man at the tap. "Welcome to the Pot," he said with another grin that Anne felt the need of even more than the first. "John Hewe's my name. You've met the wife. And you be?"

Anne gave her name, picked up her brimming tankards, returned to her work. She hadn't made it back to the table by the fire when she was hailed again from a third table: "Pigeon pie and a quart of the master's best!" From there it began to run together in her head: a quart, a pint, a bottle of Madeira, a cider, a flip, eggs and bacon, scallops, bread and cheese, a pasty, and her own film of sweat. At the end of the night, Mrs. Hewe counted out fourpence and handed it to Anne with no remark beyond "Tomorrow morning, six. Be sharp."

IT TURNED OUT THE scraps were better than the pay—a cheese rind, a strip of fat off a roast of beef, the end of a rye loaf—but there were other benefits over home. The fire was brighter, the tables cleaner, the talk merrier, and a smile drew a smile at the Penny Pot; at home Anne couldn't dig out a smile with a stick. At first Anne smiled at her customers purely for that smile back and because she was no longer so hungry and because she was out of the miserable alley, but after a time she discovered that a smile had another use. When one of the customers put a hand on her waist and she kept smiling, he gave her buttock a good squeeze and slid a halfpenny in her pocket. The other serving girl, a scowler named Patsy, never did figure out the worth of a smile, but Anne soon had the full sum in her head: A dozen halfpence and she could buy a meat pie with real meat in it. A fair enough price.

THE FIRST TIME FRANKLIN came into the Penny Pot, Anne noticed him straightaway; the Penny Pot sat near the river, right next to the shipyard, and its patrons were for the most part the men of the river—shipwrights, dockhands, corders, sailors—not men like Franklin. His looks stood him out, of course, but also the way he worked himself into the room with a crack on the back here, a pleasant word there, a smart quip almost everywhere else. Even after he dropped into a chair by the fire it kept up, one after another making their way to him to drop a word in his ear and catch a better one back—Anne could tell they got better than they gave by the looks on the faces of the ones who got. Even though he couldn't have been too many years past twenty he was *someone*, she could just tell it; she listened and soon enough learned he was Benjamin Franklin, printer, owner, and editor of the *Pennsylvania Gazette.* And soon enough again Anne noticed him noticing her, noticed him whispering a question to one of the halfpence men, the shipwright Isaac Wilkes. Wilkes whispered back with the kind of smile men used only amongst themselves; Franklin looked over at Anne and there they were—those eyes full of delight.

He waved her over and asked for a cider. She brought him one. He had a cleft in his chin that made something like a wink when he smiled, and it drew her own smile wider. That first time, as she left him, she thought she saw him tip some cider on the floor on purpose, but it was too odd a thing to believe and she decided she'd been mistaken. She'd worked her way around the room a few times before he waved at her again, and she circled back with the cider jug, but he didn't want more cider. He wanted her to look at the ants.

"Look, there," he said. "Do you see those ants on the floor, sipping at my cider? Now I want you to keep watch."

Anne watched. After a time another ant joined the first group, and another and another, which was no great mystery to her, but Franklin said, "Do you not wonder how they do it?"

"Do what, sir?"

"Communicate. Somehow the first ant has told the others to come here and feast."

Anne had never before thought about ants communicating, but she thought of it then, and discovered herself equally amazed by it. Franklin must have seen her amazement, for he laughed and gave her arm a pat. "Could it be I've found a fellow scientist?"

THE ANTS BEGAN IT, but every night after, at least those nights when Franklin was at the Pot, he'd call her over to share some other new or peculiar fact. One night over his dinner he called Anne to the table and asked for an extra glass. He had the one half full of wine already at his place, but Anne didn't question; she got the second glass, but when she went to walk away, Franklin caught her elbow and held her there. He filled the new glass a quarter full. He caught up Anne's hand, dipped her forefinger in the wine and, still holding on to it, guided it around the rim of the glass until the glass began to quiver and a sound to emerge. It was a lovely sound, a pure, mournful note, and when Franklin released her finger she kept it moving herself. He took up his own glass, rimming it as she'd rimmed hers, sipping away the wine until he'd made his own note fit hers in a perfect duet.

The next night Franklin called to her to conduct another experiment: He pulled her near to the fire to see how close she had to get before her cheeks pinked. Later, as the fire died, he called to her again and had her stand in the same spot; she stayed pale till he touched her cheek. "I wonder," he said. "Do all palms cause the same effect? But with this I'm not so willing to experiment!"

He was strange, she must admit it. But just the same she found herself watching for his coming, and when he didn't come, no matter if she worked more or less hours, it was a longer night. Whether he came or not, she kept up smiling and collecting her coins, and when he did come he watched her do it; she saw him watching and waited for him to take his own chance, but he didn't, until one night at the lag end of it he called her over and opened his palm; a British sterling half crown lay winking in it. She looked at him and he looked back and she knew well enough what that half crown was for, but she also knew how many meat pies it would get.

5

THE PAIN SURPRISED ANNE. It surprised him. He pulled back. He said, "Dear girl!" She'd never seen him discomfited, but he was discomfited then, although it didn't last long. He stroked her hair and kissed her brow and cheek; he said her name gently, and kept on. After he'd gotten where he wished, he fell away, silent, and he stayed silent so long she began to think he'd fallen asleep until she looked sideways and saw his wide-open, somber eyes.

Anne got up off the bed and picked up her skirt, pulled it on over her shift, slipped on her bodice and laced it closed. She turned back to the bed; he hadn't moved. "May I have my coin now?"

He shot upright in his shirt as if she'd doused him with cold water. He plucked his waistcoat off the floor and pulled out the half crown.

She said, "Thank you."

He said, "Dear girl," again and no more.

. . . .

ANNE SLEPT WITH THE coin in her hand all night, and in the morning stepped out into the alley on her way to Wednesday market. The nearest neighbor but one was also on her way there and no doubt in hope of a trade, for she carried a bolt of homespun linsey-woolsey under her arm. She was worn down at all her edges and appeared to be ailing by the way she dragged her steps, but Anne didn't slow for her—what could it accomplish besides making two of them miss out on the freshest goods? She pushed ahead toward Front Street, filling herself with the still-snappish March air off the river as she walked, thinking how it would soon be something more substantial than air that filled her. When she reached the stalls, she stopped first at the cages of live pigeons but moved on with regret; the half crown would get more of a dead thing than a live one. She passed up the dried venison and salt fish and ended instead at the smoked bacon. She added potatoes, beans, and Indian meal and walked home pleasantly weighted.

When Anne spread her stores out on the table, her mother looked her question at her, but Anne called up her own look, one she'd worked out at the Penny Pot for the occasional overly aggressive customer, which said, "There you *don't* go." On her mother it had the like effect. She turned away and began to measure the Indian meal into the fine, heavy crockery bowl she'd promised to include in Anne's dowry at the time of her marriage. Anne had often looked at the bowl, touched the bowl, even once put her cheek against its cooling glaze, thinking ahead to a life that she'd determined would be something different from her mother's. Looking at the bowl now, a new thought struck Anne, even happier than the old: Now her mother's life would be different too.

HE DIDN'T COME FOR a week. The next week he showed up late in the evening and searched for her the minute he'd cleared the door, but Anne couldn't say if he was pleased or otherwise at the sight of her. He said little to her through the remains of the evening, but near to closing he touched her wrist as she passed and looked his question. She nodded her answer. This time she noticed the coin he slipped Mrs. Hewe for the room, noticed the corder following them up the stairs with his eyes. This time there was no pain but she got none of Franklin's pleasure either, beyond the thought of a stewed pigeon filling her belly.

THEY WENT ALONG SO, Franklin staying away as much as a week before he again came looking. At the end of one night, he arrived late to find her pushing off the corder, and she could see it surprised and pleased and worried him in equal measure. It took longer that night, in part because he insisted she remove all her clothes, a thing she'd never done before in her life, and he lay for a long time just fondling the different pieces of her flesh. When he finally rose up and gave Anne her coin he said, "You could get more of these, you know."

"How?"

"With that corder, for one."

Anne scrabbled free of the bedding and stood. "No."

"Well then, the shipwright. Surely you see how he looks at you."

"No."

"Why *no*?"

"What need I of shipwright or corder if I have you?"

He studied her. "My single coins are sufficient?"

"Thus far."

Franklin tipped back his head and laughed. "You're no little fool, are you? Here. But don't count on the same every time you make me laugh." He fished an extra shilling out of his pocket and bounced it across the sheet.

ANNE BOUGHT A PIGEON, but no more. She was *not* a fool, and knew better than to count on the half crown, let alone the shilling, but she also knew better than to trust the corder or the shipwright or any of the other custom at the Penny Pot to treat her like a Franklin. There was an honest look to Franklin that promised to take only what was offered and in return make good on what *he'd* offered. There was also a look of through-and-through kindness in him, not like the teeth-outward-only gleam she caught in the others. The curious thing about Franklin, however, was how he came and went, and whenever he came back not looking entirely happy about it. Once he seemed to know in advance he wouldn't be coming again soon; he left her a whole crown and stayed away a fortnight. The first night of his return he didn't signal to her to climb the stairs, and she believed that the last coin had been his farewell to her, but the next night on his way out the door he reversed his course, caught her at the elbow less gently than usual, slapped his coin on the table in front of Mrs. Hewe, and tugged her to the stairs.

Once above stairs, however, Franklin's hands were as gentle as always; when he'd sufficiently pleased himself he touched her face and said, "Do you not wonder sometimes how great a sin this can be when it gives so much joy?"

"There are those who can't afford to go wondering about sin," Anne said.

Franklin looked at her for a long time. He ran his hand over each part of her and kissed her breast, throat, mouth. "I must be gone," he said.

"For how long?"

"For good. Forever. I must take my life in hand. But you're a clever girl, Anne. You'll make do." He unfolded her hand where it lay protectively cupping her belly as he spoke, and pressed some cool, heavy coins into it. Anne's fingers closed in instinct and didn't open again until Franklin had dressed himself and left. She looked down: two pounds British sterling.

. . . .

ANNE KNEW HER PREDICAMENT soon enough. It was easy to hide for a time, but then a month arrived where she seemed to spread wider each time she breathed, and the eyes that followed her around the Penny Pot held in them a new kind of look. Some of those eyes veered away but some hung on; one or two pairs urged her toward the stairs, and she hung back at first, but after thinking on it a few nights she realized she'd best get what she could while she could. The shipwright Isaac Wilkes was the first to persuade her up the stairs, after uncrumpling a fistful of the new paper money at her; Anne plucked a three-shilling note out of the lot, just high of what Franklin's half crown was worth, to make up for the discount of the paper, and discovered she could earn Wilkes's three shillings with a lot less work. He didn't wait for either of them to remove any clothes but simply pushed her onto the bed, pulled up her skirt, undid his buttons, and got it away so fast she was able to fit in the corder that same night. The corder wanted a second turn on the same three shillings and that took some sorting, but afterward he held no grudge; he and the shipwright became her steadiest customers, and she'd just begun to make up for Franklin when Mrs. Hewe came up to her at the end of a night's work and poked her swelling belly.

"I can't have it," she said. "I can't have you walking around like a signpost for the kind of place a decent gentleman won't frequent. If I'd known the goings on—" She knew better than to attempt to finish the sentence and didn't dare look at Anne as she said even that half of it—she'd taken her threepence for many a half-used bed and been glad enough for it. But perhaps it was Mr. Hewe who did the accounts; he came into the street after her and caught up her elbow. "For your trouble," he said, with some of her father's gentleness, "past and to come," and laid a twenty-shilling note in her palm.

ANNE'S MOTHER SAID NOTHING at the sight of Anne's growing belly but sent it such black looks that Anne began to imagine the fetus curdling inside her. When Anne announced she was through with work at the Penny Pot, her mother stopped speaking to her altogether, then began to rant at her nonsensically about things that had nothing to do with Anne, like the new crack in the plaster, or the turned fish, or the split in her shoe. One night after more than the usual number of hot blasts and cold drafts, her sister Mary spoke into the dark from her side of the bed. "Don't take it all to yourself, Annie. Mama never liked it when her own babies came on either."

ONE VICIOUSLY HOT DAY in August Anne saw Franklin passing by on the opposite side of Market Street. He might have seen her, he might have not, but if he did see her he could not help but note her condition; at six months, in a dress worn thin from washing and plastered to her with damp, her condition was more noticeable than Anne herself. That was how she felt most days—an invisible creature pushing a bright red wheelbarrow ahead of her—people saw the barrow and nothing else. Picking out amongst the market crowd the people who would still speak to her and the people who would not, she began to see what lay ahead. She'd figured how it would be at home—she'd take over the now discarded cradle and pull it next to her side of the bed; she'd add another hungry mouth to a house too full of them; as soon as she could wean it, she would leave the infant with her mother and go off again in hunt of work. She recalled Mary's remark. Was she, after all, to live her mother's life? Had that other life, that different life that Anne had plotted out for herself, already escaped her and her child both?

6

IN AUGUST, DEBORAH'S MOTHER died. The woman had been no more than half alive for a long time, but at her death a curious thing happened to Deborah: She began to feel only half alive herself. With her mother gone, what was left between Deborah and that life ahead, which could only be described as bleak? She pushed on in this half-dead state, putting her mother in the ground and settling her affairs; she discovered her mother's frugality had left her sufficient to live without resorting to the hatter's shop, but it wouldn't allow of a new dress or more than a single roast a month. Deborah wept tears that were only half for her mother, at times begrudging her even those; her mother was dead, but only after living the kind of family-rich life that Deborah could now only despair of. How different if she and Benjamin had been allowed to marry when they'd wished! Deborah's grief and anger mingled, each doubling each.

Sympathy callers stopped in. Deborah was surprised at the number of them—it reminded her of how remiss she'd been in paying such calls—but she'd just gotten into the habit of them when they ceased altogether, as if some unwritten rule were being followed that required so many days of attention to the bereaved and nothing past it. Deborah spent the first day without a visitor sitting in the parlor staring blindly at the back of the door; the second day she climbed the stairs and began to sort through her mother's things, few that there were. The third day she stayed in bed an hour past daylight; the fourth day, two. The fifth day she could not account for at all, or, indeed, for many of the days that followed. She couldn't recall cooking or eating a meal, or washing up, or sweeping, or any of the usual chores. She did know she had her hands in wash water when a knock finally did sound on the door, because when she went to dry them on her apron she looked down and noticed how soiled it was, how rimmed with grime her nails were. She also noticed she didn't care. She went to the door and opened it on Benjamin Franklin.

Near to, he looked different than he did in the street—more solid, more foreign somehow—more of the world and less of Market Street. For once, he seemed to have her same trouble with words. Deborah could think of only one thing to say, so she said it.

"What are you doing here?"

"I've come to express my great sadness on the death of your good mother. I was away at New Jersey and have only just returned to hear the grim news. My affection for her was always strong, as I believe hers was for me, despite some understandable reservations as to my prospects. I only hope—"

"Thank you for your sympathy." Deborah made to close the door, but Franklin gripped it by the edge and stayed its motion.

"Debby. Please. I come to make amends. I don't enjoy this weight of my past behavior on my conscience. You wrote two letters. Indeed, I attempted to answer them, but I could never come across a single proper thing to say. Should I have written that London was the world

I had always dreamed of? Should I have written how many things there were in such a city to distract a young man, that I was busy day and night and even into the next day, too busy to think of you as I ought? I told you I should not be home soon in my first letter, and the more I considered the matter, I discovered that was the only honest thing I had yet to say; having said it, what more was there to write? Then I came home and discovered your unfortunate situation, and what was there to say to that?"

"Nothing." Deborah pushed against the door again, but Franklin pushed it the other way; he won out; it opened and he stepped into the hall.

Deborah stepped back. Franklin made some study of her, and no doubt marked her advanced age, for his next words were "Do you not sometimes wish we could tinker with the clock and turn it back? Perhaps to the place where we went wrong, to begin over again and take a different turn? I should like to go back across the sea, remove the blinding glare of London from a young man's eyes, and write a different letter to a woman who deserved something better." Franklin's eyebrows lifted and Deborah almost smiled, remembering those eyebrows that talked as well as he did. "But I wonder that if I did so, would the letter be answered?"

"I answered your letter!"

"The old letter, yes, but now you're wiser and no doubt colder in your thoughts toward me. Perhaps you'd say I'd had my chance and lost it."

"You have lost it. I got married."

Franklin grew thoughtful. "Yes, yes, that damnable situation. I feel in part responsible. Or do I take too much on myself? Or do you think it possible that if I'd been better with my letters—"

Deborah threw her hands in the air. "Letters! Why do you come here and talk to me of letters?"

Benjamin raised his own hands—large, square palms upward,

miming her question. "Why indeed? Better I ask what I came to ask and take my dose, sweet or sour, whichever it might be. Here, then, is my question: Will you do something better for yourself than that regrettable apron and come out for a walk with an old friend? Or best yet, will you push what you remember of that old, neglectful friend aside and try stepping out with this new one? He's wiser and kinder and anxious to draw that awful scowl from your face to see if he can uncover the pleasanter one he remembers."

Deborah stared at him. "You come here to take me walking?"

"'Tis a small thing, I know, but we must start with something."

"I don't go about."

"You see? This is why I've come. Whatever do you mean, you don't go about? Of course you do. Come."

No, she thought; he's too late, and he offers too little. Or was it so little? To take her walking, to publicly acknowledge an interest in a woman with no honorable prospects, this would be no small thing on Market Street. She studied his face, trying to separate the new from the old, to wipe away the new confidence and find the old boy she'd once known. She failed. But in the course of the effort, she'd neglected to pay close enough attention to her apron, and somehow it had already been untied and hung on the nail; now her hand was taken up and drawn through his arm, and they were stepping out into the healthful air.

HE CAME AGAIN. AND again. He did most if not all the talking—of London, of the people he'd met, of the warmth of his reception at every foreign door he darkened. Between the words, Deborah believed she knew who was behind some of those doors, but she also believed she heard his apology for it, and as his words poured past her ears like sweet cream she began to see those London years in a way she hadn't before—he'd been young, she'd been younger—and what was one plain-faced, unfashionably dressed, rough-speaking Philadelphia girl against all of polished London?

After a time Deborah talked of Rogers, or she began to talk of Rogers, but Benjamin seemed to know the whole before she could tell the half. She made her one particular point again—that she'd left Rogers's house *before* he'd run off—and this time Franklin said, "I know it. And I'm proud of you for it," a curious echo of Deborah's small pride in Franklin's accomplishments. She began to think of her act of defiance as perhaps something not so small; she began to feel, as she walked the outskirts of Philadelphia with her arm through Franklin's, as if someone had just given her a warm quilt on a cold night.

More walks. More words. More warming. More coming to life inside that warmth like a chick in its egg. She invited Franklin in for tea and once, when she returned to the room after refreshing the kettle, she noticed something had been spilled on the hearth, the ants swarming it.

"Look at the ants," Benjamin said. "See how they communicate one with the other!"

Deborah went to the hearth, stomped on the ants, and brushed them into the fire. She turned and found Benjamin gaping at her queerly, either amused or annoyed, she couldn't distinguish. Did he think she didn't know how to keep house? Deborah looked around and for the first time noticed the dust that had accumulated on the chair rungs, the cobwebs in the corners, the dullness of the pewter. Well, perhaps he *should* think it.

The next time Benjamin came, the hearth had been scrubbed and a few other things too, and she'd gone to the trouble of making gingerbread, his favorite. The time after that he made her laugh, and the time after that she made *him* laugh, which was even better, so like the old days it seemed that she could almost forget her situation. Almost. Benjamin Franklin might fit that chair by the fire well, but he could never be anything but a visitor in it.

One evening as she led Benjamin to the door he tried to pull her into his arms, but she pushed violently against him. "We can offer each other naught but trouble," she said. "Leave me be."

Franklin drew back and studied her, dimple winking, eyebrows lifting. "We could offer each other *something*," he said.

Yes, she thought. And she'd risked everything for that something and lost.

Twice.

"Leave me be," she said.

HE DID NOT. *SHE* did not; she could blame him only partway in it. She sat in her mother's parlor cold and lonely, remembering how it had been once, especially when Franklin reminded her inch by inch, first with a thumb rubbed across the back of a hand and next with a finger drawing the line of her cheek and finally the whole hand cupping the back of her head, and without Deborah even feeling the tug somehow drawing her into those old, familiar kisses. Once there, the familiar smell of him—wool, tobacco, ink—brought back other familiar things, and Deborah, made by the earth gods and not by any saints, was soon following him up the stairs.

Deborah remembered Benjamin's strong and finely made physical self, but she hadn't remembered his utter command of *her* physical self. This was new—this was something brought home from London— and on the heels of the liquidity that always followed their successful union, she felt the first trill of fear. The Deborah and Benjamin who had begun together at nearly the same starting place were at the same place no longer, and now it was left to her to catch up. Beneath that lay the old problem, now intensified by the risks she took in sharing her body. Bigamy carried a penalty of thirty-nine lashes and life imprisonment; there could be no man and wife here—there could be nothing but shame and disgrace. And yet she could neither end it nor accept it. So it went.

IN THE END BENJAMIN solved it, although he said that Deborah did. They lay curled together in her bed, Deborah thinking how like before it was, and how she only wished it *was* before, so they could make another kind of end to it. Just as she was thinking it, Benjamin said it. "'Tis like before. That is, like before I left. How happy a time it was! And how foolish I was to walk away from it! 'Tis time to fix it."

"It cannot be fixed," Deborah said. "'Tis too late for that. Or for me," and as quick as that the old deadness filled her limbs.

"Nonsense," Benjamin said. "We do as you did before. You didn't trouble with the law when you left Rogers and took back your name; why trouble with it now? You come to my house and take my name."

Deborah blinked, stupid and frozen as a rabbit with a fox in sight.

Benjamin took her elbow and gave it a shake. "What could be simpler? All the town knows of Rogers. The sympathy will be with us."

The sympathy would be with him, she thought, for taking pity on poor, stupid Deborah Read, but despite herself she could feel the lightness, the life, flooding back into her half-dead self. She pretended to think the thing through for a time, but the truth of it was that she loved this Benjamin Franklin even more than she'd loved the old one, and she would take his love if it was love, but if it wasn't she would take his pity.

And so it was done.

7

PAIN—ANOTHER KIND OF PAIN, but somehow reminding Anne of that first virgin pain, as if it were a late-due payment. Her mother had refused to call in the midwife in a bit of economy that Anne had the time and the trouble to resent in growing waves as the event progressed and her mother stood useless at the foot of the bed. Anne made no noise, not liking her mother to know her suffering, until the very end when it all came out of her in one big gush and gasp.

"A boy," her mother said. "Not that it will help him any," and took him away to be cleaned and swathed. When he was brought back to Anne, he looked such a size that she understood better the weight she'd carried all those nine months, and the fight she'd just survived, if indeed she would survive it; the bed looked to be awash in more blood than a body could afford to lose. Anne took the babe from her mother and looked him over, thinking she could see a familiar wide forehead and clear, intelligent look; she knew the name she should give him and she knew the name she couldn't. She and Mary had been named for queens, her brother George for a king; this one would have like honors. "William," she said.

THE BLEEDING KEPT ON. Someone took the babe from her, but later, when she asked for him, no one would bring him to her; after that she remembered nothing but soft and loud, light and dark, hot and cold. After a time she heard her mother's voice.

"Will she live?"

A strange male voice answered. "She'll live, but she'll not have another. Just as well, I'd say."

The doctor. The doctor whose bill would be twice the midwife's and half as likely to be paid, which he must know if he'd ever been to Eades Alley. Anne caught a flash of an unfamiliar object shaped like a curved knife, and a new pain beyond all the others went up from Anne's womb to her brain like a bolt of lightning, blocking all memory of what came beyond, till she woke to the taste of broth on her tongue and a damp cloth on her head. She'd forgotten where she was and why she was until she heard a terrible noise and realized it was an infant crying— William crying—crying as if he'd been tossed in the fire to cook. Anne struggled to sit upright, but her mother pushed her down, rude and hard.

"Bring him." Anne said the two words with all the poor strength she owned, but she said them in her Penny Pot voice, and her mother brought him and fixed him in Anne's arms, propping him with pillows because she was too weak to hold him on her own. William took her breast and stopped crying, but not for long.

WILLIAM DIDN'T THRIVE. HOW could he? Anne was too weak and hungry and so was her milk. He cried all but the single hour after his watery meal, and the weight he'd worn into the world flaked off him as if he were a too-dry pastry crust. Anne's mother gave Anne what she could off her own plate, and from time to time Mary—thin, pale Mary—stuffed her sister's pocket with a bit of potato or a few nuts. Her father, too ill now to care about anything beyond his own comforts, fussed each time the babe wakened him, so as soon as Anne was strong enough, on those days when the December air was soft enough, she wrapped the infant in her shawl and took him out to walk, the *slap-slap-slap* of her feet against the ground being one of the few things that could soothe him to sleep.

How many days before she saw him? Not many. She spied him about to enter the clock maker's, dressed in the simple coat and breeches of old but with something of his new success in the smile he dispensed to all he passed, as if he could afford any generosity. She watched him step into the shop, and she lingered on the street opposite for no reason that made any sense, staring at his back through the window. She'd heard of his so-called marriage and had felt little at the news, so was surprised at the resentment that clawed at her. Anne had never for a minute dreamed of a place for herself alongside a man such as Franklin, but now, because of William, she *would* dream, at least enough to get William what he might need in life. But the rumors that followed Franklin made out that he'd taken on this wife in charity; if so, he'd not be on the lookout for a second case.

Franklin stepped out of the shop and had turned halfway to look behind him when he saw her. At first his eyes registered nothing particular other than the general recognition of pauper and child in the street, but it appeared he was not one to dismiss a pauper as quickly as another might. He let his eyes rest on her that second longer and that was enough for him to call her up out of his past, to register the child in her arms. Apparently he was not one to dismiss his past either. He stepped into the street and began to cross to her; he drew close enough so that if he wished to he might see what Anne had seen in that tiny face, and Anne believed he did see. His words started and stopped. "By heaven! This is . . . I daresay—"

"Mr. Franklin!"

He turned. Anne hadn't noticed the woman going into the shop, but she noticed her now, calling to Franklin as she came down its steps; Anne took note of the well-fed, square face and the firm jaw. She was not pretty, but more surprising, when she called again, even Anne, who'd been educated only as far as the Bible, could hear the fault in her grammar. "We'd best get on. The deliveries is arriving soon."

Franklin turned back to Anne. He said, "Where do you live?"

"At my father's house yet." But of course he did not know where her father lived. "Eades Alley."

"Eades Alley!"

The woman called again. Franklin turned again. He crossed the street to rejoin her, took her arm, and started off up Market Street. William began to cry and Franklin made to look over his shoulder but checked himself; Anne made no move to quiet the child—indeed, she found she could make no move at all. She stood fixed in place and watched the Franklins continue up Market Street, their heads bent toward each other as he talked and she listened. What did he talk of? Anne wondered. Ants? Singing glasses? The effect of a fire's heat on a face? She couldn't look at that woman and picture it.

WHEN THE KNOCK SOUNDED, Anne and her mother and the two next-oldest girls were in the kitchen, the three besides Anne washing clothes, with some resentful looks at Anne while she coped with William's fussing. Mary went to the door and opened it on Franklin. He seemed to have lost his old sociability; he said, abrupt almost to rudeness, "I should like a word with Anne."

Anne's mother dropped her work without question and herded the girls from the room. Once they were gone Franklin looked the kitchen over with the care of a rents agent; when he'd finished he returned to the babe, reached out and touched William's dandelion hair, felt his stemlike neck.

"Boy or girl?"

"Boy. William's his name."

"He's in health?"

"Fair."

Franklin drew his eyes from the babe to her, and proceeded to study her much as he had the kitchen. "And you?"

"The same."

He said, "Annie," but nothing more, fixing his attention again on the babe. After a time he held out a small cloth pouch, tied tight with a strip of leather. Anne put out her hand and felt a comforting weight drop into her palm. She closed her hand around it and pressed it to the babe's back.

"Would you like to examine the contents? I might hold the child while you do."

Anne shook her head.

"I should like to hold him."

Anne looked down at William; the tugs and jerks were growing stronger and he'd begun that telltale *unh, unh, unh* that would soon turn to shrieks. She held him out and Franklin took him with confidence, tucking the infant's head into his elbow, jiggling him gently up and down; either the motion or the new combination of smells widened the child's eyes and quieted his mouth. After a time Franklin removed his gaze from William and looked again at Anne. "If you examine the pouch—"

Anne set the pouch on the table, unopened. She reached for her child. Franklin handed William over and at once he began to cry. A look Anne had never before seen crossed Franklin's face: uncertainty, perhaps even shame.

He left.

8

WHEN ANNE SHOWED THE money pouch to her mother she grabbed it, peered inside, and flushed to her cap. She handed it back to Anne and took William from her arms. "We need cornmeal, oats, eggs. Salt pork. Salt beef or venison. Dare we have a fowl? Yes, yes! Pick us a good one! And sugar. Mustard and onions for your father's poultice. Chamomile." She seemed to see William in her arms for the first time. She hefted him as if weighing him. "And flour. This infant needs pap." She pointed to the pouch in Anne's hand. "There will be more?"

Anne shook her head.

"Then be sure to get your best price," Anne's mother said, but she removed nothing from the list.

THE DAY WAS WET and cold and showed the alley to its worst advantage, the sparse streams of smoke from its chimneys promising little warmth to those huddled inside. For Anne, outside, the rain slanted into her face no matter her best efforts to prevent it; the other walkers she passed had pulled hats down and collars up, and even the larger houses on Market Street, built tall and thin and close, seemed to have been pushed together as if for warmth. The stall keepers too were as cold as Anne, and impatient to sell out and close up; Anne made out well with little bickering. She completed her purchases, carrying what she could, giving directions for delivery of what she couldn't, and headed home. As she passed the Penny Pot she thought of how deeply the one day's shopping had dug into the money pouch even at storm-day prices; it was time to wean William and go back to work. But not at the Penny Pot.

ANNE BEGAN TO FEED William the pap, soaking the insides of a fresh loaf of bread in water until it had softened into a gumlike paste; almost at once the incessant crying stopped. She continued to nurse as she could but perhaps she got the more out of it—William had a way of fixing his eyes on her when he was at breast that spoke at certain times of devotion and at other times of reproach, and Anne found herself unable to look away from him, staring into the small, puckered face, trying to decide which it was. But she also found herself coming to a new understanding about love. Even amid the bustle of the house she felt as if William and she were walled off inside their own private shell; her mother could not—any other woman could not—know what it was like inside that shell. This boy, this small thing come out of nothing, despite all the trouble he had and would cause her, had wound himself around her heart like a snail around a clam, pried it open and devoured it. He'd made her glad of him, and yet when she recalled the doctor's words at his birth—*she'll not have another*—she was glad of that.

Other things in the house changed along with William. Anne could visit her father with a happier infant and soon discovered how the one's smile could draw the other's, how the father she had long cherished was still alive inside his illness. Something in the child brought out Anne's father's voice as well, and between the coughing he spoke words to Anne that she hadn't known she'd missed so much till she heard them new. "My Annie," he called her, as he used to do, and he began to call William "my boy." Despite the cheeks bright with fever and the shirt crusted with bloody spittle, Anne could see some new life in her father, and she started to hold out some hope of him after all.

So high had Anne come in those hopes that one morning when she carried William in to see her father and found him sleeping with all the flush of fever gone, she laid the back of her hand against his cheek expecting to feel the cool of health. Instead she felt the cold of death. She must have been gripping William too hard, for he began to whimper, but Anne made no move to quiet him—his noise could disturb her father no longer. She stepped back and stared at the man who had occupied that bed almost the whole of her life, who had been too much there and not enough there for years on end, and could only think in surprise how empty the house now was.

THEY BORROWED A CART from the butcher and carried Anne's father the few blocks to the Christ Church burial ground, the minister saying words of poor comfort over his grave and laying him in amongst the stones. Anne's father's grave was to be marked by a thin wood slab, engraved stone being as far beyond their reach as even the possession of a cart, and Anne examined the elaborately engraved markers to her left and right with resentment. She wanted such a stone for her father, she wanted a cart for her father that wasn't stained with blood, she wanted what only the most renowned Philadelphians had—a service of prayers right inside the elegant brick church itself. Anne wanted it known in death that her father had been more than the rotting alley that had symbolized the last years of his life.

Walking home to Eades Alley, trailing their scraps of funeral black and their funeral tears, the house felt so full of gloom and damp that Anne could barely make herself enter it. William seemed to taste Anne's bitterness in her milk; he turned away from her breast and within two days of the burial had all but weaned himself. The pap was not enough, however, and he began to lose weight again; Anne was so fearful of some dread ill in him that she found herself leaping up to watch his sleep so often she fell ill herself.

ANNE'S FATHER HAD BEEN dead a week when a man came to Eades Alley. Anne hadn't seen him at the Penny Pot; if she had she'd have remembered the distinct angles of his face and the shadows those angles cast on it. He looked no more than thirty, well but plainly dressed, with a look of newness to him, as if he'd recently come to the degree of prosperity he exhibited. The kitchen was crowded with girls and work much as before, but as soon as the man said, "I come with a message for the girl named Anne," they fled like so many geese, so it was no great trick for him to look at the babe and look at her and say, "You're Anne."

Anne made no answer. The stranger looked over the kitchen much as Franklin had done; when he said, "You may guess who sent me," she nodded.

He held out another weighted pouch. Anne saw it, but only at a glance—she'd discovered some difficulty in looking away from the man behind it. He was as finely honed as a blade, as opposite Franklin's anvil-like build as nature could have made him. He gave the pouch a little shake, as if impatient to be gone, and Anne reached out to take it, but once she'd done so he made no attempt to leave, or, in fact, to take his eyes from *her*. So, he was expected to report, then.

"I'm instructed to ask if there are other concerns," he said.

Anne could feel a fine rage building. She could see Franklin sitting at his desk, not looking up from the ledger where he'd made careful note of the sum he was handing across to this man, speaking over his shoulder as if in afterthought, *Find out if there are other concerns.*

"Do you mean do I have other concerns besides a hungry child in a leaky house in a stinking alley?"

The stranger's hair was that red-gold that explained the ready flush. "I think if you look in the pouch you'll find a not-insubstantial sum."

Anne flung her arm wide. "Enough to sweep all this away, then?"

The man said nothing, but his eyes stayed fixed on her, changing with the flushing of his face from more brown to more green; Anne would have preferred them to stay one thing or the other. Or perhaps she only preferred them to be fixed away from her.

"These are my *concerns,*" Anne said. "Report them or not. Good day, sir."

The stranger bowed—not a common sight in the alley—and left.

ANNE FOUND WORK AT the Indian King Tavern on Third and Market, two blocks inland from the Penny Pot and the alley and patronized by a less watery clientele. The work was much the same as the Penny Pot, and easier in some aspects because Anne no longer wasted time on smiling. She ran amongst the tables like the dog running inside the wheel that turned the spit at the fire; the first day she fed the dog a crust off a plate, but by the second day she examined her thin wage and thrust the leavings into her own pocket.

The work was hard, but not as hard as leaving William. The first morning Anne had left the boy dry and fed and smiling and come home to find him wet and hungry and shrieking like a crow; when she took her mother to task her mother said only, "I've got six others to care for; I can't spend all day pampering your brat." Anne tried to assign the boy's care to Mary for the promise of a halfpenny, but the money only gave Mary a better idea; by the end of the first week

Mary had put herself out to work burnishing leather at the shoemaker's for twice the wage Anne made at the Indian King.

The first time Anne saw the stranger with the money pouch at the Indian King, it was as if an imaginary figure out of some ancient tale had sprung abruptly to life. He took a table by himself and waited till Anne drew near; he asked for his rum but held her with questions.

"How long have you worked here?"

"A month."

"Every day?"

Anne nodded. She left to get him his rum, and by the time she'd returned to his table she believed she'd figured in her head his purpose. He would report to Franklin: *She's making her own wage now; she's no need of more from you.*

THE SECOND TIME THE stranger came, Anne didn't see him right away. She'd been engaged by a young and eager lawyer who'd almost convinced her it was time to think about earning a real wage again; she looked up and saw the stranger's eye fixed on her. Well then, let him put that in his report, Anne thought; if she worked it right she'd do a good deal better that night than her usual wage and Mary's put together, and after the lawyer there'd be another just as eager. She *didn't* need Franklin's pouch.

9

"YOU KNOW MY WIFE," Benjamin would say, or "Allow me to introduce Mrs. Franklin to you," and that, he believed, was sufficient.
Perhaps for him it was—the whispers followed her, not him—but
Deborah didn't care about her public life while the private one was so
exactly all she wished. They settled in above the print shop, and since
Deborah had expected so busy and popular a man to be absent most
evenings, she was pleasantly surprised by the number of nights he
climbed the stairs at the end of a long day in as much apparent eagerness for the sight of her as she was for him.

"My wife!" he would cry, with never even a joke about it; he
would surround her with strong arms, pull her against his wide chest,
and kiss all the skin of her that showed and as much of the non-
showing parts that he could reach before she pushed him backward.
But sometimes she didn't push backward, and on those nights supper
was late and often cold; always on those nights Benjamin made a point
of saying, "Delicious!" but with a look that took in all the other things

he found delicious. There were those days when Deborah did worry about her fragile status—until they'd cohabited seven years she could never be called his legal wife, and then only if Rogers didn't appear—but treated to every courtesy, wrapped inside the warmest affection, those days of worry arose less and less. Deborah's confidence grew; she began to stare down the whisperers on the street; she was Mrs. Benjamin Franklin, and woe to him who dared to question it.

THEY'D SPENT SIX MONTHS as contentedly as Deborah could imagine any man and wife to be when Benjamin came through the door one evening and approached her where she was stooped over the soup pot. He took her by the hand and pulled her away from the fire, drew the spoon from her hand and left it dripping on the hearth.

Deborah shook her elbow free, recaptured the spoon, and scraped at the brick with her shoe. "Here, now! Look at the mess you make!" She moved to return the spoon to the kettle, but Benjamin again retrieved it, this time carrying it to the table. He returned to collect Deborah's hand and drew her to the chair. By now she'd looked at him more closely and dropped readily enough into the seat, her insides hollow and ringing. "What? What is it?"

"Let me get you a glass of cider."

"I want no cider! Tell me, Benjamin! What's the trouble? Is it Rogers?"

"No, not Rogers. Here, let me get us both some cider."

"I want no cider! Tell me what the trouble is!"

Benjamin fetched the cider anyway, two large mugs, and set them on the table, settling himself with alarming deliberateness in the chair closest to Deborah. "Before I begin, Debby, you must understand one thing: What I speak of now is a past event—the mathematics will prove it to you if my word does not—'tis nothing that came during the time of our marriage."

"What, Benjamin! For the love of God, tell me this instant! What didn't come at the time of our marriage?"

"I suppose it is indeed my trouble, but now I must ask you to share in it. Believe me, my dear, I am well aware that I could ask such a thing only of a woman with a heart as large as yours."

"With a heart that's ready to burst! As you value my life, tell me!"

Benjamin took a long draft of cider. He lifted Deborah's mug to her lips but she slapped it away.

"There's a child. A child of mine. An infant. Born to a woman of brief acquaintance. His circumstance is such that he cannot thrive where he is. I ask a favor I have little right to ask—the only thing that perhaps gives me that right is my great faith in you, and my trust that you share a like faith in me. I ask you to allow this child into our home and raise it as ours. 'Tis a boy named William. In truth, I have grave doubts he will live long enough to trouble us greatly, but he is my son, and I cannot leave him to suffer and perhaps die where he is. You will understand this, Debby, or I don't know you as I believe in my heart that I do know you. You will understand and accept him no matter the pain to us, because our pain can be only a piddling thing compared to what his must be if we turn our backs."

Benjamin stopped talking. Deborah was fairly sure he stopped talking, although her head still rang with his voice—his words—but jumbled together inside her head as they were, she couldn't get them into a proper order. "I don't understand you," she said. "I don't understand you in the least."

Benjamin began to talk again, but this time Deborah couldn't hear him on account of the ringing left over from the last bit of speech making. At some point in the throes of it, she discovered she'd stood up.

"Deborah. Debby."

Deborah held up her hands, shook her head. "No," she said. "No." She began a slow walk toward the stairs, but found herself careening up them. She dashed into the bedroom, shut the door, and fell face-down on the bed. Sleep, she thought. She would sleep, and when she woke she would discover it but a dream. A nightmare.

A knock sounded on the door.

"Leave me be!"

The door opened. Deborah rolled away from it. She felt the bed sag behind her, but he didn't touch her. She imagined him peering over her raised hip, attempting to get a glimpse of her face. She pushed it deeper into the bolster.

He said, "I know I should say to you that this is your choice, but I confess some difficulty in uttering anything resembling the word *choice*. What choice do we have in this? How can we live with ourselves if we turn this child away?"

Deborah sat up and swung around on him.

"Who is this child's mother?"

"No one."

"I want to know her name."

"She's no one, Debby. I declare, I never heard a last name and would be hard pressed to remember the first. She was part of an old, unhealthy habit I've long since given up."

"Long since given up! And how old is this infant?"

"Very well then, perhaps not *long* since given up, but given up, I promise you, well before I took you to wife. I've been a faithful husband to you."

Deborah got up off the bed and walked out of the room, leaving Benjamin sitting as he was. She took the stairs and continued at the end of them until she found herself in the street. She began to walk, thinking her mind might work better with some blood pumping into it, but instead her mind stopped thinking altogether. After a time she began to notice the many passersby in the busy street, and there her mind became an unfriendly companion. At every woman she saw she thought, Is this the creature that lay with him? At every man, she wondered if he knew her husband's secret.

Husband. It was a word Benjamin had uttered, but was it a true one? The answer, of course, was no, it was not—Benjamin was not her husband by any law and therefore not in any way that bound Deborah to obey him and accept this child born of his uncontrollable lust. But as Deborah walked on and on she discovered herself looking at the question from the opposite side of it—he was *not* her lawful husband, and therefore what bound *him* to this "marriage," when out on the street somewhere walked a woman who had already borne a child for him? How objectionable must this woman be for Benjamin to cast her aside for an unlawful marriage to a woman without any great beauty or learning or means? Or was that the answer to the riddle, no doubt being asked yet throughout Philadelphia: Why should a Benjamin Franklin take pity on a Deborah Read, or a Deborah Rogers, as she perhaps still was to them? Had Benjamin known of this child and planned to drop it on Deborah from the start? Was that the bargain, then, his sudden return to her after he'd already been four years home, this hasty "marriage" where no real marriage could ever take place, all in exchange for adopting this child out of God-knows-what?

Deborah walked on and on, and after a time she discovered that her thoughts had turned the matter around again. What if Benjamin *hadn't* known of this child before he claimed Deborah as his wife? If that was the case, nothing now prevented him from leaving Deborah behind and marrying this other creature, this mother of his child, and yet he hadn't even hinted at such a course. Instead, he'd come to her and asked her to take this child as her own boy.

Her own boy. Deborah and Benjamin had lain together many times, both before he left for London and after it, but nothing had grown in her. What if this child was all that was to come to them of children? What if that cradle on that hearth she'd been dreaming of so long was to lie empty forever? Would she prefer another woman's child to no child at all? Was this then her choice?

Choice. Deborah had walked the length of the busy section of Market Street and deep into the unpopulated outskirts; she kept going, thinking on that word *choice*. Benjamin felt he had none, felt he owed this child he'd spawned a chance at a better life. He'd gone so far as to include Deborah in this lack of choice, and in truth, what *was* her choice? For whatever reason, this man had claimed her where no other man likely ever would and treated her not only as if she was his lawful wife, but as if she was a most treasured one. And what did *she* most treasure in this world? That affection Benjamin Franklin bathed her in day after day. Was that the bargain, then? In exchange for that affection, this child?

Child. Despite herself Deborah felt her heart give a little leap. Of late Deborah had secretly begun to fear a life without any children, had feared Benjamin's turning away from her because of her failure to produce one. Instead, he was offering her one, as he'd offered her everything else: his name, his protection, her life.

Deborah turned around. She didn't hasten her steps, but took them with all deliberation, letting her mind turn again and again as she walked, one minute seeing one side of Benjamin, the next seeing the other; one minute seeing one side of the child and the next the other. By the time she reentered the house, she was of no one mind on either thing. She looked in the kitchen and parlor and study but found no Benjamin, and a shudder took her; what if he'd despaired of the size of her heart and left? What if he'd gone to that other woman, whoever she was, having given his false wife her fair chance, free now to take a true wife, to take his true son into his heart?

Deborah climbed the stairs, pushed open the bedroom door she had slammed behind her on her way out, and there he lay, on their bed, hands folded across his chest, eyes closed, profile strong and stark against the weakening light. He turned to her as she entered, but she could see nothing of his expression in the shadows, no clues to either an eleventh-hour regret or a genuine relief. If only he would say something, anything, some words that would allow her to summon the right words to say back!

Benjamin lifted his hand, and that proved to be enough. It drew Deborah across the room and down beside him on the bed.

"Dare I ask? Is it *yes?*"

Deborah nodded, relieved to have no need of words after all.

Benjamin clasped her fingers in both his hands and held them tight against his chest. "My wife," he said. "My remarkable wife."

10

Philadelphia, 1731

HE APPEARED AT EADES Alley so late that all but Anne and Mary were asleep. The girls were trying to catch up on William's dirty clouts, and the kitchen smelled of scalded urine and wet cloth drying. At the knock the girls looked at each other in some alarm, but Mary was first to drop her clouts and go to the door to call through the crack, "Who is it?"

"Mr. Franklin."

Mary rounded her eyes at Anne and lifted the latch; Franklin stepped into the tiny kitchen and stood silent, stared blankly at Mary until she turned and continued up the stairs. He came up to Anne without greeting and held out a folded paper.

"Go to this address. 'Tis an upholstery shop. Ask for this man. He's got work and a room for you. Do well and you can make something of it."

Anne wiped her hands on her apron and took the paper: SOLOMON GRISSOM, UPHOLSTERER. FRONT STREET.

"He's expecting you."

Anne lifted her head. "And William?"

Franklin took in a breath that visibly expanded, then deflated, his chest. "I'll be taking William."

Anne backed away from Franklin, crimping the paper in her hand, shaking her head.

"Anne. See sense. Think what I might give him. Proper food and clothes, a good house, a decent education, a father's guidance and affection."

"And what of a mother's affection?"

"He'll have a mother's affection. I've discussed this with my wife and she's eager to take him. 'Tis best for him. Surely you see that." As if to make his point he looked around the kitchen, at the first batch of clouts hanging on a string before the fire to dry, at the next batch looped sloppily over the side of the washtub and dripping on the floor, at the sparsely filled cupboard, at the chair with the broken rungs, and, last, at the pulled stockings and split shoes on Anne's feet. "'Tis best for you," he said softly.

Anne went to the tub and gathered up the dripping cloth, tipping it back into the dirty water. She took off her apron and wiped up the spilled water with it. She went to the fire and jabbed at the expiring coals till they sparked, then began ripping the dried clouts off the line.

Franklin came up behind her and took her laundry from her. "I should like to see the boy."

How cold a thing panic was! How hot. Anne backed away from the fire, away from Franklin, away from the stairs where William lay, as if she were a hen drawing the fox away from her nest of eggs. But of course Franklin wouldn't snatch the child and walk out the door. But of course he could. A child was the property of the father just as the wife was the property of the husband; in the end, if Franklin chose to claim his child and give it his name, there was little Anne could do to prevent it. She looked hard at Franklin's face, trying to find the hidden cruelty that must have lurked in it all this time, but saw only pain—hers—reflected. He understood what he asked, then. Or he understood the half of it. He could understand nothing of what it meant in the light of the sentence the doctor had pronounced on her: *She'll not have another.* But Anne had always been glad of that, of being able to make an extra coin here and there without fear of forcing another child into the world of Eades Alley.

Eades Alley. It was as if Anne's own thoughts were making Franklin's case for him. But hadn't that been Anne's case too? Wasn't she now being offered all she'd dreamed of for William? What kind of fool could refuse that? Anne. Anne could refuse it. She would make no argument, for she had none; she would simply walk away from the man, go to her son, open up her clam's heart, and suck William safe inside it.

Anne went to the stairs and started up them.

"Annie."

She stopped.

"I know well enough how bright you are. I know you'll think over what's best for him and for you. I'll come back Friday next."

He left.

ANNE FOUND WILLIAM AS she'd left him, asleep in the cradle jammed in at the foot of the bed that Anne shared with Mary. Next to her bed she could just make out the other two beds, pushed in tight with barely a foot between them, piled double and triple with her remaining five siblings. She sat down. Mary said, "Is he gone? Did he bring more money?"

"He brought no money." She paused. Could she say the words? Could she make them doubly real by letting them into this room too? "He wants William."

Mary flew upright. "What for?"

"To raise up."

"To raise up!"

Unable to speak, Anne nodded, not knowing if Mary could see her or not, but she seemed to. "To raise up," she repeated. "Oh, Annie, what luck!"

Oh, traitor Mary!

Anne went to the cradle and picked up the boy; he was either too full of sleep to cry or already understood inside his tiny self that one person crying in so small a space was sufficient. After a time Anne felt Mary's thin arm creep around her shoulder, her sleep-knotted hair come down against her cheek. "Lucky William," she said. "Poor Annie."

Cruel, cruel Mary. She could have picked any words but those that might have left Anne with her conviction.

A WEEK PASSED AS a blink, even less when viewed through the never-ending tears. Anne raged at the tears, at Franklin, at poor Mary, at her mother, at any small child who crossed her path. The only one spared was William, but William did not spare her—he woke through the night as he hadn't done for some time; he cried even after he was fed, he pushed and struggled in her arms. But five days passed with Anne still fixed in her resolve to keep her child with her; she went to bed on the fifth night, a hot one, so stifling that when William woke flushed and fussing she was convinced he'd fallen ill. She sat cradling him in her arms and thought no one single thought that she could name, but one minute she was convinced of one thing and the next minute all was over. She'd decided. She knew. Or perhaps she'd only understood what she'd known five days before. William must go with Franklin.

Odd how it was that once the matter was settled in Anne's mind, William settled too. She carried him below stairs and sat in the dark and told him all she could dream of his new life to come; her voice seemed to soothe him and she knew it soothed her; his dead-sleeping weight grew heavy in her arms.

They sat so till dawn.

ANNE DIDN'T WAIT FOR Franklin to come back. At the end of the week she sent a note to the print shop with her eight-year-old brother, George. *Take him now.* Now while her will stayed strong. She was above stairs, folding and refolding William's fresh-laundered clouts and shifts, when the knock came. She picked William out of his cradle and changed him from wet to dry, put him in the best of the linen, took up her father's China-blue flannel scarf and laid it over her shoulder for William to rest against. Mary picked up William's clothes and they descended the stairs, but Mary only continued as far as the table, where she set down William's clothes and turned around.

Franklin was sitting alone in the kitchen in one of the better chairs, doing something to the rung of another. As Anne came into the room he set down the chair and stood up; looking from the frail babe to the man, she was aware more than ever of the strength and power in him, but she looked longest at his face, taking a final cast of it. She reminded herself that she'd never seen anything hard or cruel in it; in fact, Franklin had been fairer than most. The money, yes, but who else would have found a place for her child at his hearth or a situation for her in an upholstery shop? Not the corder, certainly. Not the shipwright. Anne thought these things as she carried William to Franklin and held him out; Franklin opened his mouth as if to speak, but she shook her head violently; she needed to get her own words out while she still had her voice. "He's full weaned. He takes a pap of bread and water but it should be milk, now we're to the season for it. He likes the air but wants good blanketing." She went to the table and picked up the freshly laundered clothes, but Franklin said, "We'll not be needing them."

Anne looked down at the stains that would never come clean in the wash, the frayed corners from so many washings. Of course; the Franklins would have better ready. But Anne had something better ready too. She took the scarf from her shoulder and handed it across. "Keep it by him. 'Twas his grandfather's."

Franklin took the scarf and tucked it into his pocket with care; he took the infant and cradled him against his waistcoat. Again, he opened his mouth to speak, but again Anne shook her head. "Go," she said.

He did so. And she hated him—oh, how she hated him—for it.

I I

DEBORAH FRANKLIN HAD SAID *yes*. She reminded herself of this over and over again through the next few days. It was done. She'd said yes. At the time she'd imagined that the first conversation with Benjamin, the agonized decision that resulted from it, must be the hardest part of it; indeed, it had been easy enough to hem clouts and shifts, to send Benjamin out for a sturdier cradle than the one he'd first purchased, but she hadn't anticipated the great upheaval that would then take place inside her head. Most often the questions came when they lay together in the dark, after they'd pleased each other and just before Benjamin had drifted off to sleep; Deborah hadn't slept in a fortnight.

"Who knows of this infant?" she asked.

"No one but Grissom."

"Grissom!"

"It was necessary to enlist him. I didn't like to get any more acquainted than I was."

Deborah could find little to argue with on that point, but she couldn't hold the main question back. "Who is she, Benjamin?"

"No one, Debby. You may guess the sort. No one who knows us could know her or know a thing about this birth, I promise you that."

"And what are those who know us going to think when a child suddenly appears in our house?"

"They may think as they like."

" 'There goes Benjamin Franklin's bastard and that fool woman who agreed to take it up!' Or perhaps they'll think another thing and say, 'Well then, that explains *that* so-called marriage!' "

"Not within my hearing, or they'll be sorry for it. Do you forget that I'm now the editor of the *Gazette*? You must get your chin up, Debby, for *his* sake. You do, and I promise you, in another six months, any questions regarding this boy's sudden arrival will be long forgot." There Benjamin pulled her close and began to comb her hair with his fingers, a thing Deborah particularly liked—the firm but gentle working of his fingers against her scalp, the soft tug at the roots—and she found herself disinclined to raise any more questions, voice any more doubts. That didn't mean that she believed all that Benjamin said—she rather believed that questions surrounding the editor of the *Gazette* might live on longer than they might if the man were, say, a chimney sweep—but only time could prove either case.

Later, however, after Benjamin had left off playing with her hair and gone to sleep, Deborah discovered that she felt even more unsettled about the idea of this boy than she had before she'd brought the subject up. She followed the thread of unease backward through all the soothing words and then forward again till she landed on the sore spot—Benjamin had said that she was to get her chin up for *the boy's sake*. Was all to be for the boy's sake now? Was Deborah's interest never to figure in it? Deborah pushed the thought away. Benjamin believed her heart large enough to hold him *and* this boy-not-her-son in it; she must believe his heart at least as large as that, large enough for a son and a not-his-wife.

LATER YET, ANOTHER QUESTION occurred to Deborah. "When this boy grows, what do you plan to tell him of his mother?"

"That here she is and always was and always will be. I promise you, Debby. Nothing more need be said."

DEBORAH PACED THE HOUSE, straightening where it needed and where it didn't, comforting herself with the touch of her things, simple as they were: this table, those chairs, that cupboard. Benjamin was a frugal man and hadn't liked her to splurge on anything beyond what necessity demanded, but it was a comfortable house, or so Deborah used to think it—the air that came in damp off the river through windows that Benjamin insisted on pushing wide might do for grown lungs but not for a sickly infant.

Deborah pulled the windows shut; she went to the cradle she'd padded with two folded sheets but it felt too full—she pulled out the topmost sheet and it felt too thin. She put the second one back. She'd already made up some pap for the child but now decided to add some sugar to it and spilled as much as she deposited. In cleaning up the sugar she stepped on her hem and pulled her skirt out at the waist; she took out her needle and thread and made as ugly a mend as she'd made since she was eight. She was wrung out and wild eyed when she finally heard Benjamin's steps climbing the stairs from the street.

Deborah leaped to her feet but didn't approach the door; Benjamin would have his arms full and could no doubt use her help, but she couldn't take a step. When he came in she was fixed in the exact middle of the room. She looked at him and took in the smile as wide as a ship's deck; she looked at the infant and saw Benjamin, there could be no doubt of it. There was the broad forehead and the dimpled chin; there, already, were the round, intelligent eyes that looked at every new thing with such great interest. But what of those things that hadn't come from Benjamin? By now Deborah knew every inch of her husband's square, solid flesh, and it couldn't account for the pointed little chin, the delicate nose, the long, slender fingers.

Benjamin made as if to hold the child out to Deborah but she took a step back, concealing her cowardice by saying, "Let me get his pap." She retreated to the kitchen and Benjamin followed; she set the bowl and spoon on the table and waved Benjamin to the chair before it, but he shook his head.

"His first meal must be from his new mother," he said, pushing gently at Deborah's shoulder till she'd backed up into the chair, placing the child in her arms. "Meet William," he said. "William, meet your mother." The small face puckered. Deborah dipped the spoon and thrust it at the infant—he took it at once in a great gulp that made him sputter; he took another and settled his surprising weight against her, his eyes—Benjamin's eyes—fixed on Deborah's. She felt as she looked at him that he knew more than she did already, that he knew better than to trust her. Yes, already his eyes had drifted away and fixed on Benjamin as he ate, as if they were long acquainted.

When it seemed to Deborah the boy had eaten as much as one of his size should eat, she set down the spoon, but Benjamin immediately reached over and picked it up, returning it to her hand.

"No, my dear, we must let him eat his fill; he'll like his new home all the better for it. He's been kept short till now and we must make it up to him as we can. There, you see? He snaps it up like a bird. What a fine boy you are, my little William!"

His little William, Deborah thought, not hers, but she caught herself up at once; she must not let herself think it. This was now her boy too. *Her* little William.

"Now you must see if he's wet or dry," Benjamin said, once William appeared sated.

"I know how to change a clout," Deborah snapped, already worn out from her efforts.

Both William and Benjamin started.

12

ANNE MAY HAVE SLEPT, eaten, worked, cleaned, cooked, laundered, slept again—she imagined she did, but she had no memory of it. She felt she'd left the Anne who lived at Eades Alley and had become another Anne who lived—or at least hovered—on Market Street, at Franklin's house. She knew the minute Franklin would have arrived home with William, the minute he would have handed William to his wife; she knew the way the wife would look down at the creature in her arms and wonder what other face in all Philadelphia could make some claim to it. All this Anne knew because she lived it in place of her own life.

Anne's mother remained patient with such absence for two days, but there either her patience ran out or she saw only a single cure for it. "Get yourself to that upholsterer's," she said. "You're no use in this house."

Anne, who'd been slaving more than three hours at the hot fire, looked up in her own kind of heat. She rapped a long spoon against the side of the stew pot that hung over the coals. "No use, am I? 'Tis my wage filled this pot."

"And you'll make a better one at that shop; with your room paid you'll be able to send enough home *and* take less out of our cupboard. After all, 'tisn't like it was when your father needed a nurse."

Well, it was true. All of it. If Anne's father had been alive, he might have had another thing to say about it, but then again, he might not. And besides, with both her father and William gone, the house was no longer the place of even the smallest comfort it might once have been.

"If a thing's to be done 'tis best to do it," Anne's mother said, and Anne couldn't argue with that either. She went above stairs and collected her father's small satchel from under the eaves; she went to her room and began to pack her few worn things in it. Her mother came in. "'Twill be better for you, Anne."

"'Twould be hard to come out worse," Anne said.

ANNE FOUND HER WAY to the upholsterer's shop and then found herself walking past it along Market Street until she'd reached the building Franklin rented for his print shop. He lived in the two and a half stories of rooms above the shop—Anne and all the rest of Philadelphia knew this; she stood across the street but at an angle so as not to attract the attention of the occupants. She studied the windows above the shop, making a map of the likely rooms in her head; there would be a parlor and kitchen at the first level and no doubt the sleeping rooms above. She looked from window to window, trying to imagine William's exact place behind them at that moment. Would he be asleep in a cradle in the kitchen next to his new mother as she worked? Would he wake crying for Anne, or would he look up at his new mother's face and notice no difference? For William she wanted the one, for herself she wanted the other. It was one thing to give up her child to a better life, it was another to be erased completely from it.

ANNE FIRST SAW THE shelves full of bolts of rich damask and glistening silk and more familiar striped bed ticking; she next saw a fair-haired boy of perhaps nine or ten years, no doubt an apprentice, hammering away at a footstool; last, she saw the man of the money pouch, stretching a rough buckram over a chair back. The pair stopped their work together at the sight of her and stared. The man collected himself first and said, "Peter, this is Anne, she's come to work alongside you; now get on with it." The boy gave Anne one last examination and resumed his hammering. The man came up to Anne, took her bag from her without further word, and walked with it toward a doorway at the rear of the shop. It opened into a hallway containing a window, a door, and a steep flight of stairs; Grissom pointed at the door.

"The necessaries."

Anne looked through the window and saw a narrow yard with a well and an outhouse at the far end; she took note and followed the man up two steep flights of stairs, looking back as she went to fix the route in her head—not just to the necessaries but to the world beyond should she find need of escape. The stairs stopped on a small landing that faced a single door to what had clearly once been a part of the eaves; the man had to duck to enter, but Anne passed with ease, and some eagerness.

Space. Low, narrow, angular, chopped up by a massive chimney and a dormered window, but space—more of it than Anne had ever had to herself. The window gave off a patch of northwest light, and the heat from the chimney would go far to counter the winter cold, if she were to remain there that long.

The man said, "Settle yourself. I'll see you in the shop when you're done."

Anne said, "Mr. Grissom, is it? What's my work, sir?"

"Stuffing ticks, to start."

"And my wage?"

Grissom lifted his eyebrows. "You were told none of this? I expected you to be told. Sixpence a day, plus the room and your midday meal."

"Very well. Thank you."

"You needn't thank me. 'Tis hard enough work. And besides—"

He didn't finish his words, but Anne could guess at them—she needn't thank him because she was a favor done for Franklin, no doubt in exchange for one Franklin had done for him. To take an untried girl of questionable character to work and live under his roof meant it must have been a considerable favor, but beyond simple curiosity it didn't concern Anne; what concerned her was the sixpence a day with the room and the part board. Anne had never excelled at sums, but she could take it far enough along to see that it would put her ahead of the Penny Pot and the Indian King Tavern, but not ahead of the whore.

WHEN ANNE RETURNED TO the shop, Grissom led her to a long table at the far end of it. Anne had already discovered how unlike Franklin the man was; he said no words that weren't absolutely demanded of him, and now he chose to demonstrate her task in silence. A striped mattress ticking lay on the table alongside an open barrel of feathers; Grissom sat himself down on the stool and began to pull feathers from the barrel and feed them through a small slit in the tick; after a large lump had appeared under the cloth, he picked up a long stick and began to disperse the lump into the corners. Only then did he seem to feel the need for words.

"The tick must be full from corner to corner, stuffed higher in the middle, dense enough so it springs back no more than a hand's width."

He rose from the stool and pointed Anne into it. Anne sat. She took a deep breath and reached into the barrel, but the deep breath had been a mistake—it drew a piece of soft down into her throat and she began to cough violently, loosing more feathers into the air to fly about the shop like gusting snow. Peter gave a snort of that pure delight that could only come from a young boy; Anne looked to Grissom to see what the grown man was likely to make of it, but although she might have sworn to a hint of amusement behind the shadows, his only response was to point Anne to the broom. She collected and made use of the tool; when she'd finished Grissom had already returned to his chair.

ANNE HAD IMAGINED HERSELF equal and more to stuffing a simple bed tick by noon and was dismayed to see that she'd filled but half the tick when an old woman appeared at the door to the shop and called out, "Dinner!"

Grissom went for the stairs to his private rooms; Anne followed Peter to a small room off the rear of the shop where it appeared the help was expected to eat. The room was full of more barrels and crates, but space had been found for a table set with two bowls of pudding, two mugs of beer, and a platter of bread and cold beef, a far better offering than Anne had been allowed at the Pot or the King. Anne was hungry enough, but Peter had dispensed with half the loaf by the time Anne had dipped her spoon into her pudding. She made quick claim to an end piece of the bread and a slab of beef before she asked, "How old are you, Peter?"

"Eleven. You were thinking ten, weren't you? Too scrawny, Pa says. That's why I've been put out to the upholsterer and not the shipwright."

"I should think upholsterers must be quite strong."

Peter considered this, nodded. "I once saw Mr. Grissom catch a whole barrel of nails that fell off a wagon."

"There you are, then. And where do you sleep?"

Peter pointed to a pallet in the corner of the shop floor.

This could have been William, Anne thought. She slid her piece of bread onto Peter's plate and he beamed at her.

THEY WORKED EACH DAY till dusk, Anne's fingers growing more and more accustomed to the movement of feathers, growing faster at stuffing ticks but still needing to rework too many. Grissom showed no anger or pleasure at whatever she'd done; in fact, he barely spoke to her at all, coming up to the table to observe her now and again in silence. With the boy he had more to say, and forcefully enough. "No! Goes the other way round. Watch your corner! Watch your corner! Fine, lad! Fine!" The blame and praise came with equal liveliness and she never heard the sound of a blow; it seemed a successful enough method—Peter worked to please and he worked hard. Anne watched him when she could and thought of William as he grew, taking his place beside his father in his print shop, being treated with like sternness and kindness. At their shared meals she continued to push a little something extra to Peter's side of the platter and soon became a great favorite of his. She wondered what William would think of her when he reached eleven, but then realized: He wouldn't.

AT THE END OF each work day, Anne walked through the dusk past Franklin's print shop, looking up at the candlelit windows. Now and then a shadow would move past the softly illuminated windows; once she believed she saw a small head resting against the shadow's chest, once she heard crying and lingered till it stilled. She heard other sounds coming from the open windows, mostly men's deep, rich voices and hearty laughter, Franklin's clearly identifiable amongst them. Once she heard a woman's raised voice, "No, I don't!" Another time she heard the same voice spiraling upward into the beginnings of a song. Or a wail.

ANNE HAD BEEN AT Grissom's a full month before she saw William. Grissom allotted her the Sunday for her own, and she'd spent the first few at Eades Alley, sharing what she could out of her wage, taking with her some of the cheese and bread that she bought at the end of each week to supply her breakfast and supper for the week to come. After one such visit she decided to risk a daylight walk past Franklin's house and was rewarded with a glimpse of mother and boy just returning home. William had put on a good deal of weight and perched in all apparent contentment against his new mother's shoulder, looking around, as had always been his way, at everything new. Did he see Anne? She believed so; the round eyes fixed on her until a loose pig ran past the door. Did he know her? Anne couldn't make a case for it; she and the pig had received equal attention.

13

THE FIRST THICK HEAT of summer had just descended when Isaac Wilkes, the shipwright, stepped into Grissom's shop. He spied Anne at her table and stopped just inside the door.

Grissom stood up from his work and approached the shipwright. "Mr. Wilkes. What can I do for you?"

The shipwright turned from Anne and faced Grissom. "I'm in need of a mattress."

"Very well. Feathers or hair?"

"Hair."

"Ours is the finest horsetail. Guaranteed clean and dry. Twenty pounds of hair to a tick."

"What's your charge?"

"Five pounds."

The shipwright nodded.

"Choose your tick, then." The two men turned to study the bolts of cloth and discuss cost; after a time a second customer entered the shop, and a moment later Wilkes was standing over Anne, bending low so only she could hear. "And what's *your* charge?"

Anne looked up at the shipwright and saw the old, familiar hunger that had led him to climb the Penny Pot stairs night after night. She thought of her sixpence a day, and her private room above, and how by simply lying across her bed for no longer than it took to pee in the pot under it she could make herself something more. She thought too of the doctor's words: *She'll not have another.* What had come at great price before came at small cost now. She looked once more at the shipwright, the thickly corded forearms, the clean linen shirt, the neatly tied queue. Why not?

Anne spoke low as she could. "Same as before. Round the back and up the stairs. Eight o'clock."

WILKES HAD CHANGED LITTLE. He came in, looked around once and back at Anne, swallowing hard. He gave her his coins and she sat on the bed, lifting her skirt; he undid his breeches, picked her up under the knees, and pulled her toward him. He sawed into her once, twice, perhaps a dozen times altogether, then grunted, rebuttoned, and left without his feet ever leaving the floor. When he'd gone Anne looked down at the coins in her hand—a week's wage in less than ten minutes.

WILKES CAME AGAIN, THIS time to purchase a small piece of braid; as Grissom wrapped it he approached Anne and whispered as before, was answered as before. He must have talked—or bragged—for next the corder came. He had none of Wilkes's sense, making no inquiries about a purchase, heading straight for Anne. "So! Here's where you've gone. What of tonight, then?"

Grissom's head swung around.

Anne said, "I'm told the meeting's Wednesday nine."

"Meeting!"

"Wednesday nine," Anne repeated. She dropped her voice. "Stairs at the back." She looked hard at the man till he caught on. That Grissom hadn't was only by luck of a distraction from Peter, but the risk to the job seemed worth it that Wednesday when Anne heard the happy clink of three shillings hit the bottom of the jar she'd commandeered for the purpose.

One night, when Anne had been expecting Wilkes, a mud-stained traveler appeared instead, who insisted when Anne tried to close the door on him, "Wilkes said! Wilkes said to take his turn!" He pulled out his pocketbook and waved it in the air. Anne considered. The mud would come off the coverlet with a stiff broom, and without Wilkes Anne would be out the night's wage, but she didn't like the idea of a stranger; she didn't like the idea that the shipwright would think he could pick her custom for her. "No," she said, and kicked closed the door.

Anne settled Wilkes when next she saw him, but just the same, her popularity grew—another man from the Penny Pot whose name and work she never did know; a friend of his she liked the look of; a poor, pockmarked man again sent by Wilkes, but this time to the shop to "inquire." A shipmaster she took up on her own after she overheard him remark to Grissom that she was the finest-looking thing in the shop. She managed to cross near as he left so she could whisper her price and her time; he was something of a risk but well kept, obviously well to do, and possessed of an honest face.

Anne had come to know something of honest faces and counted John Hewe as one; his appearance came as no great surprise to Anne, who having taken her own dislike to the wife decided the husband must likely share in her assessment. He needed more time than most but was more grateful than most, and more fun besides, entertaining her with tales from the Pot that might not have measured up against a Franklin yarn, but served her well enough in the lack.

With the new ones Anne had taken to keeping her candle lit despite the cost, just to watch out for anything nasty coming her way; in doing so she discovered that apparently it was not the habit of whores—or wives—to conduct their business in clear light. The sight of a dark triangle against white thighs appeared to be worth something to a certain kind of man; she began to charge for the extra price of a candle and met no complaint.

Of all the men who climbed her stairs, the shipmaster was the greatest surprise. At his first visit, he asked her in all politeness if she would be so kind as to put on his breeches, apparently so he might pull them off her, which Anne could see no reason not to do; at the next visit, he brought a young man around Anne's age, and paid out his coin for Anne to attend to the young man while he watched from the door. At the next visit, as the young man entered her, the shipmaster went behind him and did a thing that Anne understood from tavern talk could get the pair hanged, but it didn't seem to distract the young man from his work. Every visit thereafter there was always this same young man—Robert, he was called—between them.

BUSINESS WAS INCREASING BELOW stairs as well. A young girl named Maria was brought on to take over the stuffing of feathers; Anne took over the horsehair, winding it around wooden rods for curling, removing the curls, setting them in careful layers inside a tick sewn up on the sides like an open box. The new work required a new skill; at first Grissom hovered at her shoulder to watch over every curl, and Anne was unable to make her above-stairs appointments as freely as before. Where she could, she worked them into a regular schedule: Wilkes and the corder—whose name turned out to be Pettengill—shared Monday; Hewe kept to Wednesday; Wilkes's pockmarked friend, who called himself Mr. Black—although Anne doubted it was his name at all—came around every other Friday as he could afford. The shipmaster—

Allgood was his name—sent a boy for ribbons or braid whenever he was in town; the boy stopped by Anne with the same message each time: "Sister sends greeting," and Anne answered each message with "Tell sister to call Tuesday nine," or Thursday or Friday or whatever time remained. She kept Saturday and Sunday for herself.

Around the time Anne mastered the horsehair mattress, another penny appeared in her wage. She was eating well, her family was eating well, they all dressed better. Franklin had been right—she'd begun to make something of the job—and sometimes, especially on those nights when her hands happened to be gripping the broad, well-muscled back of the corder, she would think of Franklin and wonder if he'd foreseen both of the ways she'd manage to do it. Only later in the night, when she was too tired to stave it off, would she think of William.

ANNE BEGAN TO ENJOY her daytime work; like Peter, she found some satisfaction in pleasing Grissom with a neat and timely job, in offering a useful suggestion that was taken up with that singular, mute nod and quiet smile. This came as no surprise to her; it did surprise her that she could come to like her night work too. She found that if, when using her candle, she took some cloth away slowly, from the edges, she could turn any man breathless before he'd even touched her, and she found she liked watching their chests heave, their eyes glitter, their parts strain against their breeches. She liked deciding when and where they could touch her and when and where they couldn't, changing it up to keep the game new. She was in utter charge of these strong, proud men, smarter than them all, or so she felt until she opened the door one night to let out the pockmarked Black and found Grissom standing in the hall.

Grissom looked after the man who pushed past him, waistcoat in hand, sweat just drying on him. He looked at Anne, standing there in her shift with a shawl pulled around. He said, "Business thrives, then?"

Anne peered at Grissom and attempted to take the mood of the man. He stood with joints locked, fists knotted, brows pinched. A dark mood, yes, but how dark? Was she about to be discharged? Evicted? Accosted? But *business,* he'd said. If he'd called it a business . . .

"Do you come for your share?" she asked. "Or do you prefer to take it in goods? I've Thursday free."

Grissom's eyes flickered over her body and dismissed it. He turned and walked back down the stairs.

ANNE WAITED NEXT DAY for the summons that would discharge her or evict her, but it never came. Grissom spoke to her as little as before, but there was an ill-defined change in his tone, a new vagueness, as if he'd suddenly forgotten her name. As the days went by and he never called her to account in any way, she began to understand; he could not discharge her, he owed it to Franklin to keep her on. In time another suspicion began to take hold—that Grissom just plain didn't like her; she counted it a good day if Grissom came by her table and nodded at her progress, but that was the best she drew. Against that she could hear a "Fine, Maria, fine!" or a "Good work, Peter, my man!" It was true that there were days when a terse correction might cause a line to form between Peter's eyebrows, or an instruction delivered with an undercurrent of impatience might set Maria's fingers trembling; Grissom never called Anne to account in such a way either, but it didn't make up for the absent praise.

It shouldn't have mattered one way or the other to Anne whether Grissom liked her, but she found that in fact it did; she'd grown used to extracting whatever degree of attention she wished from men and took it as a black mark that she was unable to draw this one. But had she really tried? Or rather, had she tried in the way she was best at? One day as Grissom drew near her table to check her progress in filling a particular mattress that was to go to a new customer, Anne noticed he'd picked up some threads on the back of his jacket; she stood up to pick them off, balancing her off hand against his waist, holding out the threads to show him.

"In case you were to go out," she said, as if in apology. "How your cloth looks must hint to your customers how their cloth will look, after all."

Grissom only stepped aside to peer into the ticking box. "I want this on its way by tomorrow noon."

She attempted a like attack a week later, leaning forward and allowing her breast to brush his hand as he tested her mattress for supportiveness, but he only withdrew his hand and said, cryptically or not, "That will do."

At first Grissom's disinterest left Anne feeling as if she'd been cast adrift at sea with no idea of which way to paddle toward home, but soon enough she came to feel more as if she were floating in a still pool, surrounded by a raging stream. She took a deep breath, let it out, and set her mind to securing her place in Grissom's shop by excelling at her below-stairs work alone. She'd been good enough before; she became better now, so fast and precise in laying out the horsehair that Grissom soon had to find her other things to do. He put her to work sewing the costly bed hangings that only the wealthiest Philadelphians could afford; her first set of hangings was aligned so precisely that she never stuffed a bed tick again.

14

DEBORAH FRANKLIN SAT BY the fire hemming a new shift for William; as he neared a year or so of age he was grown out of all he'd first owned. The late September fire was the first one she'd actually enjoyed, welcoming its heat on a raw day, and had hoped that Benjamin would feel the same and come sit by her side, but instead he was dangling a ball of yarn above William's cradle and exclaiming. Again.

"You see, Debby? You see how he knows just when the yarn will swing his way? He understands a pendulum already! There! He's grabbed it again! You see?"

"He should be sleeping," Deborah said. "Leave him be."

But Franklin could not leave him be. Deborah had not expected it to go exactly so—Benjamin spending long days at the print shop, then home to play with William, then half the night at the tavern with his Junto—a group of friends who worked at bringing new things to one another and to Philadelphia by exercising their minds— this was how he described it to her. It had robbed a good deal of Benjamin's time of late because of his newest idea, the first Deborah had ever heard of such a thing—a lending library. In July his talk was all of the agreement struck; in August it was all of the fifty subscribers he'd already acquired. September was filled with lists of books he planned to order, and then he brought the books home and attempted to read them to Deborah, but who could be interested in such books? Law, astronomy, government, philosophy! She fared some better with *Gulliver's Travels,* but nonetheless, Benjamin looked so many questions at her as he read that she was sure there was something more to the thing that had gotten past her and disappointed him accordingly. It was the same with the *Iliad;* even her sense of accomplishment at having survived to its end was dashed to pieces when he came at her with another by the same author called the *Odyssey*! The books had put a new space between them, she saw that, but she knew it to be a space created by her own deficiency and could not resent him for attempting to include her in a thing so important to his very being.

The thing Deborah *could* resent was the infant. Yes, she would admit it. There were many times—indeed, most times—when Deborah was alone with William that she felt only what she should, or what she imagined she should. If the child had been hers as much as Benjamin's, she doubted she'd have felt a minute's pain over the attention Benjamin so generously lavished on the boy, but as he wasn't, she could only look at the pair of matched faces and feel the outsider to it all. There was none of her in that little face, no shape of nose or color of hair or any smile she could call her own.

And who *could* claim the other half of that face? Deborah could not leave the thought alone. She searched the boy over for some notable thing not come to him from Benjamin that she could seek out as she walked the street, but it was a difficult thing to compare an infant to a grown woman; it was difficult and it was foolhardy, for what could she do if she one day suspected a match? Nothing. Nothing at all. She might point to the woman and demand of Benjamin, "Is *that* her?" but she doubted Benjamin would say. She knew the woman must be some kind of low creature, lower than a common-law wife, but that didn't help Deborah either—if the woman hadn't been so low a thing, would she have become Mrs. Benjamin Franklin instead of Deborah? And what would have become of Deborah? There Deborah arrived each time, and each time she arrived there she resolved to be a better mother to William, if only for Benjamin's sake, Benjamin who had saved her. Sometimes Deborah was successful in her resolve, but sometimes she found herself turning away from that puzzling small face in frustration, unable to address its hidden question any longer.

AT LAST BENJAMIN LEFT the babe and came to the fire, bending to kiss Deborah on the brow, his fingers weaving themselves into the hair tied up at her neck, bringing the knot down. "Come," he said, and lifted her from the chair, his other hand already at her laces. "Come and warm your husband on this damp night; think of it—only September! We've a long winter ahead of us, my dear!"

"You don't go out tonight?"

It was an idle question—his hands had already come up under her skirt and around her buttocks—and as he caught her up and drew her toward their chamber door she thought as she thought every night: Perhaps tonight we'll make a child of our own.

THAT NIGHT PROVED NO different from the others before it; there was no child, and although Deborah did her best with William, she could not block out the idea of Benjamin and William and this other, shadowy, enticing woman forming a triangle locked tight at each corner, forbidding Deborah to enter. When callers arrived at the house it was more of the same; the callers were always men; their talk was always of matters scientific or civic, far beyond Deborah's ken. She would make her greeting and provide the proper sustenance and then retreat, but to where? To the kitchen where she could hear the comfortable talk and hearty laughter? Above stairs where she could stare at the strange child in the cradle who seemed to smile in his sleep as if he already understood the talk below stairs?

On another cold night Benjamin came in late from the tavern and slipped shivering into the sheets, tucking himself around her and warming her in a way that had become one of her favorite things about her life with him. Sometimes he didn't speak, allowing her to choose whether to be awake or asleep to him, but usually he did speak, and usually afterward he came into her, on tavern nights sometimes even as she lay, too impatient to even wait for her to roll over. So it was on this night, but afterward, thinking of the great number of times she'd collected that hot seed in her without a single sprout, she burst out, "How often, Benjamin? How often did you lie with her?"

Benjamin was not the kind of man who would pretend to need additional explanation to such a question, but he did take some time in forming his answer. Did he see the trick in it? To say *many times* would not soothe any wife Deborah knew; to say *once only* would merely emphasize Deborah's failure. But Benjamin Franklin was cleverer than most. "Once would have been too many," he said. "But look what we gain of it. Look at our fine boy."

And there Benjamin moved to a new subject, a thing he'd begun to do around her of late. "I must hire a girl for the shop," he said. "Young James and I cannot keep leaving off setting types or spreading ink to sell a bit of stationery."

Benjamin talked on in that direction; Deborah listened and took herself off on her own, a new idea that made her feel instantly more spirited. She sat up, leaning over Benjamin, straining and failing against the dark to see his face. She splayed her hand flat on his chest instead, to feel his answer.

"Give the job to me," she whispered. Yes, she felt that quick hiccup of surprise, but she kept on. "You could then hire a girl to help in the house for half what it would cost to hire one for the shop."

The chest under her hand didn't appear to breathe at all. Deborah gave it a jiggle. "I'm better at my numbers than my letters, Benjamin. You know it. I helped my father with his accounts. I could make something more of that shop for you. For instance, what of my mother's recipe for itch ointment? She couldn't keep it on hand no matter how much she made of it—someone called for it every week. And coffee and tea. They'll come in for their paper and books, but they'd take the coffee and tea if we had it. Why, we might add any number of things! I could think of many—"

Benjamin cut her short with a laugh. "I already see how you work at sales. Very well, only be kind to your master when he comes home and you may see a rise in it for you."

Was it a joke? She was so seldom sure. But there he was, rising, pressing against her. She rolled into him, gripped his buttocks, and clamped him to her, hurrying him on, not caring for her own interest, thinking that perhaps it was her heat that killed off the tender seed. He came to a satisfyingly violent end in quick time and rolled away sweating and gasping. Deborah lay still, eyes closed, legs squeezed tight to contain her husband's fluids. She thought Benjamin already asleep when he rolled over again.

"Have you noticed how our bodies' warmth increases with the speed of our pulses? I believe this is the proper measure of effective exercise, not time or distance." This drew him on to some other thoughts about the comparative effects on the pulse from a carriage ride, a horseback ride, or a walk; whatever thoughts he was drawn to next, Deborah never heard them.

THE WOMAN THEY HIRED was no girl but the gray and creased Min; she took William in hand without fuss, and Deborah, in turn, took up her new position in her husband's shop. At once her world grew by half. She'd never felt any great interest in what went on at the printer's shop beneath her home, but once in it, she spent the first part of her first day touring its workings with growing fascination. The cases of types, capital letters in the upper case, small letters in the lower case, were selected by the feel of a small notch in the metal and placed backward into a small tray Benjamin called his compositor's stick. The letters were then hammered into a larger tray, the page to be printed growing laboriously line by line. Next the tray was carried to the press and a pair of fleece-and-leather-covered objects, much like thick, sheared-off Indian clubs, were used to pat the type with ink; the fine linen paper was then placed over the tray and the heavy lever swung across to engage the press. For every question Deborah asked, she received at least a half-dozen incomprehensible answers, but at the end of it she knew what she wanted to know: It took eight hours to set a single page of type, and the *Gazette* being four pages, printed once a week, she better understood her husband's long hours.

Deborah soon discovered she had a shopkeeper's instinct for a likely sale, and added other items to the slates and pencils and quills and inks and sealing wax and various papers. Benjamin left the decisions to her, along with their success or failure. As it happened, she succeeded, making her sales and keeping her accounts, not only to her satisfaction but to her husband's. When in February she knew herself to be with child, she believed there was nothing left the world could offer her.

In October a son was born, named Francis after one of Benjamin's Nantucket forebears, and the last of Deborah's fears flew away. A daughter might have come second even to the bastard son, but a legitimate son could not. A son of theirs. It was true that a rollicking boy nearing two must be more entertaining to a father than a newborn infant who could only sleep and cry and suck, but Benjamin fussed over the cradle sufficiently to ease Deborah's mind as to his true affection. Better still, in this tiny new face Deborah could at last see something of hers, and sensing that William was now the one left out, she allowed the great, violent rush of love she felt for her own son to sweep up William too.

15

Philadelphia, 1732

ANNE HEARD THE NEWS, delivered in one of a dozen conversations that came up throughout the day between Grissom and his customers. Most of this talk Anne heard only as she heard the cartwheels rumble by in the road—the background noise associated with the day's work getting done—but the talk between Grissom and the clock maker brought Anne's head up and her needle still.

"Franklin's got his boy at last," the clock maker said. "Two years married, and now it comes. Franky, they call him. A fine, healthy infant."

Grissom cast a look at Anne—dark, changeable, unreadable. "Excellent news," he said to the clock maker. "Franklin must be a happy man. Two fine sons."

"Well, let's see what happens to that other with a legal heir on hand. Now do you have it right? Four chair casings, a bolster, two pillows—"

"I have it right," Grissom said, and he looked again at Anne.

· · · ·

ANNE TURNED AWAY THE pockmarked man that night, pleading illness; she was too distraught to play her games. *Franklin's got his boy at
last.* What *does* happen to the other one now there's a legal heir on
hand? She slept little, and next day in the shop fumbled her thread into
knots four times. At the end of the day, even though the October dark
had already fallen, she walked the three blocks up Market Street to
Franklin's house and stood outside, staring at the single yellow square
of light above the print shop. No doubt the infant Franky slept as he
should, his stomach full, his hands and feet warm. No doubt he would
have stolen the attentions of father and mother both for now, but
surely, after almost two years, that other boy must have secured his
own place in their hearts?

For a fortnight Anne walked past the Franklin house in the dark;
at the end of it she claimed an off stomach, gave up her midday meal,
and walked by the house in daylight, but she could see nothing to
either ease or disturb her mind in the blank panes of glass. Her claim
of an off stomach became true; she ate so poorly at the noon meal that
Peter began to pucker his brow as he looked at her; anyone who passed
up food was clearly dying or near to it.

At the end of the next workday, Anne held back in the shop long
enough to approach Grissom. They'd grown no more conversant over
the many months they'd been working side by side in the shop, and
Grissom looked up in some surprise as she drew near.

"I wonder, sir, if you hear anything of the Franklin household, of
the new infant. If you hear that all are well?" She'd intended no particular emphasis on the word *all* but heard it just the same; Grissom
didn't appear to.

"I hear no news to the contrary," Grissom said, his words crisp
and bare as a week-old crust. A poor offering, but Anne carried it
with care up to her room.

. . . .

ANNE HAD BARELY USHERED Isaac Wilkes into the room and closed the door behind him when a second knock sounded; she opened it on Grissom. He looked at Wilkes and made several adjustments to his features in rapid succession, as if deciding something and then deciding again anew. He said, "Leave us, please. I've some business with the lady."

Wilkes squared himself. "Have you, now? Well, I've some of my own. You just hold on to yourself and wait your turn."

Grissom didn't raise his voice or change his posture; he simply measured out his words again. "Come back another time, Mr. Wilkes."

Wilkes looked at Grissom, at Anne, at Grissom again; he walked to the washstand, slapped his hand down on the coins he'd left there, and drew them back into his palm. He walked out, jostling Grissom as he went past, but Grissom might not have felt it for all he seemed to care. He shut the door tightly behind Wilkes, turned back to Anne, and with little adjustment to his speech said, "I came to tell you I've been to call on the Franklins. I found them well. All four."

Anne's hands began to fly up; she pushed them down and buried them in her skirt.

"The infant was shown off in the usual style, but soon afterward Franklin brought the older boy into the room with as much pride as any father could claim. I played a handkerchief game with the child; he's as sturdy and healthy as you'd like. I gave out my praise at his cleverness, and both father and mother looked to be equally pleased."

Anne opened her mouth to speak but the movement loosed tears. She closed her mouth and dashed a hand at her eyes.

Grissom said, softer now, "'Tis a happy home. I thought you should like to know." He opened the door and stepped through it. Gone.

ANNE LOST SOME TIME in a spate of renegade tears, old and new crowding each other out and down her face, disregarding all her orders to cease. When she'd finally regained command of herself, it was as if the detritus had been washed away and she could see clearly the thing that was left to do. She went down one set of stairs, through the dark shop, up the other. She tapped once and no one answered; she tapped again. He came to the door in his stockings, the fire behind him casting his face in darkness but lighting his knuckles and the red-gold hairs on his wrist where his hand gripped the door. By now Anne had learned a thing or two about men; he could strike as indifferent a pose as he pleased, but she could hear his breathing and knew all she needed to know. She stepped into the room, laid her hands along the finely turned angles of his jaw, and ran a thumb over his mouth. At first his lips stayed hard, but she knew how to soften a man. She knew how to harden one too.

LIKE. DISLIKE. LIKE THE person but dislike what she's done, dislike the person but like what she's doing to him now. In Grissom's big, dense bed, the tick stuffed with the finest goose down, Anne felt the likes and dislikes rolling and tumbling under and over and around her so fast she had trouble keeping track of the up and down. She'd begun in charge of it, had begun standing in the kitchen with her hand in his breeches, but somewhere her feet had come up off the ground and she'd found herself sinking into something that felt like clouds. Grissom's mouth came looking for hers, but that was not part of the act at all, this long, deep kissing that stopped her breath; she pushed against his chest and he kicked back onto his haunches.

"Was this not the idea?"

It was, but only while it was hers. She rose up on her knees, pushing him down at the same time, drawing her hands over his chest, letting him feel the weight of her pressing him down; he must learn the rules. *She* said when and what and where, and no kissing the mouth ever; she must be allowed to breathe. She worked at him until she could hear his own breath raw as a storm in a chimney before she fitted herself over him, rising and sinking, faster and slower and faster again until all that breath came out of him in one long groan.

Anne clambered off the bed, reassembled her clothes with care, began to assemble her words with equal care. "Do you plan to visit the Franklins again soon?"

Grissom said nothing.

"I only ask because—"

"I know why you ask."

"Well then."

"I'm to see him Wednesday next, to look at some books arriving for the library."

Anne bent down and pulled on one shoe, then the other. Carefully. Carefully. "Perhaps I'll see you Thursday next."

Grissom didn't answer for so long that Anne was wondering if he could possibly have fallen asleep, but at length his voice rose up from the dark. "Thursday's your free night, then?"

"I'll keep it so."

Grissom sat up, rolled off the bed, pulled on his breeches, and began to fumble about with a jacket or waistcoat, or so it looked in the dark. He came to her, caught up her hand, and slid one, two, three cool shillings into her palm. How did he know?

"Thursday may be free," he said, "but you're not, are you?"

16

IT WAS FIXED BETWEEN the two men—every Wednesday Grissom was to call on Franklin to discuss the workings of the new library—and so it was fixed between Grissom and Anne; Thursday nights she climbed the stairs and was led silently up the second set of stairs to the big, soft bed. At first Anne did as she liked with him, but after a time he began to make requests of his own: *leave the stockings . . . stand there . . . turn so.* The game then became to discover what he would request before he could request it, but Anne's request of him was always the same: *Did you see the boy?*

Often he had; Grissom didn't say, but Anne began to wonder if Franklin made it so. She pictured Deborah Franklin attempting to put William early to bed, Franklin saying, "Oh, leave him till Grissom comes; he loves to play handkerchief with Grissom." Even the times that Grissom didn't see William he always had some kind of report to make: "I inquired. Franklin says he's well." The first time Grissom made such a report Anne suspected that he'd made it up to placate

Anne, to keep her in her giving mood; she took the report without question, but after she'd settled him she said, "Did I please you well enough, Mr. Grissom?"

He sighed a laugh. "Don't you know?"

"Very well then. If you'd like me to continue to do so, I ask but one thing in return. Whatever it is you find on your visits to the Franklins, you tell it to me as you find it. I'm no child in need of humoring. Were I to find you hid something from me—" She left the sentence to hang.

Grissom lay in silence so long Anne suspected he was forming up a numbered list of all William's ills. "I've told you naught but the truth of the boy."

"And of any concerns you might have?"

Grissom stopped again, seeming to understand that was another kind of thing. "I've kept no concerns from you."

"Nor will you?"

Grissom lifted her hand and placed it on his heart. "Nor will I."

"Well, then." Anne worked her mouth along the sinews of his neck and from there continued down.

ONCE IN A GREAT while Anne got to see for herself how William fared, spying him out walking with his father, the boy such a perfect, healthy, handsome little creature that she couldn't doubt, she mustn't doubt, he was where he belonged. Once she came upon them too close to be ignored; Franklin picked William up in his arms and began to distract him with a rapid stream of nonsense: "Shall we go to see the ships? Let's go see the ships. I wonder how many ships we'll see. How many do you think, William?"

"Two!" William shouted, and Anne was amazed that he knew the number at all until she remembered; William was two now.

Anne discovered other things as she walked about the town;

Wilkes was married and lived two doors down from his shop in a house with a hanging shutter, Mr. Black was single and favored the Indian King, Pettengill was widowed, Captain Allgood lived in the well-to-do Fairmount section of town with a pretty wife and twin daughters who often accompanied him in his carriage as he rode about town. If Wilkes or Pettengill or Black happened upon Anne while in company, they grew flustered and looked away; Allgood, on the other hand, looked straight ahead without flinching, perhaps better used to secrets—or bigger ones.

GRISSOM BEGAN TO FORGET himself in the shop, a little something more each time. One day he leaned over her and laid his palm against her back, another day he touched her wrist, on yet another he used his deeper, richer bed voice to call her. One night after Anne had climbed the stairs to Grissom's room, after she'd given him his joy and he'd begun to doze, she lingered in the warmth of that luxurious bed longer than she liked to do, the night being one of their first hard frosts. At length Grissom began to stir; Anne made to slip from the bed, but Grissom caught her arm. She turned back willingly enough—he wouldn't argue the double pay, she knew—but when she went to reach for his part he stayed her hand. He said, "I've had my turn." He took her by the shoulders and pushed her, gently, slowly backward, as if knowing just how fast and hard to go without raising the alarm. He said, "Now keep still."

Anne kept still, thinking it another part of their old game, but it was nothing like; it was a new one. When Anne discovered it she made to fend him off but by then he'd worked one hand to her nipple and one between her legs, and before she could collect herself it was too late. She was pulling him into her as hard as he was pushing; she felt the racing, racing, racing that she'd created in him so many times, and then she heard a voice—her voice—giving way with an alien sound.

As soon as she could command her limbs again, Anne pushed herself away from Grissom. The wealth of down seemed to suffocate her, to drag her back in and swallow her, but she fought her way to her feet and hurried into her clothes. Grissom called to her when she was already through the door: "Here! Anne!" But she didn't turn around. She returned to her room and by the time she got there she was trembling. She dove under her bed rug and lay there trying to comprehend what it was that had disturbed her so, but she had no words for the new feeling—only two old ones: *Afraid. Alone.*

17

THINGS WERE CHANGING AT Eades Alley. The youngest child, Elizabeth, an ailing little thing never as big as her name, died of a malignant sore throat and was put into the ground next to Anne's father. Next, two of Anne's brothers went out to work—one as apprentice to the clock maker and the other to muck out the livery in exchange for a cot in the loft. At her first visit in the New Year, Anne was greeted with the news that Mary was to be married to one of the shoemaker's customers, a man named Ezekiel Lee.

Ezekiel Lee. It was no more than a name to Anne, which she considered a good thing; if she'd known more of him, it wouldn't have been the kind of thing she'd want to share with her sister, but it did trouble her that her sister had been uncharacteristically quiet about sharing with Anne. When they were left alone in the kitchen, Anne said, "Come, Mary, what can you tell me of this Lee?"

Mary, all grown, plumper and healthier than Anne had ever seen her, turned to her sister with a strange half smile. "I can tell you he's a man of enough means to buy himself more than a single pair of shoes."

Anne smiled back. "So this is his charm, then—his means."

Mary's smile spread all the way to her dancing brows. "No."

What was this new thing in her? It was a thing Anne didn't know.

BY JUNE MARY TOO was gone, moved to Ezekiel Lee's farm at the outskirts of town, nearly into the country. When Anne made her first call, she found a small, plain home in the middle of an insignificant patch of farm—a single outbuilding with a fenced area that contained a lone horse and cow and calf, a dusting of chickens, a disorderly vegetable plot, and a hay meadow beyond; as Anne looked it over she began to think that Mary had meant her new husband could afford *only* two pairs of shoes. But there was a curious soothing air about the place; perhaps it was the regularity of the work going on, or the sense of everything growing, or even more simply, the fact that food was always at hand just outside the door. Anne found herself spending fewer Sundays at Eades Alley, leaving her mother more money in between to keep her till she returned, but with only two young boys left to feed and clothe, there were by now ample resources to go the whole way around.

THINGS HAD CHANGED AT the upholsterer's shop too. Anne had kept away from Grissom's bed for two weeks, turning away from the impatient whisper in the shop, "What's the trouble, Anne?" But she couldn't go three weeks without news of the boy. She climbed the stairs determined not to allow Grissom to overwhelm her in that way again, and for some weeks she succeeded, but eventually he managed to slip through, clever with it, sneaking in under cover of his own pleasure until it was too late for her to deny her own. The next time she went to him in utter, cold command, taking away nothing but her coins, but before too many more weeks he'd managed to level her again. And so a new game was born.

MARY GAVE BIRTH TO her own boy in the same, undecided month of November in which William had been born. Anne went to her sister's as often as she could, finding her own joy in Mary's contentment as she sat with her babe secured in her arms. One day as Anne came in after one of her visits, Solomon Grissom said, "You've been to your sister's."

"How do you know?"

"You come back all peace and roses, that's how I know."

Perversely, the remark disturbed Anne. She wanted her own peace and roses, not her sister's. Indeed, she'd time and again found comfort, if not complete peace, in the fact that three-year-old William was as strong and healthy as a child could be, or so he'd appeared when Anne had last spied him in the Franklin carriage five—no, it would have been six months ago now.

WILLIAM WAS NEARLY FOUR when Anne read Franklin's advertisement in the 1734 *Gazette* for "a servant that is a scholar and can teach children reading, writing, and arithmetic." Anne read the word—*children*—plural—and saw in it all the rest of it, all she'd dreamed for William and more. He was to have a tutor, and if he was to have a tutor he was to have a good school, and if he was to have a good school he was to have it all. The paper lay on Grissom's kitchen table; she'd picked it up and read it as she waited for him to finish dealing with the fire. When he returned to the table, he looked at her and said, "What's set you alight, girl?"

Anne pointed to the advertisement, unable to say what it was that she read in it beyond the few words, but Grissom read it, dropped a hand on her shoulder, and squeezed. No remark from him could have said more. That night Anne found something inside her opening and expanding until she lay emptied out against him, taking a heretofore unknown comfort in the arms that seemed willing to hold her as long as she lay willing to be held.

ANNE MUST HAVE RELAXED her attention then, for the days began to leap on without pause. What month was it when she began to make tassels, fringe, braid in Grissom's shop? What month when she became the one to supervise Maria and the new girl, Rose? What year did Peter's voice crack and drop? What year did Mary have the second boy and what year the girl? When had Anne stopped fighting Grissom in that big, smothering bed, some nights settling in till dawn in his arms? The unnumbered days and weeks and months and years dripped down over her into one big pool of nameless days until Anne knew every angle of Grissom's face, every red-gold hair on his body, every look and mood his changeable eyes could take on, but she knew only as much of William as the most distant relation might know.

ANNE KNEW THE YEAR—1736—WHEN the smallpox came to Phila-delphia and galloped through Eades Alley, taking her mother and the two brothers still left at home. Inoculation had been much debated about town but only for the well to do; Anne's dreams for her mother had come true in part but not in enough parts—not in the parts that would have taken her from that crowded, filthy alley. Anne's mother and brothers were buried along with the other Eades Alley victims in a common grave far outside of town; Grissom refused to allow Anne leave to attend out of fear of contagion. His fear was so great he talked over inoculation with Franklin and came away convinced that Anne should be inoculated. Grissom, Peter, and Maria had caught the disease in the natural way at the last epidemic, and Rose's father would not permit her to be inoculated, so Anne was left to consider the procedure alone.

"'Tis so new a thing," she said. "Better to wait till they've practiced it some."

"'Tis perhaps new here but the slaves have long known of it," Grissom countered. "They've been inoculating in Africa for years."

"In Africa!"

Grissom cupped the side of Anne's face, smoothed a thumb across her as yet unmarred brow. "You mustn't take the risk of a natural case, Anne. I have the greatest faith in Franklin's opinion of the process."

"And I have a greater faith in my own opinion. Tell me of this process, then."

Grissom laid it out. The stay at a house specially fitted out for the purpose, a special diet begun, a slit in the skin and pus from an infected patient slid into the wound. This most often resulted in a mild form of the disease, Grissom explained, but there were those rare exceptions . . .

Anne held up her hand to stop him. "Have the Franklins been inoculated?"

"Must I always start and end with the Franklins? Very well then—yes, yes, yes, all the Franklins have been inoculated except for Franky. He's recovering from a dysentery but will get his as soon as he's well."

"William too?"

"Did I not say all the Franklins except Franky?"

But there another kind of alarm took hold of Anne. "William was inoculated and I wasn't told?"

"He came through it fine, Anne. Entirely unharmed."

"When? When was this done? You've told me nothing. You said they were away visiting!"

"I said they were away visiting because I was told by their servant they were away visiting. Franklin only informed me this week of the inoculations." Grissom looked harder at Anne. "Why, you're trembling all over! What is this, worry over the child, or rage at me? I've concealed nothing from you."

Anne breathed, willing herself to grow calm, but oh, to have no control over even the simplest news of her child! To be forced to wait on another for this too!

That night Anne let Grissom have every part of her he desired but she kept the whole of herself to herself; she could feel Grissom's puzzlement and didn't care—it had been a mistake to let him think he could move her as he willed.

ANNE PACKED HER OWN bedding and reported to the Slade house on Arch Street, the site selected for the patients' isolation. She didn't know a soul there. The daily "diet" she was prescribed of one small piece of meat and a physic each day did not please her; she puked each morning and starved each afternoon. She considered taking her sheets and going home, but the thought of William inspired her to keep on; if so small a boy could survive it, so could she. She watched in some fascination as the cut was made in her skin and the pus slid in, then lay back and waited for whatever was to happen happen.

The fever came first and raged for two days; she continued to puke during the day and sweat during the night, but only a dozen pea-size pustules appeared on her chest and arms. Anne looked to her left and right and saw skin so covered with sores that she counted her luck on the one hand and her belated fear for William on the other.

Anne had been in the Slade house three weeks, all told, when Grissom came to collect her. He looked her all over, no doubt searching for scars, laid a finger on the single pockmark on her temple. He'd borrowed a chaise from somewhere and made to help her into it as if she were heavy and awkward with child; she shook herself free and stepped up into the carriage without his helping hand, but her legs felt like someone else's—indeed, a child's.

Grissom pulled up to the front of the shop and beckoned to Anne to come with him. She thought at first he meant for her to return to work at once, but no—he beckoned again, toward his stairs. *That* work, then. But again no. A supper of cold chicken and applesauce had been left out, no doubt by Mrs. Hyde, and if Anne could have picked the single meal in all the world that might have suited her just then, that would have been most all of it; Grissom poured out a cup of honeyed tea and that was the whole.

When Anne had disposed of a third of the food, she paused to ask, "What news at Franklin's?"

Grissom was more comfortable with silence than any man Anne had thus far ever known—he used it before he spoke and after he listened, he used it to make his point or to absorb another's, he used it to fill the space he didn't know otherwise how to fill. In Anne's new weakness she was longer in comprehending the source of the latest silence, longer still in gathering her nerve to ask, "What's happened to the boy?"

Grissom set his spoon down. "'Tis Franky."

"Franky!" A terrible relief swept over Anne, terrible in its single-mindedness, but it was also tinged with anger at Grissom's thickness, that he wouldn't know she would think first of William. "What of Franky?" she asked, but even in her own ears it sounded offhand, cold.

Grissom seemed not to notice; he seemed concerned enough for two. "The child wasn't fully recovered from the dysentery when he contracted the smallpox in the natural way," he said. "Two days and he was gone."

"Gone! You can't mean to say—?"

"Dead."

Anne sagged back into the seat. Franky. A child only—she counted back from William's six—four years old.

"You may imagine his parents' state."

Yes, thought Anne, and indeed, she could feel a sympathetic ache in her own heart now—a child removed, a hole left, the heart closing in around it, scarred and grown cold to the outside world. She looked at Grissom, ready to meet his concern now, but he looked away; there was something more. Something about William.

Anne sat forward. "You said William took the inoculation."

"He took it. He's fine." But Grissom looked away again.

Anne reached across and gripped his wrist. "You must tell me," Anne said. "You promised me. Any concern, you said. *Any concern.*"

"'Tis nothing. 'Twas painful to see, is all. I'd called around to express my sympathy and arrived at an awkward moment. Mrs. Franklin had been resting, but she got up and came into the parlor where we sat amusing William. Things were said."

"What things?"

No doubt Grissom would have gladly retreated into his silence, but he'd already gone either too far or too near. He shifted himself in his chair, he looked down and began to turn his spoon end over end, he lifted his eyes and stumbled on. "It seems she was feeling some resentment against William, that he should live while Franky died. She pointed at William and cried out something about God's mistake, his taking the angel child and leaving the devil child behind. Indeed, it was as if her grief had unbalanced her mind." But now begun, Grissom couldn't seem to leave off. "Half mad she looked. *And* sounded. And poor Franklin! Good God. He caught her up before she reached the child and carried her off to her room, set the servant to keep by her; he plans to take on another girl to take care of William until his wife recovers."

The final words seemed to bring Grissom to. He rose. "Come, Anne, I've arranged for you to stay here till *you* recover; I've brought a few things around. You're to keep out of the shop and rest here another day or two."

Anne followed Grissom to his room, allowed him to remove her shoes and bodice and skirt, to tuck her into his down and quilts like a sick child. After a time Grissom came in and curled around her like a split cocoon, smoothing her hair in a way that was no doubt intended to ease her into sleep, but Anne's head still chased after his words. *Devil child. Angel child.* She lay awake imagining William's face, frightened and pale. She heard Grissom's other words—*He caught her up before she reached the child.* What had Deborah Franklin planned to do to William when she'd reached him? Anne pictured the woman's thick hands twisting around William's throat, William's face reddening, swelling, blackening . . . She woke sweating in the November cold, with dawn just outlining the window. At first she didn't understand where she was; she looked around and saw her trunk jammed into the corner, her winter cloak and best gown hung on pegs on the wall. She looked again, frantic, and spied her pot of money on the chest of drawers, alongside her brush and hair combs and mirror, even her father's books of plays she'd brought with her from home.

Grissom hadn't brought a few things around, he'd brought it all.

Grissom opened his eyes, saw her, and smiled.

Anne said, "How long were you thinking of keeping me here?"

The smile faded, but only from Grissom's mouth. "'Tis a thing worth thinking on, is it not, staying on with me here? I'm able to keep you better than you're able to keep yourself, and you needn't—" He paused. "You needn't work at your other job anymore."

"You mean I need only work at it with you."

The smile faded from Grissom's eyes as well. As it did, Anne saw what she'd almost missed, that he'd allowed her a brief minute of reading him clear through, and she could see that she'd wounded him. But where lay the fault for that? Not with Anne. Grissom would see what he liked to see instead of what was; best he understand what was and wasn't now. She might have said so—in truth, she felt some small unease at the idea that she might be at fault henceforth if she *didn't* say so—but Grissom had already pushed back the quilt, pulled on his clothes, and left the room.

ANNE DID TRY TO stay in Grissom's big, soft bed for a time, reminding herself as she sank into it of the beaten-up straw mat she'd slept on at Eades Alley, but soon the bed began to feel like her enemy, fighting all her weakened efforts to raise herself, and she thrashed her way out of it, suddenly desperate to get out of the house too. She dressed herself, glad it was November and she could inconspicuously add the winter cloak with the hood that she could draw close around her face; she picked her way down the stairs and into the street. Her legs felt weak but they wanted to move, and she let them tug her where they would; soon enough she found herself outside Franklin's print shop, staring up at the rooms above the shop as of old, but it was no longer enough. She needed to see William, to see for herself that Grissom told the truth—that he'd come to no harm.

18

Philadelphia, 1736

DEBORAH FRANKLIN LIVED IN a discolored rainbow, gray in the middle and banded in black at both ends. The doctor had come and given her some kind of anodyne that greatly clouded her mind; she knew her darling son was dead and she knew she'd done something wrong because of it, something that had put Min in that chair by her bed and caused her husband to look at her nose instead of her eyes, but what it was she didn't know. How odd it was to forget a single thing out of all of time, especially as she could think back and remember every minute of the past five years of utter happiness. There was the shop and all she'd done to it and for it, her husband's great joy in it and in her, the sheer contentment of working so close to Benjamin's inner and outer self. To discover that she didn't need to know what was in a book in order to sell it had changed her and him; they could share in the books just the same. And the almanac—*Poor Richard's Almanac* it was, but she called it *Poor Dick* and made him laugh. He wrote about Poor Dick's wife in the almanac, and they laughed over that together, knowing it wasn't her but knowing she was part of it just the same. He always showed her his latest collection of old saws and a time or two allowed her to pick out her favorites. *Who is rich? He that rejoices in his portion. Who is strong? He that can conquer his bad habits.*

Poor Dick made them more money than all the rest of it together—the press and the shop—and even so frugal a man as Benjamin couldn't help but revel in the new knowledge that they would never starve. Deborah bought their first china porringer and silver spoon, declaring that Benjamin deserved to eat as other successful men ate, and it seemed to please him that she should think to spoil him so. Deborah wouldn't say that she was spoiled in return, but she dressed well, ate well, slept well, and then the best of all gifts arrived in the form of that sweet little boy, so good natured she might have known God would want him back.

William was around the age of two when the new child came along, and he hadn't given over his half of his parents' attention gladly. Deborah felt true sympathy for the older child; after all, she'd felt the outcast when Benjamin had first brought William home and knew the pain of watching a smile full of love directed at another. When William had first arrived, he'd put such a spell over Benjamin that Deborah couldn't help suspecting it was the memory of the mother that held him, not the child, but once they had Franky, Deborah could better understand the power an infant could hold over a parent in its own right. It was true that Benjamin continued to indulge his first son beyond what seemed suitable to Deborah, but her heart was now too full of love and pride to hold on to old resentments.

Or perhaps the core of Deborah's new sympathy for William lay in the fact that as Franky grew and shined, it became clear that it was *her* child who would carry away all prizes. William might be hand-somer, cleverer, but Franky was by far the sweeter, the kinder. Yes, William was, in the main, a fine-looking boy, but his face had begun to pinch in on itself, his eyes to follow her about, haunting her the whole day long; he never asked for a thing outright but began to sneak when her back was turned. No one comparing the two children could doubt how superior Franky was to William. Was Deborah's love equally divided between the pair? Perhaps not. But she'd like to find another woman who would have taken in her husband's bastard and treated him with as much care as she'd treated William.

A rough patch surfaced the next year; Benjamin had begun to mingle in another kind of crowd than the tradesmen's set to which he'd previously belonged. They were a better-dressed, better-spoken sort; a number belonged to the influential Quaker sect that even Deborah knew controlled most of Philadelphia politics. When Benjamin met these men in public, Deborah was untroubled; when they began to entertain him in their homes and exclude her from the invitation, her uneasiness began to grow. Benjamin excused it at first by describing these events as political and not social, for men only, "pipe-and-Madeira affairs," but once Benjamin let slip about a Mr. and Mrs. Logan arriving late, Deborah learned: Deborah Franklin—no doubt Deborah Rogers yet to those in this new circle—would not do. Deborah's pride kept her from mentioning the subject again, but she could tell that Benjamin felt its effect on her; after his slip about the Logans he stayed at home three nights in a row. On the fourth, however, he returned to whichever party sent a note around requesting that he call. What did Benjamin want with all these people? It became clear when he was appointed clerk of the Pennsylvania Assembly of Delegates. He came home overflowing with the news, the smell of spirit and smoke strong.

"You do see what it means for us, do you not?" he asked. "I'll have a clear view on all the affairs of the colony. And no little side matter, I'll be sure to get all the government printing now. 'Tis worth a few lonely nights, is it not?"

It was not, but ever since the episode regarding Mrs. Logan, Deborah Franklin had been feeling much more like the old Deborah Rogers and decided not to say so. Besides, she had Franky.

And then Franky died.

Benjamin had said to her but the day before, "He looks better today."

That night he said, "I believe his eyes less sunken this evening."

In the early hours, waking to find Deborah still sitting beside Franky's bed, he touched the child's forehead and said, "He feels cooler now."

Deborah tried to believe Benjamin even as she swabbed the boy's dry lips and saw nothing but darkening hollows around her son's eyes, as he stopped taking even the small sips she tried to drip into him, as he stopped opening his eyes, as he stopped breathing. She grabbed up Franky, shook him, clutched him, screamed sounds, not words, until Benjamin had to take him from her and hand him to Min. There came the blank space where Deborah remembered nothing until she turned and spied William standing in the corner, staring at her with that haunted look. Deborah cried out some words. What words? She couldn't remember them but she could remember the frightened look in the child's eyes. Why should he be so afraid? He lived! He breathed! She rushed at him, or she tried to rush at him, but Benjamin caught her up—Benjamin, always so confident, always so sure he was *right*—Benjamin who'd been so wrong this time. She flailed at his thick shoulders and powerful arms but couldn't weaken them; he pulled her tight against his chest with one arm, brought the other under her knees, and carried her out of the room.

DEBORAH SLEPT AND WOKE into that fuzzy gray rainbow again, but the hard black edge of it remained clear. God did this to them. Deborah knew this. Everyone knew this. And everyone knew that God did it because of her husband's sin, because of that bastard child. How dare Benjamin look away from *her* when *he* was the one who'd caused Franky to die! God would take the best for Himself. God would take Franky, the best of them all, and leave the child of sin behind.

Benjamin came into the room. He was dressed as neatly as ever, hair combed, face shaved, looking as if nothing whatever had gone awry, until she looked into the twin graves of his eyes. He fixed his eyes on the bolster behind her head, lifted a finger—a single finger—and laid it on her arm.

"Are you feeling better, my dear?"

Deborah stared at him. How could she feel *better*?

"Let me bring William in to see you. He cries for his mother so."

"*No.*"

That brought Benjamin's gaze on to hers, but now it was Deborah who was forced to turn away. She closed her eyes. She could not see William. She could not look at him knowing she should never again look at the other. Some words played in her head like a ghostly echo from another world: *devil child* and *angel child*. A terrible fear swept over Deborah. Could she have said those words out loud? Was that what she'd done? Was that why her husband couldn't bear to look at her now? She opened her eyes.

Benjamin said, "Perhaps I'd best get another girl in to help us till you're better."

Better. Again that alien word. "Min," she said, but her tongue felt lazy in her mouth and it came out more like *Muh.* She tried again. "Min. We've got Min."

"Yes, but Min needs to take care of you just now." Deborah looked to the corner of the room where Min sat in her chair, appearing intent on the stocking she was working. Deborah must admit it was a comfort to have her there. Benjamin would come and go but Min would stay, and whenever Deborah woke tied up in those confused rainbow bands, Min would come to her bed and soothe her with her anodyne and the words that Deborah had used so often to try to coax Franky to health: "Sleep now, dear."

Deborah slept.

19

ANNE OPENED THE STREET door and discovered two choices: the print shop on the left or the stairs straight ahead; she took the stairs with the kind of courage that only a greater fear could provide. She paused at the hallway at the top before knocking, thinking how best to declare herself, but discovered that pausing was sapping her courage; she stopped thinking and rapped on the door. A middle-aged servant with chapped, reddened face and hands answered Anne's knock and this told Anne nearly all she needed to know of the rightness of her decision to come. If the servant was at the door, who was guarding William? She said, "I've come to speak to Mr. Franklin."

The words had seemed enough to Anne, but she soon saw that the chapped face required more. "Tell him 'tis Anne from the—" She considered. Penny Pot? No. "Upholstery shop."

The servant stepped back and closed the door on Anne. Were all visitors treated thus? Anne doubted it. What in her appearance or manner had made this servant treat her so? Anne had worried the question a short time only when Franklin appeared and stepped into the hall, closing the door behind him. Anne noticed that he'd lost his usual color and looked heavier, weighed down. The thought had occurred to Anne that she might have to simply storm her way past him, but now she saw the foolishness of the plan. Franklin, no matter how devastated by grief, would remain strong.

And yet, he could smile. " 'Tis lovely to see you, my dear," he said, "but I'm afraid here is not the place and now is not the time."

"I'm sorry," Anne said. "I'm sorry about your boy. I'm half able to imagine what it must be for yourself and for your poor wife, but only half. You see, *my* boy—"

"I shall see that my wife gets your kind message, but just now she's not taking any calls. In fact, she's taken to her bed. But I do thank you for stopping by." Franklin turned to the door.

"I don't come to see your wife, sir; only the cloud of your grief could allow you to think I do. I come to see William."

Anne had seldom seen anyone take Franklin by utter surprise, but she believed she'd done so now. "William!"

"You can't be surprised. Under the conditions described to me, I must see how he fares."

"There are no conditions here that affect William in any way. I assure you, William is fine. William is in good hands. You may trust to me for that."

"May I? When I hear he's called devil and attacked?"

Franklin's color deepened. "You've been misinformed."

"Then you can have no objection to my seeing him. If you do object, I'll fear the worst kind of treatment of him. I'll fear the worst of your wife. Perhaps I'll talk of my fears of your wife. Perhaps I'll talk of you."

Franklin blinked.

"Make what excuse you like—say I came with a message from your upholsterer."

"My wife's in bed, as I told you. She's only just settled. I'll not have her disturbed."

"All the better then; you need make no excuse at all. Let me see my boy."

Franklin's eyes bore into Anne as if he would willingly turn her to dust there on the landing, but the longer Franklin blocked her way the more solid she felt, the more sure. She'd find her way past this man somehow, and if she saw any signs of physical attack against her child, she'd carry him out of that house if she had to strike her own blows.

Perhaps Anne's determination showed. Franklin said, "William's working at his books. I'll bring you to him and you may greet him, but if you attempt to say anything to him beyond that single greeting, I shall drag you bodily from this house and deposit you in the gutter. Is that clear?"

Anne's heart had begun to pound so hard she could barely get the word out around it. "Yes," she said.

HE SAT AT THE kitchen table, bent over a book that appeared to be way too thick for a child of six; his brow was puckered and his small jaw clenched. When Anne and Franklin entered he looked up and his brow smoothed, his eyes opening wide with curiosity. Anne hadn't glimpsed him in many months and found herself struck motionless by the sight of him sitting there with his book, so grown, so *at home*. There wasn't a visible mark on him; in fact, he was dressed in a spotless linen shirt and finely made blue breeches, his lovely, corn-silk hair gleaming and combed, and he was so obviously happy to see his father, it made Anne feel every sharp edge of her intrusion.

Franklin said, "Here is a young lady come to meet you, William. Say how do you do."

William said, "How do you do."

Anne stepped up to the table with the excuse of looking more closely at the book, but she saw nothing of it. She looked down at William's fine hair and fought with all her will to keep her hand away. She said, "You appear to be a serious student, William. You've quite a large book there."

William made no answer, which no child in his proper senses would do, but he did look up at Anne with even greater curiosity. Did he know her? she wondered. Could he possibly remember the shape of her face or the dark of her hair or perhaps her voice or her smell?

Anne said, "In truth, William, I met you once before when you were an infant, but you wouldn't remember that, would you?"

Franklin said behind her, "Very well, we mustn't keep you any longer. William, you may say good-bye now."

The boy opened his mouth to speak, but Anne took up the space. "Oh, I might stay a minute longer. I wonder, William, if you could be so kind as to take my wrap?" She slid her shawl off her shoulders and watched keenly as William rose with all the easy spring of a healthy boy of six and took the wrap from her, laying it over the chair next to him with care. Anne stepped closer and took a better look at the book. "Why surely you're too young to read this!"

William drew himself up on his knees and pointed with a lovely, slender finger at a picture of a crescent moon, then drew the finger under the two lines of text beside it. "'The *moon* gives *light* at time of *night*.'"

Anne clapped her hands. "Oh, my!" She slipped into the chair next to him. "But look here at all these numbers! Surely you don't know your numbers!"

"One-two-three-four-five-six!" William looked up at her again, beaming.

"And what a clever child you are! Now here, what do we have on this page? Oh no, I go too far. This is some sort of mathematics; this can't be for a boy your age."

"One less six is five!" William shouted, and Anne clapped her hands again.

"A little backward, son," Franklin said, but she could hear his pride despite the circumstances, despite the error.

"William answers right," Anne said. "He only reads it a little wrong. But you'll know it next time, won't you?"

"Six less one!"

Anne started to laugh, but a woman's voice, raw and slow, cut over her.

"Is this her, then?"

Anne whirled around. Franklin whirled around. Deborah Franklin stood in the doorway gripping the door frame, looking puffy, smudged, as if someone had drawn her and then tried to rub her out. Franklin was, for once, speechless.

Deborah Franklin went on. "Is this the girl you've hired to take care of William?"

"No," Franklin said. "No."

Deborah Franklin looked at Anne again, but her eyes, still crusted from either sleep or crying, seemed unable to focus. "Who is she, then?"

Anne opened her mouth, but she was cut over again, this time by Franklin. "Well, yes, my dear, she's come to inquire about the position, but we have several others to see yet. 'Tis early on." Franklin turned to Anne. "Indeed, miss, we've already taken too much of your time. We'll let you know as soon as we've talked to all the girls. Another few days only, I'm sure."

Anne made to rise, but Deborah Franklin had pushed past her husband and staggered toward Anne, staring closely at her face, so closely it forced Anne to sit back down. Deborah Franklin pointed at Anne's temple. "Is that a pockmark? Have you had the disease?"

"Just taken, by inoculation." Anne pushed up her sleeve and displayed the additional pocks on her arm.

Deborah straightened, grabbed hold of the opposite chair. "What's your name? You look familiar to me."

"Anne." Anne dropped her eyes to William's flaxen head. She pushed back her own dark hair. She said, "Perhaps what is familiar in me, madam, is that I too have lost a son."

No one in the room spoke or moved until William shoved his primer nearer to Anne and laid his perfect little hand on the page, pointing to a picture of a sun. "'When *rain* is done, out comes the *sun.*'"

Anne patted his hand, as soft and smooth as a petal. William beamed, showing a mouth full of tiny, pearly first teeth. Deborah swayed; Franklin leaped up and put an arm around her waist, with the other taking her hand. "Come, my dear, best you lie down."

Deborah pulled her hand free of her husband's, gripped harder at the chair. "What care have you taken of children?" she asked Anne.

"You needn't worry yourself about any of that," Franklin said. "I shall speak with the other girls soon and we'll find just the one for William."

"I've cared for a number of younger brothers and sisters," Anne said. "And of course my boy, till he was taken from me."

Deborah Franklin's eyes swam on and off of Anne's but never left her face. "Of what did he die?"

Anne dared a glance at Franklin. "Smallpox. Same as yours."

"And who might speak for you?"

The corder. The shipwright. The shipmaster. Your husband.

"I last worked for Mr. Solomon Grissom," Anne said.

"Grissom!" Deborah Franklin turned in her slow daze to her husband. "There you are; you need only get the endorsement of your friend Grissom. She's had the smallpox, she knows the curse I live under. Why talk to any others? I like this one." She swayed again. Franklin gripped her again.

He said, "Come, 'tis time for your bed and your dose." He called, "Min!"

Min came as if she'd been just the other side of the door. Franklin handed off his wife and Min led her out of the room.

"Ask how soon she might start!" Deborah called behind her as the door closed.

Franklin said, "William, 'tis enough study for today. Why don't you go find your pennywhistle, there's a good boy."

William slid from the chair and scurried off. As soon as he was out of sight, Franklin sank into the chair at the end of the table, dropped his face into his hands, and rubbed at his temples as if attempting to rub out the great headache that must certainly have lodged there.

Anne said, "I might start now."

Franklin's face rose up out of his hands. "Are you out of your senses?"

"Why not?"

Franklin stared at her.

"She doesn't know; she can never guess, with me so dark and him so fair. Besides, she's been told my boy is dead. Like hers. She thinks *me* like her. She thinks I can help her." Anne leaned forward and touched Franklin's hand to bring his eyes back up from where they'd fallen. She said, "I *can* help her. I can take care of William. I can keep quiet." She paused. "Or not." So short a threat. So long a one.

Franklin gazed blankly at the hand she'd touched; he lifted his eyes and fixed them on Anne with a new expression in them. She'd already identified a number of the old Franklin faces since she'd arrived: the forced calm and false courtesy at the door, the escaping exasperation at the table, the alarm tempered with patience at Deborah's entrance, and always pushing at the edges of each of them the thick gray quicksand of worry and grief. What was this new look, then? The quicksand was still hard at work, but a twist at the corner of the mouth had given the face a bitter, ironic cast, and in the eyes

she could almost believe—no, she couldn't believe—or could she—
that she saw a hint of the old, ever-speculating Franklin there.

SOLOMON GRISSOM SAT AT the kitchen table with his long legs splayed
beneath, hands and eyes on a mug that he'd drained soon after Anne
arrived but refused her attempt to refill. Anne had stood at the foot of
the table and spewed as many words as she owned into the silence, but
now the silence had not only drained her words, it had drained her
nerve; she pulled out the chair and sat down. Solomon Grissom looked
up, those not-green-not-brown eyes as indifferent as they were when
she first came; Anne was surprised by how greatly that single look
from him could unsettle her. She began to explain. Again.

"'Twas never my plan. I knew only that I needed to see the boy.
To make sure he was unharmed; nothing you could have told me
would have soothed my mind. I needed to see him with my own eyes.
But then I saw him—and such a boy! So handsome and strong and
delicate all at once! And such begging in those eyes, begging me to
look at him, to admire him. No doubt he's been much ignored since
his brother died. So I looked at him and admired and saw . . . oh, I
saw everything there was in him, that secretive, unsure thing in him,
but also the open and loving part of him; I thought how easily such a
boy could be crushed, how an angry blow or an extra scold could
crumple him."

She stopped. Grissom said nothing. She leaned forward, touched
his hand. "Solomon. I couldn't leave him."

But she could leave Solomon Grissom. And why should she not?
She was nothing but Benjamin Franklin's favor. Grissom had taken
her into the shop because of what he owed Franklin; Anne had given
what she'd given because she'd owed Grissom. The tally was even—no
less no more. Grissom had begun to think himself entitled to far too
much of her; it was time she moved on.

20

THEY WEREN'T THE FIRST words William Franklin ever heard—after all, he was five or six when they were said—but they were the ones that stuck first, shrieked at him out of his mother's splotched face, her extended arms rigid and twitching, nothing about them hinting at the comfort he'd found there in the past. His father was in the room, but he was a changed father, the smile wrung out of him and his eyes not once cast on William; besides, even if William had liked the idea of seeking comfort in this strange father's arms, it was too late—he'd already filled them with William's mother and carried her out of the room.

William didn't understand. He couldn't think why the words had been flung at him, or why his mother looked so, or his father, or why his mother had been carried from the room, but he knew it had something to do with his younger brother, Franky. Franky was dead. William hadn't entirely understood the word *dead* either, not even when Min had taken him by the hand and led him into the room where the gray, spotted thing lay on the bed. William could tell the thing wasn't his brother anymore, but he couldn't tell just why, nor could he say that he liked him any better for it. Franky had always been a small, bright light in the house that William could never outshine no matter how he tried; "Franky did it" only seemed to get a sharp word from his mother and that sad look from his father that William hated more than he hated Franky. That was the other thing William couldn't understand—he hated Franky, and yet the night Franky died William cried and cried and begged God to make his brother not dead. It did no good, of course—the next morning William crept into the room where Franky lay and found him still dead—but here was the oddest thing of all: The dead Franky was still the brightest thing in the house.

It had been clear from the first. William could not have been much above two when the infant appeared as if by magic—red, noisy, smelly. William's father bent down to where William was playing with his cups and showed him this unpleasant object as if it were one of the stableman's new kittens, or the baby pig that had shown up all of a sudden in the alley, or even a sugar paper his mother sometimes gave him to suck.

"Your brother has arrived at last," his father said, which William took to mean that his brother would eventually leave, like everyone else did who "arrived" at their house. That this thing was *never* to leave was the first shock. That William wasn't allowed to kick the cradle to silence the wailing blob was the second. His foot had only just set the rockers flying when his mother's hand came flying even faster and laid him out flat on his back.

And then Franky was dead, but instead of feeling glad, William had only felt as alone as he'd ever felt, and scared, scared, scared; nothing was normal, nothing was right. Next, William's mother and Min disappeared; they simply went into his mother's bedroom and didn't come out. William didn't mind about Min so much—she was ugly and old and she pinched him when she was cross and she was cross too much—but he grew more and more worried when his mother didn't even appear at the table to eat.

"Where's Mama?" William asked.

"Resting," his father told him the first time he asked it, but later he'd changed it to "Sick."

"Will she die?" William asked, wanting to get to the bottom of this new event in his life, but his father snapped at him, a thing his father never did. "Of course not. Go and do your numbers."

So William had been left to drift around the house, feeling like one of those leaves that fell into the river and got turned this way and that, no one caring if it ever got to the opposite bank or not.

AND THEN SOMEONE NAMED Anne came to take care of him, and William discovered that he could like this Anne. He liked the way she put a hand in his hair whenever he came near, or took his hand if they even walked from one room to the next, and when she put him to bed, she sat a long time beside him with her hand resting on his leg or his arm, whichever was nearest.

One night, as Anne sat on William's bed with her hand on his ankle, William asked if Franky was ever coming back.

"No, William. No, I'm afraid he isn't. 'Tis a sad, sad thing, and that's what's made your mother sick, but after a while she'll get better. We must give her time, though; we must give her time to make herself well again. Do you understand that?"

William said, "Time is an herb that cures all diseases."

"Where did you hear that, William?"

"I read it. In *Poor Dick*."

Anne laughed, and William especially liked that—a laugh in a house where all laughing had dried up as soon as Franky died. Then Anne said, "You're as clever as your father, William."

And those were the second words that stuck. William knew he wasn't as clever as his father, but after Anne said that he was, he began to think a little differently on the subject; he began to think he might get that clever yet.

21

Philadelphia, 1737

SPRING CAME MILD AND gray, summer came hotter and grayer; only with the August damp did the colors begin to return to Deborah Franklin's world: Min's skirt was blue, Benjamin's jacket brown, her coverlet red. Deborah left her room, clutching her husband's arm if he wasn't at the shop or Min's arm if he was, or even the new girl's arm if she wasn't occupied with William. Anne, she was. Anne with her own dead son. Every time Deborah looked at her, she saw another dead boy reflected in those cloud-colored eyes—one look and you got trapped. Deborah said something about the clouds to Benjamin, but he took it wrong and said, "If you don't trust her, we'll get rid of her, then." Deborah said no, she didn't want to get rid of her. In truth, she'd rather get stuck in that girl's gray eyes, shadowed by an unknown dead boy, than stuck in her own black thoughts of Franky.

That was Deborah's trick for the daytime—Anne—but at night the thoughts of Franky would come back to her and she'd wake crying out and flailing at the sheets until Min came and gave her another anodyne—laudanum or perhaps opium; Benjamin tried holding her tight against his solid body, but if he did she only flailed at *him* and called him things she knew—oh yes, she knew—she'd never dare call him in daylight. She was unsurprised and unsorry and not unhappy when Benjamin took to sleeping in his study, leaving his place in their bed to Min. Min and her anodyne.

Deborah did manage to go out of her room from time to time, but she was still not able to touch William or to address him as she should. She tried—oh, she tried—but every time she reached out to him, her fingers seemed to hold their own memory of that softer, younger flesh, and they'd curl up and draw themselves back into her chest. William would blink at her, as if always on the verge of tears, and she couldn't bear the sight of it; she'd turn away and let the new girl continue whatever it was she was doing with him—study or games or just silly talk. They'd begun to quote to each other from *Poor Dick,* as if testing to see who would run out of quotes first—it was the kind of game Deborah had expected Benjamin to like, but he didn't; whenever he entered a room where it was being played he walked out of it.

As Deborah's colors returned she began to notice something about Benjamin; since Franky's death he'd changed into a more solemn version of himself, darker, uncertain even, prone to odd fits and starts; now that he had Min to look after Deborah and Anne to look after William, he spent even longer hours at the print shop. That didn't surprise Deborah—she'd grown used to his hours—but it did surprise her that her husband's even longer absences came to her as something like relief. She understood that she must right herself, that the house could not function properly until she did so, but her husband's staring at her nose didn't help. He said all the words that she could want to hear: that a boy never had a better mother; that no woman on earth could lose such a son and stay sane through it; that he had the greatest faith in her strength taking her forward. When she bemoaned that they had no image of Franky, he went out and commissioned a portrait from a friend who was able to capture the child from memory; he packed away Franky's clothes himself so she wouldn't have the pain of it. He could say and do it all, but a father's grief was not a mother's, and the greatest comfort came to Deborah only from Anne's eyes, full of grief, yes, but with life in them still, promising that life for Deborah.

One day, while William was at his tutor's and Min was doing the wash, Deborah came upon Anne cleaning out William's cupboard, removing his clothes and piling them on the bed, her hands sure and strong, her back straight. Deborah lifted her own spine. She must, she *must* be like Anne. She must gather herself. But how long had it taken Anne to do so?

"How long since you lost your son?" Deborah asked.

The girl jumped, seemingly unaware that Deborah had come to stand in the doorway. She then took so long to answer that Deborah began to feel she'd been wrong to ask it. "I'm sorry," Deborah said. "'Tis not my intention to revive old pain. I wondered only if it was recent."

"Recent," Anne echoed. And then, as if she'd been reminded afresh, "Yes. Recent." But as if to prove her superior strength of mind she turned briskly to the bed where she'd formed her neat pile of clothes and began to sift through it. "I thought, being free this morning, I'd mend William's clothes." She picked up a shirt and held it out. "This is ripped at the neck." She picked up a red wool scarf. "The moths have been here. It needs a darn." She looked up at Deborah. "Unless he has another? I couldn't find one."

Deborah looked at the scarf Anne held in her hand and flushed with shame. This was her duty, and for days—perhaps weeks now— she'd shirked it. She plucked the scarf from Anne's fingers. "'Tis my task. I'll mend it."

To Deborah's surprise Anne reached out and reclaimed the scarf.

"William's my charge. As soon as you're enough recovered, your husband expects you at the shop."

"The apprentice is minding the shop."

"And causing your husband to put in longer hours at the press."

Deborah hadn't thought of that. Why hadn't she thought of that? If Benjamin had to make up for his apprentice's absence, of course his hours would lengthen. It *was* her task to mind the shop. The idea weighed first heavy and then light. The shop, not William. The shop, not this dead house empty of its most cherished life.

Deborah left William's room and entered her own; for the first time in weeks she went to the glass and looked herself over. Her hair looked greasy and dull; her skin yellow; her flesh so diminished her fine, full bosom no longer crested above her shift. She was not ready for the shop. She was not ready for the bright remarks from her customers, none of them understanding what she'd suffered. Deborah crossed to the bed and lay down on it.

Min came into the room with her arms full of fresh linen and dropped her load next to Deborah without the least hint of surprise at finding her lying there fully dressed in the middle of the morning. She said, "'Tis time for your dose." Yes, it was time for a dose, but suddenly Deborah saw herself stripped of the sympathy that had entombed her for so many days, exposed through Anne's eyes as the indulged creature that she was, collapsing into uselessness while another worked through that same grief each day without excuse.

Deborah sat up. She raised a hand to ward Min and the bottle off. She took up her comb, undid her hair, and gave it a good airing before fixing it back into its knot. She tightened the laces on her bodice, went to the kitchen, and cut a thick slice of bread. She chewed the bread into a paste that even an infant could swallow and washed it down with a cup of beer. She loosened her bodice to ease the nausea and forced a second piece in. She felt no better but trusted that she would soon enough, and that was going to have to suffice. She could do this thing. She would. She must.

WHEN DEBORAH ENTERED THE shop she discovered it was Benjamin, not James, who tended it, and she faltered. A man had just entered, a few flakes of snow unmelted yet on his shoulders—Samuel Harris. He would say he'd come for paper and ink but he'd take the almanac if she presented it, and some coffee, and twice now she'd forced him to admire the Franklin soap and believed he was near to taking a cake. Benjamin spied her over Harris's shoulder and his face opened.

"My dear! How divinely timed your appearance! I was just now worrying how to wrap up Mr. Harris's package as neatly as you do it."

Harris turned, saw Deborah, stepped across the space between them, and caught up her hands. "My dear, dear Mrs. Franklin. How my heart aches for you in the face of your terrible loss."

"You forget yourself, sir," Benjamin said. "To speak love to a woman whose husband is not two feet from you is not only rash but risky. I shall, however, overlook it this once."

Harris tipped back his head and laughed. Deborah, whose step had faltered again under the sympathetic onslaught, regained her nerve and continued. "You give away our secret, sir; I believed you to be more discreet. In payment you must take some of our famous soap."

Harris took two cakes. Deborah slid behind the counter to make his change and wrap his parcel. Her hands shook, but if either man noticed he hid it well. When Harris had gone Benjamin took Deborah's face between his hands and leaned down as if to touch his lips to hers, but his smile sat too comfortably on his mouth. Two cakes of soap did not bring Franky back; it did not suddenly return the world to the way it was. Deborah averted her face.

22

ANNE'S SYMPATHY FOR DEBORAH Franklin surprised her. It began, she knew, when she'd looked at Deborah Franklin's face and saw her own. Such pain! She would wish it on no one, even though she could likewise be glad that it kept Deborah in her chamber and away from William. The boy was again Anne's. And what a boy he was! So handsome she couldn't take her eyes from him, so bright she must struggle to keep up, and with so much love there for the taking that within a day Anne felt herself made rich from it. Talents she couldn't know she possessed emerged; she could soothe William's bewildered tears, or encourage him with his numbers and books, or simply make the poor boy laugh. On his own he began to climb into her lap or slip his hand into hers; he looked to her face for hints as to how best to respond to his mother's—was his mother angry or just sad? Anne always, always explained Deborah's behavior as nothing to do with William, and a thing that wouldn't last, all the while secretly believing—hoping—it would; perhaps that was why Anne was able to look at

Deborah Franklin's neglect of her son with so little resentment.

As to the father, Anne saw at once that William looked to him for one thing: praise. The boy did in fact receive a good deal of praise, but never evenly distributed—the irregular pattern of Franklin's attention was probably the thing that put William in such a constant state of uncertainty and need, and there Anne could only calm but never cure. To give him his due, Franklin was often distracted by business or company and, now, his grief, but unlike the situation with Deborah, Anne could find in her little sympathy for him; in his hands he held all the power that now mattered in her world. It was true that whenever Anne was able to spy on him unaware it was as if he'd run out of strength to hold up his features—they sagged against his bones, all the old delight long gone from him—but as soon as he saw Anne everything sharpened. Franklin was not comfortable with Anne in the room or, indeed, in the house, and she knew he would work to find a way to be shed of her as soon as he could. Sympathy and fear seldom walked hand in hand.

That the Franklins were not comfortable with each other either grew more and more clear to Anne. One evening Anne and Deborah were standing together at the kitchen table attempting to repair a mop when Franklin entered. He came up behind his wife and laid his hands on her shoulders; Deborah bent her knees, ducked from under him, and crossed to the other side of the table. Anne looked at Franklin and saw something flick across his face like the touch of a whip end, but still she could feel little sympathy for him. She did watch in some awe as he adjusted himself to this new wife; he was no less attentive, but his attention grew less personal; he withheld something of himself from her. For Anne's part, all her attention went to William, her heart spilling out all the years of hoarded love she'd kept for him.

AFTER A TIME INSIDE the new, blighted world in which the Franklins lived, some shadows of the old appeared. Franklin had returned to his press as Deborah returned to the shop, and this seemed to give the needed signal to Franklin's friends and acquaintances—callers began to come, not to mourn with the Franklins, but to talk to Franklin himself. Or to listen to him talk. Or to listen to him *think*, as it began to seem to Anne, and she listened too, as she'd always listened to Franklin. One night as Anne walked past the parlor door she heard Franklin explaining the workings of northeast storms; on another night she heard him exclaim, "Here now, sir, up on your chair! There, do you feel the greater heat nearer the ceiling? Now, onto the floor. You feel the air is cooler. Do you see how it is that hot air rises and cold air sinks? You see which air goes up the chimney? You see the waste?"

Anne couldn't hold herself from peering around the doorjamb, where she saw a distinguished gentleman lying prone on the floor, coat twisted up under him and wig askew.

Later that night, after the visitors had left but before the fire had died away, Anne crept into the empty parlor and stood on the chair. Hotter. She lay on the floor. Cooler. She lay there accustoming herself to this new idea until a voice said, "I see you continue as you began."

Anne leaped up. Franklin stood in the doorway, the fire lighting his face, causing an illusion of the old delight flickering across it. "You always appreciated my little experiments, did you not? I seem to recall you particularly liked my singing glasses. I have an idea to create an instrument using those glasses, fitting them one inside the other, on a rotating spindle, with a tray underneath to hold the water. But horizontal or vertical? I can never decide."

"Horizontal," Anne said, already picturing it, a thing like a harpsichord, with the broad, skillful fingers moving gracefully back and forth over the glasses.

"Yes, I believe you're right. Like a harpsichord." He wandered off.

. . . .

AT FIRST ANNE SHARED a room and a bed with Min in the uppermost half story of the Franklin home, not unlike her old space above the upholstery shop. Anne didn't mind sharing the bed, as she was used to it at home, and besides, more nights than not Min was summoned to attend Deborah Franklin by a bell on a wire Franklin had rigged to run up through the floor. But after a time Min stopped coming to the above-stairs room to sleep at all—she shared Deborah Franklin's bed, while Franklin retreated to a small bed in his study.

One night, after Anne had slept alone a number of weeks, she woke to the sound of a heavier than usual tread across the floor. She opened her eyes to discover Franklin, shirt to his knees, shawl wrapped over his shoulders, candle in his hand, standing just inside the door. Anne scrambled upright, pulling her bed rug in tighter. "What is it? What's happened?"

"My son has died," Franklin said.

The nonsensical thinking that comes with the dark put one word in Anne's mind. *William.* But before she could speak her fear, Franklin went on.

"My beautiful Franky has died, and my wife's turned half mad because of it."

Anne gathered herself. "Yes, sir, but she comes along. Perhaps you'd best attend to her now."

"Attend to her! How? She prefers Min in her bed. She can't bear to blame herself for any least little bit of it, so she fabricates a way to blame me for the whole. 'We must get the boy his inoculation,' I said, but she said, 'No, he's not well enough,' and so it went, on and on."

Franklin stepped farther into the room, and Anne could smell the wine on him.

"I'm very sorry for the situation, sir, but you do none of us any good if you're found here. You must go below and see to your wife."

"She blames me because of William. She thinks God punishes me for the old sin by taking the golden child to heaven and leaving the blackened one on earth. Good God, how she frightened me! I looked at her in her madness and actually believed her capable of terrible things. I must be half mad myself. Why, of course I'm half mad; what more proof do I need than the sight of you sitting up here under my eaves? What madness could have overcome me to allow such a thing to happen?"

All the heat left Anne's extremities. This was why Franklin had come up to her chamber—to tell her she must go. She clawed through every argument against and began to spew them out. " 'Tis no madness, sir; you're right to fear what your wife might do. She's not balanced in her mind. I'm here to keep our son healthy and unharmed. While I do it I'm bringing some comfort to your wife. If she were to discover me suddenly gone . . . If she were to learn by some mischance of my relation—"

But Franklin cut her off. "No, my dear. That trick won't work anymore. You might not flinch at causing my wife and me some trouble, but I've seen you with William now, and I know you would never do anything that might cause him shame."

"Perhaps not. But think of the greater damage to all were Deborah to discover you in this chamber."

"You needn't fear that, I promise you. Anyone in such a laudanum daze doesn't go about climbing stairs."

"Sir, I'm heartily sorry for your poor dead boy—indeed, I could hardly be more brokenhearted were he my own, but you must—"

It was as if she'd jostled a tankard of ale. The tears began to course down Franklin's face, winking gold in the candlelight before disappearing into the shadow beneath his jaw. "My poor dead boy," he said. "My poor, poor boy." The candle in his hand wobbled and tilted dangerously, casting shadows like disturbed ghosts against the walls. Anne leaped out of bed and took the candle from Franklin's hand, setting it on the floor, attempting to steady him with a hand beneath his elbow; he felt as fragile as a piece of dry straw. She led him to the bed and sat him down.

"I beg you to forgive me," he said. "But 'tis an odd thing, is it not? That you alone of all my acquaintance can best understand exactly what it is I suffer? The one boy dead, the other . . . the other—"

"The other is a fine boy. He's committed no sin. Don't allow your wife to make him carry ours. But he's like any other boy, sir—in want of his father's regular attention." Anne stressed the word *regular* but the word Franklin heard was another.

"*Our* sin! You would call it ours? No, my dear, you were no whore, at least you weren't till I got through with you. 'Tis my sin alone." Franklin dashed a hand at his wet face and pulled himself free of her grip. "I *have* tried to make it right. You must grant me that. I've tried to make it right for all. And what is the result? The four of us here together. I thought to myself, I've mastered my old passions; I'm able to manage this, such an old tale needn't be retold. And then you lay down on my parlor floor."

He *is* mad, Anne thought. And perhaps ill. He attempted to stand and staggered. "I seem to have lost my knees," he said. "Entirely fitting that I crawl about upon them, I know, but just the same, it makes for something of a difficulty when it comes to those stairs." He barked out a laugh. "Perhaps I should give over my wine and take up Debby's laudanum."

Anne took his elbow again. "Here. Rest a minute."

Franklin sat down on the bed again and leaned forward, head in hands.

"I seem to have lost all my strength just when everyone needs it most," he said. "I don't know what I'm to do for any of us now."

He was trembling. Anne stood, looking down at the top of the soft, fair hair that had left so clear a mark on her son. The boy and the man were one the part of the other, and he'd never denied it, had, indeed, tried to right it, taking on considerable trouble to himself in the righting. Anne thought of husband and wife alone in their separate beds and wondered what on God's earth she might possibly do to help them—how the pair would comfort each other with their touch, if they could only find their way there! How Franklin needed that touch! And right then all the pity for Franklin that Anne hadn't managed to conjure up in the past began to run over her like warm oil. She sat down beside Franklin and peeled away the nearest hand that still covered his face; the fingers were as cold as an unlit stove. She took the hand between hers and rubbed it, then took up the other. He drew his hands out from hers and lifted them, cupping her face. "My Annie," he said. "My sweet Annie. Can you know how I delighted in climbing those stairs with you at the Penny Pot? Can you know what utter joy and comfort it was?"

Comfort. That he would use the word Anne had just pondered seemed significant to her—that they would come to the same place at the same moment; so large a word in one sense, but also so small a one, requiring so small a thing. Anne leaned forward and touched her lips to Franklin's forehead as a mother might kiss a despairing child, or a whore might kiss an old and favored customer long after the whoring had stopped. And then she kissed him again, as the whore would.

Franklin pulled back, looked at her. "Here's the truth of it, Annie. I am, by nature, a monogamous creature. I am not, by nature, a celibate one." He smiled as bitter a smile as Anne had ever seen in him. "How fortunate that Man is possessed of reason; he may reason his way into everything he yearns to do." He reached for her but she slid away, rose and shut the door, collected the candle and moved it beside the bed. She pushed him down onto the bed tick, loosened the drawstring on her shift. She was concerned about the drink in him, but he rose to meet her as of old, only this time it wouldn't be as it was of old, this time she would be the one who said when and where and how.

· · · ·

FRANKLIN DIDN'T CLIMB THE stairs to Anne's room for another week. Anne knew something more of the man now, and could watch the old battle between his monogamous self and his non-celibate self rage; indeed, she happened to witness the exact moment when the monogamous self lost. One morning in the kitchen Deborah shrugged out from under his hand, as had become her way, and Franklin looked across the table at Anne and caught her eye as if to say, *You see, I've tried; now I give myself over to you.* Anne would admit to a kind of thrill shooting through her as she met and read that look—Benjamin Franklin, *hers*. But soon enough the fact of the thing bore down on her. Anne could never claim Franklin as Deborah had claimed him, but it didn't matter; she only needed the piece of him that kept him climbing the stairs to her room. At first Anne had feared that was the piece that would get her cast out of the house, but now she saw that it was the very piece that would keep her here, near William. She was not the Anne of the Penny Pot days. She could now do all the things that she'd learned to do so well, old for her but new for Franklin, and she could read the same fresh delight in his body as easily as she used to read it in his eyes. The Franklin that Anne now eased above stairs was not about to send her away anytime soon.

Soon enough, Franklin was climbing the stairs to Anne's room nightly, and although Anne's prime concern was keeping Franklin's interest, her secondary concern was not disturbing the sleeping woman below. But as each successive night passed with Deborah continuing unaware, Anne began to relax, and after a while she actually began to enjoy her evenings with the brilliant, entertaining, and innovative Benjamin Franklin. How could she not? She learned something new of the man—of life—each time he came.

First was the "air bath," as Franklin called it. Before coming into the bed he took off all his clothes and sat before the open window until thoroughly chilled, then plunged beneath the bedcovers and wrapped himself around Anne. At another visit he found an appropriate moment to launch a brief discourse on the method of the planets, at another the workings of the pores of the skin, the effect of the moon on the tides, how a waterspout formed. Anne devoured every bit of what he taught, and in turn Franklin paid her what she considered his finest compliment.

"There is nothing so attractive in a woman as a mind thirsty after knowledge and capable of receiving it."

BUT THE SUBJECT ANNE liked best was swimming. Franklin had begun to talk of it in a casual way one night, as he gave over his fingers to her mouth one by one, but Anne couldn't let the topic go. "Do you mean to say a sailor would never drown if he only learned this simple thing?"

"Many hundreds fewer would."

"And you know how to do it?"

"Do it and teach it. At one time I thought to make my livelihood as a swimming instructor for wealthy young men, but I took another turn."

"But certainly you must be strong to learn it."

"Certainly not. I've begun to teach William."

"William!"

"He can't swim far, but he will as he grows. Now, my dear, I do so love conversing with you, but if you would be so kind as to resume exactly where you left off—"

Anne picked up Franklin's next finger and slid it into her mouth, slowly, never allowing the waiting fingers to rush her along. When the procedure had run its usual course, from fingers to arms to neck to chest to belly and down, after Franklin had lain immobile for some time, he lifted his head to study Anne.

"Who taught you such tricks, Annie? Who came up those stairs after me? Was it Wilkes? Or that corder?"

Anne didn't answer.

"I don't see either one of them so skilled in the art of love. What of the largehearted Grissom? All that quiet pondering he does; he must have come up with an idea now and then. And how many years were you right there above that shop? I'd be a fool not to suppose he got his turn with you."

Again Anne said nothing.

Franklin chuckled and patted her cheek. "Wise girl." But in another minute he burst out, "Good God, how I dislike the thought of it!" Another second and he added, "Although I suppose I should be grateful to him."

He reached down beside the bed and fumbled about in his clothes; the next thing Anne knew she held a pound coin in her hand.

"What's this?"

"Call it something toward your retirement. What else might I give you? I can't have you walking about the house wearing a costly gown or a ruby ring, can I?"

"No."

"But if there's something inconspicuous you'd like better than a coin—"

Anne supposed she might think up a number of things she'd like, but nothing as much as she'd like the coin; in fact, her hand had already closed around it and drawn it under the bolster.

23

IT WAS DEBORAH WHO received the new gown, and a silver tea set, and a maple table; Anne saw her pass through the parlor and stroke the polished surface of the table as if it were the silky head of a beloved child. From these gifts, as well as the coins Franklin continued to bestow, Anne discovered that somehow, without her noticing, the Franklins had become well off. But Franklin didn't seem to care what his money could buy him beyond his two malleable women and more freedom; he hired more help at the press and spent more time in his study experimenting with anything that happened to come to hand.

One day Anne came upon Franklin at the kitchen table, watching William as he held a wood chip in one hand and a penny in the other, both objects thrust into the candle flame. Very soon William dropped the coin. "Hot!"

"Do you see, my boy?" Franklin said. "Metal conducts heat better than wood. The wood you can still hold comfortably in your fingers long after the heat has forced you to drop the penny. Do you understand?"

William nodded, but he would nod for his father whether he truly understood it or not—this too Anne had learned.

Another time Anne came up late to her bed, William's stomach gripe having kept her below, to discover Franklin standing naked at her washbowl, two of Anne's stockings pulled over his hands, dipping them into the water and then holding them up to the air from the open window. As Anne came in he swung toward her—still an impressive figure even without his clothes and despite the addition of Anne's stockings. He held out his hands.

"Two stockings of like thickness, one cotton, one wool. The wool stays warm even if wet; the cotton does not."

All of this was intriguing enough to Anne, but none of it was as intriguing as that one thing that wouldn't leave her alone. One night after she'd settled Franklin and he appeared to be reaching into his waistcoat for another coin, she stayed his hand.

"I've decided what I should like from you instead of that coin," she said. "I should like to learn to swim."

Franklin let out such a hoot Anne feared their discovery. "To swim!" He managed to get up and get himself dressed before he started again. "To swim! I see it now—the banks lined on both sides, Philadelphia *and* New Jersey, the ships hove to—"

"Summer's not gone. We could go at night, slip down the hall and out the door—"

"And through the streets and down to the waterfront and strip off our clothes and—" Franklin hooted again.

FRANKLIN DIDN'T COME TO her room for several nights. When he finally came he waked her from the deepest part of her sleep, carrying no candle, his form lit only by the tiniest sliver of moon from the window, holding out what looked to be Min's hooded cloak. "Come," he said. "Put this on. Go down to the shop and wait. Be *quiet*." He wrapped the cloak around her, pressed his fingers to her mouth, and left.

Anne did as he said. In the shop she discovered Franklin's apprentice, James. "Take my arm," he said. Anne did. James led her down the solemn, black-night street toward Front Street, then along Front Street until they'd passed the last of the shops. Anne pulled back, but James tugged her ahead, across the street, into the thicket of trees that lined the riverbank. He kept on until he came to a large rock and stopped. Franklin stepped out from behind it.

"Thank you, James," he said. "Two hours. No more."

Franklin took Anne's hand and led her through the trees until the river glistened in front of her and the ground turned to boggy, wet peat, then widened into hard, flat sand.

Franklin took Min's cloak from her and let it fall to the ground. He kneeled and removed her shoes, rose and brought her shift with him, pulling it over her head. She stood naked under the moon, the breeze rippling and teasing her skin; Franklin peeled away his own cloak, shoes, shirt, and breeches and stood as white and naked as she, teeth gleaming at her across the dark.

"Come," he said.

He took both her hands and backed into the water, pulling her with him. The water rose to her knees, thighs, waist, breasts, cold and thick and thrilling. Franklin's hands came around her waist and he lifted her up, pulling her to him till she straddled him, here and there freeing a hand to fondle her breasts. He eased her onto her back, hands under her buttocks, and began to coach her: "Arms wide. Arch your back. Relax your neck." They went along thus until all at once his hands fell away. "You float, Annie! Do you feel it? You see what the water is? It doesn't sink you, it carries you!"

She felt it. She felt everything. First the sheer wonder of nothing but water touching her skin, then the wild freedom, last the peacock-proud triumph before she jackknifed and sank, but Franklin only laughed and pulled her up and turned her onto her stomach. He held his hand under her belly; he told her to paddle her hands and feel the water like thread being pulled through her fingers; he told her to close her fingers tight against each other and try it again. He showed her how to push her arms straight ahead of her and then circle them back, pushing against the water with her newly closed fingers, noticing the power; he told her to kick her feet like a frog. She paddled and didn't kick. She kicked and didn't paddle. Finally she got the both of them together and she moved. She *moved*!

Franklin's hand left her belly and returned, left and returned, until she cried, "Leave me be!" and he laughed in delight. She beat against the water for a few short yards and turned and beat her way back, exhausted; she leaped into his arms and he kissed her and she kissed him back as if it were love. When she'd gotten her breath, she pushed away again and this time she felt calmer, beat less frantically at the river, let it work with her, but when she turned she discovered the river only worked with her in one direction; on the turn it became her enemy. Franklin had anticipated it, however, and was there to catch her and help her toward shore.

"Always best to cut across the tide, not against it."

"To New Jersey!"

Franklin laughed again, then sobered. "No, no, no, you must never attempt that. In the middle the river rages too strong for any man. Now come, or James will think we've drowned."

It couldn't be two hours, Anne thought, but indeed, when Anne stopped threshing the water she could hear James calling, low and forlorn, "Master! Master!" But she didn't want to leave the river. She pushed against Franklin, but he held her tight, carried her out, dried her with his shirt as if he were drying off his horse, even dressed her and wrapped her again in the old cloak. He took her hand and led her back into the woods where James waited. Anne clung to Franklin's hand an extra minute, loath to let go of the night's magic, but Franklin worked his hand free. "You mustn't be seen with me at this hour," he said, but what he meant, of course, was that *he* mustn't be seen with *her.*

James led Anne back to the Franklin home; as they entered the hall, Anne noticed Franklin's coat hadn't yet been returned to its peg and decided to wait inside the door until he appeared. This time she took *his* hand and silently tugged him toward the stairs, wanting more of him, the rest of him; she toppled Franklin into her bed and fed him into her and urged him to his end, but it wasn't, after all, any different from before. What had she expected, that it *was* love, that kiss in the river? And was that even what she wanted? What *was* this ache in her?

After Franklin left, Anne slipped out of bed, wrapped herself in her shawl, and slipped down the half flight of stairs to William's room. He lay as he always lay, curled tight around the edge of his blanket, thumb in mouth, hair fanned out behind him as if he'd been carried on the wind and dropped there, someone's pale fairy child, so unlike her darkness, and yet . . . Anne leaned down and touched his perfect ear, his delicate nose, his slender fingers. Hers.

Not hers.

THERE WERE TIMES WHEN Anne was quite sure Deborah knew what went on above her, and other times when Anne was equally sure she didn't. According to Min, Deborah had given up her daytime anodyne but continued to take it at night, which must have helped to keep her safe asleep. The notable upturn in Franklin's spirits could be explained by the fact that he might be expected to have come out from under the sharpest edges of his grief, but the shop seemed to distract Deborah too; her talk at table was all of the soaps and lamp-black and linseed oil that she'd brought new to the shelves. She was greatly improved, but Anne couldn't—and hoped Franklin couldn't—trust her with William's care even so. One morning Deborah stumbled on the hearth and spilled water from a steaming kettle onto William's foot; Anne took that as an accident, but another day she came upon the woman attempting to trim William's hair, or so she said—a long bloody scratch ran from his ear to his cheek. From that episode forward Anne haunted William throughout the house.

One early Sunday Deborah came into the kitchen dressed and combed for the world. "I shall go to church today," she said.

Franklin, taking care not to meet Anne's eye, said, "Excellent!"

"And I'll take William."

There Franklin couldn't help but allow his gaze to cross with Anne's, so hard did she stare at him. "Best take Min to mind him," he said.

"Min doesn't attend Christ Church. She's Presbyterian, like you." Deborah laughed. Coming from Deborah, the sound was so strange that it distracted Anne from its cause, but she understood it better once she came back to it; Franklin called himself Presbyterian, but he never attended services and had recently begun to contribute to every church in town, as if determined to take up every chance—or make every friend. But Franklin's chances—and friends—were not that moment's concern.

Anne said, "I'll go along and mind William."

Deborah shot Anne a new, determined look. "I'm able to mind my son. William, come, you need a clean shirt and your best jacket."

William leaped up from the table and left with Deborah.

Franklin looked again at Anne, another thought now clearly on his mind—two hours, alone—but Anne had no time for playing at housekeeping. "I'm going to follow them as far as the church," she said.

"Oh, come, Deborah's herself again; there's no need of—"

"I'm going to follow them."

DEBORAH SET OFF BRISKLY, William's hand held tight, and Anne, trailing behind, could see how alight the boy grew under that simple attention. He looked up at his stepmother again and again, smiling wider each time; he skipped a step after every two. Anne was briefly distracted by the noise from the Sunday butcher's shambles, the smell of fresh blood and raw, opened animal wafting along the street, but William's attention was fixed the other way. "The ships!" he cried, pointing to the distant masts.

At first Anne didn't notice that the woman and child had walked past the turn to Christ Church and kept on toward the river. Anne kept on after them. A number of people paused and spoke stiffly to Deborah Franklin, condoling with her; she appeared to answer with composure, but she always hastened along, each time looking down at William, as if to . . . what? Compare the dead with the living?

They walked on, William skipping higher the closer they came to the river. They passed the shops and warehouses on Front Street and continued onto the wharf; Anne took care to keep herself concealed in the crowd as she edged after them. The wind was much stronger out on the wharf; Anne watched it tug at Deborah's skirt just as William tugged at her hand, pulling her from ship to ship, pointing here and there, now pointing at a group of three pilings atop which some no doubt liquored sailor had nailed up his shipmate's bright red bandanna.

"Look! Look!" William cried, and tugged at Deborah, but she was shaking her head; she would go no closer. She let go of William's hand. He began to run toward the pilings.

It was as if Anne saw it twice—the first time in her mind's projection, the second time as it actually happened—sturdy, blue-stockinged legs pinwheeling over the planks and leaping up onto the first of the staggered pilings. Anne started to run, but she was too far back and too hindered by the crowd she'd purposely ducked behind; Deborah, far ahead of her, didn't run. Didn't move. Didn't cry out. She stood where she was and watched as William grasped the top of the second piling and began to pull himself up, hanging out over the water, connected to land by eight fingers and a knee that had somehow managed to gain purchase on that second towering piling. But no, it was four fingers and a knee now; William had let go with one hand and was reaching for the top of the highest piling, reaching for the sailor's bandanna.

Anne was still far behind Deborah and William when a spry young fellow leaped in front of both of them, danced up the first piling as if it were a stepping-stone, and plucked William out of the air just as his knee lost its purchase. William scrambled free of his rescuer and dashed up to Deborah.

"Look, Mama, for you! A kerchief!"

ANNE PERCHED ON THE edge of William's bed that night and guided him to talk of it; it was no great trick, the adventure being almost all he'd spoken of since he'd gotten back.

"Mama said *church*. She made me dress in church clothes. And then we didn't go to church! I saw the ships and she said would I like to visit the ships and we walked right past the church!"

"And you saw the ships."

"And I saw a red kerchief on top of a great post! And I climbed up and got it for Mama!"

"And what did Mama have to say of that?"

"She said how brave I was."

"She wasn't afraid you'd fall in?"

William gave a small-boy snort of dismissal. "Papa takes me to swim. But he doesn't let go." He paused. "He doesn't let go of me on the wharf either."

"But Mama let go?"

William slid down inside his sheets, grew silent.

Anne said, "William?"

William said, "I'm sleepy now."

24

DEBORAH FRANKLIN COULDN'T SLEEP. Only the night before she'd decided it was time to give up her nighttime dose and had been pleased and proud of her little experiment; she'd waked that morning feeling more alert and alive than she'd felt in some time, more able to *cope*. She'd looked sideways in the bed, half expecting to find Benjamin lying there, and had even been disappointed to discover Min still in his place. For the first time she began to consider what she might do to remedy that, to at least get back that part of her old life; what Benjamin had done all those years ago and the consequence of it was not, after all, something that could ever be erased. It was time to make the best of it and move ahead, perhaps to another child, not one who would ever replace Franky, but one who would put something living into the dead house.

Such were Deborah's thoughts that morning when she entered the kitchen and saw William at the table, noticed as if for the first time what a fine-looking boy he'd become. Indeed, it must be said that

Franky had not been so pretty a child, that if the three walked about in the street it was William who drew the eye first each time, but as Deborah examined this inherited son of hers, she saw too the look in his eye, an eye fixed on her alone of all the people in the room, an eye so full of question and hope and *expectation.* Could it be possible that this boy, after all of it, still wanted her to come to him and take him up in her arms? Could she still become that person the boy expected her to be? That Benjamin expected her to be? She could, she decided. She would. The mere presence of that thought so filled her with gratitude that she decided to go to church to give her thanks. And she would take the boy. Begin again with him as she would begin again with Benjamin. With her life.

And then Deborah had gone to the wharf. Against her closed eyelids she could still see those pilings and the water just beyond and the boy hanging there, her fear hanging there, as visible as either of the other things, veiny and red and full of fire. She'd let go of his hand, she knew that, had stood frozen, she knew that too; what kind of mother would let go of her child so near the water, no matter her own fear of it? Would she have let go of *Franky?* Would she have stood dumb and still if it had been *Franky* attempting to scale those pilings? And there lay the darkest, dankest corner in the great room of Deborah's fears. Had she *wanted* William to come to harm? In some shameful corner of her tortured mind had she seen herself as the avenging angel that would at last see Benjamin Franklin pay for his sin?

Once they got home Deborah had sent William off to play with the servant, sent him to bed with the servant, unable, once again, to look the child in the face. Was this a thing she must wrestle with all her life? No. She would not. She need not. Deborah tossed away her bedclothes and got up. She lit a candle off the kitchen fire, worked her way through the hall and up the stairs to William's room; he was, of course, asleep, but his legs and arms twitched, his small brow puckered. He'd come home elated about the bandanna, but now, perhaps, the trip to the wharf troubled his sleep as it troubled Deborah's. She laid her hand on his fine hair and smoothed it from his face, waiting until she was sure he'd settled; only then did she leave the room, turning on the landing to go down the stairs, but she paused there. A faint noise came from the direction of the servant's room, as if the girl struggled in the throes of the same vile dream that seemed to haunt everyone in the house. Well, Anne had comforted Deborah enough times to earn Deborah's comfort now; or did Deborah go in search of her own comfort? It didn't matter, she decided; comfort for someone lay at the end of those stairs.

Anne's door was closed, but Deborah did indeed hear her voice behind it, harsh and half whispered.

"She *let him go*. At the wharf's edge! She let him climb up a piling! How many times must I tell it to you? I saw him hang out over the water and—"

"Yes, you said. And I said I'll keep a closer eye on them both. What more must I say to you? But please, my dear, you must keep your voice low."

That second voice was indeed low, but Benjamin had long ago mastered the art of speaking untender things in tender tones.

Our boy is dead.

"I was in such fear," Anne continued, but quieter. "You can't know."

"Yes, yes. But hush, please, before you wake all the house. I've seen to William and he's suffered no ill effects—he's safely settled in his bed. Now if we might but do the same—"

The voices ceased. A floorboard creaked, a bed rope. Then three words she'd heard before and knew well enough where they led. "Ah, my dear—"

Deborah stood in disbelief until rage destroyed the disbelief and with it her immobility. She lifted the latch and opened the door. The candlelight barely touched the bed, and half what Deborah saw she saw from the memory of her own fingers: the long, smooth swimmer's muscles working along her husband's back, the hard, clenched buttocks pumping slowly, slowly, against the air. Against Anne.

Deborah shoved the door hard against the wall. Athlete that he was, Benjamin leaped in a single bound from bed to floor. "Deborah! Good lord!"

Deborah looked at her husband, pressing his hands over his groin, attempting to hide his nakedness from her. From *her.* She looked at the girl in the bed, shift pushed up and breasts splayed, her own nakedness of little concern to her. The girl sat up and the shift fell down of its own accord, as did her long, dark hair, like spilled ink against her shift.

"My dear," Benjamin said, and then, perhaps seeing something better of her face, even in the half dark, he stopped.

Deborah stood, her heart snapped shut like a turtle's beak, her rage beating against it, her mind refusing to think beyond the single fact that she wanted to be shed of the scene before her, the people before her—shed of Franklin as she'd shed herself of Rogers—but this time she had no mother's shelter to flee to. She couldn't demand Benjamin Franklin leave his own house, especially as she wasn't even legal wife to him. She could do nothing, *nothing* . . . but hold; she could do one thing. Deborah turned from the girl in the bed as if she were no longer there, as indeed she was no longer there to Deborah, this mother of a dead son whose eyes Deborah had believed she'd known. Had *trusted.* She turned and spoke to her husband. "Get her gone."

DEBORAH RETURNED TO HER bed and curled up next to Min. Min's hand came out and tapped her on the knee, as if to make sure she'd returned, as if to make sure she planned to stay. Everything now looking different to Deborah, she began to doubt; was this old, familiar touch less the touch of a comforter and more the touch of a gaoler? Had that been Min's job all along, to keep Deborah secured in her bed while her husband climbed the stairs to plunge himself into their servant? Had that been why the servant was hired? No, that had been Deborah's idea, to hire that particular girl with the clouded, grieving eyes. She'd been drawn into those eyes; what great surprise, then, that Benjamin had been drawn there too, Benjamin who seemed to require that release in a woman in order to breathe. What fool Deborah that she could have imagined her husband sleeping alone in his study, night after night, while Deborah lay nurturing her blame and grief with Min.

The door opened and Benjamin stepped into the room. He said, "Min." Min came awake and sat up and got out of the bed and out of the room as if in a single movement—such was his tone. Benjamin came up to Deborah's side of the bed and pointed at the space left between her hip and her knee. "May I?"

Deborah slid her leg back as far as it would go, unable to bear the touch of him. Benjamin sat down, carefully keeping to the edge of the mattress. Solomon Grissom had made the mattress. Solomon Grissom who'd recommended that girl. Or had he? Or had they even asked? Deborah could not recall.

Deborah said, "Is she gone?"

"I told her she must go. She wishes to stay until another girl is found."

"I've no interest in her wishes. I want her gone now."

Benjamin said, "Very well, I'll talk to Grissom on the morrow. Perhaps he'd be inclined to take her back into the shop."

"Do you mishear me? Talk to Grissom when you like of what you like. The girl leaves now."

Benjamin sat long enough to hear that more silence was all she would offer. He stood and left the room.

. . . .

DEBORAH WAS AS BENJAMIN had left her when he returned. This time he didn't sit down.

"'Tis done. She's packing her things."

"Has the boy waked?"

"No."

Deborah rolled away and bounced her next question off the wall; it had been too long with her and had bent its shape too many times to fly straight from eye to eye. "I should like to know why you married me. Was it for William? To make a home for William?"

The silence pushed against the back of her head. "I did not marry you to make a home for William," Franklin said at last.

Deborah whirled around. "Why then?"

"Because all the life had gone out of you. Because I felt to blame. Because I wanted to make good on my earlier promise to you. But I did it in full confidence of a long, happy future together, and I've not lost that confidence."

He crossed the room to the bed. He dropped to his knees and picked up, not her hand, which she might pull away, but a lock of her sleep-strewn hair. She might pull if she liked, but if he held on, she would only hurt herself. She lay still.

Dawn brightened the window. Out in the hall, Deborah heard a single pip from William, and a quick, answering *shush;* no doubt Min, her gaoler, hovering near the door. Had she conspired in this betrayal? The next sound Deborah heard was of the outer door opening and closing; Anne was gone.

So, that was that.

But of course it wasn't.

She pushed back the bedcovers and rose, forcing Benjamin to scramble to his feet. "I wish you'd never gone to London," she said.

"But I did. We cannot—"

"Then I wish you'd never come back!"

Benjamin gazed at her with a mix of sadness and disappointment.

Well, let him be sad and disappointed all he liked. Deborah was sad and disappointed.

Benjamin left. Deborah stood for a time, unable to fix on a plan of what to do next, until she realized she was still undressed, that there was plan enough for the next few minutes. She got up, pulled on her skirt, bodice, stockings, and shoes, and washed her face in the bowl with greater care than she usually took. She took an even longer time fixing her hair, wishing she could use up the day with it, but she could not. When there was nothing whatever left to do to herself she sat on the bed again, trying to form up the rest of the day in her head; she couldn't, for the life of her, remember what she used to do with it.

The shop. That was it. Deborah sat and listened to the house; if Benjamin had the sense of a goat he would have gone out and left her to herself, and in fact she could hear nothing but Min, now thumping about with the kettles. But what of William? Likely with Min in the kitchen, when he should be dressing and getting ready for his tutor. This, then, was how Deborah's day had already changed: She must tend to William. Curiously, the thought didn't displease her—instead, it filled her with a sense of things come right for the wrong reasons. She'd already determined to make good with William and now fate had conspired to make sure she did.

Deborah went into the kitchen but found Min alone. "Where's the boy?"

"Asleep yet."

But Deborah had heard him in the hall. Or was her guilt so roused that she'd now begun to imagine the boy's calling her? She climbed the stairs to William's room, pushed open William's door, and discovered his tousled, empty bed. Well then, he would be below stairs amusing himself with his toys or books as he so often did; she turned to go and noticed the empty peg that should have held his jacket, and the open cupboard door, also half empty, the shelves holding only a few too-small shirts, a torn pair of breeches, some old shoes.

Deborah turned and nearly fell down the stairs, but made use of the momentum to carry her the rest of the way down as fast as she'd ever dared go. She banged open the parlor door, study door, bedroom door, kitchen door, only to find Benjamin now at table, eating his porridge as if it were any normal Monday morning. He looked up.

"My dear. What—"

"The boy. He's gone."

Afterward, Deborah remembered thinking it strange how quickly Benjamin accepted her unlikely words, how fast he leaped up and pounded up the stairs and down, repeated Deborah's tracks through all the rooms. He gathered his jacket from the peg in the hall and opened the door.

"Benjamin!"

"I'll fetch him home. Don't worry."

"You know where he's gone?"

"I've some ideas where to look. You needn't worry. He's not alone."

"Anne?"

Benjamin nodded.

"But why? For spite? Does she mean to ransom him?"

"I don't think so. I think she's grown . . . overfond."

The words, spoken with such care, implied the others that mirrored them. She wanted to blame Benjamin for this too and could not, because it was true, true, true—she had not been fond enough.

25

AFTER FRANKLIN HAD GONE Anne set herself into unthinking motion, like an ox on a worn track, dressing herself for the street, putting her few things into her satchel, securing her money pouch in her pocket. She would have liked to risk a last visit with William, to explain to him that she would be looking after him even from afar, but she didn't know what kind of scene might erupt if Deborah Franklin spied her. Anne picked up her bag and made her way down the stairs, pausing before the door to listen to the last sounds of the Franklin household: Min rustling about in the kitchen, the two voices going back and forth and up and down from behind the closed bedroom door. No one would be leaving that room soon.

So why *not* say good-bye to William? What kind of coward would sneak away without a single word, a single last touch, leaving the boy to a stepmother who was as cold as a winter stone and a father who could be as warm as a bed rug, but only when it occurred to him? William shouldn't have to go through life thinking the one person who had loved him with utter constancy could disappear in a single night without even a farewell. And besides, *she* needed to see him; she needed to touch him one more time.

Anne turned and flew up the stairs as fast as silence allowed. She opened William's door and crept in, reluctant, after all, to wake him. She eased up to the bed and looked down at the boy, at his father's wide brow and well-made chin, at his mother's slender nose and hands. He belonged to Franklin, yes, but he also belonged to Anne, Anne who had given him up once and was now expected to give him up again. The first time she'd accepted the notion that William's father might provide him with the better life, but now she knew he was not loved as he should be loved, he was not being kept safe. That was Anne's first thought; the second was simpler, and with it all further thinking ended: She could not give William up again.

Anne reached out and encircled William's ankle.

"Sleepy boy! Come!"

William opened his eyes and smiled, happy at the sight of her, secure in the sight of her. Yes, Anne thought, this is right, even William sees it so.

"I've a surprise for you," she said.

William shot up. "What surprise?"

"Well now, if I told you, it wouldn't be a surprise. Hurry and get dressed and be quiet. Your parents are asleep and shouldn't like to be disturbed."

William looked at the window, faint gray lines barely streaking the shutter. "Is it morning?"

"Near enough to. This surprise requires an early start if we're not to miss it."

William leaped out of bed and took up the breeches that Anne held out to him. "I need the pot."

"Soon," Anne said. She stuffed another pair of William's breeches, two shirts, and four pairs of stockings into her satchel on top of her own clothes; she would risk a boy's wet breeches over being discovered before they'd left Franklin's home. What else did she risk? As she led William down the stairs, the word kept pace with her quickening steps. *All. All. All.*

HALF-DARK STREETS. HALF-DARK ALLEYS. Thoughts only half formed. Top it all with a child whose nature, Anne must admit, did not come entirely from her *or* his father; he was not bold. It required teasing and tempting and prodding, making up races and all kinds of other games with this fabled surprise at the end, this surprise she didn't dare name, to make William move along. Why, it took her two long, precious minutes just to get the boy to pee into a gutter! They'd finally gotten as far as the outskirts, where the houses began to thin and patches of green fields had begun to appear—indeed, they were halfway across one of those fields—when William simply buckled his knees and sat down.

"I want to go home," he said.

"We're almost there, William. Only this one more field. Do you see that pretty little house and barn at the far side? That's your aunt Mary's house! There's your surprise! And guess what, they have a horse you can ride!"

"I don't have an Aunt Mary."

"That's the surprise! A surprise aunt and uncle and three cousins. Come along now, they'll have a wonderful breakfast laid out just for you."

William looked up at Anne with that small, pinched face she'd come to love and dread together. "I want my regular breakfast," he said. "In my regular bowl. At home."

ANNE WAS ALREADY DONE in when they arrived at her sister's door, and she might have gifted Ezekiel Lee with many favors when he opened the door incuriously and ushered them in. But when Mary appeared with her newest babe in her arms she gave a little shriek and nearly crushed her infant by wrapping her arms around Anne at the same time, which startled William so much that he began to cry. The appearance of Mary's four-year-old boy and two-year-old girl only drew him deeper into Anne's skirt; Mary—blessed Mary—leaned down to William and said, "Never mind about crying babies. What say you to scones?"

William snuffed up his tears, and Anne led the boy toward the kitchen. Behind her Mary whispered, "Annie. It is him?"

Anne nodded.

There was no room to say more. They filed into the tiny kitchen and Mary dropped her infant into the cradle, settling the other three children around the table. William sat, but he kept his eyes on Anne. She smiled and smiled until she felt her teeth must fall on the floor from it, but when Mary distributed the scones and jam, William finally took his eyes away from her and turned to the table, to the two children perched on either side of him. As soon as William had his mouth good and full, Mary drew slowly backward toward the door, and Anne followed, only as far as the other side of the threshold. Ezekiel Lee came behind them.

"Whatever do you do here?" Mary began.

Anne explained, in part. The mad wife. The doubting Franklin. The boy—her boy—who must be kept safe from harm.

"Are *you* mad?" Lee asked. "You kidnapped Franklin's child?"

"I did not kidnap—," Anne started, but stopped. She would admit her reasons for taking the boy came out less convincingly than they'd first gone in; she could admit—now—that of course this is what they would all say if she was discovered: She'd kidnapped Franklin's child. What on earth had she been thinking to imagine that she could keep William at her sister's, still so near his home? She must get farther away. Soon. Anne turned and spoke directly to Ezekiel Lee. "I ask that you keep us this single night only. By morning we'll move on."

"And so must I, if Franklin discovers the boy here! Which he will, of course. Of course he will look at your sister's! What were you thinking, girl?"

"Franklin knows nothing of my relations beyond the old house in the alley, and no one's left there to direct him to you. He won't know to look here."

Lee ignored Anne, spoke directly to his wife. "My answer is no, Mary. I leave you to make your sister sensible before we all end up in gaol." He exited the hallway. Anne gave a moment's thought to what accommodation she might receive from Ezekiel Lee if she got him off alone, but Mary interrupted the thought.

"She nearly drowned him, Annie? Are you sure?"

Yes, Anne was sure. Or she had been sure. But now, her sister staring at her so, it *did* seem mad. But neither did it matter anymore. "I can't," she pleaded. "Dear God, Mary, you know how it was before. I can't give him up again."

Mary took up Anne's hands and half held them, half shook them, as if in a mix of sympathy and exasperation. But in the end she said, "I do know how it was. I do. Let me speak with my husband. Surely we might give you this single night alone with your boy. But what then?"

"What's best for William," Anne said, which proved to be sufficient answer, never mind that it meant one thing to the nodding Mary and another to her.

THERE WAS THE EXPECTED trouble getting William to settle into the bed beside his cousin, but once he did, he chose that time to tell his cousin about his papa the printer and his mama who worked in the print shop and *Poor Dick,* and how his papa was teaching him to swim. The four-year-old cousin wouldn't put the name of Benjamin

Franklin to any of that, but the adult he might speak to next certainly would; Anne must get the boy out of Philadelphia now. But how to do it, without plunging William into a state of alarm? Anne sat by the boy, her fingers gripped tight in his hand, until his rambles changed course and grew disjointed as he mumbled drowsily to his cousin about the ships he planned to visit with his father when he got home.

The ships. Anne almost swept the boy up and kissed him wide awake, but she held herself still, tight with impatience, until the exertions of the day caught William between words, he eased his grip on her fingers, and drifted away.

Anne returned below stairs. She could hear the soft rise and fall of the husband and wife talking to each other in oddly formal cadence behind the parlor door, but she had no intention of joining them yet; her interest sat there on the hall table, where the *Gazette* lay. She flipped past the editor's increasingly anti-Quaker call for arms and the mundane advertisements until she arrived at the shipping notices.

Allgood's ship, the *Nautilus,* was in dock, which meant, in the old days, his boy would be arriving in the shop with his message soon. Anne found her thoughts straying to Allgood's wife, and wondered if she were glad or not of her husband's return, thought of what the wife might think of her husband's doings up above Grissom's shop, thought of Grissom. Why on earth Grissom? Because, Anne realized, she'd just recognized a third voice rising and falling behind that parlor door.

Anne pushed open the door. Grissom rose from his chair; for a man so tight with his words he was oddly at ease with his limbs. He said, "Good evening, Anne."

"I'm surprised to see you here, sir."

"Are you? Indeed, I suppose you would be. Mr. Franklin paid me a call, thinking you might have returned to your old room with your charge; I assured him you wouldn't be likely to do so."

"No."

"And then Mr. Grissom came here!" Lee cut in. "Imagine that! Figuring to come to your sister's house! Clever man!"

Anne turned to her brother-in-law. "As you well know, while I worked at Mr. Grissom's shop, I often visited my sister. I haven't been able to get away for a visit since I began working at Mr. Franklin's. Mr. Grissom knows where my sister lives, while Mr. Franklin does not. Or rather, he did not till now."

Grissom turned to the Lees. "I must ask you to indulge a great rudeness and allow me to speak with Anne alone."

The Lees stood in tandem. As soon as they vanished, Anne said, "I suppose Mr. Franklin's sent you out to scour the town for me."

"Anne. Think. You cannot take such a man's child from him and walk away undiscovered. Nor could you possibly keep the boy better than he's kept now."

"He was near drowned by his so-called mother. And burned. And cut. What kind of keep is that? Or did Mr. Franklin neglect to report those particular bits of news? The wife has lost her wits. You of all people know this. You *told* me this."

"And I've regretted having done so every day since. Think, Anne. *Think.* Franklin would take no undue risk with his only son. He has the situation in hand. He assured me of this. I came here only to assure you of it too, to reason with you. I can take the boy back if you like, and keep you out of any danger of punishment or retribution; I believe he'll come with me happily enough—we were friends for a time."

Friends? Grissom and William? And then Anne remembered. "You played handkerchief with him."

Grissom's jaw loosened, revealing how tight it had been. "I played handkerchief with him."

"And then you stopped visiting."

"For reasons that must surely be clear to you. That isn't to say the visits couldn't be resumed."

So that was the scheme. Grissom would return the boy, and in exchange he'd get Anne back in his bed, and in exchange for *that* he'd resume his visits and his reports on William for Anne to turn over again and again until the next week's visit came around.

"You're a great friend to Mr. Franklin," Anne said. "You always were. I've long wondered what the favor must have been that requires you to repay it over so many times. First you do his nasty errands for him, next you take me into your shop—keep me in your shop when you had good reason not to—and now you come on this mission for him. Perhaps you have your own secret. Your own bastard hidden in the country. What is it, Mr. Grissom, that makes you always do his bidding? Why *did* you take me in, an unknown girl of questionable repute—just to ease his conscience for him? Why do you come here for him now?"

Grissom blinked. "Franklin knows nothing of my coming here tonight. I did so only in hope of preventing a further tragedy. I know you to be sensible over most things, but I also know that this wouldn't be the first time your feelings for this child have driven you to do insensible things. I could see you embarking on this thoughtless flight and then later, when it was too late, realizing just how thoughtless a thing it had been. I repeat, I am willing to return the boy for you, before charges are brought against you and your life ruined any more than it already has been."

Anne flushed. Her life *ruined*? This man could use those words to her, this man who had groaned out his joy to her night after night without end? Anne pulled her money pouch out of her pocket and lifted it in the air for Grissom to gauge its heft. "Do you call this ruin?"

Grissom only looked at her with those unreadable eyes. Oh, no doubt he took great pride in thinking he kept himself to himself so well, but Anne could have told him how she'd read those eyes well enough as he held her breasts in his hands. *Glorious,* Franklin had called her breasts. And the shipwright! The shipwright had said he'd give his firstborn child if he could but hang such a pair off his wife's chest . . . But Anne had no time for thinking of shipwrights—she must think of ship*masters*. She must think of William. What was best to do for William. And what was best for William required that she play another kind of part now.

Anne reached for the arm of the near chair and allowed herself to sag into it, every bit of the long day helping to bear her down. She drew a breath. She exhaled and closed her eyes and left them closed a good while; she heard Grissom shift his feet, clear his throat. When she opened her eyes, she allowed every minute of uncertainty and fear she'd ever known to show.

"You're right of course, Mr. Grissom," she said. "But the boy's had a long and tiring day; he sleeps now. I shouldn't like to send him home worn down and out of sorts. Allow him his rest and come back on the morrow."

"I dislike leaving Franklin in such a state."

"'Tis only a few hours more. Surely I'm entitled to a scant few hours in my son's company before sending him away from me forever."

Grissom watched her. Anne watched him. What *was* he thinking? She couldn't guess. He leaned forward and opened his mouth as if to say one thing, but then said another. "I'll be back in the morn."

26

ANNE ENTERED HER SISTER'S kitchen and found Mary there alone, sipping a cup of tea. She rose to fetch another cup, but Anne waved it away. "I've an errand," she said. "William's as tired as I've seen him and won't wake; on the slim chance he should, please tell him I went for a walk and will come to him as soon as I return."

Mary reached out, gripping Anne's wrist, her fingers like an eagle's claws. "Annie. You must take him back. You know this, I know you do. Only think—"

Think! Was that all Mary and Grissom could offer her? Was thinking not all Anne had done for what seemed days and weeks? Years? What could Mary know of the things Anne must think of, serene and happy in her little home with all her children about her?

"I have thought. And now I must do."

"But do *what?*"

"What I must. I've done it before, and you've gained by it; I'd think this was little enough to ask in return—that you mind my son an hour, no more."

Mary's hand dropped from Anne's wrist as if Anne had just bitten her, which she supposed she had. She didn't care. "Well?"

Mary nodded. Anne flew.

SHE CROSSED THE DAMP fields, hugging into her thin shawl, summer gone now. She knew Allgood's house and had even walked past it once with William, pointing it out to him—*a shipmaster lives there*—but the dark and her new direction confused her; by the time the pastures had disappeared and small houses had turned to larger, she began to falter. Grissom's voice, Mary's voice, Ezekiel Lee's voice hammered after her, slowing her further, but she could think and think all they liked and it would make no difference; she could not—she *would* not—give up William again. She pushed on, holding the golden image of her son in front of her like a lantern, until she recognized the impressive brick facade of Allgood's home; she allowed herself no pause but continued up the walk and raised the heavy brass knocker on the door.

As Anne had anticipated, a servant answered, her surprise at seeing a strange woman alone at that hour plain. "Please," Anne said. "Your master, at once. 'Tis an emergency; I come from his friend Robert." Robert, who'd come to see her with Allgood a dozen times or more; if Robert happened to be sitting in the shipmaster's parlor on a visit of his own, Anne's scheme was shredded, but she doubted Robert was a parlor kind of friend.

Indeed, it took Allgood under half a minute to appear at the door. As had Franklin, he stepped through it and drew it closed, but he possessed none of Franklin's charm under duress.

"You! What the devil do you think, coming here? What of Robert?"

"Nothing of Robert, sir. 'Tis I who need your help. I didn't like to say so at the door. I must leave Philadelphia. Now."

"And what in bloody hell do you expect me to do about it?"

"I thought, as you and Robert are such good friends to me, sir, you'd do what you could to assist me, and quickly, before your wife is disturbed. I took a chance on finding you home, but as you *are* home, this means your ship is still here; when does it sail next and where?"

"It goes nowhere for a fortnight. I can be of no help to you. Now get on."

"But have you no friends amongst the other captains? You must know of someone sailing to New York or Boston soon. Or shall I call again another time? Then, of course, I should run the risk of missing you and finding only your wife at home."

Allgood opened his mouth, but his brain must have caught up to it there. He closed it. "Wait in the stable." He stepped back and closed the door.

Anne headed in the direction Allgood had pointed, toward a low building pale against the thickening dark at the end of a fine sweep of lawn. She stopped outside the heavy double doors and listened, but heard no sound; she lifted the bolt and slipped into the steamy smell of wealth: horse upon horse neatly stalled on fresh hay, leather newly oiled, bins full of grain. The horses smelled Anne in their turn and began to stir, first one and then the next all down the long row. To keep from thinking, Anne tried counting them in the dark, but hadn't gotten beyond six when she heard Allgood working the door.

He stepped up to Anne and slapped a letter into her hand. "The *Falmouth*. 'Tis tied up at the Market Wharf. Give that letter to Captain Simms and he'll take you to Boston. Be gone."

Allgood left. Anne stood. There was little reason for it, this sense of a fresh-cut wound, for the whole transaction had gone exactly to plan, but in all her dealings with men Anne had seldom left a disgruntled one behind, never one anxious for his acquaintance with her to end. She was quite sure she could fly after Allgood, offering him a last three-shilling ride wherever they happened to fall on his fine lawn, even put on his breeches if it were required, but it wasn't her risk to take alone. She now had William to consider, perhaps awake and crying for her in the strange house. She now had her son.

ANNE COULD HEAR WILLIAM from outside the door. She thrust it open and ran up the stairs. Mary sat on the boys' bed, the candle on the floor casting wild, flailing shadows across the slanted ceiling: Mary's hands reaching for William, William batting them aside. "Mama!" he cried.

Anne hurried up to him and cupped his hot, damp face in her hands. "Hush, now. Here I am."

William looked up at her, pulled free, loosed a fresh gush of tears. "I want *Mama*!"

Oh, how Anne's womb twisted at that cry! But, "Very well," she said. "We were to go aboard a ship first, but if you'd rather go home now—"

"A ship!"

"Come, William. Get into your clothes as fast as you can or it will be gone."

What would Anne have done if William had refused? She would never know. The lure of a ship was enough for even this not-bold child.

BELOW STAIRS MARY STOOD between them and the door, candle in hand. "Anne."

"Don't."

"I will. Do you not see? Where can you possibly—"

Anne held up the letter. "We've a ship waiting on us. We must go." She put the same confidence into her voice that she summoned whenever she faced a new man, but it didn't have the same effect on

Mary. She took the letter from Anne's hand and broke the seal. Anne
snatched it back and read the few lines, with Mary leaning over her:

> *Honored Sir,*
> *The bearer of this note is a woman of such character as you might*
> *imagine; she has made certain threats you might also imagine, but*
> *it will serve us both to have her gone. I ask as the greatest favor that*
> *you deliver her to Boston, and if you keep her aboard till you do I*
> *shall repay you twofold on your return.*
>
> *Your obedient servant,*
> *J. Allgood*

"Anne," Mary said again.

Anne refolded the letter, carefully lining up the two halves of the
broken seal. She took the candle from Mary and touched it to the
wax, melting away its imprint but resealing the letter; perhaps Simms
wouldn't notice, or perhaps he would, but it mattered little. Either he
trusted Allgood to pay him or he didn't. Either Anne trusted to this
chance or she didn't. She had a ship to Boston and she had fifty pounds
and she could make more the minute she landed; it was as good a plan
as she could make with so little time. Anne repeated the words to
herself: *It was as good a plan,* but in truth the letter she held felt newly
flimsy in her hand.

THEY WALKED, AND THEN Anne walked and carried William, and
then William walked again, silent now, gripping ferociously to Anne's
hand. She took care to keep off the main ways, coming at the Market
Wharf along the riverbank, and managed to discover the *Falmouth*
without being discovered herself, or perhaps the truth of it was that
any who saw the muddy clothes and disheveled, whimpering child at

her side would think her just another of the city's whores and pay her no mind. The sight of the ship brought William out of his sulks at last, and he was so fast over the gangplank that Anne feared losing him amongst the crates and barrels that loomed like dark ghosts across the crowded deck. Anne approached two men hunched around a lantern reading a log.

"I'm after Captain Simms."

The nearest of the two men, short, solid, and square, as if designed for keeping upright on a slanting deck, lifted eyes so deep socketed Anne couldn't in fact say she saw them. "You have him."

Anne handed him Allgood's letter. He read it, looked again at Anne. "It says naught about a boy."

Anne made a quick assessment of Simms and decided there was little hope of winning an argument over the fare, but she also decided he was no different from any other man. She said, "I'll pay for the boy. However you like it."

Simms's head lifted; he turned to his companion. "Bleeker, give this lad a turn at the helm."

Bleeker picked up the lantern and led William ten feet aft to the great wheel. William looked back at Anne, but only once, his eye drawn compulsively to the huge wheel. It will be all right, Anne thought. It will be all right after all. She continued to say it as Simms stepped away to speak to his mate, as she was led below to a compartment fitted out with a good-size berth, mahogany cabinets, a desk, and two lamps, all bolted to the walls. The rigidity of the furnishings troubled her—nothing could move—or leave—but she stepped into the cabin, turning to speak her opening lines, and found herself in air, half carried, half shoved onto the berth, the captain's weight bearing her down.

"Hold!" Anne attempted to wriggle free of him, affecting her most confident laugh. "You must let me show you—" But Simms didn't pause. He yanked away what clothes he needed to yank away and slammed into her with a ready violence that even after all these years of teasing men into impatience came as a surprise. Very well, she thought. Very well. Let him get his job done and move on so she could see to William. It took him even less time than the shipwright, but when Anne again attempted to wriggle free he pinned her again. Began again. When he finished he got up and went out without a word; Anne barely had time to pull her skirt into place when the door opened and the mate stepped in, already working his buttons.

Anne sat up. This man could not hold the power of the captain over her, this one she could manage as she'd managed two dozen others like him. "'Tis not free," she said. "I've already paid the captain for our passage. 'Tis three shillings to you, sir."

The mate didn't slow. Indeed, he was already at the bed, his breeches riding down over his buttocks, ready as any man Anne had ever seen. He was big where the captain was small, amiable where the captain was fierce. He returned Anne's smile. "And I've already paid the captain for *you*."

Anne took in the mate's clear, hard eye above the false smile and saw the life she'd so carefully constructed begin to fade like a candle flame at sunrise, the world roll over, leaving her at the bottom instead of the top, the person begging instead of being begged. The rest blurred, swam, flickered. He went at her forever, turning her from raw to numb, and then there was the captain again. Anne's limbs began to tremble; she would admit it: She was helpless against these men. She braced herself for another assault, but the captain said only, "Fix yourself."

Anne didn't move, her limbs weren't ready; she refused to let the captain see her shaking.

"Fix yourself!"

Anne sat up. She lifted her fingers, and although they felt as if they quivered like cats' tails, she saw they were steady enough. She pulled her clothes into place. She smoothed and reknotted her hair. She slid her legs to the floor and stood; her legs were steady too, and so were her eyes as she stared back at the captain; her long practice at acting hadn't been for nothing after all.

The captain left. The new man came through the door so hard after him that Anne blinked to make sure she wasn't making up the switch in her mind. No. He stood even taller and broader inside the confines of the cabin, the boy even smaller, clinging to his father's jacket like a kitten.

"Well, my dear," Franklin said. "Here we are again." He looked around the room, selected the captain's best chair, and sat down. He kept William on his lap, the boy shrinking against his father's waist-coat as if knowing himself too big to be sitting there, as if afraid that were he noticed he'd be pushed away and ignored. All this Anne could see in him because she'd seen it before, and it pinched her heart every time. Franklin reached into his pocket and withdrew a small, intricately carved wooden horse, which he handed to William; the new toy diverted the boy's attention from his father at last.

Anne said, "Who told you where I was? Allgood?"

"Allgood!"

"Grissom, then."

Franklin's brow knitted. "Your sister Mary told me where you were. But only for a price. Like you, isn't she?"

Mary was nothing like Anne, but only because she didn't need to be. "What price?" Anne asked.

"That you wouldn't be arrested and sent to prison. That I find you new work."

"I'm able to make my way."

"Yes, you are." Franklin looked her over with closer attention. "But do forgive me if I observe that you're beginning to look somewhat the worse for it, my dear. You can't enchant us all forever, you know."

He shifted William, reached into his pocket, and drew out a paper, folded and sealed. He held it out to Anne. "You wish to go away; I shall be overjoyed to help you in that endeavor. I have a friend at Boston, a mantua maker; carry this letter and she'll find a place for you in her shop."

Anne looked at the paper. She looked at William, twirling his new toy about in his fingers, his head nestled against his father, as oblivious to Anne as he appeared to be to the conversation. She'd cost herself this boy, but she wouldn't leave him again without at least attempting to improve his condition over what it had been. "What assurance can you give me of the safety of someone who is of great concern to me? What steps will be taken regarding that person's care?"

Franklin lowered his voice, and it changed to a thing Anne had never before heard—something dark, cold, viperish. It even brought William's head out of its nest to look at his father with large eyes. "The only danger that has come to someone who is of great concern to *me* came this night, when I discovered him climbing up onto a gunwale unattended. Now you may take this letter or not, but you'll take your passage aboard this ship; if you attempt to leave it before it sails, the captain has been instructed to call the sheriff. Is that clear, or are you a greater fool than I imagined?"

Fool. Oh, how that word stung! She looked again at the paper in Franklin's hand, thicker than a mere letter should be, perhaps with a supply of paper money enclosed. She would have liked to say she didn't need it—that she didn't need Franklin's money and connections and she didn't need Mary's meddling—Mary, who'd had a dress to wear and soup to eat only because of Anne's willingness to take what came her way and make something of it. Anne had managed to keep her pride while she did it too, but only because most every man she'd ever met had been a fool.

Anne took the paper. She reached out one last time and stroked William's fine, fair hair, but he didn't even lift his face from his father's waistcoat.

27

ANNE SAT IN THE captain's cabin and made a fierce effort to collect herself. She knew she had little time; she was surprised the captain hadn't already burst through the door, claiming his next charge against her fare. She attempted to erase the image of William's face turning away from her and struggled to call up Franklin's words; she needed to concentrate on a certain few of them, like *mantua maker* and *Boston* but she heard instead *gunwale*. Was Ezekiel Lee right? Was she the mad one? Was Franklin right, that the only true danger had come to William when Anne had brought him aboard this ship? Certainly Deborah's great lapse at the wharf could be called nothing worse than what Anne had allowed this night. Perhaps Franklin was right that Deborah would never purposely hurt the boy. Anne would need to believe this if she were to depart with any peace of mind for Boston.

Boston. Anne ripped open the seal on the paper Franklin had given her and discovered folded inside it two pound notes. The letter was headed, *To Mrs. Jane Bellamy, at Frog Lane, Boston,* and began *Honored*

Madam. It went on to plead with this Mrs. Bellamy to find the bearer a situation in her shop. Unlike Allgood's letter, it said nothing of Anne's character one way or the other. It was signed, *Ever your Friend and Servant, B. Franklin.* Anne looked again at the words in the heading—Frog Lane, Boston—and discovered she misliked them. She found frogs repulsive; she didn't know this Boston, or anything of mantua making; come to that, she didn't know anything of Franklin's good faith. Philadelphia was where her family lived. Philadelphia was where the shipwright and others like him lived, people she could rely on for subsistence, by one or another means. On the other side of it, Franklin had spoken at least one true thing: She couldn't enchant them all forever. There was blackmail such as she'd used on Allgood, of course, but thus far it had not proved successful. The additional Boston advantage was that Anne was not known and could, indeed, make a new name for herself if she desired. Anne pondered the thing back and forth for a time, but soon enough realized all such musing counted for little.

William was in Philadelphia. So Anne must be.

Anne put the pound notes into her pocket; she gripped Franklin's letter between thumbs and fingers, about to rip it up and discard it in the river, but then reconsidered; for once, Franklin had affixed his name to a document, and it might yet prove useful to her.

Anne's next difficulty was going to be extricating herself from the ship unnoticed. She sat still and listened; she heard more than one tread on the deck above her, and even one would likely be enough to stop her unless she could think of something cleverer than she'd managed thus far. She tried the captain's door and it did indeed crack open, but only to expose her guard, a sailor too young to be whiskered but already thick muscled, leaning against the wall just outside the companionway. He leaped upright. "Get back in there, you cow!"

Anne cast deep into the well of her evaporating reserve and managed to draw up what she could only hope was at least a shadow of her old smile. "Come with me, sir?"

"Get inside or I'll put you inside in pieces!"

The argument was a strong one. Anne retreated, closed the door, latched it from within. She examined the cabin again. The hatch above would no doubt bring her out onto the deck and right into the middle of those treading feet; the hatch could be of no use to her. The cabin also contained a small-paned window, but on the water side, away from the dock, with nothing below it but deep, cold water. The window was no use to her. Anne turned and turned about, a new kind of panic growing in her, a new kind of helplessness that had for a long time been entirely foreign to her. She couldn't pick and choose her own space, she couldn't pick and choose what man to use or how to use him or even to come or to go; she was trapped, waiting for whichever man came next through that door. Anne's skin grew damp, her hands trembled; she turned and turned around the captain's cabin, looking for any opening, any tool to fight her way free; she spied the window again, and thought, again; it was the only chance for her.

Anne pulled a locker below the window and climbed up on it. She pushed out the glass and looked down at the water. *You see what the water is? It doesn't sink you, it carries you!* But carry her where? Anne looked to the far shore and could just make out the dark line that was New Jersey. *In the middle the river rages too strong for any man . . .* Not New Jersey, then. Anne wiggled her shoulders through the window and looked left and right; the ship was tied to the dock, but the dock didn't help her—it stretched deep out into the river and rose too high for her to reach it from the water. It must be the Philadelphia shore, then, not a dark line, but a row of dark squares—warehouses, shops. It looked a great distance away, but the waves were gentle and appeared to roll, if not directly to shore, then not away from it either. *Always best to cut across the tide, not against it . . .* But could she swim such a distance? It was one thing to do so with Franklin's strong hands hovering near; if she grew fatigued before she reached the shore, she might float all she liked but she'd only float . . . where? To some piece of shore farther along. She might be lost but at least she'd be off the ship, away from the captain.

Anne lowered herself down until she was seated on the locker. She removed her shoes, but not her stockings; she removed the money pouch from her pocket and tied it around her neck. She removed her heavy skirt and bodice but kept on her shift; she climbed up on the locker, wormed her way into the window till her weight was balanced half on each side of the sill and hovered, listening for a noisy moment. When an argument erupted on deck, she kicked with her legs and flew through the air, downward till she hit water. The cold shocked the breath out of her, but so did the fact that she continued to plunge downward. The water *didn't* carry her.

Paddle your hands! Kick your feet! Anne paddled. Kicked. She began to rise, and just as she decided she wouldn't ever be allowed another breath in this life, she broke the surface. She gulped air and water together, coughed and kicked harder, till her mouth rose higher above the water. She rolled over and floated, as Franklin had taught her, till she'd stabilized her breathing, then rolled again and struck for shore. *Paddle your hands! Kick your feet!* Anne worked her limbs as hard as she'd ever worked them, but the shore grew no closer; she felt herself sinking beneath the surface. She rolled and floated again, swallowing more water, but it gave her another few inches of air in her lungs; she flipped over and thrashed toward shore again.

Over. Breathe. Over. Kick and paddle. Her knee struck bottom first, but her feet wouldn't keep under her. She crawled onto the sand and lay on her back, panting like an overheated dog, until she found strength enough to open her eyes and look around her. She'd come up under the wharf, which would have been fine with Anne if it weren't for the company. Rats. Refuse. How hard she'd worked, only to end again where she'd begun, amongst the same dregs she'd kicked through every day of her life at Eades Alley! But Anne had gotten herself out of Eades Alley and she could get herself out of here. She looked about and the first thing she saw was the dark square of the sign in front of Grissom's upholstery shop.

Franklin knows nothing of my coming here tonight. I did so only in hope of preventing a further tragedy . . . What had it all meant? Anne had barely heard it when Grissom said it, and she could barely think it through now, but as she thought over the whole of Philadelphia she could think of no other door she could knock on half clothed and sopping wet, at an hour still considerably shy of dawn. Perhaps she hadn't made a friend of Peter for nothing—Peter, who slept on the shop floor.

BY THE TIME ANNE reached the shop she was shaking so hard that only a touch of her knuckles on the glass rattled the pane. She tried to see into the dark and seek out Peter's form, but she could make out nothing of the floor at all. She clenched her fist and rapped harder on the glass—once, twice, a third time—but the light that finally came at her came from the stairs that led to Grissom's rooms and not from the shop at all.

Grissom loomed behind the lantern, hair flying loose, shirttail dripping out of his breeches, legs bare; he peered out, fumbled the latch, threw open the door. "God in heaven! What have they done to you? Get in, will you, before the whole street wakes."

Anne didn't—couldn't—move.

Grissom reached out and caught her by both arms, half lifting her into the shop and ahead of him up the stairs. In his kitchen he pointed her to the chair near the banked fire and gave it a stir with the poker; he climbed the stairs to his chamber and returned with a blanket and, remarkably, a woman's flannel gown and shawl. He left the room and Anne changed into the dry clothes, transferring her money pouch from neck to pocket. When Grissom returned he'd done something better with his own attire, but his hair still flowed loose, glinting like escaped flame in the light of the fire. He sat across from her and studied her in silence for a time.

"How is it you come here in this state?" he said at last. "Must I assume things did not end well?"

"They did not."

"The boy?"

"His father caught up with us at the ship and took him home."

"The ship!"

Anne said nothing, but Grissom went there on his own. "A ship. Yes, that would have been your only course. And then?"

"I was bid to go on to Boston and become a mantua maker."

"But you didn't care to."

"I didn't."

Grissom pondered her some more. "You're wet."

"I was forced to swim ashore."

"Swim ashore!"

"I'd been taught."

"I see."

For reasons Anne couldn't entirely unravel she found herself unable, for the first time in a very long time, to meet a man's eye. She tipped her head forward and allowed her hair to cascade in front of her face, nearer to the fire, as if shaking it out to dry. Grissom allowed her a reasonable space of time, but when he might have expected her to straighten up and she didn't, he reached out and swung the curtain of hair aside, drawing her face up.

"What else? What else happened? Something's changed you since yesterday. Something that's driven you here. Why *did* you come here? 'Tis nine months you've been gone. If you came after your old place—"

Anne jerked her face away. "I did *not* come after my old place. I came here to discover why you sent Franklin after me at my sister's. I know why my sister sent him after me at the ship, but not why you—"

"I didn't send Franklin to your sister's."

"Didn't you! How did he find me, then?"

Grissom laughed. "Come, you're not so foolish as to think you could have hidden that child anywhere in this town and remain undiscovered by him. But of course you're not so foolish. Hence the ship." Something changed in Grissom's face. "And something happened on that ship. You're afraid, and you've never been afraid. Was it Franklin?"

Anne gripped the chair and stood, half surprised that her legs held. "If you would consider making me a loan of these clothes—"

"And just what do you think to do now?"

"I'll get by."

"Yes, I imagine you will. But as I was about to say before, if you came here looking for your old place, you may have it under certain conditions only. I've lost Maria; you were good at your work—"

Now it was Grissom who looked away, as well he might. Anne *was* good at her work. Both kinds. And she knew full well what Grissom's certain conditions might be. "If you think to have me back in your bed as before—"

Grissom barked out another laugh. "I do not. And neither does my wife, I'm sure."

The surprise of it carried Anne backward a small step; her weakened legs came up against the seat of her chair and she dropped into it, attempting a last-minute effort to look as if she meant to.

Grissom pointed at the gown she now wore. "Did you think I'd taken to wearing women's clothes?"

She hadn't thought. She couldn't think now. Grissom with a wife! But then again, Franklin had had a wife, and Allgood, and Wilkes, and how many more?

"You mentioned *conditions*," Anne said.

"Yes, conditions. Here they are. You may take up your old room but only if you occupy it alone. At all times. Do you understand?"

Anne understood. What Grissom could not understand was that whatever fear he'd imagined in her grew tenfold as he spoke those words. If Anne could take no men to her room, it removed any hope of independent means. If no independent means, then she must depend on a single man—this man—to pay her a wage and keep her fed and sheltered. A man with a wife. A man whose wife might catch them out at any time—for Grissom to keep himself away from her altogether was not amongst the possibilities Anne considered—and if the wife caught them out Anne might be sent off again to land just where she'd landed now.

That was Anne's first feeling—that fear. Her second was so overwhelming that Anne couldn't at first recognize its nature, couldn't at first see it for the thing it was: relief. She could be done with it now. No more show; no more heavy, sweaty men to be maneuvered here and there; no more cutting herself into two parts—the one to hide and the other to sell. She could go on as Mary had gone on before she'd met Ezekiel Lee, as Anne might have gone on if she hadn't met Franklin and his half crown. Franklin would not like to learn that Anne had remained in town, but what could he do about Grissom's personal choice of hire? Another question must grow out of that one though—what might Franklin try? It would surely be something. And there yet another question grew.

"Why?" she asked Grissom. "Why take me back and cross your friend?"

Grissom's mouth twitched in either a smile or a grimace or both—Anne couldn't tell. "I suppose I admire your courage."

Courage! That Grissom could speak of such a thing just at the moment when Anne felt the greatest lack of it was one knot too many, one that Anne couldn't begin to untie. She rose. "I accept your conditions. You'll thank your wife, please, for the use of her gown. I'll launder and return it as soon as I purchase another of my own. Shall I begin in the shop this morn?"

Grissom stared at her. "Courage, did I say? Perhaps I should have said doggedness." He disappeared and returned with sheets, a blanket, and a bolster, a wedge of cheese and half a loaf balanced on top. "Eat. Sleep. Get yourself some clothes. I'll see you in the shop on the morrow."

28

WILLIAM HAD NEVER LIKED sleep. Sleep was a risky thing. What if his father came home with a new treat while he slept and decided to give it to the apprentice James instead? What if something awful happened to his mother or father while William wasn't there to watch and call out for them to beware? When his mother used to put him to bed, he would hold on to her knee in hope of keeping her beside him till he fell asleep; sometimes she stayed, sometimes she didn't. Anne always stayed.

But here was the other thing William never liked: things that changed, things that didn't go according to plan. Anne, for example, waking him in the dead of night, or so it had seemed until he noticed it was really half-dark-half-light, but waking him nonetheless with all this talk of a surprise, which for William was in itself a kind of half-dark-half-light prospect. And that particular surprise had begun as dark as surprises come—a strange house with strange people in it, and children far more rambunctious than Franky had ever been.

But then there was the ship. William hadn't liked the long, dark walk to the water, or even, at first sight, the long, dark ship, so different at night from the sparkle and shine of daylight; he hadn't liked that Anne disappeared. But then the wonder of it—steering the ship! Talking to a real sailor! It was true the sailor didn't talk to him long—in fact, he didn't even stay with William long, allowing him to roam as he liked over the deck in a way that even William's mother would never have allowed, and it was that thought of his mother that turned William against even the ship. Where was his mother? Where was his father? And then, just as he was about to give in to a most mortifying blast of unsailorlike trembling and tears, his father was there.

His father, clearly unhappy with the sailor, with the captain, and even with Anne, but all that only made his extreme happiness at seeing William shine brighter. They rode home in his father's carriage, William curled in his father's lap the entire ride, petted and kissed and squeezed and told stories and promised another wonderful surprise. But William, wiser by then, said, "I don't like surprises."

"You'll this one," his father said.

And he did.

Pirate—a horse of his own—a thing none of the other boys he knew had yet achieved. Pirate didn't come till later the next day, but that was all right, because that night and the next morning William's father *and* his mother spoiled him in the most satisfactory way, and later he was taken to the stable to meet Pirate, and then the very best times of William's life began.

Each morning before he went to his tutor, William went down to the barn and visited with Pirate; when he came home from the tutor he visited again. He made a lot of new friends by trading rides, but he always sent the other boys away when his father came to take him riding, which his father did a lot at first but then not so often and then almost not at all. All of the extra fussing over William began to fall away too, and after a time the old witch Min took him up to bed most nights before his father had even come home. At breakfast his father would say, "How's that old Pirate?" and William would struggle to think up some Pirate news that might interest his father: he ate William's hat, he stepped in a hole in the street and almost threw John Pettigrew, he'd learned to yawn.

William's father would laugh, or say, "Indeed!" or "Silly old Pirate!" or "Clever old Pirate!" and then leave for his shop and not come home the whole day or night long, or if he did come home he had other men with him, who took William's father away behind a closed study door.

William loved Pirate, but he loved his father more. One morning he got up early, sneaked away to the stable, opened the door to Pirate's stall, and shooed him through. He went home, raced up the stairs and into the kitchen where his father sat eating his breakfast, and shouted, "Pirate's gone!"

That was a wonderful time too. Each morning William's father took him up behind his saddle and they combed the streets, but Pirate was not to be found. At the end of the week William's father took him to the print shop, and William was allowed to watch as his father set the types for the advertisement: "Strayed from the Northern Liberties of this city, a small bay mare . . . She, being but little and barefooted, cannot be supposed to have gone far; therefore if any of the town boys find her and bring her to subscriber, they shall, for their trouble, have the liberty to ride."

In due time Pirate was returned, but William's father no longer took William to ride; instead he was taken to the print shop to do some job of work that was either hot or smelly or dirty, and in time William balked.

"I don't *like* working in the print shop," he said.

"Well, my boy," his father answered, "it appears you're not my son after all."

William didn't like the words. He didn't like them at all. He cast a worried look at his father, but the matter was only made worse by the shocked look on his *father's* face, as if he'd just gotten his hand caught in the printing press. William's eyes began to fill. He picked up the inking tool. "I shall like the print shop, Papa," he said.

To William's horror, his *father's* eyes filled with tears. "Oh, my Billy," he said, roughing up his hair. "Remember always, no matter where or who you are, I'm your father and I love you."

William heard and believed—he did—but he'd also heard and learned; it was not a good thing to disappoint his father.

29

WHEN DEBORAH HAD GAZED on her rutting husband, her rage had indeed been great—at a husband who was not a husband; at the friend who was not a friend; at the rutting itself, since in it she saw the kind of vigor that had been lacking the last time she and Benjamin had attempted it. If William hadn't been stolen, Deborah's rage might have lived a longer, more violent life, but with William gone she'd been so terror struck—for the boy, for Benjamin, for herself—that another, separate, violent emotion consumed her. She'd not loved the boy as she should; God saw, God punished; it was Deborah's fault that the boy was gone, and at that particular moment, two-pronged blame was too unwieldy a thing for Deborah to manage.

William came back from his ordeal tired, pale, nervous, and full of himself all at the same time; he talked of a house he didn't like and a ship he did, but he could remember no one's name except for the vile Anne. Benjamin took care not to vilify Anne, a consideration Deborah appreciated only while she kept her thoughts on the boy and what he'd been through. Later, Benjamin surprised William with his own horse—an uncommon thing in their tradesmen's circle—but Deborah said no word against it and made much of the boy in her own way, serving up his favorite foods, petting him, taking him up to bed at night instead of leaving it to Min, as before she'd left it to the vile Anne.

As a matter of course, however, after William's safe return and the resettling of the household, Deborah found herself less able to keep her thoughts fixed on the boy's ordeal and let them drift to the larger villainy, as she saw it. The questions bubbled forth.

"How long?" she asked one morning at breakfast after William had gone off to his tutor and Min had left them to their silence. "How long were you at that girl? Since the day she first came?"

"My dear," Benjamin started, "I see no purpose to—" But looking closer at Deborah, he went on. "Only of late. I might add, as well, only after many nights of finding my own bed full."

"Full of the keeper you set on me."

"Out of concern for you."

"Bah!"

Silence, except for the scrape of Benjamin's silver spoon against the china porringer Deborah, as a token of her husband's due, had purchased for him. The sound of that costly spoon against the elegant china began to go through her head like the pain she'd once experienced with an abscessed tooth; she reached across the table and swept the porringer to the floor. The china cracked in three pieces; the thick gruel spattered on the floor, the walls, the chairs, and Deborah's skirt, but none of it touched her husband.

Benjamin stooped to pick up the pieces of the bowl and began to fit them together. "I shall mend it," he said. "I'm most fond of this bowl. And the woman who gave it to me." He looked at her. "I know better than to inquire after your affections just now. 'Tis only necessary that you know I've held fast to mine."

"Oh, I know well enough what you've held fast to!"

"A drowning man will hold fast to whatever's near at hand that will keep him afloat, Debby."

As was the way of it with so many of their arguments, Deborah could call up no matching answer to Benjamin's poetic rebuff. She left the room.

THEY FIXED ON WILLIAM during those long days, keeping him between them as if he were a stiff bolster. Benjamin accompanied the boy to the stable at any hour of the day, to ride or to visit his horse; Deborah made sure William stayed with them at the table till the last plate was cleared and sat with him even after he slept, attempting to form up her questions for the next day's answers.

"What's become of that creature?" she asked Benjamin one morning.

"She's gone from Philadelphia. I've seen to it."

"Gone where?"

"Boston."

Another day—week—fortnight—another question. "What others besides her have you been at?"

Benjamin's eyes widened in convincing surprise. "Good God, woman, what kind of hound do you think I am?"

Deborah should have found this at least partially comforting, but somehow she did not; it only made this Anne more special, more chosen. And there Deborah's thoughts turned to the vile Anne— just how vile a creature was she? Had her supposed friendship with Deborah been all sham? But for that question there was no one she could ask.

In time Deborah's questions ran down, but her rage did not. Another fortnight or two or four, however, and Benjamin seemed to have run his own calculation that told him his penance had now been paid. He'd left her alone behind her closed door every night since the discovery, but one evening he caught her hand as she walked past on her way to their room. There wasn't a stern line anywhere in his features and yet his voice bore a note that was new, that drew from Deborah a greater attention.

He said, "I've not done right by you, Debby."

"No."

"I begin the count at London."

Deborah considered. "Yes."

"I continue on to William. I should have better appreciated what I asked of you there. And I end . . . Well, we know where I end. But I wonder. Do you think you've done right by me? I speak of the time since Franky's death. I speak as a man with the usual number of basic flaws and needs. To be denied the chance to give and take any kind of comfort . . . We might have helped each other as husband and wife are meant to help each other, but this you would not allow. I caused the next breach and I admit to it in full, but now we must look beyond. Can we not declare these last mistakes canceled one by the other and put forward our best efforts toward each other, toward William, toward our children to come?"

Our children to come. That had been just the spot Deborah had come to that night when she'd found Benjamin in that vile creature's room.

Benjamin leaned forward, all intensity now. "Are you my wife yet, Debby? 'Tis time for you to decide. Yes or no."

And there it was, the old worm that had been eating away at Deborah, gnawing closer and closer to her core, camouflaged by her anger and her questions, ever since she'd discovered the servant lying under Benjamin just as Deborah had so often lain. For she was *not* in fact Benjamin Franklin's wife and never had been. Not in law. What claim did she hold over him greater than the claim of any servant who might reasonably expect to be housed and clothed and fed? What prevented her being dismissed along with any servant who failed to please or provide as requested? To make an even more specific point, what separated Deborah from Anne? Were they not, in a sense, both whores? Deborah would insist on one large difference—she hadn't befriended or accepted confidences from another woman and then betrayed her without a blink, but where else lay the difference? If Anne—or Deborah—wished to keep dry and warm under Benjamin Franklin's roof, if she wished to eat a decent supper and wear decent clothes, she'd open her door to him when he knocked. Deborah had certainly done so. So had Anne. *Were* they not both whores? But the question Benjamin had asked was *Are you my wife yet?* Did she feel so? Or more to the point, did she wish to be so? If she did, there was but one direction in which to go.

Deborah walked to the bedroom and left the door ajar. Benjamin followed her through. He liked to be naked, he liked her to be naked—so foreign a thing, but one Deborah had grown used to—but now he made no attempt to remove her clothes, only taking off his own breeches, socks, and shoes and sliding between the sheets in his shirt, as if they were strangers again. Deborah kept her shift on as well—she could not imagine lying so exposed and raw to him. Awkwardly they worked their way back to the old touchstones—his broad, smooth-muscled back, her heavy, responsive breasts—but the anger didn't stay where Deborah had stashed it, and it would appear that Benjamin had hoarded some of his own; they clapped together at the end in a shared fury, and neither would let go, because to let go meant they must look each other in the face, a thing neither appeared ready to do.

30

GRISSOM'S UPHOLSTERY SHOP HAD changed. Peter had mastered enough of the trade to be put over the girls, now assigning them their tasks more often than Grissom, Grissom spending fewer hours in the shop. After meeting Grissom's wife, Anne decided this wife was the cause of Grissom's absence; on those rare occasions when they toured the workings together she hooked herself to Grissom's elbow and didn't let go, lifting her face in total attention every time he spoke, but Anne couldn't hold such intense effort against her—Grissom would take some work to know.

That first day they came directly to Anne's table, but whether it was Grissom's or the wife's idea, Anne couldn't tell because they were entwined so. Anne made to set down her work and rise, but the woman held out a hand to stop her. "Oh, dear me no, keep on as you were, you're Anne and I'm Mrs. Grissom and that's all my husband wished to say, and all I wished to say is good luck in your new employment. You appear to have a knack for the handling of horsehair, I must say." So there was the marriage's first lie—as far as the new Mrs. Grissom was concerned, Anne had never worked in the shop before, known Grissom before. All right, thought Anne, fair play.

"May I wish you good fortune in your new marriage," she answered.

"The fortune is all mine," Grissom said, and Mrs. Grissom looked up at him in all solemnity, as she should have; from a Franklin such a remark might be taken as a pleasantry, from a Grissom it must be taken as an oath. And there Anne discovered the thing that had changed Grissom, lightened him and weighted him together. Anne couldn't say that in her recent dealing she'd seen a good deal of it, but now that she saw it she knew it for what it was—a man in love with his wife. He would come to her yet, of course, but perhaps not so soon as she'd first believed, perhaps not this very week. The couple looked at each other in silent unison and in silent unison turned for the stairs.

Perhaps not this month, then.

ANNE HAD BEEN BACK at the upholstery shop a week only when Franklin walked in. He strode toward the table where Anne was working—in fairness to Rose, Anne had been put back to the bed ticks again—but before he'd managed to quite reach her Grissom intercepted him and clapped him on the shoulder, steering him to the back of the shop, through the door where Anne and Peter and Rose shared their noonday meal.

The voices rose and fell, rose and fell, rose some more, until Peter, who was nearest, rounded his eyes at her. He got up and came to her table. "They're at odds over you! Come help with my chair and hear all!"

Anne rose and joined Peter at his station, pulling and holding a bit of damask as he tapped the nails home, softly, sparingly, the better for listening.

"I've no doubt your wife *should* dislike finding her in town, Franklin, but that's not my concern. My concern is that she's a fine worker and I've no wish to see her moved along."

"No doubt you have other reasons to keep her."

"No doubt you have yet to hear of my happy marriage, sir."

"As I should like mine to remain."

"And good luck to you, sir."

Anne choked down a burst of laughter that broke off the conversation in the next room, but by the time Franklin reappeared Anne was already back at her table, wrestling her curls of horsehair into their form. For a second Franklin only stared at her and frowned, but he couldn't let her be. He crossed the room. He leaned down and spoke low.

"I could have you arrested yet, you know."

"You must do as you like, sir. But if I *were* arrested, I should be forced to explain my reasons for stealing the boy away. The reasons I felt he was not safe in your home." She waited, but as Franklin made no response, she asked—she couldn't help but ask—"Is he well?"

Anne watched a new battle twist and turn inside Franklin, one that seldom concluded as this did, with a silent admission of defeat, a moving on. "He's well," he said at last. "I pledge to you I will keep him so; will you make me a pledge in return?"

"I don't know."

Anne's old friend, the dimple, flashed. "Wise girl. Don't promise a thing till you know what the thing is. I should only like you to take some extra care in avoiding Mrs. Franklin about town. For the boy's sake."

"And yours."

Franklin dipped his head, but soon after, the old, familiar speculation crept into his eyes. "I wonder, this marriage of Grissom's, what chance do you give it?"

"The best."

"Meaning you plan to leave him be?"

"I plan to leave all of you be. I work only at upholstering now."

Franklin surprised her by breaking out into a full-blown laugh. "But do we plan to leave you be? Ah, Annie my girl, despite what trouble you've caused me, I believe I mourn the loss of you even harder this second time. You gave me life after death, and I shan't forget it. I shan't forget the rest either, or forgive it, but I find myself wishing you well just the same. Now for God's sake, keep shy of my wife." He bowed, hat swept wide in the kind of exaggeration that might have been mocking or not, and departed the store.

After Franklin had gone Anne stared at the empty space that he'd left for some time. She was already deep in mourning for William, but was shocked to discover that she was able to find in herself a pale shadow of that feeling for the father too. Of all her men he'd been the easiest to please, his pleasure seeming so much greater than that of any other man she'd come to know. Well, and why not? His talent lay in making her feel, even when she could not believe, that he loved her alone, and he no doubt made every other woman who'd ever pleased him feel so too. Before the act, after the act, just her presence seemed to please him, her presence and her talk, no matter what she talked of. Or was that *his* act? If so, it was an act that had succeeded in forcing this peculiar regret on her now.

Anne returned to her mattress with a half laugh, half sigh. Grissom approached, but she was so cloaked in her own thoughts she didn't see or hear him until he dropped a finger on her hand to still its darting about amongst the curls of hair. She looked up, startled. He dropped his voice low.

"Does our friend give you trouble?"

"No, none whatever."

Grissom studied her. "Very well. I trust you'll alert me if he does."

"To what end?"

Grissom pointed to her hands, already busy again. "Such nimble fingers don't come my way often. 'Twould be worth a fight to keep them."

"And how would you go about fighting Franklin, especially as he has the law behind him?"

"I'd leave it to you to show the way. You seem to be mastering it thus far."

31

BY THE FALL OF 1737 Deborah had cohabited with Benjamin Franklin for seven years and could now be declared his legal wife. Benjamin said nothing of it, and neither did Deborah, at first, but some weeks after the milestone had been reached, Deborah walked into her husband's study at night, a thing she seldom did. Benjamin lifted his head from his book in surprise; if his forehead wrinkled briefly with annoyance he soon smoothed it.

"Did you know we've been under this roof together seven years?" she asked.

Benjamin's eyebrows rose. "Indeed! Now there's a thing!"

"This means I may now be declared your legal wife."

"And this means William will have been with us seven years and may be declared my legal heir."

It was not the response Deborah might have wished for.

. . . .

THE NEXT NEW THING in Deborah's life was the next new thing in Benjamin's—his appointment as postmaster general of Pennsylvania. He began to keep the post office in his shop, which meant Deborah often kept the post office while Benjamin traveled to map out postal routes and post offices throughout the colony. The post office suited Deborah well; she could consult Benjamin's new chart and offer up the proper charge for the collection of the letters, depending on how far it had come; she could take the money and mark it down and direct other letters along their route. The shop brought certain people Deborah's way, but the post office brought them all, including the ones who hadn't spoken to Deborah before. But it was different from before—now Deborah was Benjamin's legal wife, and she could claim her official place.

One night after some months at the postal work, Deborah interrupted Benjamin at his evening study, a thing she'd begun to do with greater comfort. "I should like to invite some of your friends to dine."

"My friends eat too much already," Benjamin answered. "Better they're encouraged to skip dining from time to time." He returned to his book.

"I shouldn't think, looking at the shape of Mr. Grissom, that he needed to skip dining. And he's brought in a new wife, from Virginia, I'm told. I should like to meet her."

Benjamin's head shot up. "Haven't I told you my rule? Never torture newlyweds by making them leave the comfort of each other's company only to inflict them with ours."

"But I should like to meet her."

"She's the perfect match for Grissom—that is, she's on the retiring side. She doesn't care to go out in company any more than he does."

"He used to come often to see you."

"To poke about amongst my books, not to dine."

"He was most kind to William."

Benjamin said nothing.

"Besides, I heard the Grissoms were at Peale's just last week."

"Fulsoms. The Fulsoms were at Peale's." Benjamin stood up. "I believe I'm done with this day. Time for us to find our bed."

"Just the same, I should like to call around to Grissom's and meet the wife and ask them to dine."

Benjamin peered at Deborah as if she were someone new, as indeed, perhaps, she was. "As it happens, I have business with Grissom in the morn," he said. "I'll carry your invitation along."

"Thank you."

There Benjamin, apparently forgetting it was time for bed, sat down, opened his book again, and began to flap about amongst the pages.

THE NEXT MORNING DEBORAH had just finished stocking her shelves with some new offerings—palm oil, mustard, and cheese—when Benjamin returned. "I regret to say the Grissoms have declined our invitation. As I suspected, his wife is not disposed to go into company. Grissom sorely regrets missing the evening, and plans to come to talk books again soon."

To talk books. Which Deborah could not do. And so where was her entertainment in it? "The Fulsoms, then," she said. "We know *they* go out to dine."

Benjamin looked to prefer the idea of books with Grissom, but Deborah had made up her mind. Was it not, by now, her house too, at least in part, at least to use as she liked now and then? She pushed on. "I shall invite the Fulsoms."

MIN WAS SENT AROUND to the Fulsoms with a note, and a note was returned; the Fulsoms were unable to dine on account of an ill child. Deborah sent an answering note with a pot of chicken soup and a repeated invitation for any date as soon as the child was well, but heard nothing from the Fulsoms regarding the soup or the invitation. Deborah sent another note to the Greens, who couldn't dine and didn't trouble to give a reason. She tried the Larchwoods, who had entertained Benjamin a number of times in the political vein, but was again refused, although that answer was most polite: A painful attack of gout was anticipated to keep Mr. Larchwood indisposed for some time. The next morning Deborah saw Mr. Larchwood out riding. In hindsight, Deborah wondered at her foolishness in expecting Philadelphia's society to abruptly take Deborah Read-Rogers-Read-Franklin into its bosom just because she'd crossed that magic seven-year line. She sent no more notes around.

IN TIME, HOWEVER, DEBORAH began to think again of Solomon Grissom. She'd always felt an affinity for the man, as he seemed to possess as few ready words as she did; he appeared completely at ease with her own lapses into silence, and she very much liked the idea that his wife might be the same. If the woman was shy, all the more reason to attempt to bring her out, to make of her a friend of Deborah's own. Besides, Grissom was a successful shop owner and certainly pleasant enough to look at, and Deborah had never been able to imagine why he'd remained so long a bachelor; she wanted to meet the woman who'd brought him to this end. If Mrs. Grissom wouldn't come to see her, she would just have to go there and see her for herself.

The next morning Deborah told Benjamin that he and his apprentice must take care of the business of the shop and the press and the post office between them; she had an errand to run. She made up a basket of gingerbread, biscuits, and jam and stepped into the street. She looked west and saw a woman who'd been caught picking pockets now tied to the courthouse rail for her shaming. She looked east and saw the sky pierced with mast after mast, from London, Genoa, Lisbon, Cadiz, Ireland, Newfoundland, and the West Indian islands, or so her husband's *Gazette* had recently reported. The new trade had brought new sights and sounds and smells to Philadelphia—the stink of the overworked slaughter houses, tan yards, and lime pits that lined the Dock Creek; the competing shouts of the corders and fishmongers on the wharves; the blur of different-colored costumes and faces all around her; she could even feel the change in the overtrodden mud slipping about under her shoes. She would speak to Benjamin about that mud—he ran the *Gazette* and *Poor Dick* and had started a library and a fire company and was now clerk of the assembly—surely he could do something about too much mud on the shoes!

So it was that Deborah stepped into the upholsterer's shop looking down at her shoes, uneasy about the mud ending up on Grissom's floor; when she lifted her eyes they were met by a pair of gray ones she'd once claimed to know well. The eyes neither dropped in shame nor blinked with nerves; Deborah, the legal wife of Benjamin Franklin, would not be the one to avert her eyes. She lifted her chin and stared at the girl, that brazen, vile, witch of a girl, that kidnapper who had supposedly been banished to Boston instead of being thrown in gaol, a thing that Benjamin had explained would have called unwanted attention to poor William. Poor William! That was what Benjamin had said. *Poor William.* As if Deborah had suffered nothing at all.

After a time Deborah became aware that Grissom stood at her side, that he touched her elbow, that he in fact tugged at her elbow.

"Mrs. Franklin, I'm most pleased to see you."

Deborah turned to face Grissom, glad for the excuse of looking away from those gray eyes that had once stolen Deborah's compassion, but as usual she found herself without speech.

Grissom tried to help. "How do you fare, Mrs. Franklin? How fares your delightful boy?"

And William may be declared my legal heir. That was the other thing Benjamin had said.

"*My* boy is dead, Mr. Grissom." Deborah handed him her basket. "Please give this to your wife." She walked out, stamping the mud off her shoes and onto the floor.

DEBORAH RETURNED AS SHE came, but this time smelling nothing, seeing nothing, hearing nothing of Philadelphia. She walked into the shop, through the shop, and out the back to the press, where Benjamin stood in his leather apron, his compositor's stick cradled in his hand as if it were a jewel-encrusted sword. He looked up. "My dear!"

"I've come from Grissom's," she said, and waited.

Benjamin handed the compositor's stick to his apprentice; he came over to Deborah and took her by the elbow. She was tired of people tugging at her elbow. She was tired of the shop and the press and Benjamin and William and the whole great lot of them. She pulled free, left the shop, and climbed the stairs. Behind her she heard Benjamin's heavier tread.

THEY SAT ON EACH side of the cold parlor hearth, Benjamin leaning forward with his hands on his knees, just as he sat with his important friends whenever he was attempting to appear at his most earnest, coddling them into a vote for a militia, or a hospital, or a school. "Of course I knew she was there," he explained oh-so-reasonably to Deborah. "I called on Grissom and discovered her. I saw her on the Boston ship myself but she came back, Grissom took her back. I tried to talk Grissom into sending her away again, but I failed. Apparently she's good at her work. Better than most. He'd not had a girl—" Somewhere in amongst his ramblings, Benjamin saw his mistake. He stopped. "Debby," he said. "I haven't been back to Grissom's shop since I found her there. I shan't go again. I'm in the bed I wish to lie in with the woman I wish to lie with, as you well know, or if you don't, I'm not the fellow I think myself to be. And such hard work I put into it too!"

He smiled. Deborah did not. His brow pinched in impatience and she could read his thoughts as if they marched along the grooves. *I've left James in charge of the composing . . . there's no one to attend the shop . . . I wonder if anyone's waiting for his post . . .* "Now come, Debby," he said. "You're not going to be silly over this, are you?"

Deborah stood up. "Yes, I am. 'Tis the best word for it too. Silly to object to being deceived over this lesser thing after having been deceived many times over the larger. You never did even ask them to dine, did you? No, of course you didn't. Because you were afraid he might—no, your friend Grissom never would, but his wife just might—mention that girl in the shop. Last time you deceived me you gave—and I took—some blame for it to myself. This time you alone may take the blame for my shut door."

Benjamin, even in the great rush of the day, sat where he was for some time, as if pondering what she'd said, which would be the first occasion for it. Perhaps Deborah was getting better with her words.

32

Philadelphia, 1740

WHEN WILLIAM WAS APPROXIMATELY ten or eleven, his parents moved into a more fashionable home, still on Market Street, but a home that even to a boy spoke of something finer than what had been.

William also noticed that as they moved four doors along Market Street the spinning wheels and looms didn't come, that his mother began to buy her cloth from the shops, her meat fresh instead of dried, their bowls made of china instead of pewter. William noticed these things, but none of them changed his life to any great extent, until the following year when his father enrolled him in Alexander Annard's Classical Academy, a school far above the reach of any other tradesman's son. One day William was lording Pirate over all his horseless friends, the next he was looking for a friend who *didn't* have a horse; he was amongst the rich Quaker boys now, the oldest, most influential families in Philadelphia—the Graemes, the Shippens, the Penns.

But William was glad enough for the change. At the old school a word had just begun to shadow him as he fought his way among the sons of bricklayers and smiths and cordswainers, a word he understood only in its sense and not its exact meaning—*bastard*—but at the academy the word got magically left behind. For a time William did have to struggle to fit in, but he was sharp and he was quick; soon enough he'd learned what clothes to wear and what words to speak, and one day one of the boys invited William to his home. William had thought his new Market Street house was fine but soon saw its lack of space and glitter and *lawn*. It was true, he did overhear his friend's mother: "Only think what he comes from!" But the boy's father countered, "He's polite enough and pretty enough; he'll get on."

William took even greater care with his dress and his manner after that and he did get on. Other invitations came, to horseback rides and skating parties and sleigh rides; soon enough he began to think of himself not as a printer's son but as that other kind of boy, the kind who might expect to go to Eton or Oxford, to become a merchant or a lawyer or a politician if he chose.

And then one morning, coming down the stairs early, he heard his mother's voice from behind the bedroom door.

"I'd like to know what you think you're doing to that boy, puffing him up so full of himself, as if he belongs with that kind, when it's a printer's trade he's to inherit. He's already past the age of half the apprentices in this town; he should be at the press learning his job. What's that school costing you? And you've another coming soon to feed and clothe."

Soon after, William's sister, Sarah, was born. The sister was a blow; by then William had come to understand something more of the meaning of the word *bastard,* and saw at once that if he was one, his sister wasn't; he also saw that his mother preferred the one who wasn't. As to his father, William could not have foreseen how eagerly his tall, strong, proud father could debase himself over a cradle of uncomprehending pink flesh, even if it was his own. His own and Deborah's. Theirs together. So. What more did William need to know of it? He understood things now. The charmed Franky. His mother's wild raillery at this "devil child" who was never hers but the product of some other passion between her husband and . . . *whom*?

Many nights William approached his father's study ready to ask the rapidly all-consuming question, but each time he began his faltering sentence, something in his father's eye dried out his mouth. One night he finally managed to get a single sentence out.

"I should like to know who my mother is."

"Your mother is Deborah Franklin. And this is no longer a subject between us."

And so it wasn't.

All the while, the child Sally grew and sparkled and charmed her father, pulling him to her as if she were a flame and he a light-seeking insect. "My Sally!" he would cry, and scoop her up and tease her into giggles and words and soon—William must admit it was precociously soon—even letters, the father exclaiming over the daughter's little slate as he so rarely found time to exclaim over William's ever-denser pages.

But worse was yet to come. Shortly after Sally was born, William's father took him out of Alexander Annard's Classical Academy, where he'd worked so hard to achieve and *belong*, and put him to work in the print shop. As much as William liked being at his father's side, printing was still messy, smelly, strenuous work, and William still hated it. Feeling for the letters, in constant fear of picking the wrong one, the lining up of the letters—*backward*—into a word, the words into sentences, the sentences into a page, the inking, the hefting about of ream after ream of paper, the swinging of the heavy arm of the press time after time. His father, William decided, had way too much to say. But beyond that he would not blame his father for this new life chained to the print shop. He knew who to blame. He'd heard Deborah's words.

Deborah. Inside his head, William stopped calling her *mother,* and started to think of her by her given name, but the game was only a satisfying one at the start—soon it turned on its inventor, grew talons and horns, butted at him night after night. If Deborah should not be called *mother,* who should be?

One night, after William had painfully clawed his way into his teens, he came home from the shop tired, hot, ink stained, out of sorts with the world in general and with one person in particular. He'd been so hot and tired he hadn't made proper use of the turpentine rag to clean the ink off his hands, and as he gripped the doorjamb to swing himself through it, he left an inky smear on the woodwork. As luck had run for him of late, his house-proud mother stood just on the other side of the door.

"Get your filthy hand off the paint!" she shouted at him.

That was the moment it first occurred to William that perhaps Deborah was speaking of ink and perhaps she wasn't speaking of ink; in either case she'd spoken it at the wrong time. He leaned more heavily into the hand where it rested against the doorjamb.

"What did I say to you?"

"William," his father said, "listen to your mother."

William dropped his hand and looked straight through Deborah at his father. "I should like to," he answered, "if someone would only tell me where to find her."

The room turned still.

His father broke through the quiet first. "Your mother stands there. And it would behoove you to remember your duty to her."

"She's not my mother. Since the whole town knows it, I'd have thought you'd know it too."

"I shouldn't like—," his father began, but Deborah rounded on her husband, damp, red, raving.

"Do you see? Do you see what he is? The greatest villain that ever lived! Oh, that I must ever claim him as mine!"

William turned, stepped back through the door, and slammed it closed. Behind him he could hear his father, his voice raised as it rarely ever was.

"Debby! Dear God! Think of the boy! Where's your heart?"

"Tired. My heart is tired and sore and sick to death of the sight of him."

And somewhere inside another door—the bedroom door, most likely—slammed closed.

LATER THAT NIGHT WILLIAM'S father came to his room. "I expect you to apologize to your mother."

"And who might that be?"

"Below stairs lies your mother," his father said, in that voice that William could never find it in himself to cross.

The next day William apologized to Deborah, but Deborah retracted none of her words.

THAT SAME YEAR WAR with Spain was declared from the courthouse steps, and the cannon on the hill fired off round after round all day long. Soon the French had entered into it, stirring up the Indians along the frontier, attacking settlements nearer and nearer to town; William's father became the loudest voice in favor of building a militia for the defense of Philadelphia and the surrounding towns, but the solid Quaker voting block against all things militaristic held sway. William ground out the rest of the year at the print shop, but at the beginning of the second year, when the privateers began sailing up the Delaware into Philadelphia and flashing about their gold, William began to make some plans of his own.

33

Philadelphia, 1745

ANNE WOKE TO A late-night tap on her door, by now such an alien sound she wasn't sure she'd heard it; she'd kept her promise to Grissom and entertained no men in her room or anywhere else. At first there had come the expected random knocks from those former, overfond patrons who could not latch on to the idea that this particular door was now closed. In time, however, the message was absorbed, and Anne was left alone. The fact that Anne was indeed alone required some adjustment on her part, but soon enough she discovered a new serenity in the falling away of all pretense; she began to practice pleasing herself of an evening, and found she could excel at that too. She borrowed books from Solomon Grissom and now and then dipped into her pouch to purchase a special one; she took more pains with her sewing, and with a bit of trim here and there managed to turn her wardrobe—and her room—into something that told another story of Anne than the one she'd told before. As for the daytime, she worked as she'd worked before and soon made her way back from bed ticks to

tassels to hangings, from there to being trusted with the running of
the shop now and then.

But Anne was not the only thing in Philadelphia that had changed,
and from what she heard from Grissom's customers as they came in
and out, much of the change could be laid to Franklin. The streets had
been paved and culverts run under them to divert the water. A thing
called a "fire engine" had appeared, to be used by the fire company
Franklin had formed for the express purpose of responding to alarms,
and it came just in time, containing a terrible fire at the warehouses
along the wharf. A learned society had been formed, "to promote useful knowledge amongst the British plantations of America." With the
announcement of war and the news of repeated Indian and French
attacks on the Ohio border had come an even bolder move: Franklin
defied the pacifist Quakers who controlled the assembly and began
lobbying to form a private militia. But perhaps the most talked about
of all Franklin's innovations was the "Pennsylvania Fireplace," an
invention he refused to patent so that all could share in its benefit, the
benefit being the reduction by two-thirds of the amount of wood
required to heat a home. What the corders at the waterfront had to say
about this Anne didn't know, but she knew what everyone else said of
it: Franklin was now called genius *and* philanthropist.

Other, private changes in Franklin's life had come to Anne's attention as well—the move to a more fashionable home, the birth of a
daughter, a partner brought into the printing business. It was rumored
that much of Franklin's new free time was spent on experiments
regarding a thing called electricity, and Anne found herself regretting
one single aspect of her old life: the chance to hear firsthand what such
a thing was and what it could mean—what it could mean for William—
for this was how she took note of everything regarding Franklin.

Anne always watched for William as he made his way about town
but rarely saw the boy near to; if she was seen first, mother or father
or Min took care to either turn him around or distract his attention

another way. In time William grew into a tall and finely made young man who began to go about on his own, but whenever he passed Anne he did so without a single flick of recognition. Anne lay awake many of those early nights debating the gain and the loss of making her identity known to the boy, but in the end decided that when she did so, she must do it as someone who would cause him no shame; there were still too many about town who remembered the whore. Give it a few more years, she decided, until no one remembered any-one but the upholstery worker—then would be the time.

Solomon Grissom too had changed, taking to married life so well he'd fathered a child every odd year, pausing at a current tally of two girls and a boy. Anne had been exceedingly pained at the arrival of that first girl, the memory of William's earliest days in her arms brought fresh to life with every cry of hunger or distress, but in time the child had come into her own red curls, her own way of dimpling, her own distinctive voice. So had the next girl. They were not Wil-liam. But then came the boy, and by the cruelest act of fate he came as fair haired and bright as William; Anne couldn't keep her eyes from him whenever he happened into the shop hand in hand with his father. Elisha, he was called, and Anne went out of her way to make a friend of him, tying up a yarn dog for him, or sewing a stuffed cat, keeping a piece of molasses candy in her pocket to treat him. When he became ill with dysentery and didn't appear for a week, Anne's attention fell off and she bungled the accounts; Grissom, already gray from lack of sleep, had to keep late in the shop to sort them out.

Another thing occupied Anne's mind in addition to William and Elisha: Solomon Grissom's marriage. Contrary to her prediction, Grissom *had* left Anne alone, and as glad as Anne was of it, she was just as puzzled. She began to make a study of the pair, watching the Gris-soms together and apart, and noticed how they listened for the other's tread and lit up when the other appeared, how well they attended not only each other's physical selves but each other's looks and words.

Through the wife, Anne came to a greater understanding of the husband; she learned that his silence was not always empty, that his acuteness was not always barbed; she began to feel freer in his presence now there was no doubt his heart had rooted firmly in some other ground. Anne watched Sophie too, and learned something of those other things that could be given to a man besides that single thing that was all Anne had ever allowed. The other things were things Anne had never seen the point in learning, but it fascinated her just the same, and at times, at night, she would warm herself by hovering in her imagination over the Grissoms' hearth.

SO FIVE YEARS HAD gone by, and here was the old *tap, tap, tap.* Or more accurately, as Anne had failed to move at the first sounds, *Crack! Crack! Crack!* Grissom at last? Her thoughts too disordered to sort, Anne threw back her bedcovers, wrapped her shawl around her, lit a candle, and went to the door. Franklin stood there, but not the same old Franklin of the confounded and confounding half smile, the smile that could never decide if she were angel or devil—this Franklin had decided what she was.

"Where is he? Where've you got him?"

"Grissom?"

"Grissom! So that's how this happy marriage works! No, not Grissom, blast it! William. Is he here?"

"Why on earth would he be here?"

"He's run off. I know you told him who you are. Where else should he go but here?"

"I've told that boy nothing."

Franklin stopped looking frantically around Anne's room and brought his eyes back to her face. Anne looked back without a flinch. At forty Franklin had grown even wider in the shoulders and back but had begun to thicken at the waist, his hairline had begun to creep backward, slightly lengthening his forehead, but his chin remained firm, his eyes keen. The decided look in them softened to a rare confusion.

"Do you mean to say you've said nothing to him? Not when you took him or any time since then?"

"He knows nothing of our relation. He knows nothing of me at all. He doesn't even recognize me when we pass."

Franklin took a visible breath and it gusted into the room like a small tornado, lifting the loose hairs that lay on Anne's neck. He peered at her a time longer. "I find I must believe you in this, although I was quite convinced otherwise. He'd begun to ask questions, abuse his mother. I assumed you'd explained yourself to him and painted her black in the process. It seemed the logical—" Franklin stopped, and looked at her in new defiance. "It was no ill usage at home that brought him to this, I promise you!"

"And it was nothing I said that brought him to it, I promise *you*."

Franklin, calmer now, studied her longer. He may have decided to believe her, but he wasn't through blaming her. "God's breath, woman! It was madness to take him!"

"Yes, it was. I admit that to you now. I saw it aboard the ship, when I realized that *I'd* carried him into danger—" Anne stopped. "The ships."

Franklin stared. "Good God! The ships! Of course it would be the ships! 'Twas all he ever talked of! What can be wrong with me that I shouldn't think of a ship, with the pirates running all over town flashing their gold and calling for crew." Franklin wheeled for the door.

Anne dropped her shawl, picked her gown off the peg, and pulled it on over her shift. She wrenched open her case of drawers in a hunt for a pair of stockings and Franklin heard the complaint of the wood—he swung around, saw her standing with the stocking in her hand and plucked it out of her fingers.

"My dear Anne, you can't think to come with me at this hour."

"I might help you search. Think of all the ships tied up just now at the wharfs! I might—"

"He'll be on one of the privateers—there are but four of them in port. Think how it will look. You must keep here."

Of course he was right. Of course she couldn't help search. Again, as Grissom once told her, it was more of that madness only love for her son ever drove her to. Franklin tugged the stocking free of her hand, crossed to the bed, and, taking into account the circumstance, laid it out with considerable care.

"You must send me word at once," Anne said.

"I shall." Franklin strode to the door a second time, stopped a second time. He came back into the room, picked up her hand, kissed it. "God love you, my girl," he said, "for God knows I cannot."

ANNE SAT UP WITH some of her mending, waiting for a message from Franklin, thinking about what he'd said of pirates. She might have thought of the ships, but she hadn't thought of pirates, and she didn't like to think of it. She'd heard of them, of course, seen them, in fact— privateers authorized under the king's letters of marque, set loose to rob and plunder any ship sailing under a French or Spanish flag; she'd also heard of some of those men—and boys—killed, some of the ships sunk. It was true that some came home rich as kings; Anne could imagine the fifteen-year-old William as she'd known the seven-year-old William, eyes alight at even the thought of a ship, but she could also imagine the fifteen-year-old William lying on a ship's deck, painted all over in his own blood. She'd once thought William not bold, and here he was, ready to sign on to as bold an adventure as could be, while she—a woman whose courage had once been admired—sat trembling.

Anne sat up watching the dawn come on, but no message came from Franklin. She dressed herself and went to the shop, but what work she did was a poor effort. At noon a messenger came to the shop, carrying a letter to Grissom. Grissom opened it and crossed the shop to Anne's table. He handed her a separate, sealed piece of paper and Anne saw her name scratched across it in Franklin's familiar hand. She tore it open.

He was discovered aboard the Wilmington and removed. A thousand thank yous. You took and now you give back—the score is settled between us for this life.

The letter was unsigned. Of course.

34

WILLIAM FRANKLIN DOUBTED THAT his father would ever understand what it had taken for him to board that privateer. To a man like
Benjamin Franklin, who could take an idea—any idea—and leap after
it with the confidence of one who saw exactly where it led long before
anyone else had even registered the words, such a step would seem
small enough, but to William it was as large as the sum of his young
life. As large as death.

It was Deborah who drove William out of the house day after day,
but as he wandered through the stark, late-day streets he felt no great
affection for his father either, a father who'd allowed his wife to stand
there and call William a villain, who'd told *William* to apologize for
doing nothing but attempting to find out the simple truth about himself, a truth his father had long denied him, continued to deny him,
even after his own wife had as much as admitted how false the original account was. Deborah Franklin was not his mother. She was
ashamed to call herself his mother. And instead of thinking of himself

as the legitimate offspring of one of Philadelphia's most admired citizens, William must now consider that he was likely the bastard son of that man and . . . whom? *Whom?*

William left the house one day driven by a particularly violent storm of mortification and rage; he walked and walked and ended, as he always ended, at the wharf, and there he saw the *Wilmington*, bathed in the shine of the gold she'd brought to the Philadelphia streets. In front of the ship the Delaware River stretched toward the horizon as smooth as a well-worn road, leading . . . away. That was all William cared about. It would lead him away.

William found the shipmaster, a taut, sun-blackened man lit by his own fire, whether made up of greed or glory William couldn't tell and couldn't care; the shipmaster's reasons were his as William's reasons were his, and neither was asked nor offered. The deal was struck and William returned home, sneaking in without speaking to or seeing anyone, going to his room and putting together what he hoped at least faintly resembled a sea kit. He considered and decided that his father, at least, deserved the courtesy of a brief note. In writing the note, a sense of the finality of the words brought on a rush of affection that in truth had seldom waned, and the pen stuttered over the paper, leaving rough starts and stops that William had little time to remedy. *Honored Father*, he wrote. *I'm gone to make my own way. I'll not burden you again in this life. Your devoted son, William.*

It was dark by the time William boarded the ship, any aura of gold long gone, the river no longer a bright, glimmering road to fortune but an empty black void, suddenly reminding William of a much smaller boy, a seemingly much bigger ship, a darker night. Who was that servant who'd whisked him away in darkness and taken him aboard that ship? He could no longer remember her face or her name, only the way she'd begun to frighten him. He did remember the early, wild excitement of actually being on a ship, being allowed to steer a ship! Had he understood that a ship tied to a dock didn't need steering? He doubted it. He'd believed in it. All of it. But next had come that hollowing fear when he realized the servant and even the strange man had disappeared, and he was alone in the dark on the enormous ship with the black water far below him. What next? The crashing relief at the sight of his father coming up the gangway and striding across the deck to scoop him up and take him home.

Much as his father did again aboard the *Wilmington*.

Shouldn't William have foreseen the same old conclusion to the same old play? But this time there was no relief, just more of that burning shame, intensified by a jeering crew and a screaming captain, with William's father as William's father always was, the voice in William's ear as gentle and sensible as warm pudding, the arm around his shoulder as hard and irrefutable as a fireplace crane.

THE EPISODE DID LITTLE to improve the mood at home. William entered rooms and walked out again if Deborah was the only occupant; he spoke to her, where possible, through his father, or even the baby Sally, deciding the best way to show his stepmother how little he cared if he pleased her or not was to put all his efforts into pleasing Sally. Most of these maneuvers only caused Deborah to lose more and more control of her tongue, which only caused William to act more and more hateful, with the single exception being that he developed a true affection for this little sister, who was fast becoming, in her innocence and ignorance, his best ally.

But it turned out William in fact had another ally, neither innocent nor ignorant: his father. He saw, he heard, he tried and failed to smooth it; in the end he understood that there would be no peace at home with both son and wife under the same roof and he came up with a solution that pleased most parties. He enlisted William in the king's army.

. . . .

OH, HOW WILLIAM LOVED the army! The order, the neatness, the single focus, the chance to succeed and to advance to a legitimate title that drew him honest respect, even from his father. William had achieved the rank of captain, as high as he could advance without a purchased commission, an investment his father was disinclined to undertake, and there it seemed to William that his army career had ended.

But somehow, somewhere, in amongst all the pacifist Quakers of Pennsylvania, William's father managed to prevail in a plan he'd long nurtured of building defenses along the western frontier; the expedition was actually put forth in the assembly and accepted, and Benjamin Franklin, chief defender of defense, was asked to head it. No one dared object when the father then turned around and enlisted his army captain son to aid him—in fact, to lead him, for what did William's father know of armies? It was William who planned and executed, but of course on their return to Philadelphia it was the elder Franklin who was praised and cheered, although to give him his due, he asked for none of it, and in fact rode seventy-five miles in two days in order to sneak into town ahead of a parade that was rumored to be forming to honor him. The end result of the expedition? As William remained stopped at captain in the king's army, his father was made colonel of his own home-grown militia.

But William refused to be stopped at home, where the words *devil child* and *villain* could too easily haunt his days. He began to think of another profession that prized order and rules, that preferred neat rows of books with well-ordered shelves over his father's method of unclassified piles and unlabeled crates and boxes. With his father's reluctant permission, and no doubt his stepmother's relief, he moved out of his father's house and began to study law with a friend of his father's named Joseph Galloway.

35

Philadelphia, 1748

DEBORAH FRANKLIN TOOK UP the letter from Boston and announced without looking at her chart, "One shilling."

Fulsom fished out his coins and counted. "Ah, Mrs. Franklin, I find myself sixpence short."

"Then it shall be delivered to you on the morrow in the penny post. To help you in your accounting, that will make it seven pence you'll need to scrounge out."

Fulsom stared at her. "I assure you, Mrs. Franklin, you may count me good for the sixpence and give me my letter today. I've waited on it a fortnight."

"Then another day shouldn't mark so great an addition to your waiting, should it?" Deborah turned to the next customer. "Good day to you, Mr. Hughes. How many do you leave with us? Two for Boston, three hundred ninety miles. We now run three mails a week this time of year; you may expect it to arrive Thursday next. And one for New York, one hundred six miles, that should arrive by Sunday."

Out of the corner of her eye Deborah observed Fulsom leaving the shop and stopping in the street to lay out his mistreatment to one of the Shippens, not friends of Benjamin's since he'd organized the militia, but Shippen seemed to hold enough respect for the Franklins—or his mail delivery—to listen without taking a side in it. That was the best Deborah got from Philadelphia society, but it was better than she'd gotten before now, and she liked it. She liked her life. She liked working in the shop with Benjamin so near, she liked those evenings when she had Benjamin's undivided attention as they discussed the day's accounts; above all, she liked her daughter, Sally.

It had taken seven long years after the death of Franky for Deborah to bear herself another child. After four years—the length of time it had taken her to get Franky—she decided that God was not through punishing Benjamin for his old sin, and something jagged and unlovely began to grow in her in place of a child: When she looked at William she saw only those old sins and resentments that could never be held to account. But when Sally was born, Deborah could look at her and see all that was good in Benjamin and herself, as if it had been saved up and let free in this one sparkling, amiable child who was sure to win every heart she encountered. Sally was not as pretty as William, but her stolid features and sturdy limbs were Deborah and Benjamin together, and Deborah would insist to any who would listen that Sally was nearly as bright as William ever was. Benjamin was determined that his daughter would learn what a young girl should learn in order to best serve her role in life, but Deborah was determined that she would learn what a young girl might learn of *all* of life; unlike the mother, the daughter would not be left out.

So it was that Deborah sat, taking stock of all that had finally come right with her world just before it all flew apart.

. . . .

FIRST WAS THE SHOP. Benjamin came home one night lit up with more than just the milk punch at the tavern; he pulled Deborah out of her chair, spun her around, and kissed her. "Meet your newborn husband," he said, "fresh out of the printing business forever. I've turned it all over to my new partner, Mr. Hall—press, shop, *Gazette*—together."

At first Deborah couldn't comprehend it. "Turned it all over! What on earth do you mean to do with yourself?"

"I mean to sit back and collect my share of the income from Mr. Hall and otherwise do as I like. Step up and make something useful of myself. Lie down and celebrate it." He caught up her hands and attempted to tug her toward the bedroom, but Deborah shook herself loose.

"And the post office?"

"William can manage the post office."

William can manage the post office. William, who would want her help the least of anyone's in it. "And what of me? What am I to do? Retire to our rooms and—"

"The rooms go with the shop. I've rented us a new house on Race Street, away from the bustle of all this commerce, so I may do my thinking in peace."

"Thinking about *what*?"

"About it all, Debby. About the what and the why and the how and the *what if*." And as if he suddenly realized how behind he was already in all this thinking, he floated away from her and into his study.

DEBORAH SLEPT LITTLE THAT night, her mind in turmoil as she attempted to chase after all that Benjamin had said and what it likely meant to her life, but Benjamin appeared to have no such difficulty. He slept and rose at the usual time and went into his study again, until a message arrived that drew him out of it in some haste. Later, when Deborah went into the room to collect his empty cup, she spied a half-finished letter lying on his desk. The letter was addressed to Cadwallader Colden, a frequent correspondent of Benjamin's in New York.

> *My Dear Friend,*
> *I am settling my old accounts and hope soon to be quite a master*
> *of my own time. I am in a fair way of having no other tasks than*
> *such as I shall like to give myself, and of enjoying what I look upon*
> *as a great happiness, leisure to read, study, make experiments, and*
> *converse at large with such ingenious and worthy men as are pleased*
> *to honour me with their friendship or acquaintance, on such points*
> *as may produce something for the common benefit of mankind,*
> *uninterrupted by the little cares and fatigues of business.*

Deborah stood as she was, reading and rereading that letter for some time. What could she make of a life that held no other tasks but those she would like to give herself? She couldn't begin to imagine such a life, for it required a shadow Deborah to follow her around and do all the rest of the things she would have to abandon in pursuit of her own enjoyment. She knew better than to imagine herself *producing something for the common benefit of mankind,* but as she read through the letter a second time, and a third, she discovered that its beginning was by far the least disturbing part of it. *Reading. Studying. Experimenting. Conversing with ingenious and worthy men.* Where were Deborah and Sally in any of it?

NEXT CAME ELECTRICITY. IT was true that the move to the new house occupied much of Deborah's time, but it hardly slowed Benjamin in the plan he'd laid out in his letter. For many years Deborah had gotten used to all the odd things that leaked out of Benjamin's study and got strewn about the house: a dark cloth and a white one laid side by side on the south windowsill to see which absorbed more heat (the dark one); the dead flies he'd found drowned in his bottle of Madeira and set out on that same sunny windowsill to see if they might revive (some did, some didn't); the plants that cropped up in every room for the purpose of purifying the air (not so far as Deborah could determine); an empty honey jar hung from the kitchen ceiling on a string that was to have proved something or other about ants if Deborah hadn't removed it and thrown it out. But now all the experiments were about a single thing: electricity. *Electricity.* Deborah couldn't comprehend the workings of it, nor could she think of a single use for it; worse, it took up more of Benjamin's time than press, shop, and post office put together. And worse than that, along with the electricity came William.

William. Deborah had tried with the boy. She had. Perhaps if her own boy had lived, or if William hadn't been stolen, or if he'd only stop looking at her that way . . . perhaps if William's *father* would only stop looking at her that way every time she made the slightest correction of the child, as if she were about to hold his hand in a flame. Perhaps if his father would stop fussing over William's every remark while leaving Sally—and Deborah—to speak only to each other or to the increasing silence. Whatever the cause, William had grown from a spoiled boy to a sullen and angry adolescent, most of his anger directed at Deborah.

William was fifteen and as obstinate as a boy could be—at least around his mother—when he ran away and shipped aboard a privateer. After Benjamin had retrieved him Deborah waited for the meting out of some long-overdue punishment, but none had come. The boy had gone off to his bed without a word spoken; Benjamin and Deborah had gone off to their bed, and Benjamin still said nothing, until Deborah could no longer keep hold of it.

"What do you plan to do, give him another horse in reward for it?"

"It was mortifying for the lad, being hauled off the ship. He's been through enough."

"And we haven't? You would excuse him going away like that with no thought for us?"

"I'll speak to him."

"And I'll wait for it."

But the next morning it was Deborah, of course, who ended up railing at William as he sat spooning her porridge into a mouth that managed to look disdainful even as it opened eagerly enough to swallow it.

"I wonder if you have the least idea what worry you've caused us," she began. "I wonder what your plan was. Were you to disappear without a trace? What were we to think happened to you?"

William set down his spoon and stood. "I don't know, Debby, but I'm quite sure you'd have thought neither long nor hard on it."

So Deborah had answered: "Do what you will then, and see what I care of it! See what I ever cared of it!"

WILLIAM NEVER SLEPT UNDER his father's roof again, going from the army to the residence of Joseph Galloway, Benjamin's lawyer friend, and Deborah was glad of it, a thing she could admit only in the silence of her own mind. Benjamin, on the other hand, couldn't seem to reconcile himself to the boy's absence. Here he had his little daughter, so amiable, so bright, so lively, already so helpful around the house, and all Benjamin could think about was how to lure William back into it.

The answer proved to be electricity. The pair closed themselves inside Benjamin's study, and whatever it was they did, Deborah's part in it was only to keep Sally out of it. After a time lightning entered the mess; Benjamin configured a system of wires that resulted in the ring of a bell when an "electrical event," as he called it, passed overhead, and after six months Deborah had had enough of those bells to last her life. She might be crossing the room with a mug of cider and the bell would ring and startle her so, she'd slosh the drink onto her skirt; she might get Sally to sleep at last and the bell would wake the child; *Deborah* might be drifting to sleep and the bell would jolt her awake so violently she was lucky if she could sleep again the whole night.

Glass tubes began to appear. Glass jars. Boxes of glass jars. Benjamin was particularly proud of that box, calling it his "battery," after the military term.

"But what does it do?" Deborah asked.

"It captures and stores electricity."

"For what purpose?"

But Benjamin had already moved on to a peculiar wooden frame with a wheel and more glass jars. "And this is my electrical motor."

Deborah tried again. "Do you see in this some kind of employment for William?" This was the latest subject of discord between them, for on William's return from his enlistment he hadn't been returned to the print shop, or, in fact, to anything, except reading— *reading*—at Mr. Galloway's.

"He studies law," Benjamin explained, which was fresh news for Deborah, but there Benjamin hastened away from the conversation *and* the house in search, he said, of a turkey.

The turkey was electrocuted. So was Benjamin, but he appeared to sustain no permanent damage, although the turkey was killed instantly. "'Twas quite a jolt, I must tell you," Benjamin offered afterward, to all appearances quite pleased with both the purposeful and accidental halves of the experiment.

"I might have wrung the turkey's neck for you and saved you both the pain," Deborah said, after which Benjamin looked at her as he'd begun to look at her more often of late, as if she were no older than Sally.

Electricity brought other changes—a houseful of friends and strangers who ate Deborah's food and then left her alone in the kitchen with Sally, while they returned to the study and the latest experiment. A great deal of mail began to travel back and forth to London—letters and packages—but now, if Deborah inquired about any of it, she received a single-word answer: "Electricity." Benjamin no longer attempted any explanation whatever. He did manage to find time to lobby for a free school and a hospital and to get himself elected to a seat in the Pennsylvania Assembly. He also perfected a new kind of lantern for lighting the streets of Philadelphia and wrote a piece for the *Gazette* that got talked of all through town and brought more strangers calling: If England planned to continue to export their convicts to the American colonies, it was time for the colonies to export their rattlesnakes to England. Deborah assumed that pieces like that made her husband no friends across the ocean, but the opposite appeared to be true. Benjamin and William erupted into great excitement when word arrived that some of his electrical experiments had been published in an important scientific journal in London, but Deborah couldn't see the benefit of such distant fame. They lived in *Philadelphia*.

Flying away: not just Deborah's life, but Benjamin himself, leaving her behind to chase after him as she could, and as if to make the point, Deborah came into her kitchen one morning to find the table strewn with twine and sticks and paper and cloth.

"For kite making," Benjamin said.

Deborah hadn't witnessed the end result until it came home torn and sodden, but it wasn't the kite that drew her eye, it was her husband's face—as alight as she'd ever seen it. "We've done it, Debby," he said. "We've pulled electricity from the sky."

By now Deborah knew better than to ask *why,* but she could think it.

NEXT CAME "POINTS"—METAL RODS affixed to houses and churches and even ships, to protect them from the dangers of lightning. As he'd done with his stove, Benjamin made no effort to patent the objects, preferring the world to reap the benefit, and for a time Deborah hoped that his interest in his experiments might fade, that he would now turn to things the rest of Philadelphia found less fascinating, that she might get him back to herself, for at least the odd hour of an evening. But no. Benjamin was made deputy postmaster general over all America, and that set him on fire just as much as had electricity. He increased routes, put up mile markers, added nighttime riders, set up a common system of rates throughout the colonies. Indeed, the post office Deborah could and did understand, and she could and did see the immediate worth of all of these innovations, but of course Benjamin saw something else as well.

"I've long wished we might bring these disparate colonies into one cohesive unit," he said, not to Deborah, but to William. "The post office is our opportunity to do so. With communication opened up amongst the colonies we might form a general council, with members from each colony elected by popular vote, with a president to preside over all."

But this time it was William who asked, "To what purpose?"

"To manage all our common concerns—Indian treaties, trade laws, taxes."

"Is that not the job of Parliament?"

"Parliament's grown too distant. They've lost touch with our concerns here, allowed us no voice there. Just look at their utter disregard for our commerce in their system of taxes. 'Tis a right long acknowledged by all Englishmen that they be taxed only by their own consent, given through their own representatives."

William answered with a thick silence, but even William's silence could steal more of Benjamin's attention than Deborah or Sally could ever borrow with their words.

36

Philadelphia, 1757

WILLIAM'S LIFE WAS COMING along satisfactorily. At Joseph Galloway's he learned there were other intelligent men in Philadelphia who
didn't live as his father did, running in dashes and spurts after this idea
or that, catapulting from invention to invention and scheme to scheme,
men who would allow William to settle into a steady course of his
own thought. William read the law and the more he read the more he
liked; he found himself back in the company of his old friends from
the academy instead of the tradesmen's sons of his father's set, and he
again began to copy his friends in their dress and talk. But his charm
he'd learned at home, and he soon found that both men not his father
and women not his mother found him an agreeable companion, an
excellent partner for sharing a bottle of Madeira or a fancy-dress
dance; he became a member of that social circle his father had managed to only just brush up against. That most of the members of that
circle were pacifist Quakers and his father's political enemies didn't
greatly trouble William's sleep.

Yet William's favorite times remained those that he spent with his father. No discovery in *Blackstone's Commentaries* could match up to the day he tracked the path of lightning in a burned-out house and reported to his father that it traveled from metal to metal, not straight to earth. No dance with Philadelphia's most sought-after belle equaled that dash across the soaking field clinging to the string of his father's electrified kite, while his father hunkered down, safe and dry inside the barn door, and watched. No evening spent amongst Philadelphia's most influential Quakers topped a quiet hour in his father's study, hearing the latest news from the floor of the assembly even before it appeared in the press.

And yet, as smooth as William's path appeared, there was a single stone in the road that he could not seem to miss no matter how often he feinted left or right, no matter how hard he tried to distract himself with dewy, giggling young ladies or rich wine and exotic, imported fruits.

William Franklin wanted—needed—to know who his mother was.

Most of what William knew he learned by—literally—listening behind closed doors. He was at his father's house assisting with a demonstration of his father's electrical battery; his father had sent him below to the print shop to gather up some treatise he wished to show off, and as William was about to exit the shop he heard two of his father's guests, either just arrived or just leaving, talking privately on the stairs.

"What's said nowadays of that lad's mother?" the one gentleman asked.

William froze where he stood in the dark shop, on the other side of the partially closed door, his ears canted backward.

"'Tis said she's the agreeable sort," a second voice answered.

"No doubt." The pair laughed. The first voice kept on. "No one he could have taken public notice of, I take it?"

"I'd say not. But some provision was made for the creature, as I understand it."

"The young man's a lucky devil. Most would have left him to rot."

"But the brass! To drop his ill-gotten gains in his wife's lap, and then look you in the eye, daring you to say the first word about it!"

"And no one does."

"Well, not to his face."

The two men laughed again. The first voice took it up at a new spot. "But this so-called *wife*."

"Yes. I suppose 'tis there Franklin's paid for his sins."

More laughter, followed by a more somber note. "You know I've heard it said she's his real mother after all, the brat got too soon and so denied till after they were wed."

"But why not claim him now and put an end to all the talk? No, I don't give that much credence."

"Nor I. A common street whore she was."

"I've heard 'twas a kitchen maid, the deed done right under the wife's nose, and the maid continued to work in the house!"

"Or perhaps 'twas the governor's wife."

They laughed again, moving on to another rumor about the governor's wife and the new customs officer.

WHICH WAS THE TRUTH? No matter the nights William fretted his sheets while he pondered, no matter the legal concepts lost as his mind wandered away to consider this other case, he could never resolve himself to any of those overheard hypotheses. If his mother was a common street whore, why was his father so convinced of his paternity that he would take the infant to raise as his? And why would his *stepmother* agree to take in such a child? Likewise, if William's mother was a servant who delivered a bastard child that his father then claimed as his, knowing his stepmother as he did, neither servant nor child would have remained many days in his stepmother's house. And Deborah Franklin William's natural mother? If so, then William knew nothing of a natural mother's love. Which of course, as William considered it now, he did not.

SUCH WAS THE STATE of William's existence until one night in the spring of 1757 when William's father appeared at Joseph Galloway's door with an extraordinary offer that catapulted William into what he would ever after consider his real life.

37

BENJAMIN CAME HOME EVEN later than usual from the assembly, his features pasted over with that particular calmness that always meant there was a great wave roiling underneath. Deborah set down his favorite supper—cold beef, bread, and pickles—and filled his mug with his favorite milk punch. He ate for a moment or two, set down his fork, and held out his hand. Deborah came around the table and allowed herself to be drawn into the seat next to him. "I've news, Debby. Important news. Delightful news. I've been asked to represent the Pennsylvania Assembly as their agent to the Crown. We leave for London next month."

Deborah said nothing. First she needed to make sure she wasn't deep in one of her old nightmares; next she needed to make sure that Benjamin did indeed mean to include *Deborah* when he said the word *we*. He so seldom did these days.

"You wish me to accompany you to London?"

"Of course I do. What should I be without my Debby?"

"How long should we be gone?"

"Three months. Perhaps six. As long as it takes to get the job done. William will enter the Inns of Court to formally take up the study of law, so he will of course stay on after we depart."

Of course. Of course William would come along. "And what of Sally?"

"What of Sally! Why, she's almost a woman already; what polish London will give her! What shine!"

Polish. Shine. Two things Deborah was long past hope of claiming.

Benjamin continued to speak. "I promise you, Debby, you'll find London fascinating. The shops will amaze you. And the people! The variety is endless."

Benjamin went on about this scientist, this author, this publisher, all of whom had been his correspondents for some time, until Deborah began to see the picture, but not the one Benjamin wished her to see: Deborah in some rented rooms with none of her own furnishings about her, with even Sally pushed out into the London social whirl, Deborah expected to either keep up or stay behind.

Yet none of this Deborah could say. "You know my dislike of traveling over the water."

"Which would vanish entirely should you let me teach you to swim. But let me assure you, these ships are safe as houses nowadays—there's not been a soul lost between Philadelphia and London."

But there had been souls lost between Boston and London and New York and London; this Deborah knew because she'd read of them in her husband's paper, and that he would give her such a quibbling kind of answer took away that argument and his next together. But what choice had she? She felt like a horse pulled behind a cart, futilely attempting to dig its hooves into the earth to slow its forward progress.

DEBORAH MADE EVERY EFFORT to ignore the subject of London, but by the next week Benjamin had begun to scold her about the need to begin her packing. He'd commissioned a new suit of clothes for himself already, and three new shirts, and new shoes, and a half-dozen pairs of stockings. Deborah began to sort through her most fashionable things and layer them into her trunk, her spirits sinking lower as the level in her trunk rose higher. She did not want to go to London. She was tired of trying to keep up. Indeed, she was more tired of keeping up than she was afraid of staying behind.

Staying behind. The words came at Deborah with enough weight to cause her to sit down on the bed amongst her unsorted clothing. She was *not* a horse. There was no rope tying her to Benjamin's cart. Why *not* stay behind? A mere three months it was, and she'd been without Benjamin that long a number of times: when he'd gone off to the frontier on his famed military expedition, when he'd ridden his postal routes, when he'd gone to visit his sister in Boston. She sat utterly still, thinking it out from both sides and top to bottom and around again until she was quite sure of her mind. This one thing she *could* choose. Or could she?

Deborah considered. Benjamin couldn't physically carry her aboard, but he could cut off her keep if she stayed behind, although it would result in a public scandal that he would surely wish to avoid. What more clever means of persuasion might be brought to bear on her she couldn't guess at, but to give him—and her—a clear sense of her determination, she reached into the trunk and piece by piece began to return every already packed item to its original place.

Benjamin came in. He found Deborah unfolding her favorite quilted petticoat and shaking it out. "Ah! My old friend! Yes, yes, yes, you must be sure to take that along—'tis quite damp in London. Are you near finished with your packing? You amaze me. And here I've just received word that we're delayed a week. We leave a fortnight Monday."

"Then 'tis just as well I didn't start your washing."

"True." But there Benjamin happened to peer into Deborah's

trunk and saw bottom. He lifted his eyes. "Now here, you don't seem so far along after all. Was it not half full this morning?"

There had been a number of times in Deborah's life when Benjamin had something important to say to her—*The governor wants to send me to London . . . There's a child . . . Are you my wife yet*—and before each of those times he'd taken up her hand first, as if to signal the import of the words before he spoke them. Deborah now took this lesson from Benjamin and turned it back on him; she sat down on the bed, reached up and took her husband's hand, drawing him down beside her, but there all subtlety failed her.

"I don't want to go to London," she said. "I've considered long and just now decided. 'Tis best Sally and I stay here in Philadelphia."

A line that usually indicated a mild disturbance—or annoyance—creased Benjamin's brow. "Come now, Debby. We've little time for this; there's much to be done."

"Yes, there is much to be done. This is how I've thought of it too. Best you go and take care of your business at London while I stay here and take care of your business at home. Manage your accounts, collect your rents, look after the post office."

"I've arranged with David Hall to manage my affairs."

"Mr. Hall has enough to do with the shop and the press. 'Tis the thing I'm best at. Leave it to me."

Benjamin folded his other hand over hers; Deborah looked down and couldn't see her fingers at all. "Debby. My dear child. Of course you must come. What shall I do in London without you?"

"Just what you should do with me. And don't forget you'll have William."

Did he detect the jibe? No.

"William is not my wife. And you must think of Sally."

"How do I not think of Sally? She'll be all that's left to me. Sally can't sail."

"I know you have fear of this crossing but only because this is an unknown thing to you; here's the beauty of an unknown thing—it becomes a known thing with such ease! You only step aboard the ship and there—'tis known."

"No, Benjamin. I should be put to better use here."

"Nonsense! You'll be put to better use by my side."

"'Tis only three months."

"I can't promise three. I told you. Perhaps six."

"Three or six. 'Tis no great stretch when looked at amongst the whole. What of those printers you set up in Carolina and New York? And your tenants on Market Street? To leave them to strangers—"

"Better than leaving me to strangers."

"They won't stay strange long. Not to you. To me they should stay strange forever."

Benjamin leaned in to peer more closely at her—at fifty years of age he'd begun to wear glasses for close work and to complain of the lack of clarity in the images afar. Deborah sat in the space between the two problems, a third problem, but a problem for him, not her; she could not go on being pulled after Benjamin anymore. He was clever enough to see the truth in what she'd just said, and she watched him see it, consider it, shift things around inside his mind; when he began to speak again, the tone of the conversation had changed. He talked of the pain of parting and the debilitating effects of loneliness and the great drag of time he must now live through till he was again by her side. In other words, he'd heard and seen the truth of it and he'd accepted it; he would depart for London without her.

38

PHILADELPHIA HAD CHANGED. EVERYWHERE Anne looked there seemed to be another new industry or shop of some kind—a rum distillery, a steel furnace, a glassworks, a brass button shop, a mustard and chocolate works, even an Italian sausage maker. The streets were lit and paved. The Godfreys, Shippens, Hamiltons, Norrises, and Logans had all built new mansions with sixty-foot frontage and foreign columns and—or so Anne had heard—fancy papering glued to the walls. The Quakers who'd once controlled the town were down to a quarter of the population, the Anglican Christ Church had a new, majestic steeple; the Presbyterians, Lutherans, Moravians—even the Catholics who had never till now been permitted public worship—all had churches or chapels of their own.

Other changes: Isaac Wilkes had died, crushed by an overturned cart. Allgood, and no doubt Robert, had been lost at sea. Two corders and a shipwright had been brought down by the yellow fever, some said come from the filthy water in the Dock Creek. And yet when

Anne passed Benjamin Franklin now and again she saw that past fifty he remained as fit and strong as ever, wigged now and more fashionably dressed, an important man in Philadelphia. Whenever he appeared at the distance in the street she felt the queer pull of the man; they couldn't be separated by more things—background, education, wife, past adversity—and yet the things that tied her to him were so strong. Franklin was the first man to seek her, to open her, to change her life course for good or ill; he taught her things she could have learned from no other and he could, she knew, teach her more. She could make music from a glass, she understood the travels of heated air, she could swim; but she didn't understand what this new thing called electricity was, or why sparks were being collected inside jars, or how a metal rod could keep a house safe from fire. She wanted to understand. She wanted to *know*.

And then there was the thing that connected them forever and above all: William. The hungry boy had drained her breasts and her heart and now the hunger was all hers—she'd watched, listened, even prowled, and discovered her boy—*her boy*—growing only handsomer and smarter and more polished every day, meshing seamlessly with the highest social circles. This new air, this study of law he'd undertaken, the shimmering young beauties he took about all seemed to suit him; a good deal of the old sourness had left his features now. Anne still saw nothing in William's face that told her he remembered her, but she could also tell herself that was just as well; she gleaned what news she could and took a silly pride in her son's success. It was enough. For now.

Solomon Grissom had fared well for a time, fathering seven children all told, but his wife, Sophie, had not recovered well from the last. Grissom had brought his son Elisha into the shop to work at an early age, and when Peter moved on to his own shop, Grissom allowed his boy, now sixteen, to take on much of the management role, setting Anne back into her place along with the other new seamstress, Grace, who'd been brought on to meet the increased demand. The change did not sit well. Anne could ignore Elisha's apparently forgetting every toy or piece of candy Anne had ever bestowed, but she couldn't ignore his increasingly sharp tongue when Anne resisted his urgings for speed over quality. Grissom, preoccupied with his wife's health, made only brief appearances in the shop, and when he did appear he didn't seem able to concentrate his mind; customers began to complain and fall off, but if Grissom even noticed, Anne couldn't tell.

Anne had passed forty but had been lucky enough in it, her hair silvering but her health good, her back straight, her teeth sound. She told herself it little mattered what happened to the shop as long as her work continued as it was, but already her long hours had begun to fall off, and she was able to leave the shop well before sunset. Oddly, the shorter the days became the longer they felt, the more restless her spirit grew; since her enforced swim she'd spurned the river, but now she found herself taking long walks along it at the end of each day, moving northward to the sand spit where Franklin had once taken her. At first she only looked and moved on, but one early summer day she found herself shedding her clothes and swimming, drying stretched out in the sun. One day, however, she found her walk taking a turn in another direction, until one turn and another brought her to Eades Alley and her old door.

The alley looked the same, smelled the same; the door looked the same. Anne leaned forward and laid her palm against the splintered wood, curious to discover how uneasy she felt as she touched it, as if her connections to this one unchanged place hadn't been severed as irreversibly as she'd imagined. She left the alley and found herself following the old route to the Penny Pot; she stood at the corner and watched the Pot traffic, about to move on when John Hewe stepped out the door.

Hewe had been one of Anne's most disappointed customers when he'd discovered she'd given over her old occupation; he'd come back three times before she'd finally convinced him *no* meant *no*. She heard he'd lost his wife in the yellow fever epidemic, which no doubt accounted in part for him looking at her now with something of the old hope resurrected, but she could little account for the pleasure she took in seeing him.

"Here now!" he cried. "Will you see what I see! Have you come to visit me? Perhaps to tell me you've fallen back on old habits?"

Anne couldn't help but smile. "I'm afraid no." And yet she stood there looking at the hungry John Hewe, feeling something of the old days stirring her. She'd honored her promise to Grissom, understanding better and better with the passing of the years just what he'd done for her, and not just as a debt owed Franklin—he'd faced down Franklin, after all. John Hewe, though, could be no violation of Grissom's rule about taking men into her room above the shop; this was something from before the rule, something of the old Penny Pot way of doing that had never involved Grissom at all. And standing in front of the tavern as she was, the older memories began to blank out the ship ones—she could recall the satisfaction of the dance, the game, a game for which she made the rules. But no. "I'm sorry to say—"

"Oh, bosh! You're sorry, I'm sorry, we're all sorry. Come have a bite with me." He lifted both hands in the air to stop her next refusal. "I won't pester you anymore about the other. All I'm after is to sit across from you for an hour and remember finer times. Come, eat. A piece of whortleberry pie and my finest wine and a chance to make a lonely old man happy. What's to argue there?"

Anne couldn't help but laugh at the idea of a lonely tavern keeper, but even as she laughed she realized as she stood there in the street that *she* was lonely, that she'd always liked John Hewe. And she'd always liked whortleberry pie. She followed Hewe inside.

"TEN SHILLINGS."

"Ten shillings! Cheaper to marry you! Come now."

Anne pushed back the chair from the private table John Hewe had set up in his private room. The wine had turned the room soft and warm and the bed hangings that framed the bed in the corner—hangings she'd made herself in Grissom's shop—took on the look of old friends. John Hewe took on the look of an old friend. That didn't mean that business wasn't business, and Anne had heard the fancy whores in the London shop windows charged a guinea for a lie down. Perhaps she wasn't so fancy and she wasn't in London, but she knew her trade with the best of them.

"Ten shillings," she repeated.

"Gah!" But even as Hewe roared he fished a ten-shilling note out of his pocket, dashed around the table, and grabbed Anne in a fierce embrace.

"Hold now," Anne said. "Let me show you the full ten's worth."

Hewe eased back, gave himself over to Anne, and let her lead him as she liked, help him through his old man's problems, bring him to his desired end. Afterward, as Anne got up from the bed and began to reconstruct her attire, Hewe spoke from behind her.

"'Tisn't so bad an idea, you know."

"What isn't?"

"Us marrying."

Anne laughed.

"'Tis no joke! I mean what I say! Marry me, Anne! Why not? I'll keep you fed and clothed and warm and you'll keep me from dying alone. Either the work or the yellow fever will kill me soon enough, and I'd rather you kill me. Come here, feel what you've done to my heart." He caught up Anne's hand, pulled her back to the bed, pressed her palm against his sinewy, hairless chest; his heart beat like a pigeon's just before its neck was wrung.

"Marry me, Anne."

Anne shook her head, kissed Hewe's temple, teased his ear with her tongue, and left, but as she walked back to the shop she thought of that frantically beating heart and the chance that perhaps she'd seen the last of John Hewe alive; the unexpected gloom that followed the thought made her step heavy on the stairs. Or was it simply that Anne was now getting old? She'd always thought her former way of life was there to catch her if she needed it, but as Franklin had once said to her, *You can't enchant us all forever, you know.* Could that explain this suddenly acquired affection for John Hewe? Could she settle herself into a couple of rooms above a tavern with a man? No, Anne decided; she'd left it too long.

SOME WEEKS LATER ANOTHER late-night knock sounded on her door.

"Are you alone?" the familiar voice inquired.

Ironically, Anne was sitting reading *Pamela,* the first novel published in America—by Franklin, of course—and finding nothing in the woman's stupid virtue to remind her of herself; she had, indeed, been feeling herself quite alone. She opened the door. Franklin came in and took up both her hands; he kissed the back of each and then kept hold of them, but only because Anne let him keep hold.

"I come in the heartfelt hope that I find you well."

"You do."

Franklin nodded. "As I see." He reached out and lifted a stray lock of hair from her cheek. "How is it, I wonder, that this silver only adds more spark to your flame?"

Anne pulled back, freeing herself of both his hands. "We all like silver."

Franklin laughed. "Anne. My dear Anne. Quite the same, I see. May I sit or do you prefer me to be gone?"

"It depends why you've come."

Franklin studied her, seemed to decide some degree of talk must come before the chair, settled his heels a little farther apart and began. "I'm to go to London in a month's time. I act as assembly agent to the

Crown, bearing a petition for a more reasonable arrangement with our colony's proprietors in regard to taxes. They own vast holdings in this colony and yet they pay no tax toward its maintenance or defense. Would you call that fair?"

"No."

Franklin nodded, pleased. "Would you call it fair that my wife refuses to come with me?"

"On what ground?"

"She dislikes the idea of traveling over water."

"And?"

"And nothing as you might like to imagine it. I've been naught but true and kind to her since . . ." He let the sentence trail. "She says London should feel too strange to her."

"Yes, I imagine it would, to her."

Franklin studied her. "Would it to you?"

"Philadelphia already feels strange to me."

"So London would be no great shock, then."

Anne peered at him.

"Will you come to London with me, Anne?"

Anne was so surprised she sat down; Franklin seemed to take it as an invitation and sat too.

"So you're in need of a bed warmer now your wife won't come."

"You may say."

"And how long do you expect to be gone?"

Franklin looked down at his shoes, leaned over, picked a piece of straw off a toe. He straightened. "Six months. Perhaps a year."

"Or more?"

He studied Anne. "Mebbe so."

"And if your wife changes her mind and decides to travel with you?"

"Then my invitation to you would be withdrawn. Understand the nature of my offer, Anne. As I told you once before, I'm a monogamous creature, not a celibate one. If Deborah stays behind, as I'm quite sure she will, I'll pay your passage to London and keep you in food, clothes, and rent, in exchange for the usual favors. This arrangement isn't entirely foreign to you."

Yes and no. But that wasn't the necessary question. The necessary question was, yes *or* no?

Once again, Franklin appeared to read the words as she thought them. "Before you answer yes or no, allow me to add one more argument—William comes along to take up a place at the Inns of Court." He leaned forward, took up Anne's hands again, and began to guide her onto his lap in the Franklin way of old, even as he did so appearing to allow her to decide where to sit on her own, but Anne had copied the trick too many times to be fooled now. Still, she allowed herself to be settled on Franklin's knees, allowed him to kiss her mouth and lift her breast, might even have allowed him to warm his hand between her thighs if he hadn't stopped of his own accord, set her back on her feet.

"In Philadelphia I'm married yet," he said. "You see how I stick to my rule. I sail from Philadelphia to the London ship at New York; best you travel to New York ahead of me, by land. I'll provide the transport; I'll arrange for the inn along the road."

"And who is William to think I am?"

"Just who you are. An old servant, met by coincidence on shipboard. Whatever else goes on between us won't trouble him. His mother and he—" Franklin stopped. "He's a fine boy, Anne. He'll go far, surpassing me in the end. You may trust that we've done right by him. All of us. In London you'll have a chance to see for yourself what he has and will become. But hold—you've not said yes or no!"

And so Anne allowed Franklin his new little game, pretending she hadn't answered the minute he'd said William's name.

39

ANNE WROTE OUT THE short, bare sentence with care: *In a month's time I leave for London with a friend.* She read the note over and found its bareness its greatest fault but could find no way to make it more. She tore the paper across and wrote on the small piece that remained: *I should like to speak with you alone.* She waited three days to find him in a quiet corner in the shop where she could slip the note into his hand.

He came that night, and she recognized even in his knock what a different man he was from Franklin; two strong raps, no more, as spare with his raps as he was with his words, but each with its own conviction. As he came in she remarked the change in him, more noticeable here in the privacy of her room than amongst the commotion of the shop: the drawn face, the coat looser on the lank frame, the eyes on her face but the attention elsewhere. She began, as she hadn't intended, at the end.

"In a month's time I leave for London."

The eyes snapped back to the room, to Anne. "Alone?"

"With a friend."

Grissom said nothing.

"A mutual friend."

"You're sure?"

What did he mean? Was she sure she would go or was she sure of the friend? But what matter his meaning? In either case, the answer was the same. "I'm sure."

"Very well." Grissom turned to leave, but Anne reached out and touched his arm to hold him. She felt the need of more words, the need to add that Grissom had more than enough girls in the shop for the work that was coming in, that he didn't need her, that it was best she go, but none of it would form up just as she wished it. She said, "May I ask how your wife fares?"

"She begs to die, that's how she fares."

"What does the doctor say of it?"

"He says her heart is strong. Over and over he says it, and she grows upset when he does, thrashing about, weeping. This last visit she refused to see him. She said to me, 'Tell him to go away and let me die.'"

Anne stood struggling for words that might be of any comfort, but finding none, decided to take her lesson from Grissom—to leave words alone. She returned her hand to his arm—a brief touch only— but it seemed to loosen him. He went on.

"She doesn't even want me near. She pushes me away. She begs to die and I beg her to live."

"But if she lives only to suffer—"

"I wish her to live as she was before! Alive and happy in my arms!"

A child's wish, thought Anne, which must have been what moved her to speak to Grissom as if he were a child. "You must gather your-self. You must get back to your shop. Elisha isn't yet ready to manage it alone. If you busy yourself—"

"Busy myself! Busy myself! Do you not think I try to work? I stretch and tack the cloth and think only what change I might find above stairs when I return. I climb the stairs and find a little less of her each time, as if I take something of her away whenever I leave her side. Elisha is not ready, you say! Busy myself, you say! As if it was so simple a thing. But you who don't allow of love, how are you to know?"

Grissom stopped. A visible effort to tamp down one line of talk and heave up another overtook him, and after a time he seemed to succeed. "I beg your pardon. You do allow of one love, and I of all men may attest to the power of it. William does well?"

"He goes to London with his father to study law."

"I see." Another pause. "And does he know of the relation—?"

"He does not."

"Perhaps, then, in London he will learn of it."

Anne could not deny that the plan had crossed her mind. Away from Philadelphia, away from Deborah, Anne would have her chance at last—or so she'd thought before—but now, hearing the idea come out of Grissom's mouth she heard its flaw: To reveal herself to her son in London, she must reveal herself in the guise of what he'd no doubt believed her to be all along—his father's whore.

A fierce urge to ask Grissom's advice over this conundrum overwhelmed Anne—surely this man of all men would understand how she longed to claim her son in some small way without disgracing him— but as she looked at Grissom again she saw that a man so tortured could be of no help to her; he could understand nothing right now but his own suffering. For perhaps the first time it was Grissom who needed Anne's help, and thinking this, understanding this, she discovered in herself a desperate wish to help Grissom in return. But what could she possibly do for such a man in such a way? She lifted a hand as if it might even be possible to wipe out some of the pain that was carving up his features, but Grissom caught her hand and pushed it away, pulled it back, pulled her back, into him, crushing her inside his arms.

"Sophie. Oh, God, my Sophie—"

Again Anne could find nothing to say, but Grissom wasn't after any of her words; she held him as he held her, murmured as he murmured, answered his mouth with her mouth, his hands with her hands, allowing herself to be Sophie for Grissom as she'd doubtless been other women for other men so many, many times before. What was different here? Nothing, she told herself; perhaps it was a different kind of want, but the answer to it was the same.

But it was the wrong answer. Anne saw it as soon as Grissom reared up over her on the bed, even as he released into her, a new traitor's anguish now painting his features in place of the old. He pushed himself away from her, recovered his breeches, folded himself into them still wet from her, and shuffled out the door, unable to even turn and look at her.

It was good that she would soon be gone, Anne realized, away from these uneasable burdens that weren't her own.

FRANKLIN SENT A NOTE via messenger.

> *Enclosed herewith please find stage and room fare for the road.*
> *I've further secured the driver's interest in your welfare—should*
> *trouble arise you need only look to Mr. Finn. At New York it will*
> *be necessary to engage a carriage at the livery next the stage stop; go*
> *direct to the White Horse Inn where a room has been arranged. I'll*
> *send word to you there when we're to sail. Godspeed.*

Anne packed her trunk and prepared to make her good-byes. Mary should have been her first visit, but Anne hadn't spoken to her sister since her betrayal, despite the fact—or perhaps because of the fact—that over the years Anne had come to think Mary right all along. Mary would like these new plans no better than the old—there could be nothing for either of them in laying down worse blood on top of bad—she'd write to Mary from abroad. She next climbed the stairs with heavy feet to bid farewell to Sophie Grissom, undoubtedly for the last time.

The woman lay in Grissom's big, soft bed, nearly buried in its folds, the terrible knowledge of her fate plainly visible in her eyes. How *did* Grissom bear looking into them day after day? Sophie peered at Anne a long time, as if unable to identify her. At length she said, "You go away," and closed her eyes, but whether she meant it as a statement of fact or an order of dismissal Anne couldn't decide; as she wished to go away anyway, she went.

The last call she made—surprising herself—was to John Hewe. He saw her coming through the door as if she were the only person in the crowded room and came after her, herding her into the quiet of the hall. "Tell me you've come—," he started, but Anne wouldn't let him finish a vain hope.

"I come to say good-bye. I travel to London soon."

Anne was surprised when his eyes filled with tears, so surprised she found herself saying a thing she'd not intended to say the minute before. "I've time to go above and say a more thorough good-bye." When Hewe seemed not to hear, she said, "A gift is what I mean."

Hewe surprised Anne even more by giving his head a violent shake. "Be off if you're to be off."

Anne left with Franklin's old words chasing after her again: *You can't enchant us all forever, you know.*

THE STAGE WAS CLOSE, dirty, smelly, and already filled with an overweight couple and a violently coughing young man. The driver who Franklin had assured her was her friend took no notice of her at all, staring ahead at the road as if it was his sole concern.

She stepped to the front of the coach and looked up at him. "Mr. Finn? I believe you've had a word—"

The man looked down at her from the seat's height, a position that might cause a look of disdain in any man, or so Anne told herself. "Finn's come into money, took himself off. Shandy's the name. Get on if you're going; we're an hour behind."

Anne considered. Resolved. What did she care for this Finn? He might have arranged to seat her beside the overweight woman instead of the coughing man, but little beside. Anne climbed in next to the coughing man, turned her face to the window, and pretended to fall asleep at once, then surprised herself by actually falling into a half doze.

It was long after dark when the stage pulled into the courtyard of a poorly lit inn; the overweight man began to joke with the cougher about who should share a bed with whom, grinning all the while at Anne. Anne pushed ahead of the three of them and entered the inn, walking straight up to the innkeeper. The bed he offered Anne was in fact but half of one, in a quarter of a room, a couple occupying one of the room's beds and an old woman occupying the other. The old woman stirred as Anne dropped her shoes and slid into the sheets. She smelled of spirits, overused linen, and another thing Anne could only describe as slightly turned ham.

"Where are you coming in from?"

"Philadelphia. And yourself?"

"Here I was born and here I am now. Thirty-four years in."

The man in the opposite bed called across, "Quiet, there!"

"Ah, stuff yours!" the woman shouted back. "If she is yours!" She cawed.

Whatever the man might have answered, his woman—if she was his—shushed him.

Anne's bedmate rolled away and began breathing in starts and stops through a congested nose. Anne closed her eyes, but this time she couldn't even come close to a doze. Thirty-four years. An "old woman" not as old as Anne, intoxicated and foul mouthed. Most likely an old whore. What was it in an old whore that forever showed?

Was there something in Anne that had prompted that lewd exchange between the men as they approached the inn, something that had convinced the innkeeper this was the bed in which she belonged? Was this woman what Anne was to become?

Anne slept beside her shadow self perhaps an hour, no more.

THE STAGE RATTLED INTO New York, a place as narrow and cluttered as Pennsylvania was wide and ordered, yet somehow more somber while at the same time sounding twice as loud. The streets turned this way and that as if commanded by the buildings and not the reverse, but Anne found the livery and the White Horse Inn, and a pleasant widow innkeeper who seemed well acquainted with Franklin and interested in taking good care of Anne. She was given a bed of her own, as clean as her own, and fresh water to wash; when she recounted her exhaustion, a plate of bread and cheese arrived at her door. Anne ate, and although it was not four o'clock, climbed between the cool sheets and slept till dawn.

FRANKLIN'S NOTE CAME THE following morning and said simply: *We're aboard. Come.* Anne read the note with damp palms. How odd, she thought, that she should remain cool all this long journey till now.

The carriage arrived to collect Anne; her trunk was loaded in and they set off for the wharf, the sunlight beating sporadically through a line of high white clouds, adding and subtracting shadows so fast Anne couldn't capture any sense of New York's tumbled-together streets and buildings. To ground herself, she moved her thoughts from where she was to where she was going: London. With her son.

The wharf was mad with carts and carriages and vendors and foot traffic; the tide must have been at the flow, for the ships rode high above the dock. The driver pulled Anne as close to the gangway as he could maneuver, leaped out, and set her trunk down. She swung around for a last word, perhaps only to delay him while she accustomed herself, but already he was back in his seat, whipping the horse ahead through the crowd. Gone.

Anne turned back to the ship, scanning its bustling deck, holding out little hope of finding either of the Franklins in such a swarm, and was surprised to find the elder almost at once, a tall, broad-shouldered man standing at the gunwale, also scanning the crowd. Did he truly tower over all the others aboard the ship or did it only seem so to Anne, as if he might reach up and pull his lightning from the sky where he stood? Once at London, how high might he reach? Standing below on the wharf, it suddenly struck Anne exactly why Deborah Franklin would have wished to stay behind.

But Benjamin Franklin was not the reason Anne stood on the wharf about to tread the gangplank. William was. And there he was, joining his father at the rail, even taller than his father now, similarly dressed in a dark suit meant for traveling but with a flare all his own—a ruffled stock at his neck instead of a plain one. Here was a man grown, ready to follow his father across the sea, but once there, his own life would be waiting for him, his reach for the heavens also unlikely to exceed his grasp. Anne could see his future before him as sharply focused as if it were hers.

But it wasn't hers; how clear it became as he stood above and she below! And as Anne stared up at the two men a curious thing happened; she heard, as clearly if he stood beside her, Solomon Grissom's words. *You're sure?* She'd begun to lift her hand to signal one of the crew to attend her trunks, but now she dropped it to her side. What was it *Anne* reached for? A London rooming house somewhere, the kind of house that would allow of gentlemen callers at stray hours, the kind of house where William would likely never go. His father would, of course, but for how long? *You can't enchant us all forever, you know.* Anne thought of the guinea-a-lie whores and how long she might carry on that kind of trade; she thought of the woman of the previous night, lying old and stinking in her bed at the inn, perhaps waiting for the chance traveler to drop her a coin. She thought of the solitary man's interest that might ward off that end, and how long she might count on that interest to hold. *Was* he a friend? Was she *sure*?

She wished to answer other. Indeed, she stood some time attempting to call up that other answer, but in the end she could give but one only.

No.

Anne turned her back to the ship, scoured the crowd for a carriage just emptying its fare, and flagged it down. The driver loaded her trunk and pulled away; Anne turned for one last look at the two tall sentinels at the rail, but from that distance she could no longer determine father from son.

40

London, 1760

WILLIAM FRANKLIN WOKE EACH morning asking himself the same thing: Is it a dream? London! If he only ignored the strangling smoke from the coal fires, the beggars, the heaping manure piles that ringed the town, there was nothing of it he didn't adore. The ancient architecture; the shops full of everything from the finest lace to pistols and swords; the coffeehouses in which he and his father could instantly strike up scintillating conversations with erudite, educated men; the fine English homes whose doors were eagerly opened for this American Benjamin Franklin, already more famous abroad than he was at home.

And then there was the Inns of Court, the most renowned legal institution on earth, where William could walk across six-century-old courtyards, dine under Van Dyck and Titian portraits of kings and queens in the same hall where Raleigh and Bacon had dined, then retire to his comfortable rooms and read in *Blackstone's Commentaries,* "The King can do no wrong . . . The King is and ought to be absolute . . . all-perfect and immortal," and know that he walked over the same ground as this immortal king. Oh, what didn't William owe his father now?

It was true that the Franklins' rooms were on the cramped side, that the landlady fluttered about them too much, that she had a prim little daughter William's father had already begun to push his son's way. Polly Stevenson was, to all appearances, unencumbered with a single asset beyond her obvious admiration for the elder Franklin, and William had other ideas in mind. He'd seen the whores on the street corners and in the sex shops; there were also any number of women who appeared to be nothing more nor less than willing, and clearly Polly Stevenson was not, or at least not in the manner William had in mind.

IT DIDN'T TAKE WILLIAM long to find someone who was. He first saw her in one of those dusty London coffeehouses that was tucked up in the back of nowhere; she sat with a number of men and it was clear from the look of her that at least one of those men had expectations that might likely be met before the night was done. William might have moved on at the first words out of her mouth, but the mouth was so plump and it had just been wet by some dusky Madeira; then she leaned down to straighten her shoe buckle and gave William an extended view of as fine a bosom as he'd seen in the entire decade since he'd begun to notice such things. William sat down at the table and struck up the kind of easy conversation he'd first learned on his father's lap. It soon became clear to the others at the table that they were outmatched; they drifted away, and William purchased his new acquaintance another bottle of wine, accompanied by a barely edible roast duck. When he discovered she lived in a room above the coffeehouse, he offered to make up for the poor meal with another bottle of claret and an escort upstairs to her room—there were few men alive who wouldn't at least have chanced it—and he was unsurprised when she accepted.

HER NAME WAS MAUDE. The coffeehouse belonged to her brother-in-law, who in exchange for her help in the kitchen allowed her the use of one of his rooms. The room was as expected—passably clean, cheaply adorned—but Maude was both more and less than anything William had anticipated. The utter lack of inhibition, the way she melted open almost as soon as she was touched, this was thrilling and flattering to any man, but he was taken aback by her utter passivity after the thing was done. She didn't seem to know how to get from *undressed* to *dressed*. She didn't seem to care if he stayed or left. She didn't seem to understand that another girl might ask for something in exchange for the service provided—at the very least, a promise to return.

Nevertheless, William did return. He called again and again over the next two months, expecting but never encountering any of the other men he'd seen sitting with her at the coffeehouse. The best thing about Maude was that she never seemed to want anything more from William than he wanted from her, and so they went along, until William met Elizabeth Downes.

HE FIRST SAW THE lively flash of her green eyes over the sea of heads at one of those London parties to which William had early been inducted by his fellow classmates. The green eyes locked with his but didn't dwell; they came back, drew off. It was hopeful, but it wasn't enough. William cast about for something better in the way of introduction, and as he did so he happened to look down and spy a green velvet hair ribbon, either discarded or lost, lying on the floor. He picked it up and worked his way through the young men stacked up around Elizabeth Downes like termites, waiting for a gleam from her eye, a touch of her hand, a closer view of her lovely neck.

"I believe you've lost this."

The girl lifted a graceful arm to her hair and touched the black satin ribbon wound into it; she touched her neck, where an enormous emerald hung from another satin ribbon, also black. "'Tis not mine," she said. "You must try another."

William gripped one of the silver buttons on his new silk waistcoat, gave it a vicious twist, and held it out, not smiling. "I believe you've lost this."

Elizabeth Downes laughed. But no, that wasn't the way to say it: She tipped back her head, closed her eyes, and began to bubble up with a melody so full of life that William believed he might survive a month on the sound of it. But William would admit—no honest man wouldn't—that when the green eyes were disguised under those richly fringed lids, his own eye went next to the green emerald at her throat, calculating the weight of it.

Elizabeth opened her eyes and held out her hand for the button. "Forfeit."

William handed over the button. "Now you must offer me a chance to redeem it."

She pondered him, as somber now as she'd just been light—clearly a woman of intensity in all things, an intensity that William determined to get to know.

"Thursday next," she said at last. "Six o'clock. My father's house."

ELIZABETH'S FATHER PROVED TO be a wealthy Barbados sugar planter, which explained, in part, the golden luster of Elizabeth's skin, the air of expectation that all things—and all men—would come to her simply on her command. When William appeared at the Downes mansion he was duly impressed—beginning with the gatekeeper's cottage, the gates, the glistening stone drive, then the mansion itself rising up and up and up into a sky that seemed to bend low in deference to meet it. The massive oak doors themselves were bigger than his father's shop front, the hall bigger than his father's house, the servants in better clothes than William had seen most days on his father's wife.

Mr. Downes had many questions for William, mostly about his father and his now-famous experiments, but he asked enough about William to allow him to shine; William could, in fact, recount some of his father's most interesting experiments firsthand, having assisted in their execution, but neither was he shy about speaking of his own prospects. Once he completed his studies at the bar he intended to seek out a political appointment; indeed, as William announced this, Elizabeth's father nodded as if he might have had a similar idea in mind.

That night at the Downes mansion led to other days and nights filled with music, literature, dancing, cribbage; walks in St. James's Park along broad gravel paths that ran beside glistening canals lined with geese, ducks, deer. Soon those walks began to involve the kinds of kisses that hinted at a promising future ahead; William rode off on fire at the thought of that future with Elizabeth, straight into Maude's present, to have that fire put out. William told himself he would never have contemplated such a double life if he'd possessed more confidence that a bastard son of an American printer could actually ever secure a woman like Elizabeth, or if Maude had been anything else but Maude.

BUT EVENTUALLY TWO THINGS together caused William to end his double life: his sense of a growing seriousness in Elizabeth, coupled with a growing seriousness in Maude. Elizabeth began to start more and more sentences referring to the future with the word *we.* She spoke often of her father's belief that William would go far. Maude, on the other hand, took to lying next to William with her head propped in her hand, studying his face. She began to drop into awkward silences if William mentioned going out to another coffeehouse or tavern or party, as if she actually expected to be invited along. William had already been calling on Elizabeth more and Maude less, and now he simply stopped calling on Maude at all.

One day some weeks after William had stopped calling on Maude, he spied another kind of low woman, "the street whore" his father's compatriots had once decided might have spawned him, and he thought of Maude. Conventional sensibility might rank Maude a cut above the street woman, but William found himself thinking of the street woman with greater respect; at least she demanded something for her time. Thinking so, a wave of compunction overtook William. He stopped at the goldsmith's, selected a brooch that he could hardly afford on his father's strict allowance, and sent it around with a note that said, *For Maude. A remembrance.* He'd poised his pen to add his name but thought better of it—if she knew who it was from it would mean what it was meant to mean—if she didn't it would work just as well in easing William's conscience.

COMING HOME ONE NIGHT, several months after he'd stopped calling on her, William found Maude lurking outside his landlady's door. For a moment he didn't recognize her; the plump lips had been absorbed inside a bloated face, the eyes were hooded, the hair and bosom wrapped tight in an unbecoming brown shawl.

"What the devil! Maude!"

She collapsed into bawdy, convulsive tears. He swept her out of sight into the shrubbery, stroking her shoulders while holding her away from him at the same time. "What's the trouble, Maudie?"

In almost the same instant her tears dried and her eyes flashed at him in fury. "What's the *trouble*? Can you not guess? You come and come and then you don't and now here I am! Here I *am*!"

"Yes, yes, I see that. I should have explained myself perhaps, but I hadn't taken you for the sort of girl that might wonder about a fellow in that way. I see now how unkind it was and I apologize. I should have explained."

"Explained *what*?"

William was still holding Maude by the shoulders, but more for defensive reasons than anything else; the steel in her arms—and, indeed, in her eye—surprised him. It was past time for half measures. Swift and sure and out. He gripped a little harder to ward off any possible blows. "The fact of it is, Maudie, I've met someone else, someone I plan to marry. You know we neither of us took our arrangement as a serious thing—"

Somehow Maude pulled free of him and took a step back. For a minute she appeared to have lost her footing, and William expected to see her next on the ground, in a swamp of more tears, but instead she simply restacked her spine and drew herself up. "Well, Billy," she said, "'tis a serious thing now. We've got a child coming on."

WILLIAM FOUND HIS FATHER, as he so often found him these days, in his sitting room poring over a book with his landlady's daughter, Polly, his landlady hovering near to refill his teacup whenever desired. His father sat barefooted, his wig absent, one hand circling his cup, the other tossed easily across the back of Polly's chair. He looked . . . at home, William thought. As if this were his family now. Polly raised her head, saw William, and did something with her face that made it appear even more unfortunate. She blushed. Despite William's best efforts at ignoring the girl, he'd for some time now suspected that she shared the elder Franklin's dreams of an attachment with him, which only made William's current predicament all the more awkward.

"Billy!" William's father cried. "Come look what this nimble-minded young lady has discovered in Rousseau."

The girl looked at William's father and smiled, all that was wrong with her face almost righting itself.

"Father," William said. "May I have a word?"

Give the nimble mind its due—the girl was up, collecting her mother and herding her from the room before either Franklin was required to ask her to do so.

"What, son? 'Tisn't ill news from home?"

"Nothing of the sort. 'Tis trouble here. I come to you because—" William hesitated.

"You come to me because 'tis where you should come. Out now, what is it?"

"A child. Due in six months' time."

William's father studied him, as William studied his father. What did each read of history on the other's face?

"'Tis yours, then?"

For a time, it was true, William had eagerly considered that point, casting back over his many unscheduled visits to Maude's room, searching his memory unsuccessfully for the odd pipe lying around, the echo of fast-disappearing footsteps on the stair, even launching a delicate question here and there. But Maude's answers had been so adamant, so *consistent,* that William had been forced to admit the lack of evidence against anyone but himself.

"I believe 'tis mine."

"What sort of woman?"

"A . . . an agreeable sort." Oh, how those overheard words continued to haunt him!

"The wife sort?"

William took a deep breath. "There's talk of a political appointment. Were I to marry this woman, it would limit my prospects considerably. Besides—" Should he add here that he had another in mind?

He'd yet to mention Elizabeth Downes to his father, but he hesitated. Bringing Elizabeth into the conversation at that particular point somehow seemed the greater crime.

But his father seemed to understand the dilemma as it stood. After all, weren't William's dreams for his future his father's dreams for him too? "Very well," he said at length. "Tell me the woman's name and where she keeps herself."

"Why?"

"Why! What the devil do you mean, *why*? Because you've come here, as I assume, for my help. The child must be taken care of, and as you've little means of your own, I'm willing to take on whatever expense is required until you're able to assume such responsibility. Now the first decision that must be made is whether the child would be better served removed from the situation it will fall into at birth; if so, a fostering family must be found. As to the woman, if she keeps the child, or even if she doesn't, it would be best to leave her better off than worse off, wouldn't you say? Depending on her circumstance she might be satisfied in coin—" His eyes dropped to the floor. "Or she might be positioned to earn her own way."

William stared at his father; when else in William's life had his father failed to meet his eye head on? "Is that what you did with my mother?"

The elder Franklin's head came up. He looked at William as blandly as if he'd just been asked if he'd scraped his boots before he came into the room. "The irony of this situation has not escaped me."

A BOY WAS BORN. The results were much as William anticipated: Maude had no means—or apparent wish—to keep the child; she would give it over—and keep quiet about its parentage—in exchange for a loan to set up in a milliner's shop, which William's father was able to arrange. In fact, William's father arranged it all, as anxious as

William to keep his name clear; how odd, then, when it came time to collect the boy, William's father insisted that William go along. When they arrived at Maude's room, her sister—a sharper, harder version of Maude—answered the door, and it was the sister who took charge of the money and the key to the shop. William had so anticipated and dreaded any kind of scene with Maude that he felt oddly off-kilter when she chose not to appear. Did she stay behind the scenes because she cared too much for the child or because she cared none at all?

Maude's sister disappeared through a door at the side of the parlor and returned carrying the infant; she moved toward William, but William's arms hung numb at his sides while his father's reached out, his eyes starting with tears. "Dear God, he's you all over again!"

And suddenly there was Maude, hovering briefly in the doorway in a state of undress, heavy breasts hanging loose under her shift, two damp circles marking the cloth with either the remnants of the infant's last meal or the anticipation of a next one that would never get delivered. William took a step toward the door but the shadow flew off, and William pursued her no further; afterward—long afterward— that last image of Maude pursued *him*. Why had she appeared at the door in such a state? Had she wished a last word with William? A last look at her child? Had she perhaps changed her mind and then changed it back again? Had she wanted to send her boy away with some final words of instruction? *Don't swaddle him too tight. Don't feed him every time he cries. Tell him his mother loved him.*

In the dark carriage William's father handed the boy across, and for the first time William felt the terrible weight of that minute lump of flesh, about to be cast off into the world by his own hand. But to what fate? All William could say—indeed, perhaps all his father had managed to say—was that the boy was going to a better fate than the one he'd left behind. And at the least, this boy was not going where he was unwanted by anyone.

The Mortensens were waiting in their parlor, just inside the door, the pair standing stiffly side by side like matching chessmen, beaming like matching suns the minute they first glimpsed the boy. William's father began to speak, first warm words of gratitude followed by cooler ones about terms: sums of money to be paid to an account, the address where reports were to be sent. These reports would go to a friend of William's father and never refer to the child by his legal name—William Temple Franklin—but by the name of William Temple, the name under which he would be raised.

As the negotiations ran on, William stayed silent, looking around at the unpretentious table and chairs, the simple pewter filling the shelves, the well-stuffed wood box beside the fire, the waiting cradle that sat opposite. He looked down at the child in his arms and saw his infant self and a similar room and a similar couple standing by; the room began to shift, the people to blur; he handed the boy to Mrs. Mortensen and grabbed hold of a chair; when he looked again he saw that tears of instant love and joy had started up in Mrs. Mortensen's eyes.

No, William thought, this was not how he had begun his second life—that much, at least, he could know of it; there had been no such tears in his stepmother's eyes. He leaned down low to Mrs. Mortensen. "Thank you," he whispered. He touched the boy and felt as if a rope drawn tight had just snapped and whipped back and lashed him. He turned abruptly and left the house.

William's father lingered behind.

41

London, 1761

WILLIAM'S LIFE BLAZED ON, the sheer brilliance of it, the sheer speed, making it easier and easier to mentally leave Maude and the child behind. He made barrister; he began to write anonymous political treatises for his father that were lauded far and wide; he grew closer and closer to Elizabeth Downes and her family and friends, as a result forming his first important political connections that weren't his father's. In fact, when one of those new connections spoke the right word in the right ear, William was invited to march in the king's coronation procession while his father was left to watch amid the hordes that lined the streets on either side.

The coronation spectacle was grander than anything William had ever imagined on this earth—first came the herb women sweetening the streets before the tread of the hundreds of dignitaries who led the parade, then the magnificent display of glinting swords, orb, scepter, and jewels. Last came the king himself, glowing in gold, silver, and fur, followed by row upon row of trumpets, drums, and fifes. Walking in step beside London's most famed barristers, directly behind the courtiers, dukes, and earls, William felt as if he'd found the place, the people, the culture where he belonged. Later he would toast again and again, as deep and as long as any true Londoner: "Long live the king!"

THE ELDER FRANKLIN DIDN'T approve of William's new social set or his growing political connections, or, indeed, the new slant to his political writings, more full of Crown and Parliament than America, but in his father's disapproval William detected the whiff of spoiled grapes. The elder Franklin's own mission in London had not gone well, his petitions to the Penns ignored, his petitions to the Crown outright denied. In fact, to anyone who paid attention, Benjamin Franklin's official work in London had come to an effective end the year before, but even to those who paid attention he was not considered a failure. In between bouts of defending the increasingly unpopular America in the London press, Benjamin Franklin managed to invent a fireplace damper and a musical instrument called an "armonica," based on the musical glasses with which William had played so often as a child; the elder Franklin also continued his electrical experiments, testing the effect of applied current on the paralyzed limbs of war veterans and perfecting the design of his "points," as they were called. In scientific circles and beyond, Benjamin Franklin became *the* American to know, honored with a doctorate in philosophy from Oxford University for his work with electricity. William's honorary master's for assisting his father with his experiments went largely ignored.

Perhaps no wonder then that William's father, settled in contentedly with his London "family," was in no great rush to go home. What he did with his landlady, William could never prove or disprove, but neither did he really care; he found the close relationship between his father and the landlady's daughter the more disturbing circumstance. The appearance of Elizabeth Downes hadn't cooled his father's schemes of William and Polly marrying, no matter how often William declined any invitation where Polly was likely to be present, but it didn't stop his father from cultivating the girl as if Elizabeth Downes were but a figment of William's imagination. No wonder, then, his apparent shock when William announced his official engagement.

William's father rose from his chair and paced and near shouted, not his usual method when attempting to carry a point, but of course this point was already lost. "Elizabeth is a lovely creature. She's wealthy. She's brought you important friends. She shines at court. Only *think*, William, think if she'll shine in America. If she'll be content in America. Think what kind of a wife, what kind of a companion she'll make for you."

Curious, William thought, coming from the man who'd married Deborah Read. But then again, look who William's father would have chosen for his son instead of this delight of all London, Elizabeth Downes: Polly Stevenson, the landlady's daughter. In other words, Benjamin Franklin would look no higher for William than he'd looked for himself.

BUT WILLIAM BELIEVED THAT in time Elizabeth Downes would conquer his father as she'd conquered him; indeed, his father was as charming and polite to Elizabeth as he was to any other woman of his acquaintance, and perhaps that was why William underestimated the intensity of his father's disapproval or disappointment, whichever it should be called. After two years of stalling about London essentially unemployed, William's father booked a passage to America that would put him well out to sea on September 4, 1762, the day William and Elizabeth were married at St. George's in Hanover Square with all the pomp and splendor such a couple deserved.

. . . .

ONE WEEK AFTER THEIR marriage, with Elizabeth by his side, William marched past more gilt and jewels and towering murals and tapestries to kiss the king's ring and accept his appointment as royal governor of New Jersey, swearing to uphold his oath of allegiance to the Crown till death. Even as he backed away from the king's presence, William felt utterly changed; he'd achieved this prize by hard study both inside and outside the Inns of Court, by doggedly pursuing the right kind of advancement with the right kind of people, by displaying his increasingly impressive political skills. This was his and his alone. At last, William Franklin was legitimate.

And then William stepped outside those glittering, magnificent halls to face the smoke and filth and ugly rumors: His appointment had come not because of his qualifications and connections but because of his *father's* connections, despite his father's diplomatic failures, despite his father's disapproval of the appointment, expressed so eloquently with his public and private silence on the subject.

42

Philadelphia, 1763

BEFORE HE LEFT ENGLAND, William Franklin made out a will providing for his wife, Elizabeth, and his bastard son. He pressed the Mortensens to continue to keep the child's identity a secret, not wishing to arrive at his new post burdened with unseemly gossip or to distress Elizabeth; he could not have foreseen—or perhaps he could have—of course he should have—that the older, private gossip would gain its first public audience, fanned into flame by his royal appointment.

Without the supposition of some kind of backstairs intrigue, it is difficult to account for that mortification of pride, affront to the dignity and insult to the morals of America, by the elevation to the government of New Jersey of a base-born brat, wrote John Adams of Massachusetts. Philadelphia's John Penn chimed in. *I am so astonished and enraged at it that I am hardly able to contain myself at the thought . . . If any* gentleman *had been appointed it would have been a different case . . . I make no doubt but the people of New Jersey will make some remonstrance upon this indignity put upon them.*

Such was Elizabeth Franklin's introduction to America. The

papers caught up with them at the wharf, but as Elizabeth had already lost almost every meal along with most of her courage while at sea, newspapers appeared to be of little interest to her. The couple stepped out into an icy Philadelphia winter rain to the welcome sight of their father's enclosed carriage. As William's father leaped out of the carriage to assist the obviously weakened Elizabeth, a good deal of William's hurt at his father's refusal to attend the wedding dissipated. The pale and stumbling Elizabeth was in no condition to charm anyone, but it soon appeared there was no need, for William's father set out to charm her instead, and it took less time than it took to drive the carriage to the Franklin residence.

Even William's stepmother did her best with Elizabeth, hurrying her into bed and waiting on her with soup and tea as her digestion grew to tolerate it, but he could see that his stepmother's trademark on-again off-again attentions and often inappropriate comments and questions were wearing Elizabeth down further. When William made what he thought was a tactful suggestion to allow Elizabeth her sleep, Deborah, ever on tenterhooks around him, shot back that she wasn't used to the kind of luxury that allowed for a woman's sleeping in the daytime.

Had Elizabeth heard? Apparently. That night, as they lay back to chest against the cold, she said, "William, is there some trouble between you and your mother?"

William, himself worn down by the crossing, his concern for his wife, his anxieties over meeting his father and stepmother after prior acrimonious partings, his digestion no longer accustomed to Deborah's heavy buckwheat cakes, blurted out, "She's not my mother."

Elizabeth rolled over, touched William's face. "I know this. Do you think I can't read a newspaper? Who was she, then?"

"I don't know. He's never said."

Elizabeth reared back. "You never asked him?"

"Of course I asked him. He said that Deborah was my mother and wouldn't go past that."

"Well, you must demand the truth of him."

A surprisingly fierce wave of resentment took hold of William. How dare this new wife of his take his lifelong struggle and bring it down to this single, clipped sentence, as if it were so simple a thing, so easily remedied?

"Why?" he retorted. "I know who my father is. The rest is of no consequence."

Elizabeth drew farther back from him; he could hear a new, raw edge in her breath; she reached out and touched the dimple in his chin. "This is his," she said. "And your fine height. And some say your charm." She drew a finger down his long, narrow nose. "But whose is this? The newspapers also called you 'the handsomest man in America.' That didn't come from your father alone."

William struggled to turn the mood. "You think my father unhandsome? Come now, Elizabeth, surely you're the littlest bit smitten; after all, most women are."

William reached for his wife to give her a playful squeeze, but she stretched farther away. "You see what you do, William? You make your father all. All! I've long noticed this. Whatever he is, he's but half what you are. You have a right to know what the other half is."

"I told you," William said, irritated again. "Who bore me is of no consequence."

"It was of consequence to her," Elizabeth shot back. "And it was of consequence to the one who raised you up. Everything, William. *Everything* is of consequence to everything else."

Elizabeth rolled away from him. William attempted to listen to her breathing to determine if she slept, but his own was so labored it blocked out any other sound.

THE NIGHT HAD EXHAUSTED William more than it had rested him, but in the morning his concern was all for Elizabeth. He'd held out hope of her speedy recovery and a quick resumption of their journey to New Jersey, but it turned out that his wife's lungs were having some trouble adjusting to the clean Philadelphia air after the coal smoke in London. The doctor was sent for and advised against stressing her lungs further with winter travel, but William, already anxious about his pending reception in his new colony, could not risk any additional ill will by languishing for weeks in Philadelphia. Neither could he face telling Elizabeth she must stay in this single cramped room in his parents' house, eating Deborah Franklin's pancakes and listening to her carp at William's father. This was not the life to which Elizabeth Downes was accustomed. This was not the life he had promised her.

Once again, William took the problem to his father, who saw the situation so clearly and quickly that William was embarrassed. "You've grown too fine for us, have you?"

William began to stutter out a half-backtracking, half-forward-moving explanation, but his father stopped him before he'd managed to stumble into too great a danger. "I understand the difficulty for you under this roof, William. I also understand who your wife is, and who you've become, perhaps something better than you do. I further understand the political situation; you cannot cower in Philadelphia with a new royal appointment awaiting you in New Jersey. Ask our friends the Galloways if they'd like to host Elizabeth—they keep more to your new style of living and have even had a nurse in lately for the daughter's confinement; then you and I may travel in clear conscience to New Jersey."

William peered at his father. "You and I . . . together?"

"Unless you feel I should be of no use to you."

Opposing answers pummeled William from both sides. What would the Franklin prudential algebra say here? His father the much admired editor and writer. His father the famous scientist. His *father*, in whose shadow he must forever travel.

"Thank you, Father," William said. "I should be honored to have you by my side."

WITH GUT-CLENCHING RELUCTANCE WILLIAM left a teary Elizabeth behind in Philadelphia and set out with his father for New Jersey. Filled with trepidation after the derogatory accounts in the papers, admittedly still somewhat uneasy in his father's presence since his abrupt London departure, frozen and bone jarred by icy ruts in the ill-kept roads, William had imagined another kind of start to his new life. He had not imagined starting it, again, as that bastard boy who had been whispered about in Philadelphia's hallways and streets. As they drew through town, William found himself fallen back into his old habit of scanning every strange woman's face, looking for something of himself. *Everything is of consequence to everything else.* Damn Elizabeth, he thought, for bringing all that up again.

William looked sideways at his father, also apparently on edge in this new, close quiet after such bustle and commotion in the Philadelphia house. "Thank you, Father," he said. "'Tis an uncomfortable time of year to make such a trip."

"Nonsense. I should like to see you launched."

"Into a position you'd preferred I didn't take."

"I make it a rule that when a thing is done, I don't go back and worry it to death. We make our decisions in this life and we live by them, good or ill."

Was this an opening offered? But even if wasn't, what next chance would William have?

"I assume you've seen what's written about in the newspapers," he started.

"I have."

"I should like to know . . . I think I have a right to know . . . there

was something said of a kitchen maid named Barbara, of a . . . of a
street woman left to starve to death, of—"

"We had no kitchen maid named Barbara. No one has starved to
death. The whole of what you need to know is that you have a father
and mother who have done the best for you they could in keeping
with their individual circumstances. For a man of your resources, that
should be—it must be—enough. But as you raise the topic, tell me
what arrangement has been made for your son."

The cold carriage grew warm. For a moment William's throat
failed to work. "I've provided in my will," he managed at last. "His
bills are to be forwarded through a friend. I left instructions that until
I'm settled into my new post his true identity should remain secret; I
didn't wish to jeopardize the people's regard until I'd proved capable
of doing them some service."

"And then? Do you intend that he come to live with you?"

William hesitated. "I've a new wife to consider."

"Yes," William's father said. He might have added, *As did I,* but he
did not, for if he had, William might have added, *And* my *son will not
suffer as did I.*

Everything is of consequence to everything else, William thought, as
they rode on in silence.

WILLIAM'S FEARS—THE IMMEDIATE ONES—were assuaged when a
troop of cavalry with swords drawn and plumes high rode out through
driving snow to meet them, followed by sleighs full of cheering ladies,
with bonfires and salutes lighting the roadside as they entered the
capital. William's speech was welcomed heartily, he suspected both
for its content and its brevity, and later, at the nearby tavern, his health
was drunk along with the king's.

. . . .

WHEN WILLIAM FINALLY MANAGED to collect Elizabeth and show off her new home, the proud moment was dulled somewhat by the fact that Elizabeth's lungs appeared to like New Jersey no better than they did Philadelphia. She arrived in the "wilderness," as she called it, shivering and barely able to breathe; she spent the first two weeks in the governor's mansion under a thick bed rug with hot poultices on her feet and chest, while William plied her with biscuits and sherry and largely useless words of encouragement.

AS THE FIRST MONTHS ran themselves out, William dashed about with his new duties and then came home to attempt to soothe his wife. William could never quite decide whether his wife's nerves caused her attacks or whether the attacks caused the nerves; if she started up in her bed at the howl of a wolf her breathing would grow labored, but was it because of the sudden draft or her anxious state? Whatever the original cause, once the lungs began to struggle, her nerves began to fray, causing the lungs to struggle more, and around and around they went. William did discover a thing or two that helped: He would draw his wife back inside the blanket's warmth, ease her down onto her right side, and rub her back in gentle circles, talking quietly and steadily, until the lungs under his hand stopped working like the gills of a near-dead fish.

WILLIAM'S FATHER WROTE HIM a letter, or rather, he pretended to write him a letter; it appeared obvious from the formal style that the composition was in fact a first draft of an autobiography. He claimed he sent it to William "imagining it may be agreeable to you to know the circumstances of my life," and William was forced to admit that it was. Oh, yes, it was, but the real meaning of the letter soon became clear: William's father wanted to remind him of his humble beginnings and the benefits of the Spartan lifestyle in which his father had been raised. Just the same, William tore into his father's words, chewing and tasting and swallowing each one before finally spitting them out, but the particular words he was after weren't there. William was mentioned but a few times, first in 1755 and last in 1757. His mother wasn't mentioned at all. His father did confess to a youthful affinity for "low women," despite the "great inconvenience"; was that what William's mother had been, a "low woman"? Was that all William had ever been, a "great inconvenience"? Almost as disturbing were the passages about his stepmother: "I pitied poor Miss Read's unfortunate situation," Benjamin Franklin wrote. "I considered my giddiness and inconstancy when in London as in a great degree the cause of her unhappiness." And so he assumed a married state with her, "and thus corrected that great erratum as well as I could." Having recognized the obvious disparity between mother and father, having witnessed the overwhelming resentment of the mother, a new horror began to torture William: Where was he at the time of this "correction"? He must have appeared at around the same time; had he in any way influenced it? Could his father have married this near-illiterate Deborah Read only to give William a proper home? If he had, there was nothing on this earth that William could do to make up to his father for such a sacrifice. And worse, if Deborah Read was the better choice, what must his real mother have been? The old rumors began to take on more verity; William's father's silence on his mother's identity only seemed to prove the case more fully.

William was a bastard, yes; now he must add to it that his mother was likely a whore.

43

Philadelphia, 1763

DEBORAH FRANKLIN PULLED OUT the packet of her husband's old letters and began to read them from the beginning again.

LONDON, JULY 27, 1757
My dear Child,
We arrived here well last Night, only a little fatigued with the last Day's Journey being 70 Miles. I write only this Line, not knowing of any Opportunity to send it. Billy is with me here at Mr. Collinson's, and presents his Duty to you, and Love to his Sister. My Love to all. I am, my dear Child, Your loving Husband,

B. Franklin

LONDON, NOVEMBER 22, 1757
My dear Child,
I have now before me, your letters of July 17, July 31, August 11,

*August 21, September 4, September 19, October 1, and October 9.
I thank you for writing to me so frequently and fully. The agreeable
Conversation I meet with among Men of Learning, and the Notice
taken of me by Persons of Distinction, are the principal Things that
sooth me for the present under this painful Absence from my Family
and Friends; yet those would not detain me here another Week, if I
had no other Inducements, Duty to my Country and Hopes of being
able to do it Service . . .*

LONDON, DECEMBER 13, 1757

Dear Madam,

*Having had the pleasure for several months past, to be personally
known to what you will readily allow, to be your better half, having
had for many years a very high opinion of Mr. Franklin; I must
confess it was very unequal to what I now know his singular merit
deserves. Now madam as I know the ladies here consider him in
exactly the same light I do, upon my word I think you should come
over, with all convenient speed to look after your interest . . . Dear
madam, I am Your most affectionate, Humble servant,*

William Strahan

LONDON, JANUARY 14, 1758

Dear Debby,

*Strahan has offered to lay me a considerable wager, that a letter he
has wrote to you will bring you immediately over hither; but I tell
him I will not pick his pocket; for I am sure there is no inducement
strong enough to prevail with you to cross the seas. I would be glad if
I could tell you when I expected to be at home, but that is still in the
dark; it is possible I may not be able to get away this summer . . . I
am, my dear child, Your ever loving husband,*

B. Franklin

LONDON, JANUARY 21, 1758

My dear Child,

I begin to think I shall hardly be able to return before this time twelve months . . .

LONDON, JUNE 10, 1758

My dear Child,

I have no Prospect of Returning till next Spring, so you will not expect me. But pray remember to make me as happy as you can, by sending some Pippins for myself and Friends, some of your small Hams, and some Cranberries. Your answer to Mr. Strahan was just what it should be; I was much pleas'd with it . . .

LONDON, MARCH 5, 1760

My dear Child,

Mr. Strahan is very urgent with me to stay in England and prevail with you to remove hither with Sally. I gave him two Reasons why I could not think of removing hither. One, my Affection to Pensilvania, and long established Friendships and other Connections there: the other, your invincible Aversion to crossing the Seas . . .

LONDON, MARCH 28, 1760

My dear Child,

I have now the Pleasure to acquaint you, that our Business draws near a Conclusion, and that in less than a Month we shall have a Hearing, after which I shall be able to fix a Time for my Return . . .

LONDON, JUNE 27, 1760

My dear Child,

I am concern'd that so much Trouble should be given you by idle Reports concerning me. Be satisfied, my dear, that while I have my

Senses, and God vouchsafes me his Protection, I shall do nothing
unworthy the Character of an honest Man, and one that loves his
Family . . .

Deborah pushed the packet of letters back into their box, having
received little more satisfaction from the reading the second time—or
third or fourth—than she had at the first. Three months had turned
to six, to twelve, to two years, to four, and Deborah might have
reconsidered braving the seas if she'd only been told her husband
should be gone even longer, but that information—or invitation—
never came.

THEN ABRUPTLY, IF THE word *abruptly* could be used five years after
the man had first sailed, Benjamin Franklin came home, carrying
extra weight, the first wrinkles, an expanded forehead, and clothes
much finer than those he'd taken across. There was something different in his speech too—a polish that made him stranger to her than had
the altered features or clothes; before, the words were the things that
had escaped her—now added to those was this new, strange tone.

Benjamin came in, grinned, and opened his arms wide, lifting a
questioning brow as if to say, "Well, here is what I am and what I'm
not—are you ready for it again?" At her first glimpse of all the strange-
ness, Deborah might have said *no,* but at the sight of the open arms she
saw that what was important in him was the same; she ran into his
arms and the nineteen-year-old Sally came running and hugged them
together.

A family again.

DEBORAH FOUND COMFORT IN Benjamin's older, looser flesh—it
reminded her that she hadn't aged alone. They found their old, famil-

iar places, more slowly, less violently, perhaps coming to a lesser end, but it was as it should be and no more. Over the coming days Benjamin and Sally played duets on the harpsichord and the new-fangled armonica that Benjamin had shipped home from London; he read aloud to them out of new-fangled books that Sally grasped more quickly than Deborah, but that fact only made her proud. In due time it seemed all Philadelphia came to their door, taking Benjamin off into his old life again, but Deborah was more patient with it this time; he was here.

And then he was gone, this time on a six-month tour of his postal routes. Sally and Deborah were invited to visit William and his new bride in New Jersey, and although Sally went, Deborah elected to stay home. She'd heard enough about the new Georgian house with the fancy white fieldstone facade, the elegant furniture, the visiting artists and high-society Brits whom William now called his friends.

She'd met Elizabeth.

THE POSTAL SURVEY TOOK up most of that first year, but when Benjamin returned he excited Deborah by ordering construction begun on a new house on Market Street—the first house they would ever own. The happy bustle and commotion of planning and building took up most of the next year; part of Deborah's joy over the house was the sense of permanence it implied, but she soon discovered that even though a house couldn't move, a man could.

Two years from the date of his arrival home, Benjamin appeared at the bedroom door with the news as before. London. Again. This time, no mention was made of Deborah's coming along; how could she, with so much work on the new house yet to be done? But she was worried. William was in America this time, and in his few visits to his father, Deborah had grown concerned. William may have matured into his proper filial duty in his years gone, but that could twist both ways; she heard him talking over his father's business with an alarmingly proprietary tone. A letter had come, out of which Benjamin had read aloud:

> *Please tell my mother I am not so very great a distance away if she*
> *should require my aid at any time.*

With Benjamin gone, Deborah feared William's interfering hand. But those seven years spent as an unlawful wife had taught Deborah the power of a bit of paper.

Deborah approached her husband. "You've gone over the books I've kept since you were gone?"

"I have."

"There's naught amiss?"

"Naught amiss. My child, you do me proud!"

"As I shall this time you're gone."

"I've no doubt of it."

"Should you not write it down, then, so those who might question my authority may read of it in your own hand?" She did not say the name *William*. Benjamin did not. But at the week's end, Deborah tucked an official document called a *power of attorney* into a desk where she also found William's next letter, which Benjamin had elected not to read aloud:

> *As you appear to have found your own reasons for keeping your*
> *business in her hands, I will only add here that I am ever your*
> *dutiful and grateful son and should the need arise, ready and willing*
> *for you to command.*

44

ANNE CAME DOWN THE stairs and stepped into the Penny Pot's common room. Familiar heads came up and waved or smiled, but Anne had seen a table of new custom—better dressed than the usual Penny Pot crowd—and she began to work her way there. As she moved amongst the tables, returning each greeting with a smile, she remembered her first days at the Penny Pot, and how much—and how little—she'd learned in all the years that had stretched between now and then. Odd that she was in fact thinking about those early years when a general cry went up, and she turned to find Franklin sailing through the door.

Anne hadn't seen Benjamin Franklin since the New York wharf; she'd returned from that aborted journey and gone straight to the Penny Pot, laying her proposition down in front of John Hewe. Beside the marriage contract there must be another—a will that on John Hewe's death would bequeath the Penny Pot to Anne. Hewe had made a brief, weak argument.

"The Pot's been promised to my grandson."

Anne had looked around the tavern. "And where is he?"

"Williamsburg."

"Ah," Anne had answered. "And yet here I am."

In the end the two contracts were drawn and signed, and Anne had given Hewe three years of hard work both above stairs and below, a faithful wife to him while he lived, washing and feeding him in his last illness, holding his hand while he died. Now the Penny Pot belonged to Anne alone. It was true that after John Hewe died, she often lay awake in an uneasy, exhausted state, pondering the many things she might have forgotten to do . . . or say. Then there were those nights when she woke thinking of William, and whether in her life she would ever see him again, and what she might say were she to do so. She knew he'd returned from London with an English wife and an English appointment as royal governor of New Jersey, that when he visited Philadelphia he didn't stay at his parents' home. She knew all this and she knew nothing; she hadn't laid eyes on him in more than seven years.

There were times too when Anne had thought of Franklin. She'd read in the papers of his receiving this or that honorary degree from the most respected European institutions; she read his oft-quoted essay, "A Defense of Americans," first printed in the *London Chronicle* and later reprinted in the *Pennsylvania Gazette;* she followed every report of his scientific innovations—watertight compartments for ships, iceberg watches, a phonetic alphabet—and read with amusement that he was reportedly climbing every tall building in Europe and fixing them with his electrical "points."

Anne also listened to every report of Franklin's pending return that never came true. As she followed these London doings via newspaper and rumor, she gave passing thought to what kind of witness she might have been to all of it, even what possible influence she might have had, but she never regretted her last decision regarding him, no matter how many times she might question an earlier few.

And now here was Franklin, home again, but by the time he strolled into the Penny Pot, he'd in fact been home for some time, still filling the papers and the rumor mill by making his own news. As trouble brewed between the white settlers and the Indians on the western front, as rumors of a planned slaughter of Indians circulated, he wrote a pamphlet defending the six Indian nations, joining forces with the Quakers at last and forming six militia companies to provide for the tribes' protection.

The next Anne read of Franklin he was gaining more Quaker friends and losing political ones by defending Negro education. Undaunted by the criticism, Franklin ran for his old seat in the assembly, but lost by eighteen votes in the face of a campaign against him composed of false—and true—rumor: An Indian lover. A hatred of Germans. A bastard child.

FRANKLIN SPIED ANNE AND made straight across the tavern floor to her. "Ah, my old friend." He caught up her hand. "Or the Widow Hewe, as the name is now?" He lifted an eyebrow.

Anne chose to ignore the eyebrow. She retrieved her hand and led Franklin to a seat by the fire. Without asking she went away and returned with a tankard of milk punch. Franklin pointed to the chair opposite, but Anne waved at the restless crowd around them. She must stay on her feet.

"I hear you leave for London on a new mission soon," she said. "With your wife this time?"

"No."

Anne waited, sure that the old invitation would be renewed, but it wasn't. In fact, Franklin soon began to exhibit those signs of increased intensity, which meant he was approaching the true reason for his visit.

"What news have you of Grissom?" he asked at last. "I understand he's widowed too."

"Yes," Anne said, but again nothing more, for there was little more to be said of it. At his wife's death Anne had written Grissom a heartfelt letter of condolence, but the next time she'd passed him in the street, he'd avoided meeting her eye. For many months little was seen or heard of him, but she continued to make the occasional excuse to pass the shop, and one day was surprised to see him back in it, taking his son to task by shaking out an apparently improperly filled bolster onto the floor.

Anne returned her attention to Franklin and found him leaning forward in his seat, staring fixedly at her. "Tell me, then. Why didn't you come with me to London? What did you get for yourself by staying behind?"

Anne circled the room with her arm. "A tavern. What do you suppose I'd have gotten if I'd gone to London with you?"

Franklin sat back, attempting to look offended. "You'd have gotten—and given—a fine old time!" He continued to gaze at her darkly, but after a while he began to laugh, and much to Anne's surprise and his obvious delight, she laughed with him.

Franklin pointed again to the chair, and this time Anne pulled it out, sat down, and waved to the girl for another milk punch. Once they were alone again, Anne said, "Now tell me of William."

All mirth evaporated; Franklin's brow creased. "I could tell you a thing or two of William." But then the brow eased. "Yes, I *could* talk to you of William."

He began. William lived beyond his means, blaming the poor salary set by the New Jersey Assembly, declaring his extravagant lifestyle necessary for the sake of his position. He was courting the wrong friends. He was ignoring his father's good advice as to the proper handling of his constituents. But he was also building better roads, feeding and clothing the poor, treating fairly with the Indians, banning gaol for debt.

My son, Anne thought, but didn't say.

Never said.

45

Philadelphia, 1774

BENJAMIN HAD BEEN WISE enough this time not to promise Deborah any three- or six-month return, and Deborah had been wise enough to refuse to allow Sally to accompany him; what would her days have been like if both Benjamin *and* Sally had gone? This second absence had now stretched far beyond the first, entering its tenth year, with no definitive word on when Benjamin might come home, and here sat Deborah, rereading his letters and looking for hints. Again. But this time as she reread the letters one after the other, she was better able to notice the steady change in tone—it was all business between them now.

I have sent six coarse diaper Breakfast Cloths; they are to spread on the Tea Table, for nobody breakfasts here on the naked Table . . .

There is also 56 Yards of Cotton printed curiously from Copper Plates, a new Invention, to make Bed and Window Curtains; these are my fancy . . .

The Oven I suppose was put up by the written Directions in my former Letter. You mention nothing of the Furnace . . .

I received the two Post Office Letters you sent me. It was not Letters of that Sort alone that I wanted; but all such as were sent to me from any one whomsoever . . .

Send me a little draft of the Lot you have bought that I may see the Dimensions, and who it joins upon. Who have you for a Tenant in the House, and what Rent do they Pay? Have you got the Carpets made? Have you mov'd everything, and put all Papers and Books in my Room, and do you keep it lock't? As to oiling the Floors, it may be omitted till I return: which will not be till next Spring . . .

When Deborah came to the letter dated August 1765, she paused. On Benjamin went about carpenters and paint and rents, never knowing as he wrote how close he'd come to losing it all. The Stamp Act had come to America, and Benjamin, in London, had at first underestimated the violent hatred of the act at home. While riots broke out from colony to colony, he wrote making recommendations of his friends for the positions of stamp agents; it was therefore believed that he defended—or perhaps even crafted—the hateful law. Rants against Benjamin Franklin appeared in the newspapers, and a rumor flew about that his new house was to be burned to the ground, filling Deborah with rage. This was Philadelphia's thanks for her husband's years of service, for Deborah's sacrifice?

William had heard the threatening talk in New Jersey and sent a carriage to fetch Deborah and Sally to the safety of the governor's mansion; Deborah read the letter that came with the carriage and all her old resentment, long at the simmer, began to boil.

Honored Mother, This carriage will deliver you and Sally to New Jersey where you must stay in safety until this fuss over the Stamp Act blows past. There is no need of staying in town and suffering such humiliation as Father's enemies would inflict upon us all.

Humiliation, was it, to stay and defend her home? Deborah called it *humiliation* to run to New Jersey. But Sally, all there was left for Deborah on her home soil, Sally who at twenty-two was fast growing into the kind of companion that Benjamin might have been had he only retired at home like most sensible men—Sally must be kept safe. Deborah contrived the kind of excuse that was like as not true—William's wife was ill and he'd asked Sally to come nurse; the girl was packed off.

Soon the warnings began to roll in in earnest; a cousin, the cousin's brother, even a neighbor came to tell her an actual mob had formed and was approaching her home. Deborah sent the men home for weapons, and while she stationed herself with a loaded musket at the upstairs window, the men waited below behind the barricaded door. Just past dark she heard them, the catcalls and hoots like a barn full of drunken owls; next the torches came into view. Deborah got up and lit the lamp beside her; let them see who they tormented! Let them remember who her husband was and all he'd done for them and their town!

The tactic appeared to have some effect. As Deborah resumed her seat, musket held high, the mob slowed; the collective nerve seemed to fail. The catcalls grew halfhearted, several torches sputtered out and weren't relit, the crowd began to thin at the edges, and within the half hour the street before her door was empty again. Deborah went below and handed her cousin his gun and her thanks; the men went home and Deborah went to her bed, lying down fully clothed, until her heart had returned to its normal rhythm. Then she rose and began a letter to Benjamin.

WHILE DEBORAH WAITED FOR Benjamin's answering letter she had time—three months—to write four more. She believed herself to be a dutiful correspondent, not only in the letters she'd sent but in the ones she hadn't: She'd told Benjamin every detail of her handling of his business affairs but left out any mention of the angry answer from William over her refusal to come to New Jersey, of his disapproval of a young man named Richard Bache of whom Sally had grown fond. She tried to conceal from Benjamin her growing gloom, but she couldn't answer his numerous questions about curtains without admitting her indifference to the matter; she was forced to respond to his repeated inquiries about his friends that she seldom went out anymore.

Finally, in November, Benjamin's letter came.

> *I honour much the Spirit and Courage you show'd, and the prudent Preparations you made in that Time of Danger. The woman deserves a good House that is determined to defend it.*

Deborah's spirits lifted at the receipt of that letter, and again when news came that after a speech Benjamin made to Parliament arguing against the Stamp Act, it was repealed. Her spirits flagged again after an altercation with the workmen, who refused to carry on without the master of the house on hand; her mood dipped again after harsh words from William over her decision to allow Sally to marry Richard Bache; they dipped again, and again . . .

DEBORAH FLIPPED THROUGH THE packet of letters faster, stopping only at those hints that might tell her what her future might hold.

> *It seems now as if I should stay here another Winter . . .*
> *I this Morning am to set out for a Trip to Paris . . .*
> *I shall chuse to leave England about May or June . . .*
> *I must stay a few Weeks longer . . .*
> *I hope to be able to return about the middle of next Month . . .*
> *As you ask me, I can assure you, that I do really intend, God willing, to return in the Summer . . .*

And here it was winter again. Deborah thrust the pile of letters aside and picked up the pen, despair and anger mixing now, taking charge of her words.

> *Varius air the Conjeckters of our nabors sum say you will Cume home others say not. I cante say aney thing as I am in the darke and my life of old age is one Continewd State of suspens. I muste indever to be Contente but fear I lose all my reseylushon and this verey dismall winter will be verey long.*

Sally came into the room. "What, Mother, are you not ready? We must leave soon! Mr. Whorton expects us in time to dine."

Deborah laid down her pen. "I'm ready." She got up, fastened her shawl, and followed her daughter and her new husband outside. Ahead of her on Market Street, Deborah could see the crowd; ever since the trouble over the Stamp Act, Deborah had stayed shy of any such large gatherings and she lagged behind.

Her son-in-law tried to ease her. "'Tis only a whipping, Mother. Come along."

But Deborah had never been able to stomach a whipping either, and by the time they reached Mr. Whorton's the poor victim's cries had brought on one of her fiercest headaches. Mr. Whorton came to the door himself to hurry them in out of the ice and cold, and Deborah found herself leaning more heavily than usual on his arm. He spoke and she didn't hear; she tried to speak and her tongue wouldn't move. There were people around her, more people gathering around her, but she couldn't tell who they were. Oh, she was so tired of all of it! So tired of trying to make sense of it, of trying to be heard! That was what she thought of—her extreme tiredness—and then the blackness came down.

46

ANNE WAS PASSING BETWEEN tables on her way to mind the fire when she heard one of her patrons speaking Deborah Franklin's name. She slowed.

"An apoplexy," the patron said. "She was dining at Whorton's and they had to carry her home."

"Dead?" a second patron asked.

"Not dead, no. I called there this morn. But she's insensible—no speech, recognizes no one in the room."

"And Franklin in London yet."

"Of course he can't say he wasn't warned. 'Tisn't her first, and the doctor wrote him after the last, hinting that if he wanted to see his wife again he'd best come home."

"Well, he didn't come home."

"But the daughter's with her. And the son's come racing over from New Jersey. She's not alone."

Anne moved on with her work, fumbling tankards, forgetting

names, mindless of all but those overheard words. *The son's come . . .* Three streets away he was. Now. It was no place for Anne to be, of course—under normal conditions she wouldn't be welcome—but if this report was true and the woman wouldn't recognize her, and as the son never had, what could be the harm? But what the gain? None, except to see him, perhaps for the last time. Reports from New Jersey had been sparse, but on the whole, complimentary, even after the bloody stamp crisis. William had taken a circumspect course by refusing to either attack or defend the act, thus avoiding much of the turmoil engulfing a number of the other American colonies, but when Boston emptied three shiploads of tea into Boston Harbor, William supported the royal line, that Boston must pay for the tea; until they did, British warships would blockade Boston's harbor. Philadelphia, and apparently the main of her sister colonies, responded by sending food and fuel overland to the beleaguered Bostonians as fast as they could load and dispatch their oxcarts, and the day Anne heard that bit of news, a steady pressure developed behind her eyes. A line was being drawn, and William appeared to be positioning himself on the other side of it—the king's side; how would such a line ever be crossed? William's father, according to the chatter at the Penny Pot, despite some early wavering, was now firmly with the Bostonians. The line became a trench, dug deeper with each new issue of the *Gazette*. The pressure behind Anne's eyes grew. *Would* she ever see her son again? And then he arrived in Philadelphia to attend his stepmother's illness and for the second time Anne found herself walking the streets toward the Franklin home, uninvited, unwanted, undaunted. She must see her son.

A FANCY ARCHWAY MARKED the entrance to the courtyard where Deborah Franklin now lived, and back on Market Street, Anne walked through it just as brazenly as she'd once walked through the print shop door. She approached the house and knocked. The servant who opened the door was not Min, the older woman no doubt long dead and unremarked; this one accepted her pronouncement, "Widow Hewe. Come to call on Mrs. Franklin," without question and waved her in.

SALLY FRANKLIN—SALLY FRANKLIN BACHE—met Anne in the front room. She'd collected her mother's earthy features and heavy body and her father's clever eyes; she seemed little concerned with Anne's fumbled words of her connection to the family and would have ushered Anne into the sickroom at once had not William exited it at nearly the same time.

"My brother," Sally said, and no more, as if Anne's name had already been forgotten. A queer, garbled sound erupted from the other room. "Excuse me," she said, and left Anne and William alone.

Anne's first glimpse of her son after seventeen years would of course be a hungry one. She raked him over from head to toe, noticing that he'd grown more solid; that his hair had silvered much like Anne's; that the open, hopeful smile the boy had once turned on her was now replaced by the man's public one. As Anne gazed at him she realized that if she could wish for any one thing on earth, it would be for that boy's smile to light him—and her—once again.

"The Widow Hewe," Anne said. "Or so I'm called now. You knew me by the name of Anne. I minded you when you were young."

"Of course," William said, but the empty smile didn't change. "'Tis most kind of you to call. I'm afraid my mother's confusing faces yet, so you mustn't expect—"

Anne waved the concern off. "'Tis been a long time since I've seen you, Mr. Franklin. I hear of all your accomplishments and they come as no surprise to me, considering your cleverness at your early lessons."

Some of the blankness left William's features, but only to be replaced by wariness, confusion. Did she dare go on? She was the

Widow Hewe, as respectable as she'd ever be—if he was to learn of her now it could hardly cause the turmoil the word *whore* might have done. It was not the proper time or place, but would the right one—or even another one—ever come? Anne took a quiet, steadying breath. "There are infants who bear in themselves a look of such brightness one sees their future greatness in them at an early age. One might look at such an infant and know he deserves the best one has to give him, and if perhaps one's best isn't enough, one must make way for something better. I wonder if this is something you might understand."

But William wasn't hearing. He wasn't even listening. He stood halfway turned to the room behind him, where the garbled sound had broken out again but in a more strident tone. Anne's fingers itched to reach out and grip William's arm, to shake him, to draw him back to her and what she was trying to tell him. *You're my son.* Anne did, indeed, lift her hand, but before she could bring her fingers as far as William's arm, he swung around.

"I do beg your pardon," he said, "but I must return to my mother now. Please do come and pay your respects." He gestured toward the sickroom door, the long, elegant body inclining after the gesturing arm, the rules of his adopted gentility no doubt the only thing that kept him in the room with Anne at all. What to do? She could take her last look at William and leave the house now, or she could accept his invitation and step into a room where she didn't belong.

Anne stepped into the room. It was dim, close, and overly crowded, but she recognized only two people in it: Sally, at her mother's bedside, and Solomon Grissom, leaning against the wall in the far corner. At the sight of Anne, his eyes widened in a surprise close to shock, reminding Anne, if she needed reminding, of how foolish it was of her to come.

But Sally Franklin was lifting a hand and pointing at Anne. "Here, Mother, 'tis the Widow Hewe come to call. Can you say hello to the Widow Hewe?"

Anne took a small step forward. Deborah Franklin lay so still and her flesh had melted so lifelessly into the bed tick that Anne considered for a mad second that the woman had died and no one but Anne saw. Anne said, "Mrs. Franklin."

Deborah opened her eyes and looked straight past Anne. Anne, following her gaze, spied William's tall frame where it hovered just inside the door. Deborah Franklin's limbs began to twitch, a hand to half rise from the coverlet. She struggled to make a sound.

Sally leaned closer to the bed. "What, Mother? Are you comfortable? Should you like a drink?" She reached for the pitcher but Deborah rocked her head, left, right. She grunted again, something with a little more form to it, her eyes again fixed on William's tall shape, so strikingly outlined against the light from the door. "Buh." She tried again. "Bud."

Dear God, thought Anne, does she struggle to call him *bastard*? Was she to carry her old resentments all the way to the grave? Anne lifted her eyes to meet Solomon Grissom's and had little trouble reading the same thought in them. But just as Anne had begun to feel so sure of the word, Deborah Franklin struggled through another revision of it. "Budin." The twitching grew more violent. She lifted her trembling hand and stretched it toward William. "Buh-min. Beh-min."

Benjamin. As Anne caught it, so did the daughter. "No, Mother, Papa's in London yet. This is William just come in."

William took a step away from the door, edged closer to the bed, and there he was again, as if three decades had been instantly washed from his face—the small, unsure boy, looking at this woman for the thing she'd never managed to find it in herself to give him. Of course he hadn't remembered Anne, or heard a word she'd said to him, or cared who she was or why she'd come. What William craved was for Deborah, not Anne, to call him *son*.

Anne backed toward the door.

47

Perth Amboy, New Jersey, 1774

PAST MIDNIGHT AND WILLIAM Franklin had been sitting at his desk since eight, a candle on each corner, two letters set out side by side in the middle. The left-hand letter was dated October 1773, written in his father's unequivocal hand, smudged with lampblack and dog-eared from much rereading.

> *From long and thorough consideration of the subject I am indeed of the opinion that the parliament has no right to make any law whatever binding on the colonies, but you, a thorough courtier, will likely not agree.*

The letter on the right-hand side, dated May 1774, was only slightly more crisp, the hand of Lord Dartmouth only slightly more equivocal.

I believe that in your position and with your connections a secret and confidential exchange of letters with the Crown Office might serve your king and country well and further secure your political future in the American colonies.

No two letters, taken together, could make the thing more plain. William's father had gone to the rebels; the Crown Office knew it and now demanded that William make clear where his loyalties lay. William might have taken his father's letter as written in a moment of pique if it hadn't been followed by the letter about the tea.

Tea. William still cringed at the word, although it didn't stop him from drinking it—the rebellion's nonimportation agreement had made real English tea a scarcity for most colonists, but not for William; it came by the same secret route as his dispatches went back—but he cringed at the word itself because of the sheer audacity of the rebels who had darkened Boston Harbor with it. It had also caused an outright argument with William's father. At first the elder Franklin had agreed with William that it was a shameful act that should be paid for by the Massachusetts colony at once, but later—*after* William's father had received a humiliating dressing-down in the Privy Council for making public some correspondence that further damaged the Crown's reputation in the colonies—William's father sent a letter in which he declared the *king* owed Massachusetts—and indeed all the colonies—recompense for their illegal taxes! How clear it was which Franklin had stayed true to his principles and which one had decided to run rampant! William had answered his father's letter in a most temperate fashion, hinting that perhaps the incident had at least given his father, safely tucked away in London, some idea of the kind of risk every loyal colonial subject must now ward against. In reply William's father had called him obstinate. *William* obstinate!

Well then, so be it. William rang the bell. "A cup of tea, please, Hamilton." He pushed his father's and Lord Dartmouth's letters aside;

they had failed to distract him from or assist him in the more important letter he needed to write now. He took out a fresh piece of paper and began to write.

> *Honored Father,*
>
> *It is with great sadness that I must tell you of the death of our mother this December the nineteenth. She was buried on the twenty-second with a very respectable number of the inhabitants in attendance. She told me in October that she never expected to see you again unless you returned this winter and I heartily wish you had happened to have come over in the fall, as promised, as I think her disappointment preyed a good deal on her spirits. I do hope that you are able to return soon, and with a particular cargo dear to me in hand.*

But William, always sensitive to his own disappointments, decided in the end to cross that last sentence off.

SUCH WAS THE WAY of that twisted, smirking thing called fate that William and Elizabeth had had no child of their own. The matter was a disappointment to William in that the legacy he strove to achieve was best effected if another generation could step in to carry it forward, but Elizabeth dismissed all such talk of legacies; her disappointment took the form of a vacancy behind the eyes whenever the subject arose. William had kept careful track of that gray film, thickening and thinning over the years, perhaps becoming thickest when nature made it clear that the odds in favor of parenthood were worsening fast. During those grayest days William had spent many nights in thought of his son in London, and when it neared time for the boy to enter school, had even written to his father. Perhaps this was the time to bring the boy across, have him take up his proper name, introduce him as the son of a poor, deceased relation for whom William had stood godfather and now intended to bring up as his own? But William's father had answered with another plan, bringing "William Temple" into his London circle as the son of a friend, although after his father's description of the boy's strong family resemblance, William doubted anyone was fooled. Compounding William's disappointment, his father enrolled the boy in a new, radical school not at all to William's liking, but as the elder Franklin took on the expense, which William could ill afford, he said nothing.

But the more William thought about the boy, and the longer he watched Elizabeth, it began to seem less and less likely that William's son should suffer the same humiliation that William had suffered both inside and outside his home. Now, with his stepmother dead, the matter seemed even simpler, if all the more urgent; he decided to press his father again to send the boy across. But first, William must decide how best to tell his wife of the child. Of Maude.

William chose a quiet winter evening when Elizabeth sat reclined on the love seat before the fire, reading a letter just come from her father, an activity that almost always created a certain melancholy in her that sent her in search of William's arms. He pushed aside the fluff of skirt that covered the love seat and settled beside Elizabeth, picking up her hand. With Elizabeth, any delayed overture only allowed her active imagination to conjure up worse horrors than William could ever dream of; he'd practiced the words long enough through one unending night after another; he leaped in.

"There is a boy," he began. He pushed on. He told the tale—mostly—as it had occurred, with perhaps a slight adjustment to the time line; he hadn't gone far when Elizabeth withdrew her hand and sat staring straight ahead; as he wore down she rose from her seat and approached the fire, revealing nothing to William but the back of a rigid neck.

"Elizabeth?"

She whirled. "Why did you not tell me this till now?"

"I . . . I didn't know what you should think of me. Or him. I couldn't have borne it if—"

"If I'd turned out like her?"

"No. *No.*"

"Can you not see the difference between us? Can you not think of your poor mother's circumstance as something different from my own? She took you in to keep him—'tis clear as day to me and has been since the first minute you told me the tale. An abandoned woman of little means, not even a lawful wife, how strong she would have to be to refuse to take you in! How strong to not resent you day after day—a child born to a woman whose bed her husband chose over her own! And ever after, to watch this man's infallible ability to make himself agreeable to every woman he passed—don't look so, William, you know 'tis true—to feel herself under such constant threat, whether real or no, and then to have her own boy die . . . Oh, William, you've told me and I've heard what pain it was for you; I've seen that boy's portrait, displayed so prominently in the parlor even as they move from home to home, with nothing of you on show anywhere. I know what it was for you. But I know what it was for her too. *But I am not her.*"

William stood stunned, not over any particular thing his wife had said to him but at the sheer force and weight of the whole of it together, at the certain implication that she'd thought and perhaps dwelled on this woman—his stepmother—so long. He could think of nothing with which to defend himself except "And I am not him, Elizabeth."

Elizabeth waved an impatient hand. "I know this too. Although I find it—" She stopped, reconsidered whatever word she'd almost used. "I find it *remarkable* that you should insist on imitating him in so many ways. In this particular way. Who was she?"

And there was the question William had been waiting for. All his life he'd craved a single name and it had been withheld from him; here was his chance to prove that he wasn't his father, that this particular version of the same old story was his own. And yet . . . why had his father not told? Shame, William had long believed. Shame at the connection to someone that his father would not like to admit knowing. But for the first time, William could think of another reason. What if the woman was someone William—and Deborah—knew? The conviction to keep such a name secret could only grow stronger as Deborah's resentment grew, as William's relations with Deborah frayed. William could see this now. But Maude was an ocean away; her name revealed could neither help nor harm her. The larger question was, would it help or harm Elizabeth? And Temple? William could only know what the lack of a name had cost him.

"Her name was Maude. She was . . . she was not a royal governor's wife. But I promise you, I was no more to her than she was to me, and she was happy enough to trade her silence for a milliner's shop."

"And her child? She was happy enough to trade her child?"

And there was the other question that had haunted William throughout his life. Had the woman who'd borne him ever shed a tear for him, or wondered about him, or even tried to discover if he'd grown up as she'd have hoped? This woman had chased him through every year of his life; had he ever chased her in a like way?

But Elizabeth seemed to sense what her last question might have done to William, and she answered it for him. "I know she wasn't happy. But what choice had she? And it was her mistake too, wasn't it? You must live with its consequence and so must she." She paused and added, "But must the boy?"

Elizabeth. His cherished Elizabeth. She went on. "We should be able to do more for him here with us, William. Surely you must have thought of this. You must inquire."

"You would have him here?"

"I would have him here."

48

WILLIAM WROTE TO HIS father. The letter was heartfelt and honest, conveying Elizabeth's eagerness to take in William's son, adding in William's concerns for a father so distant in such tumultuous times. Indeed, according to the domestic and foreign papers that William perused, his father's popularity was declining abroad in direct proportion to its rise at home. William told his father this too. Whether his arguments won the day, or whether—as William heard it rumored—his father was just barely able to escape England with his scalp, that May he came home, bearing the newly named—or renamed—Temple Franklin with him.

The timing was poor. While his father was at sea, a small skirmish at a village called Lexington in the still-troublesome colony of Massachusetts had set all the local militias out marching and drumming and fifing, but William had been too distracted by his son's and father's pending arrival to perhaps pay it the attention it deserved. Indeed, he was taken aback when father and grandson first stepped into the governor's parlor and the elder Franklin stopped just inside the door, staring up at William's full-length portraits of the king and queen.

But then Elizabeth appeared. She went up to William's father, kissed his cheek, took his arm, and led him past the portraits toward the best chair. As soon as she had him properly settled, she turned to Temple, who stood motionless himself but still outside the parlor door, looking around at the massive staircase, the polished floors, the gleaming sconces, the lovely black-and-white mural of Passaic Falls that William had had painted. The falls were the first thing he'd fallen in love with in New Jersey, but not the last, and here, finally, was Temple to enjoy it.

"You're so like your father I feel I know you already," Elizabeth said. "Come in and tell me what you think of your new home."

Temple took several slow, thoughtful steps into the parlor; he too fixed on the portraits of the king and queen in their gilt frames. "'Tis quite fine," he said. "Not at all what I thought America to be."

Elizabeth laughed. "Nor I."

Temple brought his eyes back to Elizabeth. "But you like it here? You don't wish to go home?"

"My husband is here. And now, my son. *This* is home. Come. Sit down. This, I think, will be *your* chair, here."

ELIZABETH. HIS ELIZABETH. OH, how she shined! All through dinner she refused to be disconcerted by the elder Franklin's stiffness, by her husband's nerves; she directed the conversation to neutral things—Temple's London school, his interest in law, his impression of Philadelphia, of America. William had expected some hint of accusation from Temple—*why did you not think to send for me till now?*—but none came. William glanced sideways at his son as often as he could do so unobtrusively, but it was soon clear that his father had delivered to him a fine-looking, well-mannered, well-spoken boy. It was going to be all right, William thought. It was going to be fine.

And then Elizabeth headed up the stairs linked arm in arm with an exhausted Temple, leaving the other father and son pair below. William led his father from the dining room back to the parlor, where on his instruction his father's favorite brandy had been set out, but once inside the door, faced again by the portraits, the elder Franklin paused.

"I find it curious that you choose to honor our oppressor so."

The word *oppressor* drew William up in surprise; he hadn't heard so strong a word out of his father's mouth before. And that these should be amongst Benjamin Franklin's first words to the son he hadn't seen in ten years might have foreshadowed for William what was to come. Fool that he was, it did not.

"They only occupy their rightful place, sir. This is, after all, the royal governor's residence."

William's father drew solemn eyes from the portraits to his son. "Indeed, they do occupy their rightful place. 'Tis you who do not. 'Tis time you give over this unnatural life of toadyism and become your own man." The eyes hardened. "Past time."

The words were not new ones, but when conveyed in a letter already months old on its arrival, the conviction must have gotten lost; the knife buried under the words in this face-to-face declaration took William as much by surprise as the word *oppressor* had. But the fact that his father could utter them standing in the royal governor's house, paying the governor none of that which he might consider his due, rankled William as much as or more than the portraits had rankled his father. Further, that his father could expect—no, demand—that he resign a post that was his sole source of income, identity, and purpose, only to support a doomed cause, meant to William that his father had lost all sense.

William drew himself up and answered his father in the clear, concise manner of discourse he'd first learned from him. "In the past we've agreed that Parliament has erred, but I hope we might likewise agree that we may trust in it to correct its course and continue to govern America with more discretion and freedom than is currently enjoyed by any other nation on earth."

William was dumbfounded when his father exploded.

"Under what hill of horse dung have you shoved your head? Parliament hasn't enough discretion to govern a herd of swine! Resign your post! Get out now before you're dragged out wearing a tar-and-feather coat!"

"I've taken an oath of allegiance to the Crown! Nothing these mad zealots do will ever induce me to swerve from the duty I owe His Majesty!"

"And what of the duty you owe your father? What of the disrespect and humiliation you heap on me by keeping this course?"

"Yes, I keep my course! I have not changed! 'Tis you and these madmen who fly about with any wind that humiliate *me,* make me assert my loyalty over and over to those who should never have cause to doubt it!"

"And your loyalty to your father goes for naught? You, of all people, would put a king who cares nothing for you or your countrymen before that?"

You, of all people. Oh, William knew what his father meant by that, as would Elizabeth, who had just then come to the door with eyes glowing wet but flashing hot at the same time. She came into the room trembling, and William was flooded with love of her and of her courage—only one who feared so could truly possess it.

Elizabeth stepped up to her father-in-law and spit out her words like bitter seeds. "Sir! I ask you to mind where you are. At the head of those stairs is a boy only a few hours arrived into his father's home for the first time, and this is the impression he is to receive?"

William's father fell silent. "I apologize to you for my heedlessness of the situation," he said at last. "You are quite right to chastise me. But if I were able to shake your husband free from this place, you would thank me for it eventually. Now, as I find myself far more tired from my journey than I first seemed, I must beg leave to retire for the evening."

FOR THE REST OF the visit, William's father remained at his charming best—when in the company of Temple and Elizabeth. On his final night he came to William's library, stood square in front of his desk, and began it a second time, but with a chill that William found vastly more terrifying than the former heat.

"Is this your final word? You'll stay at your post? You'll continue to bow and scrape and play toady to these madmen?"

"I dispute who the madmen are, Father. If you and your friends think the most powerful monarch on earth will allow these colonies to be ripped out of his hands by an ungovernable mob, then *you* must keep hold of that title."

"My son," William's father said, but only as if he was marveling at ever having claimed him as such.

William was still struggling to decide on the meaning of those two ponderous words, as well as the best way to respond to them, when his father continued. "Now we must talk about Temple."

William relaxed. "Nothing could have gone more smoothly. He and Elizabeth get on famously. She's remarked to me every night what a fine boy he is—well educated, well mannered, so likable. I must credit you, Father. You've clearly taken considerable time and trouble with the boy."

"Yes." A crisp sheet of paper, black with narrow, densely filled columns, floated out of the elder Franklin's pocket and dropped onto William's desk. "Here's my latest accounting for Temple's expenses while he was with me at London. You see I've made separate note of food, clothing, schooling, books, miscellaneous items. You should find it a handy guide going forward as you will no doubt be moderating your own lifestyle to accommodate it."

William looked down at the paper and blinked. "Thank you, Father. I . . . I am unable at just this time . . . The legislature has again refused my request for a rise in salary, and what they allow me at present wouldn't support a pair of oxen let alone a governor and his wife."

"Not this particular wife, surely. And now it must support a son as well. What plans have you formed concerning his schooling?"

"I'd thought Eton—"

"So you would send him back to England. And how would you pay for a school like Eton on your governor's salary?"

William couldn't. Of course he'd thought of Temple's schooling, but he'd hoped that his father would continue as he'd begun, fronting Temple's expenses until William was in a position to repay them. Looking up at the elder Franklin now, his face so scarred with bitterness at even the mention of the words *Eton* and *England,* William was shocked by the change in him. How had they come to these opposite poles? It was just not possible that his father actually believed something good for America could be spawned by this rebellion.

But neither was it possible that his father would pay for Temple to enroll at Eton.

"Perhaps New York," William tried, thinking of his Loyalist friends there, but apparently his father was thinking of them too. His face hardened further.

"I should like to enroll Temple in the academy."

William looked down at the ledger on his desk, so carefully inked, with such deadly purpose. His father would enroll Temple in the academy that he had founded. In Philadelphia. The *free* academy. The money was the convenient excuse, of course; he had come here to discover how fixed William was in his Tory views, and now he was determined to get Temple away from them. But the money was the thing that would tie William's hands. He had none. He had a wife. And a son?

"I've only just begun to know the boy," William said.

"He must keep with me during the school season, of course, but he would stay with you the remainder of the summer, and return to you at the school holidays. You must think what's best for him."

"I must talk with Elizabeth," William said, although both men knew the matter was done.

WILLIAM'S FATHER LEFT FOR Philadelphia the next morning.

"I hope next time we meet events will have moderated enough to allow us a better accord," William said at the carriage door.

"The only event that can bring us into accord is for you to resign your royal appointment and honor the father and the country to which you were born," his father answered.

WILLIAM WROTE TO HIS father the following week, apologizing for any disrespectful words he might have spoken, trusting that neither man would allow a difference in their politics to affect their personal relation, promising his continued gratitude to a father who had done so much for a son who could only struggle harder each day to deserve all he'd been given.

William's father never answered his son's letter. In August he wrote to Temple, sending him instructions and travel money to Philadelphia.

49

Philadelphia, 1776

THE PENNY POT HAD changed; Anne had changed it. The old smoke-filled, beer-soaked main room remained, but in the back Anne had added a smaller room and filled it with cloth-covered tables, upholstered chairs, a Pennsylvania Fireplace on the hearth. Here she began to draw another kind of patron, one who wished to assemble with like-minded gentlemen for thoughtful, constructive discussion that was best kept apart from the general public. Privately, Anne called it the "Common Sense" room, after the recently published pamphlet that seemed to provoke the most conversation. She was therefore unsurprised one day when into it walked Benjamin and William Franklin.

But of course it wasn't William. William was grown and gone, the royal governor of New Jersey, and this was a boy not older than sixteen, surely, but just as surely a Franklin by blood and manner, if not wit.

"Allow me to introduce to you the Widow Hewe," Franklin said to the boy. "Widow, may I introduce to you my son's godson, Temple Franklin?"

The boy dipped his head with perfect form but said nothing. Anne said nothing. William-but-not-William had cost her her own wits.

"We come for some pudding and pie. Shall we sit here by this wonderful fireplace? What clever fellow contrived that thing? I wonder. And what clever lass decided to purchase it?"

The two men settled in front of the fire. Anne retreated to the stairs, but there were his steps, heavier but just as nimble, behind her. She turned.

"And how fare you, my dear Annie?"

"Well. And you, sir?"

Franklin's face, still so strong, so changeable, sobered. "You must know I've lost my old and faithful companion. I every day become sensible of the greatness of that loss, which cannot now be repaired."

"Yes, well." Anne paused. "This boy. This *god*son. Yours?"

Franklin studied Anne as he'd been known to study her before, assessing her risk to him, but he certainly knew that whatever her risk to him, she was no risk to William. "William's. We say he is the child of a close relation. Deceased. Thus far no one has dared question."

"So. He takes after his father, then."

"Godfather, please."

"I speak of William. William takes after his father. And this boy's mother?"

Franklin looked down the stairs, up at the ceiling, back to Anne. "I should like to think she's as well settled as you are. I did my best to make it so."

"A Grissom's shop for her?"

"I had naught to do with Grissom's shop. That was his own suggestion. But I kept an eye, Annie. I kept an eye. I would never have left you worse off than before."

"And now you have this boy with you, and you bring him here. Why?"

"I bring him here because I'm proud of him, and I wished you to see how straight and tall and fine this little seedling grows."

"And what of William?"

Franklin's features moved again, locked, darkened. "William grows in his own direction. He is lost to me now."

"Lost! Lost? What do you mean by lost? You've always worked to see him well."

"I can do nothing for William. He hears nothing but his own counsel. But I *can* make sure his boy sees a better example."

Anne sank down onto the stair. "I hear such talk. I hear it every day, such rumbling! Do you agree with this fellow Paine who writes with such certainty about independency?"

"Any man with the wit to read must think so."

"But William. What will become of William?"

"God knows." Franklin picked up Anne's hand, squeezed it, and dropped it. How unsettling that change in her skin, from cold to hot to cold again!

50

Perth Amboy, 1776

IT WAS PAST MIDNIGHT when the knock sounded on William's library door. As royal governor he was used to being disturbed with matters both trivial and monumental at any hour of the day or night, but there was something about the insistent tempo of this knock, as well as about the particular time in which he now lived, that caused a small thrumming to set up in his throat.

"What!"

Hamilton stepped into the room. "I've news, sir."

William Franklin looked at his servant in irritation, but he couldn't have said whether his irritation was with Hamilton or with the letters to his recalcitrant assemblymen that he'd been attempting to write. "Then give it, Hamilton."

"Your father's passed through Woodbridge in a fair-size convoy; the word goes he's on a secret diplomatic mission to Canada to treat with the French."

William stood up. He'd noticed a marked change in his son's letters from Philadelphia of late, a dutiful neutrality that not only avoided all mention of the grandfather's politics, but avoided all mention of the grandfather himself; the fact that the dough-faced Hamilton should carry the first news of the man in months galled William almost as much as the news itself. But that news was, of course, too insane to even credit. First was the intended purpose of the mission—as if anyone in his right mind would credit the French in Canada with taking such a fool's leap; second was the fact that his father, at his age, would ever undertake such a mission in March. March in Philadelphia or New Jersey was one kind of thing; March in Canada was altogether something else.

"Where do you hear this nonsense?"

"From Fitch at the King's Arms." Hamilton pinched his lips. "Not to say the likes of such a party would stop there. But Fitch knows Potter at the Dog—the Dog's more in the rebel way and they stopped there. Potter told Fitch he overheard talk of a diplomatic mission to Canada to enlist the aid of the French in their cause, which is to say, in the rebellion."

"Who's of the party?"

Hamilton unnecessarily and offensively named William's father again. "Dr. Franklin, and one Samuel Chase, a pair named Carroll. And a Jesuit priest."

William knew the names Chase and Carroll from his own spies, but it was the unnamed Jesuit priest that convinced William of the rumor's validity; only someone as cunning as his father would think to bring along a priest to deal with the Catholic French. But that wasn't the worst of it. Despite their violent argument, William had not until this minute truly believed that his father could cast him off so completely as to travel within a few insignificant miles of him and not stop with him, to stop at the Dog instead. The *Dog*. Christ in heaven!

Hamilton left, and William climbed the stairs to his room. Elizabeth was sitting up in bed—the sheet, her shift, her skin all the same stark white in the glow from his lamp, as lovely as the Greek Venus and as easy to shatter into sparkling shards.

"William, I heard Hamilton talking to Cobb and Percy; they say your father's passed through Woodbridge without stopping here. It can't be true, can it?"

Damn Hamilton. And Cobb and Percy too. Elizabeth had remained in poor health almost continuously since that first altercation between William and his father; it had worsened again when Temple left to live with his grandfather in Philadelphia. The latest physician William had called in had told him to keep her away from smoky rooms, dusty roads, violent winds, extreme cold, but he'd said nothing about the state of nerves that seemed to accompany each attack. William sat on the bed and looked his wife over with care, noting her somewhat accelerated breathing but as yet no gray or blue tinge to her skin. He held out his arm and she came into it, leaning against him. He began to absentmindedly rub her back, but she shrugged him off.

"William. Tell me it can't have come to this."

William started in attempting to explain his father's actions—*urgent business, haste, secrecy essential*—but halfway through he found himself out of temper and, in fact, out of caring anymore what Elizabeth might think of his father. "I don't know why my father does what he does, Elizabeth."

Elizabeth pulled back and studied him, not liking what she saw in him if her cobbled brow could be taken as fair hint of it. When she spoke again her tone had changed from one of alarm to one of conciliation. "Well, I do, now I think of it. He's afraid. If his cohorts discover him in communication with you, they'll think he gives you their secrets. They'll think him disloyal. 'Tis all it is, William; how silly of us not to see it."

But if Elizabeth meant her words to soothe William, she'd picked the wrong ones; her argument only worked to prove the opposite point. Other royal governors had simply retired to their country estates to wait out this doomed rebellion, but this was a luxury William could not enjoy. His father being who he was, it was essential that William prove to king and Parliament again and again that his loyalties were unaffected by his unfortunate personal connection to one of the rebellion's leading activists. Indeed, if all Perth Amboy knew of his father's trip to Canada and the purpose behind it, what was to keep the news from reaching Lord Dartmouth at the Crown Office? And if the news reached Lord Dartmouth from other than William's own pen, what would—what *should*—Lord Dartmouth think of it? That William's loyalties were divided. That William would pass on some but not all of the rebel activity in his colony, and none of it that involved his father. Conversely, if William did write of this secret mission to Lord Dartmouth, if he did put his father's name to paper, if the rebellion failed—*when* the rebellion failed—his father could be hanged as a traitor.

William stood up, now as unfairly irritated with his wife as he'd been with Hamilton. "I've work to do," he said.

WILLIAM HAD JUST PUSHED aside the empty sheet of paper for the fourth time when the library door opened and Elizabeth entered, trailing a pair of shawls over her nightdress. One of the shawls was an airy, becoming thing, the other ugly and coarse and much more practical for a chilly night. William looked at the shawls and thought how much they were the essence of Elizabeth now: The airy shawl had come from a fancy London shop, the wool one from a New Jersey farmer's wife.

Elizabeth came up to William and slid onto his lap, encircling him inside her two shawls. "You work too long," she said. "Come to bed."

As if he'd heard them, Temple, home on a short break in his schooling, appeared framed in the library door behind Elizabeth. Only Temple could sleep through Hamilton's and Cobb's and Percy's chatter on the landing outside his bedroom door and wake at a conversation one floor below him, William thought. Elizabeth slipped off William's lap to give him an impulsive hug, the kind of hug that William had looked for in vain most of his childhood, and all William's previous annoyance with his wife was washed away by a mad rush of love.

"Why is everyone up and about?" Temple asked.

"Your father's up because he's working. I'm up because I wish him to stop working. Come, if we leave him be he might finish before dawn breaks."

Elizabeth and Temple moved toward the library door, arm in arm. Although William had found little time to spend with the boy, Elizabeth took every minute she could capture, but even so, William had barely cast his eyes back to his desk when Elizabeth returned, alone.

"William," she said. "Something's more wrong than your father's stopping at the Dog and Whistle. What is it?"

"Nothing. A bit of trouble with my assembly. Nothing of any consequence."

Elizabeth bent down, touched her lips to his lips, smoothed the collar of his coat. "William," she said. "My poor, dear William. Have you not yet learned about consequences? Now hurry up and finish so I might get some sleep."

IN THE END ELIZABETH slept and William lay awake, comfortable between crisp, warm sheets in his down-filled bed, thinking of his father at the Dog and Whistle, perhaps sleeping on bare tick, perhaps sharing his bed with another of his party who would no doubt stink of rum and smoke and God knew what else. William reached out and touched Elizabeth's powder-soft skin, inhaled the scent of her English soap, imported yearly at greater and greater trouble and expense; his father still used the caustic soap his family manufactured in Boston and sent to him by the crate. Was this great divide between them perhaps first brewed in soap? Whatever the brew, it was his father's making, and now his father must pay the price, as William had already begun to pay. Oh, how he was paying! His only relief was that he'd managed, thus far, to keep the extent of the damage from his wife.

Elizabeth did not yet know that the New Jersey Assembly was no longer paying heed to William's admonition that *they* should be molding public opinion, not allowing the people—the *rebels*—to mold the *assembly's* opinion. Neither did Elizabeth know—he hoped to God she did not know—that calls for the governor's resignation had begun to come from others besides his father, within the New Jersey colony itself. William could tout a long list of successes as governor and, looking ahead, had begun to form another long list, but now his goals had shrunk to one, keeping his post by whatever means necessary. Keeping Elizabeth as she should be kept. Elizabeth Downes may not have fallen in love with the royal governor of New Jersey, but that was certainly whom she'd married, with every expectation of a lifestyle similar to the richness she'd left behind in London. Bad enough that she'd discovered herself married to a bastard, that she'd read for herself what that prig John Adams had written in the papers, what Penn had written. But was that not also his father's fault? Only last fall a mutual friend had shared with William something out of one of his father's recent letters, thinking it a kindness to apprise William of how the state of affairs—read state of the estate—now sat: *My son is lost to me forever,* William's father had written to this friend, and he had gone on to announce that he was altering his will to favor Sally's oldest boy instead. So there it was—from bastard to legitimate heir and back to bastard in the course of a single life.

There was but one thing, one *legitimate* thing, that William could now call his, and that was his royal appointment. His governor's post. But if William were to remain in it, his father must be hung out over a cliff. But whose fault would *that* be? Not William's! Not! William had never done anything but his duty and he would never do anything but his duty; if his father chose to treat with Canada, he put a noose of his own making around his neck.

Unless . . . A mission to Canada. An effort to enlist the French. *Could* the mission succeed? Could the Americans and the French in Canada combine forces and wills and together actually succeed in driving the English army, the greatest in the world, from the North American continent? And if they did, then what? Thirteen colonies adrift, ruled by nothing but a gaggle of politicians loosely assembled into a thing they called a congress. The English governors set in place in all the other colonies would go home, of that William had no doubt, which would leave William, the only American-born amongst them, to his singular fate. But what fate? Could it mean the younger and not the elder Franklin might end up dangling from the end of the rope?

No. No and no and no. It was not possible. Loyalty could never fail to be rewarded—William's father had taught him that. His friends at the Crown Office would see to his safety and that of his wife and son. Unless he lost his friends at the Crown Office for failure to do his duty. For disloyalty, for it could never be called anything other than that. William's duty was plain; he must write to Lord Dartmouth of his father's mission to Canada, and his father must take the consequences of his decisions on himself. His father, who'd left William caught in such a position in the first place. He had been forced to write to Lord Dartmouth after the Stamp Act riots, after the nonimportation agreement, after Boston's destruction of the tea, the same tortured words each time: "No attachments or connections will ever impel me to swerve from my duty to my king." And afterward, and since, he'd sent the Crown Office specific evidence of the rebels' contact with the Spanish and French, the ports they were using for smuggling gunpowder from the French islands, the names of known smugglers.

But now William must write something worse. Far worse. But

what choice did he have? How else to keep the only accomplishment that could not—it could *not*—be credited to his father—this governorship? How to keep his *life*? William wished only to go on as they'd gone on before; it was his father who wished to change it all, ruin it all, cast William into obscurity for all time as the "great inconvenience," the "base-born brat," to elevate himself as "the great genius of the day," as he was already being called in the newspapers.

William got out of bed, relit his lamp from the fire, returned to his library, and sat at his desk. He drew the blank piece of paper toward him again and began to write.

It has come to my attention that a secret delegation moves
northward through New Jersey with plans to prevail on the Canadians
to enter into the confederacy with the other colonies. The delegation
consists of: Samuel Chase, Charles Carroll, John Carroll and

There William stopped. He could not. But he could not not.

William set down his pen, covered his letter with his arms, dropped his head onto his arms, and wept.

51

Philadelphia, 1776

THE BOY CAME BACK, without his grandfather but with a girl, one who'd served at the Penny Pot for barely a month before she'd run away with a deserter off one of the ships. Anne had seen this girl about town since, showing some wear but still shining bright enough to latch on to the occasional man for a month or two before casting him off in the face of a better offer. But Temple Franklin? What kind of offer could a boy his age make to such a girl?

The same old one, as it turned out. They ate a platter of bread and cheese and drank a bottle of wine while Anne took note of Temple Franklin's long, slender fingers, his long, delicate nose. Just as Temple's father had grown to be handsomer and taller than his father, so Temple had grown to outshine them both in looks, and both the younger Franklins seemed to have captured at least a measure of the elder's charm; Anne watched the way Temple leaned into the girl and whispered, then drew back and smiled, then leaned in again and whispered. The girl laughed, shook her head, laughed again, and then Anne saw it, the glint of silver passing from boy to girl, the girl's hand opening and closing and opening, looking from the coin to Temple Franklin and back again, as if to determine which shone brighter, or whether, if added together, the shine would grow bright enough.

Temple stood up and walked toward Anne where she lingered yet, at the foot of the stairs. He smiled at her as another had smiled at her, as sure of the result as the other had been. "How much for a bed?"

"Full up," Anne said.

The boy gave a sheepish grin and shrugged, perhaps his most charming performance yet, and would have turned away, but Anne caught his arm.

"Perhaps your grandfather never mentioned to you that I used to care for your father when he was young."

"No! He made no mention!"

"How fares your father?"

The boy's face, so open the moment before, took on a wary look. "He writes he is well."

"And you answer his letter as fast as all dutiful sons do, which is to say never quite fast enough?"

The boy smiled again, familiar again. "Next you'll tell me to go home now and write my letter."

Anne looked behind Temple; the girl had gone, taking Temple's coin with her, as Anne had hoped she would do—nothing like receiving a cheap lesson while still young. And oh, this boy was so young! He was William in those years when Anne could discover all that was new in him only glimpse by glimpse; William when he ran away to be a pirate, William when he turned to soldiering and she fretted over his fate as his father never seemed to do.

"You'll find your own time for your letter," Anne said. "Come and join me for a plate of mutton stew and we'll talk of your father."

But again, the face turned wary. Had his father or his grandfather warned him of talking of the family to strangers? "I thank you for the kind offer," he said, "but indeed, I must go." He picked up her hand and bowed over it.

52

Perth Amboy, 1776

WILLIAM'S FATHER HAD ONCE taught his son a method he used when addressing any difficult decision—"prudential algebra," he called it—a listing of the pros and cons of the case, canceling one against another of equal weight until only one option was left. With something like hope William set aside his half-written dispatch and pulled a fresh sheet of paper from his desk. He labeled the left side pro, the right side con, and sat considering the matters that might be worthy of a list with such deadly intent. Any such columns of his father's would no doubt be filled with world affairs and discoveries that would shatter long-held suppositions and beliefs—William hadn't a prayer or an intention of competing with that; let the son's list read like the boy's it was, for there in the boy he was stuck.

Pirate, William wrote under pro, and *Alexander Annard's Classical Academy,* but before he could name a third thing his pen had already traveled across the page to the right. Across from *Pirate* he wrote *Privateer,* and drew a line through both, the one canceling the other out.

And what of *Annard's*? Had not his father listened to his stepmother, pulled him out, and returned him to the hated printing office? Across from *Annard's* William wrote *Printing Office* and lined that pair of entries out. But he returned to the pro column and quickly, before he could drift over to the right side of the page, he wrote *King's Army, Law Studies with Joseph Galloway, Inns of Court, London, London, London,* set down his pen, and sat back in his seat.

For what came next was Elizabeth, the royal appointment, the royal oath. William had become who he'd become, and in the end, prudential algebra couldn't solve that. For William, now, there was no choice. He was who he was. He picked up the columned sheet and tore it down the middle, tore it again, crumpled it. He pulled into place the letter he'd begun so many hours ago and read what he'd written thus far:

> *It has come to my attention that a secret delegation moves northward through New Jersey with plans to prevail on the Canadians to enter into the confederacy with the other colonies. The delegation consists of: Samuel Chase, Charles Carroll, John Carroll and*

William picked up his pen, inked it, and carefully etched the last name into the paper: *Dr. Franklin.*

THE FIRST REAL THUNDERCLOUDS rolled toward William at the beginning of June, when a new, illegal Provincial Congress was formed, William's own legitimate assembly declared void, and his salary stopped. The storm broke on June nineteenth at two in the morning, when someone began to pound violently against the thick doors of Proprietary House.

William was sitting at the small desk in his bedchamber writing a letter to his son, Temple, unwilling to leave Elizabeth to do his usual work in the library because of the increasingly poor state of her health. William began by confirming plans for the boy's summer visit, and continued by inquiring after the health of Sally and her family. He paused. Went on. *How fares the old man after his Canada travels? Was his health greatly impaired? Nothing ever gave me more pain than his undertaking that journey.* Just remembering that pain had caused William to set the pen down, just as the pounding on the door commenced.

Elizabeth sat up in bed. "William! What is it? Who knocks at this hour?" But William was already at the window. A half-moon lit what was on most days an impeccably manicured lawn, but on this night fifty mounted and armed militiamen were churning it to mud.

"Nothing, my love. One of my father's overly dedicated mail couriers. You know what they say of them—ride all night without a stop for a cup. Go back to sleep." William crossed to the bed and kissed his wife's forehead, already clammy, but he couldn't afford her a second more.

He left the room and met his servant Hamilton at the top of the stairs, as white or whiter than Elizabeth.

"'Tis the rebel militia, sir! Come with an order from—"

"Shut your mouth," William hissed. "Alarm her and you'll be mucking out the stable."

As William stepped off the last stair and saw the militiaman standing in the foyer, it gave him pause to consider how swiftly he'd chosen to blame a mail carrier—and indirectly, his father—for the early-hour disturbance, but he took care not to let any hint of that old bitterness reach his face for fear the obviously nervous militiaman at the foot of the stairs might find some courage in it.

William greeted the man by pointing to the dispatch he held in his hand, acknowledging neither his illegal rank nor his right to be standing in the royal governor's house. The militiaman stepped forward and handed William the sealed and folded parchment. "From Colonel Sirling, First New Jersey Regiment."

First New Jersey *rebel* regiment. William Franklin, who'd kissed the ring of King George himself, who was an appointed officer of the British Crown, William Franklin was to have his wife's peace disturbed by this? William broke the seal on the document in disgust, read in disbelief. One of his couriers had been intercepted carrying "a treasonous letter" to the Crown, and William had been declared "an enemy to the liberties of this country." Colonel Sirling had ordered William's arrest, and he was to be transported to Burlington, to await the "will and pleasure of the Continental Congress."

The will and pleasure of the Continental Congress. Good God, that it had come to this! That one of the king's own royal governors must sit and wait on the whim of an illegal mob that dared to call itself a congress! It could only be considered proof of a world gone mad, proof that all William was and all he stood for was now to be tested to the utter limit. It was proof—and there it took William some time to even spell out the thought in his head—it was proof that the rift between William Franklin and his father, who now sat on the Continental Congress, was complete.

William worked to keep any hint of his mental disarray from his face, to focus on the document. He read it again, so enraged that the black letters turned red and wavered on the page; he waited till his vision cleared and read it a third time; this time he saw that he needed to swallow what he needed to swallow until he was able to marshal some support. He was not, after all, friendless.

"You will allow me to inform my wife?" Without waiting for an answer he turned for the stairs, making sure to take each one with an even, measured tread. They would not see him run. Not yet!

Elizabeth was at the window, gripping the sill, leaning forward as if to peer out, but William had long experience in identifying the nuances of posture and knew that she also leaned so in an effort to capture her fleeting breath.

"Soldiers, William!"

"Yes, my love." William had already gone to his desk in the corner and begun to write furiously. "And I must go with them until the court clears the matter up, and so I must get this letter off at once to the chief justice. I promise you, it shall be resolved and I shall be back home almost before it's been dispatched."

"But, William! At night!"

"Hush, Elizabeth. Keep your breath." William finished his letter to the chief justice. He grabbed another sheet and began to write, this one for the press, for his people.

> To be represented as an enemy to the liberties of my country
> merely for doing my duty to their future happiness and safety is
> sufficient to rouse the indignation of any man not dead to human
> feelings. I appeal to every individual in the province to vouch
> for me. Let me exhort you to avoid, above all things, the traps
> of independency and republicanism now set before you, however
> tempting they may be baited. No independent state ever was, or
> ever can be, so happy as we have been, and still might be, under the
> present government . . .

He sealed and addressed both papers, went to the landing where the other servants were hovering, and handed Hamilton the pair of envelopes, peppering him with instructions he'd no doubt forget by the time he reached the stairs. He returned to Elizabeth, folded her into his arms, began the circles against her back.

"I do not—"

"Hush, now. Hush."

Elizabeth fell silent, but the breath came no easier under his hand; it didn't matter, he couldn't wait. Already, here came the steps on the stairs, and he would not allow them to upset Elizabeth by arresting him in her presence. His Elizabeth. Dear God, what was to become of Elizabeth? But as he tore down the stairs that question had already become supplanted with another: Had his father, from his seat on the congress, sanctioned this illegal act, or had he stood as a lone dissenting voice of reason amid a pack of rabid wolves howling for the arrest of the only American-born governor on the continent?

William reached the bottom of the stairs just as sixteen soldiers with guns and bayonets drawn charged through the doors, but down the stairs behind him hurtled Elizabeth.

"William! Dear God in heaven! What do they do to you?"

"You mustn't fret, love. 'Tis all show. They won't dare harm an officer of the Crown."

"But, William, tell me, what shall I do? Shall I send word to your father?"

"Yes, write to my father," William answered, but only to ease her, for of course his father already knew of it.

53

THE JOURNEY TO BURLINGTON, to the seat of the Provincial Congress, was long, exhausting, and mortifying; William was paraded under
guard past the laughing, spitting crowds of farmers and shopkeepers
who'd once cheered his arrival in a colony he'd done nothing but better.
The Brunswick inn where they stopped for the night only heaped more
humiliation on William; he was confined to a filthy room and so rigidly
guarded he was forced to relieve himself into a bucket in public view. At
daylight he was kicked awake and without food or drink thrust back into
the carriage and delivered to another filthy inn at Burlington.

But William was not yet defeated; when the guard came to bring
him before the tribunal the next day he said, "I have no legal business
with your congress," and refused to leave his room.

The guards didn't trouble to argue with him; they left and returned
with thirty more soldiers who carted him off at gunpoint, and at gunpoint he was brought before the tribunal.

. . . .

IT WAS LIKE A play, thought William, or a puppet show, these supposed five "justices" acting out their impostor roles in neat wigs and shined buttons, simpering drivel to one another only to make him wait and seethe and wait more. At length the central figure on the stage took his first good look at William, and William returned it evenly.

"Mr. Franklin, is it true that you tried to convene an illegal assembly during this month of June?"

"I know of no illegal assembly beyond this one. And on the grounds of its illegality, I have nothing further to say. You may do as you please."

The puppets looked at one another in such perfect unison William was more than ever convinced of sticks pushed, strings pulled; one puppet in particular grew red faced as William continued to sit in composed silence.

The lead player resumed. "A letter of yours has been intercepted, sir, written in March of this year, addressed to Lord Dartmouth at the Crown Office. It names certain gentlemen, diplomats on an official mission. Do you recall this letter and who it named?"

So this was the intent—not to elicit already known facts but to humiliate William by making him say his father's name, by making him repeat the words by which he'd been accused of convicting his father of treason and by doing so convicting himself of the same.

William felt the old rage first, but next the oily sweat of fear. *Say nothing.* He held himself straight and still, and it proved to be all that was needed to bring the red-faced inquisitor leaping to his feet.

"How dare you! How dare you sit before us with your fine airs and pretend yourself a gentleman when everyone knows out of what baseness you were got!"

There all semblance of due process fell away. Several other justices rose from their seats, someone called for quiet, another called for the guard; a third attempted to insert a motion into the pandemonium ordering William's return to the inn to await his verdict, and someone managed to holler a second. William laughed out loud. Had these fools not heard? The verdict had been delivered. He was his father's base-born bastard. There was nothing more to be said.

BY NIGHTFALL WILLIAM HAD become ill, fevered. When he was told to expect no word till the tribunal reconvened in four days, he begged for paper and pen to write to Elizabeth, couching his words in careful terms that he hoped would slip past those who vetted it.

> *My dearest Elizabeth,*
> *I am well; do not be concerned. I am held at the Burlington Sword and Shield, my room tight and cozy under the northeast eaves, kept company by a half-dozen cheerful and attentive guards. As I shall be here four days more at the least I should like you to inform Hamilton to cancel my meeting on the twenty-fifth.*
>
> *I am ever your loving,*
> *W. Franklin*

If the letter got through, Elizabeth would know what to do; she would alert William's friends and they would know where William was and under what kind of guard and that they had four days to effect an escape.

But the letter didn't pass. It was returned to William in half-inch shreds, accompanied by a good deal of cursing and slamming about of swords. In his fevered sleep he dreamed of Elizabeth pinned at the end of a militiaman's musket, gasping for air, shouting at him between gasps, "Bastard! Bastard!"—a word she'd never once used, despite having double the cause.

. . . .

ANOTHER OFFICER, A CAPTAIN in the rebel militia, arrived at the inn bearing the answer from congress, which he read aloud. "'As the said William Franklin by this and his former conduct, in many instances, appears to be a virulent enemy to this country and a person that may prove dangerous, therefore, it is unanimously resolved, that the said William Franklin be confined in such place and a manner as the honorable Continental Congress shall direct.'"

"Such place" proved to be a gaol in Hartford, Connecticut, a place as far away from William's friends—and Elizabeth—as the Continental Congress could get him. William was carried on the rough, two-hundred-mile journey and displayed along the route to jeers and catcalls like a caged bear. Perhaps the worst moment came as they entered the outskirts of Hartford, and one of his guards decided to taunt him by handing him a local newspaper. William was described as "a noted Tory and ministerial tool exceedingly busy in perplexing the cause of liberty."

Ministerial tool. William looked at the top of the paper to make note of the date: July the fourth, 1776. The date could never signify anything to anyone but William, but to him it would forever mark the day he'd been robbed of his freedom and his reputation. Of everything.

54

Philadelphia, July 8, 1776

THEY WERE ALL THERE, gathered at the steps of the State House—
the Germans, the Scots, the Irish, the Quakers, the free Negroes, the
English. The Americans. Toward the front of the crowd stood Franklin and four others, one of them extraordinarily tall, with the kind of
peppered skin that didn't like the sun; the other three were so easily
lost in the crowd that Anne couldn't remember one of their faces the
minute she turned away. Later, she discovered that they were the members of the committee that had drafted the extraordinary document
that was now being read aloud from the balcony above. Anne had
come to hear the declaration, but she'd also come to speak to one of
these now-famed authors of liberty about his incarcerated son. She
reached again into her skirt pocket and withdrew the bit of paper she'd
torn from the *Gazette* but hours before.

William Franklin, a noted Tory and ministerial tool
exceedingly busy in perplexing the cause of liberty, has been

arrested; he is the son of Doctor Benjamin Franklin, the great patron of American liberty . . .

The unknown orator had begun to read what he billed as a unanimous declaration of the thirteen united states of America. Anne folded her bit of newspaper into her palm and gave her best effort to attending the spoken words, words she could once have believed in, and yet how blackened they were now by the printed words she held in her hand!

> *Separate and equal station* . . . with William in gaol. *Life,*
> *Liberty* . . . with William in gaol. *All experience hath shewn, that*
> *mankind are more disposed to suffer, while evils are sufferable* . . .
> *But when a long train of abuses and usurpations evinces a design to*
> *reduce them under absolute Despotism, it is their right, it is their duty,*
> *to throw off such Government* . . .

To throw off William.
The list of royal abuses rolled on.

> *For taking away our charters, abolishing our most valuable*
> *laws and altering fundamentally the forms of our governments, for*
> *suspending our own legislatures* . . .

But how could William not be one of "ours," born not a half dozen streets away, born to one of the crafters of this noble document, born to Anne?

> *We, therefore, the Representatives of the united States of America,*
> *in General Congress, Assembled . . . do, in the Name, and by*
> *Authority of the good People of these Colonies, solemnly publish and*
> *declare, that these United Colonies are, and of Right ought to be Free*

*and Independent States . . . And for the support of this Declaration
. . . we mutually pledge to each other our Lives, our Fortunes and our
sacred Honor.*

At the cost of *William's* life, *William's* fortune, *William's* honor?
This, then, was the question that Anne had come to ask. As the
crowd cheered, roared, raged in that bloodlust way only a declaration of war could bring on, Anne pushed through the bodies to the
front, running afoul of elbows, knees, mouths. To her surprise,
Franklin looked more somber than most; to her even greater surprise, before she could reach him he detached himself from the tall
man and began to make his way down the street toward the water,
alone. He moved at a good pace; Anne took after him as soon as she
could free herself from the entangling crowd, but she couldn't catch
him up without breaking into a conspicuous run. She followed
behind him; to her amazement, he turned at Christ Church and
entered the graveyard.

Anne might have given Franklin his moment to make his peace,
or to do whatever it was he'd come to do there, but her shoe
crunched over a stick and he turned and discovered her. So there
they were, and Anne saw no sense in pretending they weren't. She
drew closer.

"We think the same once again, I see," Franklin said. "A day to
share with them, is it not? In my case, to ask forgiveness, to ask if she
might agree that it was worth the sacrifice. And what do you plan to
say to Mr. Hewe?"

Anne thrust the crumpled bit of newspaper at Franklin. "How can
you do this to your own son?"

Franklin glanced at the paper, and all that had been solemn and
vulnerable in his features the minute before hardened into a thunder-
ous black mask. "He is not my son."

"He is your *son*."

"He is a son who would have stolen his father's life, his livelihood, his good name!"

"And so you steal his."

"I! I! 'Tis the business of Congress. Nay, nay, 'tis *William's* business. He was warned again and again and yet he goes ahead in disregard of the consequences, accusing his own father of traitorous acts. And you come here and stand before my wife's grave, my wife who tried day in and out to make something honorable out of our vile spawn—" He stopped, trembling. He held up his hands to keep Anne from speaking—or to keep himself from speaking; he breathed in and out, gathering himself.

He began again. "I . . . forgive me. Dear God, you see what he brings me to. Never was I prouder of a boy, never have I stood in anything but full admiration of you. Well, perhaps there was an instance, aboard ship—" He smiled bitterly. "Would you have done better with him? God's truth, I don't know."

"But what is the charge? Can it be they'll charge *him* as a traitor? For that he would hang. Surely you cannot stand by and allow your son to—"

"There's naught I can do."

"Naught you can do! You who sit in the Congress that voted to hang him?"

"We voted to jail him."

"'We'! You mean to say that indeed you voted so?"

"Understand this, Anne. William's fate was his own then and 'tis his own now. We are through." He turned back to his wife's grave. "Perhaps if I'd left him here at home and insisted Deborah come with me to London . . . I should have insisted . . . in truth, if I'd even asked her a second time—"

Franklin turned back to Anne. "But what does this day teach us? There's no going backward now. God alone knows how we shall all end." He paused. He seemed to study Anne for a long time. "Although

I suspect I know where I shall be when it all ends. I'm an old man. How likely am I to return from this next mission? You must speak of this to no one, Annie, but I go to Europe soon, to plead with the French for aid. I plan to take Temple along. If I'm to die in a foreign land, I should have a relative on hand to close my eyes. But 'tis for the boy's good too. He spends time with his stepmother, who loves him as her own, but presses him to visit his father in gaol. I tremble to think where that might lead. I must take him away from his father's influence and his father's friends and put him to work at a better cause." Franklin looked back at the grave and gave a bitter chuckle. "What *she* might have said of crossing the sea to *France,* with my bastard son's bastard son along, I think I might know."

The words chilled Anne; she'd never heard Franklin use the word *bastard* before.

Anne was still attempting to interpret its meaning when Franklin turned to her again, with that old, speculative look in his eye. "What the devil, Annie, why do you not come with me?"

"Come where?"

"Why, to France!"

Anne stared at Franklin, seventy years old and looking it now, his hair receding, his waist expanding; she'd heard rumors of gout, rheumatism, kidney stones. And yet he was ready to travel across an ocean in wartime, to France, to help win this war he'd helped to start, and he wanted her to come. What was he after this time, lover or nurse? Or did he simply prefer a woman's softer hand to close his eyes?

As if he'd read her thought, as he'd appeared to do so often in the past, Franklin began to grin. He scooped up her hands. "Come! Let's do it this time! And right, for once! The pair of us unencumbered, with a new boy along to make into an honorable man!"

Anne noted—indeed, how could she not?—there was no mention of making her into an honorable woman, but she didn't care—she'd already made herself respectable without Franklin's help. But France!

She must admit, he'd caught her with the idea. And Temple—Temple had caught her the first minute he'd stepped into her tavern. It had been William who'd almost lured her to England, hoping to lay some claim to him there; could William's son now lure her to France? *Could* she claim something of William's son, if her own son was indeed to be lost to her forever? Anne could still feel the dampening ball of crumpled paper she'd been holding clenched in her fist; she could not give up on William as easily as his father seemed to have done, but she could do nothing for William alone. Surely the Great Patron of American Liberty could do something for his son if he chose, and perhaps in France, with Franklin's now ailing flesh once again in her hands . . .

Other people began to enter the graveyard. Franklin looked around. "I must go," he said. "Indeed, I shouldn't have left, but this day . . . This day of all days—" He looked to the grave, then away. "Say you'll think on it; say that at least, Annie. Let me call at the tavern tomorrow for your answer. You and I and Temple and France and a new country to be nursed into life. Think on it!" He kissed her hands and took himself off, looking fifty again.

Anne left the graveyard, but paused before stepping into Market Street. The street was busy now, the crowd from the State House dispersing, heading toward their homes or their favorite taverns; indeed, Anne spied a number of her patrons heading toward Vine Street. She spied Grissom heading toward his shop. *I had naught to do with Grissom's shop. That was his own suggestion.* But why? Because he admired her courage, even back then? Or had he foreseen the other use Anne might be to him in time? Or was he simply largehearted, as Franklin himself had once called him?

Anne stepped into Market Street and paused, waiting for Grissom to catch her up. They greeted each other and walked together in the old silence, toward the water, toward the upholstery shop and the Penny Pot, Anne pummeled by her own thoughts of old worlds and new, Grissom no doubt wrapped in his. She was startled when at last he spoke to find his thought her own, that the trick did not belong exclusively to Franklin.

"I cannot decide, on such a day, if the world really is new, or if it only seems so."

"'Tis officially at war; there's all I know of it."

"Yes."

They walked in silence again until Anne started to feel its weight. She looked sideways at Grissom and saw him more clearly now in the brighter light by the river. The angles of his face had softened slightly with age, but the eyes had greatly livened since she'd last been so close to them.

"I see you're back at your shop," she said.

"I am. You were right. I was needed there." He cleared the damp from his throat. "I see you do well with your tavern."

"No thanks to your custom."

"I dislike interruption while I eat."

"I now have a quieter room in the rear."

He looked at her, then away. "I further dislike going back and finding someone else in my chair; I've grown used to having my own."

"I see. That makes it the more difficult."

They'd come level with the shop, but Grissom made no move to turn in, continuing on with Anne toward the Penny Pot.

"Do you remain friends with Franklin?" he asked.

Friends. The word stopped Anne, the surprise echo of it. "I've spoken to him but twice since his return."

"He's a busy man. Elected to Congress almost the day he got off the ship, seemingly on every committee, and now this declaration. I recall reading some of his advice to Parliament in the London papers. 'If you send troops to America you will not find a war, but you will make one.' Prescient, was he not?"

"I don't suppose there's such a word as *instigent*."

Grissom slowed, peered at Anne, smiled. "You know your friend well."

They'd reached the tavern. Anne looked out over the river, its surface summer smooth and blinding in the midday light. She thought of her first swim in it, of her second. She thought of the man who'd been with her on that first swim, the man she'd turned to at the end of the second. She thought of friends, sons, sons' sons. She thought of how long—how very long—she'd attempted to cling to that other life that was never her own; she thought of the immense waste of it.

"Mr. Grissom," she said, "I have an even more private room, above stairs, in which, since my husband's death, I'm never interrupted. Would you care to come up and share supper with me? If you like, you may bring your own chair."

Grissom smiled that indefinable half smile. He paused, as he always and forever would. But if Anne were to live another kind of life now—her own life—there should be more room in it for waiting, for defining.

Anne waited, and in time Grissom reached around her, pushed open the door for her, and followed her through.

55

Litchfield, Connecticut, 1777

WILLIAM FRANKLIN LAY IN his dark cell, for once undisturbed by the lice and the flies and the rats, the letter that had just been slid through the hole in the door crushed in his hand. Elizabeth, his beloved Elizabeth, who had struggled alone through a year of hell in New Jersey until she was forced to escape to New York with only such possessions as she could gather as she ran, had died, brokenhearted and alone. William had been informed of her decline and had begged to be allowed to see her; he'd written to General Washington, who had appealed to Congress; the request had been denied. They'd seen a contrite William Franklin before; they'd moved him out of gaol into a private home, with the freedom to ride about the countryside, a freedom he'd used to marshal the local farmers to the Loyalist cause. Now, in punishment, he was back in a cell even more foul, his latest and most urgent request denied.

William lay shivering with the perpetual fever that gripped him now, thinking backward, again. *Had* he been wrong? If he'd yielded to his father and resigned in 1775, if he'd but acknowledged wrongdoing to the Burlington tribunal in 1776 and accepted a gentleman's parole, if on his release he'd renounced the Crown instead of inciting the Loyalists, would Elizabeth be alive? If he'd married Maude and raised Temple as his own, would his son be with him now instead of in France with his grandfather, working for the rebel cause? Would Elizabeth have married an Englishman and be alive and well and a world away from this war that would forever be blamed on the wrong side?

Right. Wrong. The words tipped back and forth, up and down, side to side in William's fevered mind, coming to rest where they'd first begun. The one constant in William's life had been and would forever be his king. He'd not been wrong in his loyalty to the Crown; if he'd been wrong in other things, he'd not been wrong alone. He'd done what seemed best at the time, or he'd done the best he could at the time; perhaps now he could grant that his father, his stepmother, even that phantom woman who'd given him birth and pursued him down the years to land with him here could all say the same. What wrong turns they'd made belonged to all of them together; the lives they might have lived had escaped them all together. But what could any of it matter now? Elizabeth was dead in New York, Deborah Franklin was dead in Philadelphia, his father and his son were a continent and a cause away; any words that remained unsaid amongst all parties would remain unsaid through time. Oh, what he should have liked to say to Elizabeth! But what should he have liked to say to Temple, to his father? To explain himself, perhaps, to find just the right string of words at last, but as William had never succeeded at finding them before, what hope should he have of finding them now? The great irony of it all, of course, was that he *had* found the right words once, and had even managed to speak them aloud—to Deborah Franklin.

. . . .

SHE'D LAIN SLEEPING WHEN William first arrived. He took his turn of the room, speaking to all present—the minister, the upholsterer, the new press man, several others he didn't know, leaving his sister, Sally, to last, Sally the best of them all. He took a seat a distance away and watched his stepmother sleep, watched her chest rise and fall and stutter and rise and fall again, but when Sally got up to greet a new visitor, William took his excuse and followed her from the room. Worse luck, he ended up standing trapped, listening to some no doubt well-meaning and yet meaningless babbling of a former servant; better off back inside the quiet torture of his stepmother's sickroom. At his first chance William ushered the visitor into the room and followed behind her, only to discover his stepmother now awake and staring at him, struggling against her sheets, striving to speak to him. To *him*. At last. William had even taken a tentative step forward when he heard what his stepmother was saying—not his name but his label—the only thing he'd ever been to her all his life. William froze, hardening his shell against her as he'd done so many times, but suddenly the word softened, rounded, turned into what William should have guessed it would be all along.

"Beh-min! Beh-min!"

Benjamin.

William stared at the addled woman in the bed, struggling to reach that tall form that had just walked in the door, so sure it was her husband come at last, ignoring all the years of lessons that had been forced on her up to now. What kind of love was this that could hope so violently, right up to the end? Well, William's. Here he'd stood at the door and believed his stepmother struggled to call his name, forgetting about that boy who'd stood in so many other doors, waiting for a similar word. William had hurt, but he'd never understood how Deborah might have hurt until Elizabeth had explained her mother-in-law's heart to him. But now, standing in the sickroom door, listening to his stepmother's struggle, William understood something else too: He and his stepmother were the same in another way, each wanting the attention of a man who too many times had too many other things to do; perhaps that further explained a good deal of the resentment that had built up between them. Perhaps too, each had found it easier to blame the other than to blame the man around whom their hearts and minds had perpetually orbited.

William looked again at the woman lying twisted and struggling in the bed. It seemed in keeping with so many of the ironies of his life that he should come to a final understanding of her when she lay so close to death and so uncomprehending, when it was too late to make amends or to ease her mind. Or was it?

"Beh-min," Deborah cried again.

William stepped up to the bed, sat down, and took Deborah Franklin's hand between his. He dropped his voice to that hearty register he'd listened for in his childhood bed for fifteen years. "Hush, Debby," he said. "I'm here."

AFTERWORD

THE IDENTITY OF William Franklin's birth mother remains
unknown. In creating the character of Anne I sifted through the
rumors flying around Philadelphia (and parts beyond) at the time,
discarding what seemed highly improbable or obviously politically
motivated, combining what seemed most probable with the few
known historical references—old and new—that survive. I studied
and took into account what the record revealed of the characters of
the individuals involved and have presented here what I consider to
be a plausible version of the various scenarios offered through time,
as pondered by William Franklin and others in these pages.

This is, of course, a work of fiction, but dates, events, and portions
of the dialogue and most of the letters attributed here to the three
Franklins are, in the main, historically accurate. For plot purposes,
however, certain liberties have been taken, perhaps the most glaring
the fact that Deborah Franklin's mother did not predecease her daughter's "marriage"; she and her other children and Benjamin Franklin's

nephews and apprentices all lived under the Franklin roof at one time or another. William Franklin did attend his stepmother through an earlier stroke, but at her final illness only managed to arrive in time to see her into the ground. Benjamin Franklin was, as stated here, still in England when William's chastising letter announcing the death arrived two months later. Benjamin Franklin's regretful remarks to Anne at the Penny Pot were, in fact, his remarks at the time.

The following additional historical facts round out the tale:

In 1776, at the age of seventy, Benjamin Franklin did indeed take his grandson Temple to France on a diplomatic mission to enlist the aid of the French in the American cause. Franklin was successful—and hugely popular—in France; numerous accounts exist of his scientific, political, social, and amorous escapades while there. In 1785, fearing the end of his life was growing near and disliking the idea of dying so far from home, Franklin returned to Philadelphia. A lifelong slaveholder, he spent a good part of his remaining years agitating for the abolition of slavery. He died in 1790, lauded by all for a list of scientific, philanthropic, social, and political achievements, any one of which would have placed him amongst the greats for all time. He chose for his and his wife's tombstone the simple words: *Benjamin and Deborah Franklin 1790*—a curious notation, since Deborah had died sixteen years before.

After a prisoner exchange in 1778 finally set William Franklin loose in New York, he continued to annoy General Washington and the Continental Congress by serving as president of the Board of Associated Loyalists, organizing raids on American forces and even becoming involved in a revenge hanging of a rebel captain. In 1782, as the war drew to a close, he escaped to England, possibly to avoid being hanged himself. In France that same year, Benjamin Franklin signed the treaty to end the Revolutionary War, with Temple serving as secretary to the delegation.

In 1784 William Franklin wrote to his father:

> *Ever since the termination of the unhappy contest between Great Britain and America I have been anxious to write to you, and to endeavor to revive that affectionate intercourse and connection which until the commencement of the late troubles, had been the pride and happiness of my life . . .*

This was a letter that might have had better results if he hadn't then gone on to defend his conduct.

> *If I have been mistaken . . . it is an error of judgment that the maturest reflection I am capable of cannot rectify; and I verily believe were the same circumstances to occur again tomorrow, my conduct would be exactly similar to what it was.*

Not surprisingly, the elder Franklin answered with his own defense:

> *I am glad to find you desire to revive the affectionate intercourse . . . It will be agreeable to me . . . [But] indeed nothing has ever hurt me so much as to find myself deserted in my old age by my only son; and not only deserted, but to find him taking up arms against me, in a cause wherein my great fame, fortune and life were all at stake . . . few would have censured your remaining neuter, though there are natural duties which precede political ones.*

In 1785, at William Franklin's urging, Benjamin and Temple Franklin traveled from France to England to meet with William on their way home to America. The meeting did not go well. Old monetary debts were settled but not old grudges, and William was not invited to Benjamin's farewell fete. The next morning Benjamin and Temple sailed for America, avoiding a final good-bye.

William Franklin remarried in England and lived out the rest of his life there, never returning to America. He continued to champion the Loyalist cause, lobbying for reparations for financial losses the Loyalists incurred during the war, and although recompense was made for civilian losses, Benjamin Franklin fought successfully against compensating those who "bore arms against [us]." In other words, William.

Temple Franklin, following in his grandfather's and father's footsteps, fathered an illegitimate daughter with William's new sister-in-law, but then abandoned the family, leaving his seventy-year-old father to claim the child as his own. Before his death in 1813, William Franklin followed in his father's footsteps once again by disinheriting his son in favor of his granddaughter/adopted daughter, Ellen.

The identity of Temple Franklin's birth mother also remains unknown.

ACKNOWLEDGMENTS

MY THANKS GO OUT to the folks at the Historical Society of Philadelphia, who put in considerable effort to deliver unreadable text in readable form; to everyone involved with the Massachusetts Interlibrary Loan System, who got me just the right material at just the right time; to my agent Kris Dahl at ICM, for opening new doors and adding a fresh and insightful point of view to this work; to my editor Jennifer Brehl at William Morrow, who never quits until it's right; to her indefatigable assistant Emily Krump; and to my family of early readers who egged me on without mercy—you know who you are.